LIGHTNING

*Published outside the UK under the title PASSION'S PROMISE

LIGHTNING

Danielle Steel

CORGI BOOKS

LIGHTNING
A CORGI BOOK : 0 552 13749 9

Originally published in Great Britain by Bantam Press,
a division of Transworld Publishers

PRINTING HISTORY
Bantam Press edition published 1995
Corgi edition published 1996

5 7 9 10 8 6

Set in 10.5/12pt Monotype Plantin by
Phoenix Typesetting, Ilkley, West Yorkshire.

Corgi Books are published by Transworld Publishers,
61–63 Uxbridge Road, London W5 5SA,
a division of The Random House Group Ltd,
in Australia by Random House Australia (Pty) Ltd,
20 Alfred Street, Milsons Point, Sydney, NSW 2061, Australia,
in New Zealand by Random House New Zealand Ltd,
18 Poland Road, Glenfield, Auckland 10, New Zealand
and in South Africa by Random House (Pty) Ltd,
Endulini, 5a Jubilee Road, Parktown 2193, South Africa.

Reproduced, printed and bound in Germany by
Elsnerdruck, Berlin

To Popeye,

My first chance, and my second,
and my only chance.
May life only smile on you and
bless you.

With all my heart and love,
forever,

Olive

LIGHTNING

Chapter 1

The voices droned around the conference room as Alexandra Parker stretched long legs beneath the huge mahogany table. She jotted a note on a yellow legal pad, and glanced across the table briefly at one of her partners. Matthew Billings was older than Alex by a dozen years, he was in his mid-fifties, and one of the firm's most respected partners. He rarely asked for help from anyone, but it was not unusual for him to ask Alex to sit in on a deposition. He liked to pick her brain, admired her style, her sharp eye for the opponent's fatal weakness. And Alex was merciless and brilliant once she found it. She seemed to have an instinctive sense for where the point of the dagger would do the most damage.

She smiled at him now, and he liked what he saw in her eyes. She had heard just what they needed. A different answer from the time before. The very merest inflection. She slipped him a note on her yellow pad, and, with a serious frown, he nodded.

The case was an extraordinarily complicated one, and had already been in process for years. It had been to the New York Supreme Court twice, with various motions, and involved the careless dispersal of highly

9

toxic chemical pollutants by one of the most important corporations in the country. Alex had sat in on these depositions for Matt before. And she was always glad that this particular case wasn't her problem. The suit was being brought collectively by some two hundred families in Poughkeepsie, and represented millions of dollars. The case had been referred to Bartlett and Paskin years before, just after she had become a partner.

She liked her cases tougher, shorter, and smaller. Two hundred plaintiffs were not her cup of tea, although more than a dozen attorneys had worked on it, under Matthew's direction. Alexandra Parker was a litigation attorney too, and she handled an interesting assortment of difficult cases. She was the firm's first choice when the fight was going to be hard and dirty, and you needed an attorney who knew case law and was willing to spend a million hours doing meticulous research. She had associates and younger partners to help her of course, but Alex wanted to do as much of the work as she could herself, and she had a remarkable rapport with most of her clients.

Her real forte was labor law and libel. And she did a fair amount of litigation in both fields, though certainly, a lot of cases were settled. But Alex Parker was a fighter, a lawyer's lawyer, someone who knew her stuff and wasn't afraid of hard work. In fact, she loved it.

They broke from the deposition for a recess, and Matthew came around the table to talk to her after the defendant from the chemical company left the room with all his attorneys.

'So what do you think?' Matthew eyed her with interest. He had always had a soft spot for her. She had a fine mind and great skill as an attorney. Besides which, she was one of the best-looking women he knew, and he liked just being around her. She was solid, she was smart, she knew the law, and she had great intuition.

'I think you just got what you wanted, Matt. When he said that no one knew back then of the possible toxic effects of their materials, he was lying. That's the first time they've come right out and said it. We have the government reports from six months before that.'

'I know.' He beamed. 'He walked right into it, didn't he?'

'He sure did. You don't need me here. You've got him.' She dropped her legal pad into her briefcase, and glanced at her watch. It was eleven-thirty. They'd break for lunch in another half hour. But if she left now, she could get a little more work done.

'Thanks for coming in. It's always nice having you around. You look so innocent, you throw them off-guard. While he's staring at your legs, I can throw the net over him and grab him.' He liked teasing her and she knew it. Matthew Billings was tall and attractive, with a full head of white hair, and a beautiful French wife who had been a fashion model in Paris. Matthew Billings liked pretty women, but he also respected talented and smart ones.

'Thanks a lot.' She looked ruefully at him, her red hair pulled back in a severe bun, her face so lightly made up you could hardly see it, and her black suit in sharp contrast to the vivid natural colors of her red hair and green eyes. She was a striking woman. 'Just what I went to law school for, to become a decoy.'

'Hell, if it works, go for it.' He laughed, teasing her again, as one of the defense attorneys drifted back into the room, and they lowered their voices.

'Do you mind if I leave now?' she asked Matt politely. He was, after all, one of the senior partners.

'I've got a new client coming in at one, and I've got a few dozen cases to cast an eye on.'

'That's the trouble with you,' he pretended to frown at her, 'you don't work hard enough. I've always said that about you. Just plain lazy. Go on, go back to work. You've served your purpose here.' His eyes twinkled at her then. 'Thanks, Alex.'

'I'll have my notes typed up and sent to your office later,' she said seriously before she left. And he knew that, as always, her careful, intelligent notes would be delivered to his office by the time he got back there. Alex Parker was a remarkable lawyer. She was efficient, intelligent, capable, wily in just the right ways, and beautiful into the bargain, not that she seemed to care about her looks particularly, or notice the attention they brought her. She seemed to be completely unaware of herself, and most people liked that about her.

She left the room quietly, with a brief wave at him, as the defendants came back into the room, and one of the attorneys glanced admiringly at her retreating figure. Unaware of it, Alex Parker hurried down the hall, and down several corridors to her office.

Her office was large and well decorated in quiet grays, with two handsome paintings on the wall, a few photographs, a large plant, some comfortable gray leather furniture, and a splendid view up Park Avenue from the twenty-ninth floor where Bartlett and Paskin had their offices. They occupied eight floors, and employed some two hundred attorneys. It was smaller than the firm where she'd worked before, on Wall Street, when she'd first graduated from law school, but she'd liked this a lot better. She'd worked with the anti-trust team there, and she'd never really liked it. It was too dry, although it taught her to pay attention to details and do thorough research.

She glanced through half a dozen messages when she sat down, two from clients, and four from other attorneys. She had three cases ready to go to trial, and six more she was developing. Two major cases had just settled. It was a staggering workload, but it wasn't unusual for her. She loved the pace and the pressure and the frenzy. That was what had kept her from having children for so long. She just couldn't imagine fitting children in, or loving them as much as she did her law work. She adored being a lawyer, and thoroughly enjoyed a good fight in the courtroom. She did defense work primarily, she enjoyed difficult cases, and it meant a great deal to her protecting people from frivolous lawsuits. She loved everything about what she did. And it had eaten most of her life up. There was never time for anything more than that, except Sam, her wonderful husband. But he worked just as hard as she did, not in law, but in investments. He was a venture capitalist, with one of the hottest young firms in New York. He had come into it right at the start, and the opportunities had been remarkable. He'd already made several fortunes, and lost some money too. Together, they made healthy salaries. But more than that, Sam Parker had a powerful reputation. He knew his stuff, took amazing risks, and for twenty years now, almost everything he touched turned to money. Big money. At one point, people had said he was the only man in town who could make fortunes for his clients with commodities. But he was smarter than that now. Sam was never afraid of a risk, and he rarely lost funds for his clients. He'd been deeply involved in the computer world for the past dozen years, had made huge investments in Japan, done well in Germany, and had major holdings for his clients in Silicon Valley. Everyone on Wall Street agreed, Sam Parker knew what he was doing.

And Alex had known what she was doing when she married Sam. She'd met him right after she graduated from law school. They'd actually met at a party given by her first law firm. It was Christmas, and he'd arrived with three friends, looking very tall and handsome in a dark blue suit, his black hair flecked with snow, his face bright from the frigid air outside. He'd been full of life, and when he stopped and looked at her, she felt weak in the knees as she watched him. She was twenty-five years old, and he was thirty-two, and he was one of the few men she'd met who wasn't married.

He tried to talk to her that night, but she'd been distracted by another attorney from the firm, and Sam had been called away by his friends to talk to someone they knew, and their paths hadn't crossed again, until six months later. Sam's firm had consulted hers on a deal they were trying to put together in California, and she'd been called in with two other associates to help a senior partner. She'd been fascinated by him then, he was so quick and so smart and so sure. It was hard to imagine Sam being afraid of anything, or anyone. He laughed easily, and he wasn't afraid to walk a tightrope of terrifying decisions. He seemed to be unafraid of any risk, although he was fully aware of the dangers. And it wasn't his clients' money he was willing to risk, it was the whole deal. He wanted it his way, or to walk away from the deal completely. At first, Alex thought him a brazen fool, but as the weeks went on, she began to understand what he was doing, and she liked it. He had integrity and style, and brains, and that rarest of all things,

14

courage. Her first impression of him had been correct, he was afraid of nothing.

But he was intrigued by her too. He was fascinated by her intelligent, thoughtful analyses, her perception of a situation from three hundred and sixty degrees. She saw all sides and expressed the risks and the advantages brilliantly. Together, they had put together a most impressive package for his clients. The deal had been made, and the company had done brilliantly and been sold for an astronomical amount five years later. By the time Sam and Alex met, he had a reputation for being a young genius. But she was gaining a powerful reputation too, though she was building solidly and more slowly than Sam was.

Sam's business allowed for more glitter and dazzle, and he liked that about it. He thrived on the high life, and the enormous power of his high-flying clients. In fact, the first time he took Alex out, he borrowed one of his clients' private jets and took her to Los Angeles for the world series. They'd stayed at the Bel-Air, in separate rooms, and he'd taken her to Chasen's and L'Orangerie for dinner.

'Do you do this for everyone?' she had asked, amazed at all his little attentions. She was more than a little in awe of Sam. She'd had one serious relationship with a boy her own age at Yale, and nothing but a series of meaningless dates during her brutally hardworking years in law school. The relationship while she was at Yale had dissipated by her junior year, and he had long since gotten married. But Alex didn't have time for relationships. She wanted to work hard and be someone. She wanted to be the best lawyer in her law firm. And Sam's wild flash and dash didn't quite fit with that profile. She could see herself with attorneys like the ones in her firm, who had gone to Yale Law

School, like her, or Harvard, sober, quiet guys, who spent a lifetime as partners of Wall Street law firms. In his own way, Sam Parker was a wild man, a cowboy. But he was great looking, nice to her, and fun to be with. It was hard to remind herself that he wasn't really what she wanted. Who wouldn't want Sam? He was smart, gorgeous, and he had a terrific sense of humor. She would have had to be crazy not to want him.

They had driven to Malibu before they left L.A., and walked along the beach, talking about their families, and their lives, and their futures. Sam's experiences had been interesting, and very different from Alex's. He had said, almost casually, but with a tense look in his jaw, that his mother had died when he was fourteen, and he had been sent to boarding school, because his father didn't know what else to do with him. He had hated boarding school, detested the kids, and missed his parents. And while he was away at school, his father seemed to have drunk himself to death and spent the last of his money. He died when Sam was in his senior year, though Sam didn't tell Alex what he had died of. Sam had gone to college then on the small amount of money his grandparents had left him. His parents had left him nothing. He'd gone to Harvard and done well, and he didn't say anything to Alex about being lonely when he was in college. He made it sound like a great time, though thinking about it, she knew that it must have been rough for him to have no family at all by the time he was seventeen. But it didn't seem to have hurt him.

After Harvard undergraduate, he had eventually moved on to Harvard Business School, and had been totally enamored with venture capital. He'd found a job the minute he graduated, and in the eight years since he had made fortunes for several of his clients.

'And what about you?' she had asked quietly, watching his eyes as they walked along the beach at sunset. 'There's more to life than venture capital and Wall Street.' She wanted to get to know him better. She had just had the most exciting weekend of her life, and she hadn't even slept with him. She wanted to know more about Sam Parker before they disappeared back to their own lives after they left California.

'Is there more to life than Wall Street?' he laughed, slipping an arm around her. 'No one's ever told me. What is there, Alex?' He had stopped walking and looked down at her. He was enormously taken with her, even then, but a little bit afraid to show it. Her long red hair had been flying in the breeze, her green eyes looked deep into his and made him feel a stirring he had never felt before. In some ways, it scared him.

'What about people? Relationships?' She knew he had never been married, but she didn't know more than that. She assumed, just looking at him, and watching his easy style, that he must have had hundreds of girlfriends.

'No time for those,' Sam teased, as he pulled her a little closer and they continued walking. 'I'm too busy.'

'And too important?' she asked pointedly, fearing that he might be conceited. He certainly had every reason to be, but so far she hadn't seen it.

'Who said that? I'm not important, I'm just having a good time.'

'Everyone knows who you are,' she said matter-of-factly, 'even here. Los Angeles, New York . . . Silicon Valley, for sure . . . Tokyo . . . where else? Paris? London? Rome? It's a pretty big picture.'

'And not exactly a correct one. I work hard, that's all. So do you. No big deal.' He shrugged his shoulders and smiled down at her, but they both knew there was a lot more to it than he admitted.

'I don't fly to California in my clients' planes, Sam. My clients come to me by cab. If they're lucky. The rest of them come by subway.' She grinned and he laughed.

'OK, so mine are luckier. Maybe I am too. Maybe I won't be lucky forever. Like my father.'

'Are you afraid of that happening to you too? Losing everything?' It was an intriguing side to him, and clearly a motivating factor.

'Maybe. But he was a fool . . . a nice fool . . . but a fool. I think it killed him when my mother died. He gave up. He lost his grip, he was like that when she was sick too. He loved her so much that he just couldn't handle it when she went. It killed him.' He had long since decided that he would never let that happen to him. He would never love anyone enough to let them pull him down with them.

'It must have been awful for you,' Alex said sympathetically, 'you were so young.'

'You grow up fast when you're the only one you have,' he said soberly, and then he smiled sadly, 'or maybe you never do. My friends say I'm still a kid. I think I like that. It keeps me from getting too serious. There's no point getting too serious in life. It's no fun when you start to do that.' But Alex was, she was serious about her work, and her life. She had lost her parents by then too, although less dramatically than Sam had. But, in her case, it had sobered her, made her feel more responsible. She had to be more grown up, more alert about her career, more intense about her work. It was as though she felt obligated to live up to their expectations of her, even now that they were gone. Her father had been an attorney too, and he had

18

been so happy when she'd gone to law school. And she wanted to be the best attorney she could now, for him, even though he wasn't there to see her do it.

They were both only children, they both had important careers, they both had a lot of friends, which for both of them replaced family in some ways, though Alex spent a lot of time with friends of her parents, and families of her friends from law school. Sam's friends were mostly bachelors, people he worked with, clients, or women he'd gone out with.

He had kissed Alex for the first time on their walk down the beach in Malibu, and he had slept most of the way back to New York, with his head on her shoulder. She had looked down at him pensively, thinking that he looked like a long, lanky boy as he lay there beside her, but she was also thinking how much she liked him. Too much probably. She wondered if she would ever hear from him again, if this was a beginning or an interlude for him. It was hard to tell with Sam, and he had admitted that there was a young off-Broadway actress he was currently going out with.

'How come you didn't take her to L.A.?' Alex had asked candidly, shy, but never afraid to ask important questions. It was too much a part of her makeup not to.

'She was busy,' he said honestly, 'and I thought it would be more interesting to get to know you.' He hesitated and then turned to Alex with a smile that melted her heart in spite of her best efforts not to let it. 'To tell you the truth, I didn't ask her. I knew she had rehearsals all weekend, and she hates baseball. And I really wanted to be with you.'

'Why?' Alex had no idea how beautiful she was when she asked him.

'You're the smartest girl I've ever met . . . I like talking to you. You're bright and you're exciting, and you're not exactly hard to look at.'

He had kissed her again when he dropped her off at her apartment, but there was no commitment in the kiss, no promise. It was quick and casual, and in a moment the cab was gone, and Alex felt strangely let down as she walked into her apartment with her suit-case. She had had a wonderful time, but she figured that he was in a hurry to get back to his off-Broadway girlfriend. It had been wonderful, but she knew it didn't mean anything. It was just another fun weekend in the life of Sam Parker. She didn't think there was much room in his life for Alex Andrews.

Until he sent her a dozen red roses at the office the next day, and called her that afternoon and asked her to dinner. Their romance began in earnest after that, and, in spite of the heavy cases she had to prepare, she could hardly concentrate on her work during her four-month courtship with Sam.

He asked her to marry him on Valentine's Day, almost four months to the day of the first time he'd taken her out to dinner. She was twenty-six by then and Sam was thirty-three. They got married in June, in a small church in Southampton, with two dozen of their closest friends in attendance. Neither of them had families, but their friends provided the warmth and celebration to make it an extraordinary day. They had gone to Europe on their honeymoon, and stayed in hotels that Alex had only read of. They went to Paris and Monaco, and spent a romantic weekend in Saint-Tropez. Sam had a client who was dating a minor movie star there, so they had a fabulous time, and went to a party on a yacht and sailed to Italy and back by morning.

They went to San Remo, and then on to Tuscany, Venice, Florence, Rome, and then they had flown to stay with a client of his in Athens, and then to London for the last few days, where they went to Annabel's, and all of Sam's favorite restaurants and nightspots. They looked at antiques, and jewelry at Garrard's, and he bought her all kinds of fun clothes in Chelsea, though she said she had no idea where she'd wear them, surely not to the office. It was the perfect honeymoon, and they had never been happier than when they got back to New York, and she moved into his apartment. She'd been staying there anyway, but she had kept her own apartment until after the wedding.

She learned to cook for him, and he bought her expensive clothes, and a beautiful simple diamond necklace for her thirtieth birthday. He could have afforded to buy her a lot of things, but there was very little she wanted. She loved her life with him, their love and romance and friendship, their mutual respect, and passion for their work. He had asked her once about giving up her career, or at least putting it on hold to stay home and have kids, and she had looked at him as though he were crazy.

'What about not retiring, and having kids?' he had modified his previous offer. They had been married for six years by then, and he was thirty-nine years old, and once in a while he thought about having children. Most of the time, it would have cramped their style, but still, he thought it would be too bad if they never had them. But Alex had said she wasn't ready.

'I just can't imagine having anyone be that dependent on me, I mean all the time. I'd feel guilty working as hard as I do now, I'd never see the kids, and that's no way to bring up children.'

'Can you see yourself slowing down eventually, working less?' he asked. But he couldn't see her doing that, and neither could Alex.

'Honestly? No. I don't think you can be a part-time lawyer.' She'd seen other women try it, and they always drove themselves crazy. Eventually, they either came back to work full time, and felt guilty as hell toward their kids, or retired completely. And she didn't want to do that either.

'Are you saying you don't want children at all, ever?' It was the first time she had ever really thought about it, that seriously, and she wasn't ready to say that either. Their conclusion was 'not now, maybe later.'

The subject came up again when she was thirty-five, and by then it seemed like everyone they knew had had children. They'd been married for nine years by then, and they were very comfortable with their life as it was. She was already at Bartlett and Paskin, she had made partner, and Sam was something of a legend. They flew to France every chance they got for holidays, and California at the drop of a hat for a weekend. Sam still had a lot of business in Tokyo, and quite a lot in the Arab states, and Alex found his life fascinating, but her career wasn't unimpressive either. And there just didn't seem to be room in either of their lives for a baby.

'I don't know, I feel so guilty about it sometimes . . . like it's unnatural of me . . . I don't know how to explain it to anyone, but it's just not for me, at least not now,' she concluded with him, and they put the subject away for another three years, until she was thirty-eight and he forty-five. An alarm had gone off on her biological clock, albeit briefly, and this time she brought the subject up to him, after another partner at the office had a baby, and this time she conceded it was

22

just adorable, and her friend seemed to be handling both career and child well. It had made Alex think seriously, for the first time, about having children.

But this time, Sam could no longer imagine it. Their life was too set, too well regulated, and too easy without kids. After twelve years of marriage to her, he thought it was too late, and it would no longer enhance anything. He wanted her to himself now. He liked things just as they were, and she surprised herself at how easily she gave the idea up again. Obviously, it was just not meant to be. She had an enormous trial to handle right after that, and the subject of children in their lives went out of her head completely until four months later.

They were coming back from a trip to India, where she had never been before, and she was feeling seriously ill, and afraid she had caught some dread disease, when she went to her doctor. It was the first time she had felt really sick in years, and it scared her. But what he told her of her malady scared her even more. And that night, she looked at Sam and told him the news in bleak desperation. She was pregnant. She had really put it out of her head, this time permanently, after the last time the subject had come up, and so had he. And they looked at each other like two victims of the crash of '29 when she told him.

'Are you sure?'

'Absolutely,' she said miserably. It was the first time she'd ever been pregnant. And she now knew what she'd never been completely sure of before. She didn't want children.

'It's not cholera or malaria, or something like that?' A near fatal disease would have been more welcome news to either of them than a baby.

'He says I'm six weeks pregnant.' She had been late on the trip, but she'd thought it was from the extreme heat, or the malaria pills, or just the rigors of travel. And she had never looked as miserable in her life as she did now, staring unhappily at her husband. 'I'm too old for this, Sam. I don't want to go through it. I just can't.' Her words surprised him too, but he was relieved to hear them. He didn't want the baby either.

'Do you want to do something about it?' he asked, startled by her adamant dislike of the situation. He had always suspected that she might want kids someday, and, lately, he had begun to fear it.

'I don't think we should. It seems like such a spoiled rotten thing to do. It's not like we can't afford to have a baby . . . I just don't feel I have the time, or . . . not the energy,' she thought about it carefully, 'but the interest. The last time we talked about it, I just figured that was it. The conversation was over. We're happy like this . . . and then, *blam* . . . we're pregnant.'

He grinned ruefully at her. 'It's ironic, isn't it? We finally decide not to, and you get pregnant. Life certainly has its little curve balls.' It was one of his favorite expressions, but it was true. And this was a doozy. 'So what do we do?'

'I don't know.' She cried when she thought about it. She didn't want an abortion, or a baby. And after two weeks of agonizing about it, they decided to go ahead and have the baby. Alex didn't feel that they had a choice, morally, and Sam agreed, and they tried to be philosophical about it, but they were anything but enthusiastic. Alex was depressed every time she thought about it, and Sam seemed to forget about it completely. And when they did discuss it, which was as seldom as possible, they sounded as though they were discussing a terminal illness. This was certainly not anything they looked forward to. It was something that had to be faced, but they were clearly dreading everything about it.

Exactly four weeks later, Alex came home from the office early one afternoon, throwing up uncontrollably, and with such acute pains in her abdomen that she was literally doubled over. The doorman helped her out of the cab, and carried her briefcase inside for her. He asked if she was all right, and she insisted that she was, although her face was the color of paper. She got upstairs in the elevator, and let herself into the apartment, and fortunately her cleaning lady was there, because, half an hour later, Alex was hemorrhaging all over their bathroom and barely conscious. She had taken Alex to the hospital herself, and called Sam at his office, and by the time he got to Lenox Hill, Alex was already in the operating room. They had lost the baby.

They both expected it to be an enormous relief. The source of all their anguish was gone. But from the moment Alex woke up in a private room, crying miserably, they knew that it wasn't that easy. They were both consumed with guilt and grief, and everything she had never allowed herself to feel for their unborn child, she felt now, all the love and fear and shame and regret and longing she had never felt before. It was the worst experience of her life, and taught her something about herself she had never known or suspected. Maybe it had never even been there before, but it was there now. All she wanted, to fill the aching void the miscarriage had left, was to fill the void with another baby. And Sam felt it too. They both cried for their unborn child, and when Alex went back to work the following week, she was still feeling shaken.

They had gone away for a few days over a long weekend, and talked about it, and they both agreed. They weren't sure if it was a reaction, or real, but they knew that something major had changed. Suddenly, more than anything, they wanted a baby.

Sensibly, they decided to wait a few months, to see if the feelings stayed. But even that was impossible to do. Two months after the traumatic miscarriage, Alex sheepishly told Sam the news with barely concealed glee. She was pregnant.

And this time, unlike the first, it was a celebration. A cautious one, because there was always the possibility that she would lose this one too, or that she would never be able to carry a child to term. She was thirty-eight years old, after all, and she'd never had a baby. But her health was excellent, and her doctor assured them that there was no reason whatsoever to anticipate another problem.

'You know what? We're nuts,' she said, lying in bed one night, eating Oreo cookies, and getting crumbs all over their bed, but she claimed they were the only things that settled her stomach. 'We are completely crazy. Four months ago, we were suicidal about having a kid, and now we lie here talking about names, and I keep reading articles in magazines in the doctor's office about what kind of mobiles to buy to put over the crib. Have I lost my marbles or what?'

'Maybe.' He smiled tenderly at her. 'You're definitely harder to share a bed with. I had no idea that cookie crumbs would be part of the deal. Do you think you'll have this fixation for the whole time, or is this just a first trimester addiction?' She giggled at him, and they cuddled in bed. They made love more frequently than they had in years. They talked about the baby as though it were real, and already part of

26

their lives. She had an amnio, and, as soon as they knew it was a girl, they decided to call her Annabelle, after their favorite club in London, but it was a name that Alex had always loved, and it had good memories for them. This pregnancy was completely unlike the first one. It was as though they had learned an important lesson the first time, and felt as though they had been punished for their indifference and hostility to that baby. This time, there was no question of anything but unbridled excitement.

Alex's partners gave her a shower right after the New Year, and she left the office reluctantly that week, only two days before her due date. She had wanted to work right up until she went to the hospital, but it didn't make sense to continue working on cases she couldn't complete, so she left on schedule, and went home to wait for their little miracle, as they called her. Alex was afraid that she'd be bored, but found that she enjoyed setting up the nursery, and was surprised herself at how much time she spent folding little undershirts, and arranging diapers in neat stacks in the changing table. For a woman who struck fear into most lawyers' hearts when she entered a courtroom, she seemed to have changed in a single instant. She even worried sometimes that it might dull her skills when she went back, maybe she wouldn't be as tough, or as focused, but in spite of her concerns about that, all she could think of now was the baby. She could imagine holding it, feeding it, she wondered if she would have red hair like her own, or dark, dark hair like Sam's, blue eyes, or green. Like a long-awaited friend, she could hardly wait to see her.

They had arranged to have the baby in a birthing room at New York Hospital, Alex wanted everything to be natural. She was planning to savor every moment

27

of the experience. At thirty-nine, she couldn't imagine doing this again, so she didn't want to take any of it for granted. Despite Sam's aversion to hospitals, he went to Lamaze classes with her, and was going to be at the delivery with her.

And she and Sam were having dinner at Elaine's three days after her due date, when her water broke, and they left quickly for the hospital, and were then sent home, until labor had started in earnest. They did everything their coaches had told them to do. She tried to sleep for a little while, then she walked, Sam rubbed her back, and it all seemed very pleasant and very easy. There was nothing difficult about this, nothing they couldn't handle, or she couldn't do. They lay in bed and talked, about how amazing it was that after thirteen years of marriage they had come to this, and Sam glanced at the clock, and tried to guess in how many hours they'd have their baby. They both fell asleep eventually, and when the contractions woke Alex again, she took a warm shower, as she'd been told to do, to see if labor would stop or get harder. She stood in the shower for half an hour, timing the pains, and then suddenly, with no warning, hard labor began for real. She could barely stand as she got out of the shower, and when she went to wake Sam, he was dead to the world, and she started to cry in panic as she shook him. He awoke finally, and gave a start when he saw the look on her face.

'Now?' he said, leaping out of bed, with his heart pounding, looking frantically for his trousers. He had left them on a chair, but suddenly in the dark, he couldn't find them, and Alex was doubled over in pain, gripping his arm, and crying.

'It's too late . . . I'm having it now . . .' she said, panicking, forgetting everything they'd told her. She was too old for this, it hurt too much, and she no longer wanted natural childbirth.

'Here? You're having it *here*?' He looked terrified as he stared at her, unable to believe it.

'I don't know . . . I . . . it . . . oh God, Sam . . . it's awful . . . I can't do this . . .'

'Yes, you can . . . we'll get you drugs at the hospital . . . don't worry about it . . . go put some clothes on.'

In the end, he'd had to help her dress and find her shoes, and he had never seen her as vulnerable, or in as much pain. The doorman had found them a cab instantly. It was four a.m., and she could hardly walk when they got her to the hospital. The doctor was already waiting for them there, and the labor nurses were well pleased with Alex's progress. She, on the other hand, was a lot less pleased with the process they referred to happily as 'transition.' She sounded like someone Sam didn't even know as she shouted for drugs, and got hysterical with each contraction. But as labor progressed, she calmed down finally, and two hours after they'd gotten to the hospital, Alex was hard at work pushing out their baby. She'd had an epidural finally, and was calmer, as Sam held her shoulders and everyone in the room cheered her on. It seemed to take forever, but it was only half an hour before Annabelle's little face appeared. She had bright red hair, and she let out a huge yell, and then as though she'd surprised herself, she looked up at Sam, as tears coursed down her parents' cheeks. Annabelle just stared at Sam, as though she had been looking for him for a long time and had finally found him. She was introduced to her mother then, and Alex held her, overwhelmed by emotions she had never even dreamed of. She felt complete in a way she had

29

heard people talk about, but never believed, and she couldn't even imagine what her life would have been like if she'd missed this experience. Within an hour, she was holding Annabelle as though she were an old hand at it, and happily nursing her baby. Sam took a thousand photographs of them, as he and Alex cried, unable to believe the blessing that had been bestowed on them, the miracle they had almost missed, and fortunately hadn't. They had been spared from their own stupidity, they felt, by a wiser Power who had showered them with good fortune.

Sam spent the first night in the hospital with them, and he and Alex spent most of it staring down at Annabelle, taking turns holding her, wrapping her and unwrapping her, changing her diapers and her night-gown, and Sam watched raptly as Alex nursed her. He thought it was the most beautiful thing he'd ever seen, and as they looked at her, they both agreed, what they wanted now was another baby. They couldn't believe that they had almost deprived themselves of this. And Sam could hardly believe that Alex was willing even to think about it so soon after the ordeal of labor, but she said it to him as they kissed over Annabelle sleeping soundly between them.

'I want to do this again.'

'You're not serious.' He looked stunned, but pleased. He had been thinking exactly the same thing. He would have loved a son, but another little girl would be fine too. Their little girl was so perfect and so beautiful. He kept touching her tiny toes, and Alex kept kissing her tiny fingers. They were completely enamored with their daughter.

It remained a passion with them once they got home, and Annabelle flourished in the unbridled adoration of her parents. Sam came home early as often as he could. And Alex went back to the office, with regret, when Annabelle was three months old. She tried to continue nursing her even after that, but it became impossible with the pressures of her schedule. What she did instead was come home for lunch as often as she could, and she made a promise to herself to leave promptly at five, whenever she wasn't in trial, and work at home at night after Annabelle went to bed. And on Fridays, she left at one o'clock, come hell or high water. It was a system that worked for them, and she was religious about coming home promptly whenever possible. And in exchange for their love and efforts, and their incessant appreciation of her, Annabelle adored her Mommy and Daddy. She was the light of their lives, and they were all that mattered to her. Carmen took care of her in the daytime, but Sam and Alex took care of her themselves the moment they got home from work, and Annabelle lived for that moment. She would squeal with excitement and delight whenever she saw them.

Carmen liked working for them. She was crazy about Annabelle, and they were nice people. She bragged a lot about Alex and Sam, about how important they were, and how hard they worked, and how successful. Sam was in the financial columns a lot. He had made a big splash early on, and had continued to make news frequently with record-making deals for important clients. And Alex had been on television more than once, with exceptionally newsworthy or landmark cases. Carmen loved that.

And there was no question in Alex's and Sam's minds that Annabelle was not only beautiful, but absolutely brilliant. She walked promptly at ten and a half months, spoke clearly shortly after that, and spoke in sentences long before it was expected.

'She's going to be a lawyer,' Alex always teased Sam, but neither of them could deny how incredibly she resembled her mother. She looked just like Alex, and even her mannerisms looked like a miniature version of her mother's.

In fact, the only disappointment to them was that their efforts to get pregnant again had been surprisingly unfruitful. They started when Annabelle was six months old, and had tried for a year after that. Alex was forty by then, and decided to go to a specialist to see if anything was wrong. But she and Sam had both checked out, and there was no problem with either of them. The doctor had just explained that, at her age, conception often took longer. At forty-one, they had put her on Serophene, a form of progesterone, to 'improve' her ovulations, and for the past year and a half she had taken the drug that seemed to add more stress to her life than she already had. They were making love on schedule, using a kit to tell them exactly when her LH surge was, and when the optimum time was for conception. Alex had to add her urine to a series of chemicals, and when they turned blue, it was time for Sam to rush home from the office. They laughingly called it 'blue day,' but there was no doubt that the pressure it put on them didn't make things any easier in lives that were already filled with stress and tension provided by their clients, and, in Alex's case, her opponents.

It was not an easy time for them, but it was something they both agreed they wanted very badly. And it seemed funny to both of them that after so many years of emphatically not wanting children, they were now willing to go to any lengths to pursue having them. They had even talked about her taking Pergonal shots, which was a more extreme solution than the

Serophene pills, with other side effects. And they also considered in vitro fertilization. They hadn't ruled out either of the more elaborate treatments. But at forty-two, she still felt she had a chance for conception without such heroic measures, particularly with the hormones she was currently taking. That in itself was already a big commitment, because taking them was anything but easy for her. She was one of those people who reacted severely to medication. But she felt it was worth it, because she and Sam both wanted another baby so badly. Annabelle had taught them many things, mainly how sweet life could be with the bond of a child between them, and how much they had missed in their years of childlessness. They both had impressive careers to show for it, but now she felt that they had missed something far more important.

Annabelle was three and a half years old by then, and Alex's and Sam's hearts melted every time they saw her. Her hair was a halo of coppery curls, her eyes were huge and green, just like her mother's, and her face was dusted with a thin veil of what Alex called 'fairy dust,' which were her freckles.

There was a huge photograph of her, holding a shovel on the beach the summer before, in Quogue, as Alex sat at her desk and glanced up at it, with a quick grin. She glanced at her watch again. The deposition she'd sat in on had cost her the better part of her morning, and she had less than an hour now to go over some papers before she met with a new client.

She glanced up as Brock Stevens came in. He was one of the young associates in the firm, and he worked exclusively for her and one other attorney, doing research, and legwork, preparing cases for trial for her. He'd only been with Bartlett and Paskin for two years, but she was impressed with him, and his handling of her cases.

'Hi, Alex . . . got a sec? I know you've had a busy morning.'

'That's OK. Come on in.' She smiled up at him. At thirty-two, he still looked like a boy to her, he had sandy blond good looks, and looked like everyone's kid brother. He had gone to a state law school in Illinois, and she knew he came from a simple family with very little money. But he had worked his way through school, and he burned with a real fire for the law. It was a feeling that had always governed her life too, and she had a lot of admiration for him.

He strode across the room, and sat down across her desk from her, with a serious look, his shirtsleeves rolled up and his tie askew, which also made him look younger. 'How was the depo?'

'Pretty good. I think Matt got lucky. His principal defendant let his slip show, and I think Matt may have gotten just what he wanted. He's wearing them down anyway, but it's still going to take forever. That case would drive me crazy.'

'Me too, but it's interesting making history with it. They're setting a lot of precedents. I like that.' He was so young and alive and filled with dreams, sometimes she thought he was naive, personally, but he was also an extraordinarily fine lawyer.

'So whatcha got? Anything new on the Schultz case?'

'Yup.' He smiled happily at her. 'We hit pay dirt. The plaintiffs been cheating on his taxes for the past two years. He's not going to look great to the jury. That's why they've been resisting giving us his records.'

'Nice. Very nice.' Alex smiled at him. 'How'd you find out?' They had had to file a separate motion to get the financial records, and they had finally come in that morning.

'It's pretty easy to figure out what he did. I'll show you later. I think this might open us up for a settlement, if you can get Mr Schultz to settle.'

'I doubt it,' she said thoughtfully. Jack Schultz owned a small company that had been sued twice, unfairly, by previous employees. It was the latest game to win fat settlements from employers who didn't want to be hassled. But settling had created precedents for him, and now he was being sued by another previous employee, who had been skimming money from the company and taking illegal kickbacks, but was trying to sue Jack Schultz for discrimination. And this time Schultz did not want to settle. He wanted to develop a reputation for fighting and winning.

'I think we've got what we need anyway. With that testimony about kickbacks from the guy in New Jersey, I think we can bury the plaintiff.'

'I'm counting on it.' She smiled at him. They were set for trial the following Wednesday.

'I have a feeling the plaintiff's attorney will call you about a settlement sometime this week, now that we've got their financial records. What are you going to tell them?'

'To take a flying leap. Poor Jack deserves a win on this one. And he's right, you can't keep rolling over to settle. I wish more employers had the guts to do what Jack is doing.'

'It's cheaper to settle, most of them don't want to be bothered.' But they both knew that there was definitely a growing trend among businesses to fight and win, rather than to buy off their opponents with settlements that rewarded plaintiffs for filing bad lawsuits. Alex had won several of those cases the year before, and she had a great reputation for defendants' work in suits like this one. 'Are you ready for trial?' he asked her, but he also knew that in Alex's case, that was a foolish question. She was always extraordinarily well prepared, she was extremely knowledgeable about the law, did all her homework, and then some. And he always tried to back her up in every way he possibly could so that there would be no surprises for her in the courtroom. He liked working for her. She was tough, but fair, and she never expected anyone to work harder than she did. He didn't mind the hundreds of hours he spent working, preparing cases for her, he always learned a great deal from her strategy. She never put herself out on a limb unless she was absolutely sure she wouldn't hurt her client by taking risks, and she always warned them fully of the risks she was taking.

Brock wanted to be a partner like her someday, and he knew that time was not far off. He also knew that, given their successful working relationship, Alex would be more than willing to recommend him. Although she complained occasionally that once he made partner, which she hoped wouldn't be soon, she would have no one decent to do her grunt work. He also knew, from the other partner he worked for in the firm, that Alex had already put a good word in for him to Matthew Billings, though Alex would never admit it.

'Who's the new client you're seeing today?' He was always interested in what she did. And what's more, he liked her.

'I'm not sure. He was actually referred by another firm. I think he wants to sue an attorney, in another law firm.' She was always leery of those, unless she felt they were truly justified. Being a litigator frequently had its downside. She wound up with a lot of people

36

across the desk from her who were looking to take out their anger against the world on people who did not deserve it. The miserable and the bitter and the greedy frequently thought that their lot in life could be improved by a lawsuit, and Alex never took those cases, unless she felt their claims were justified, which they usually weren't.

'Anyway, do whatever you can to wrap up Schultz, and why don't we spend tomorrow morning going over it. It's Friday tomorrow, so I'm leaving at one, but that should give us enough time to sum it up pretty squarely, and I'll go over the files again this weekend. I want to read all the depositions again and make sure I didn't miss anything.' She frowned as she made a note on her calendar to meet with him at eight-thirty the next morning. She had no other meetings scheduled for the entire day, and she usually saved Fridays for in-house business.

'I've been going over the depositions all week for just that. I made some notes I'll show you tomorrow. There's some real good stuff in there you'll want to use, and I made some indications about the videos too.' They had videotaped some of the depositions. It was a tool which she sometimes found useful, and if nothing else, it aggravated the opponents.

'Thanks, Brock.' He was a godsend for her. As busy as she was, without a good associate to work for her, she'd have been lost in a sea of cases. She had an excellent assistant too, a law clerk who spent as much time with Brock as he did with Alex. They were a good team, and they all knew it. 'I'll see you at eight-thirty tomorrow. Thanks for the diligent preparation.' But it was nothing new for him, it was his style, just as it was Alex's. He was thorough and smart, and a nice guy. And it also helped that he wasn't married. He had lots of spare time to spend on work, late at night, over holidays, on weekends. He was willing to do what he had to to build an important career. At times, he reminded her of her and Sam in their early days. They worked just as hard now, but differently, there wasn't that blind hard push that kept you in the office till midnight, as it had for them years before. Now they had Annabelle and each other, and they wanted more out of life than just careers. But fortunately for her, Brock Stevens wasn't there yet. She knew he had seen someone in the firm for a while, another associate, a very attractive girl who'd gone to Stanford, but Alex also knew that Brock valued his career too much to risk getting too involved with anyone from the law firm. There were rules against that, and getting serious with another associate, or a partner, might keep him, or her, from making partner. And Alex knew that both he and the other associate were too ambitious, and too sensible, to let that happen.

She met with the new client shortly after that, and she was very lukewarm about what she heard from him. It was an ugly case, and she was not at all convinced that the plaintiff in this case wasn't lying. Generally, she preferred defense work. She told him that she'd think about it and discuss it with her partners, but that she felt that her own schedule at the moment, and the number of cases she had pending trial, could well keep her from giving him the kind of attention she felt he deserved, and was certain he wanted. She was very diplomatic with him, but very firm, and promised to call him in a few days after a meeting with her partners. She had no intention of meeting with anyone. She just needed some time to think it over, but she doubted very seriously that she'd take it.

And at five o'clock sharp, she looked at her watch, buzzed her secretary, Liz Hascomb, at the desk outside, and told her she was leaving. She left at five o'clock every day, whenever she could, and her schedule allowed it. She signed a few letters her secretary had left, jotted a few notes, and buzzed her again with a few instructions. A few minutes later, Elizabeth Hascomb came in to pick up the notes from her, and she and Alex exchanged a smile. Elizabeth was a widow who was approaching retirement age, and she had had four children of her own. She admired the fact that Alex thought enough of her little girl to go home to be with her as early as she could every night. It proved to Elizabeth that she was not just a good lawyer, but she was a good woman, and a good mother. And she liked that. She had six grandchildren of her own, and she loved hearing stories about Annabelle, or seeing photographs of her when Alex brought them into the office.

'Give Miss Annabelle my love. How's she doing in school?'

'She loves it.' Alex smiled, dropping the last of her papers in her briefcase. 'Don't forget to send Matthew Billings my notes from this morning, please. And I'll need all the Schultz files on my desk when I come in tomorrow. I have a meeting with Brock on it at eight-thirty.' There were a thousand things she was going to have to think of. The Schultz trial was set to start the following Wednesday and she was liable to be out of the office for a week or more, which meant she had to take care of as much as she could before that. It was going to be a grim Monday and Tuesday.

'See you in the morning.' Alex smiled warmly at Liz, who also knew that if an emergency arose after Alex left, she could call her at home, or send papers

39

up to her by messenger if she had to. As devoted as Alex was to Annabelle, she was never completely out of contact. And when Alex was in court, she always wore a beeper.

'Good night, Alex.' Liz Hascomb smiled at her as she left, and five minutes later, Alex was on Park Avenue, plunging into five o'clock traffic. The rush hour had just begun, and it took real spirit to grab a cab before anyone else did. She got one headed uptown, and noticed with surprise what a beautiful day it was. It was one of those splendid October days with bright sun and a hint of warm air, but a brisk breeze that carries with it just the merest suggestion of autumn.

It was the kind of weather that made her want to walk uptown, except that she didn't want to waste a minute getting home to her daughter. Instead, she settled back in the cab, thinking about Annabelle and her mischievous little face with the freckles. It was hard not to think about getting pregnant again too. They'd been trying for three years, and it was discouraging that it just hadn't happened. But on the other hand, she wasn't ready yet for more dramatic measures. She wondered how, with her schedule, she would ever manage either in vitro fertilization or even Pergonal. It all seemed so complicated with everything else she had on her plate. It would be so much easier if it just happened. Her progesterone was high enough, her FSH, or follicle-stimulating hormone, was low enough . . . but there was still no baby. And thinking about it reminded her that she had to run a test with the 'blue kit' as soon as she got home, just to make sure they didn't miss the ideal moment. According to her calculations, she was due to ovulate sometime that weekend. At least she wouldn't be working, or in trial, thank God, she thought to herself, as the cab lurched and darted through the traffic around them.

They wound up in a traffic jam on Madison and Seventy-fourth, and she decided to get out and walk the last three blocks. The air felt good on her face after being cooped up all day. And there was a real spring in her step, as she swung her briefcase beside her, and thought about getting home to Annabelle. Maybe Sam would even be home. Her smile deepened as she thought of him. She was still crazy about him after more than seventeen years of marriage. She had everything. A fabulous career, an adorable little girl, a husband she loved deeply. She was the luckiest woman alive, and she knew it. That was the best part. She never took any of it for granted. She was grateful for every blessing in her life, every day. And if she didn't get pregnant again, it wouldn't be the end of the world. Maybe they'd adopt. Or maybe they'd just have Annabelle. She and Sam were only children, it hadn't done them any harm. On the contrary, people said only children were smarter.

Whatever happened, she knew they had it made. Just thinking about it made her smile broadly as she reached their building, and smiled at the doorman as she strode confidently into the lobby.

Chapter 2

As Alex opened the front door, the apartment seemed
strangely quiet. There was not a sound anywhere, and
she wondered if Carmen had taken Annabelle to the
park for longer than usual. On most days, they were
home by five o'clock, and then had a bath before
dinner. But when Alex walked into her bathroom,
she found Annabelle sitting like a little princess in
a mountain of bubble bath that almost hid her
completely. Carmen was sitting on the edge of the
bath, watching her, and Annabelle was pretending to
be a mermaid. She wasn't saying a word, she was just
'swimming' up and down the tub nearly hidden by the
huge froth of bubbles. Using her mother's deep marble
tub had been an extra treat, and was why Alex hadn't
heard her as she came into the apartment. The master
suite was at the end of a long hallway.

'What are you doing in here?' Alex grinned broadly
at both of them, happy to see her baby. She was the
cutest little girl Alex had ever seen, and her bright red
hair shone like a beacon in the bathtub.

'Shhh . . .' Annabelle said seriously, holding her
finger to her lips. 'Mermaids don't talk.'

'Are you a mermaid?'

'Of course I am. Carmen said I could use your bathtub and your bubble bath if I let her wash my hair tonight.' Carmen smiled at her employer and Alex laughed. Annabelle loved to make deals, and Carmen was as much putty in her hands as her parents were, Annabelle didn't take unfair advantage of it, but she knew that she was everyone's darling.

'How about if I take a bath with you, and we both wash our hair?' her mother suggested. She wanted to take a bath anyway before Sam came home for dinner.

'OK.' Annabelle thought about it for a minute. She hated to have her hair shampooed, but she was beginning to suspect there would be no way out this time.

Alex slipped out of her black suit, and high heels, and Carmen went to check on dinner, while Annabelle continued to play mermaid, and a moment later they were both in the big tub, having a conversation about their respective days. Annabelle liked the fact that her mother was a lawyer, and her father was an 'invention capitalist,' as she called it. She always explained that it was sort of like a banker, and he gave away people's money, which was not exactly the way her father described what he did, but it satisfied Annabelle. She knew her mother went to court and argued with the judge, but she didn't send people to jail, which was simpler.

'So how was your day?' Alex asked, luxuriating in the warm water and the bubbles, feeling like a mermaid herself after a day at the office.

'Pretty good.' Annabelle looked at her with obvious pleasure. Her mother had kissed her hello when she got in the tub, and Annabelle was happily sitting beside her.

'Did anything special happen at school?'

43

'Nope. We ate frogs though.'

'You ate frogs?' Alex looked intrigued, but was familiar with her daughter's shorthand and knew there was more to the story. 'What kind of frogs?' Surely not real ones.

'Green frogs. With black eyes, and coconut hair on them.' The 'coconut hair' was the tip-off, as Alex wondered how she had ever managed to live without her.

'You mean like cupcakes?'

'Yeah sort of, Bobby Bronstein brought them. It was his birthday.'

'That sounds pretty good.'

'His mother brought gummy worms and spiders too. They were pretty gross.' She was delighted at the scary report that had intrigued her mother.

'Sounds yummy.' Alex smiled down at her as Annabelle shrugged, unimpressed by the culinary delights she had encountered.

'It was OK. I like your cupcakes better. Especially the chocolate ones.'

'Maybe we'll make some this weekend.' . . . after Daddy and I make love and try to make you a baby brother or sister . . . She reminded herself again about the blue kit.

'What are we doing this weekend?' a familiar voice asked as they both looked up to see Annabelle's Daddy, watching them from the doorway with obvious amusement. It was an appealing scene, and his eyes met his wife's with all the love he felt for both of them, and then he leaned down to kiss his wife and his daughter. Alex caught him by the tie and held him there for another kiss, and he didn't object as he kissed her.

'We were talking about making cupcakes, among other things,' Alex said seductively, as he raised an eyebrow, and then stepped back from the tub and took off his tie and opened his collar.

'Any other plans for this weekend?' he asked casually, he had also remembered the blue kit.

'I think so,' she smiled at him, and he returned the look in her eyes with pleasure. Almost fifty, he was still a strikingly handsome man, and looked ten years younger than he was, as did Alex. They were a good-looking pair, and it was obvious that Annabelle had done nothing to dim the passion between them.

'What are you two doing in the bathtub with all those bubbles?' he asked Annabelle, and she looked at him matter-of-factly.

'We're mermaids, Daddy.'

'Any interest in having a big whale join you?'

'You're coming in too, Daddy?' she giggled, and he took off his jacket and started unbuttoning his shirt, as the three of them laughed, and, a minute later, he had locked the door so Carmen wouldn't come back in, and he was in the tub with his two mermaids. He splashed and they played, and eventually Alex did wash Annabelle's hair. And then she got out of the tub and dried her off and wrapped her in a big pink towel, while Sam took a shower to wash all the soap off. He stepped out of the shower and grabbed a big white towel, which he wound around his waist as he surveyed his two ladies with pleasure.

'You two look like twins.' He smiled again at the bright red hair. Alex had complained lately about finding a few gray hairs, but you couldn't see them, and her hair was still as bright as her daughter's.

'What are we going to do for Halloween?' Annabelle asked as her mother dried her hair, and Sam opened the bathroom door and walked into their bedroom to put on jeans and a sweater and a pair of loafers. He loved coming home to them, playing with Annabelle, and spending time with Alex. He didn't even mind if she worked late at night, he just liked being with her, as he had for the last seventeen years. Very little had changed between them, except that he seemed to love her more each year, and Annabelle had only strengthened the bond between them. He was only sorry they hadn't figured out how great kids were a little sooner.

'What do you want to do for Halloween?' Alex asked her, as she fluffed up the bright red curls with gentle fingers.

'I want to be a canary,' Annabelle said firmly.

'A canary? Why a canary?' Alex was smiling at her.

'They're cute. Hilary has one. Or maybe I'll be Tinker Bell . . . or the Little Mermaid.'

'I'll go to F.A.O. Schwarz on my lunch hour next week and see what I can find. OK?' And then she remembered the trial. She'd have to do it before Wednesday or wait till the trial was over. Or maybe Liz Hascomb could call them and see what they had in Annabelle's size. Alex always had to be artful about using her time to its best advantage.

'What are we doing for Halloween?' Sam had strolled back into the room in jeans and a dark green sweater.

'I thought we'd go trick-or-treating in the building, like last year,' Alex explained, and he nodded. She was wearing a pink terrycloth bathrobe with a pink towel on her head, and she put Annabelle's nightie on, and turned her over to Sam, so she could go out to the kitchen and check on dinner.

There was a chicken in the oven, baked potatoes in the microwave, green beans sautéing in a pan, and

Carmen was about ready to leave them. She stayed later when they went out, but if they were staying home, she often started dinner for them, and then left. Or Alex and Sam would cook dinner themselves when they both got back from the office.

'Thanks for everything.' Alex smiled at her, and Carmen smiled back. 'I'm going to need lots of help next week, Carmen. I'm going to trial on Wednesday.'

'Sure. I help you, I can stay late. No problem.' She knew about their efforts toward having another baby too, and she was disappointed it had not yet happened. She loved babies, and kids. At fifty-seven, she had had six kids and two husbands, and at last count she had seventeen grandchildren. She had a full life in Queens, but she loved working for the Parkers in Manhattan.

'See you tomorrow,' Alex called out when Carmen left. The table was set, the dinner smelled wonderful. Alex went to put on jeans and a shirt herself. And five minutes later, she called Annabelle and Sam to dinner. They ate at an old rustic table in the kitchen, the place mats were clean and pretty, and the candles were lit. Sometimes they ate in the dining room, but most of the time they ate in the kitchen, and most nights they ate with Annabelle, except when they came home late, or went out to dinner. But they both enjoyed their meals with her. She was good company and they thought their time together was important.

She chatted on busily through the evening, and Sam helped Alex clean up the dishes, while Annabelle played, and then he watched the last of the news, while Alex read Annabelle a bedtime story. She was in bed and asleep by eight o'clock, and the evening was theirs. Alex was about to sit down next to him on the leather couch in the study when she remembered the ovulation detection kit again and went to do it. It

47

showed only that she had not yet had the hormone surge that preceded ovulation, and there was no way to predict when it would happen. Except that she knew that with the hormones she was on, it was likely to be fairly regular and happen, as she had predicted, on Saturday or Sunday, which was still two or three days away. They had been advised to be sure not to have been abstinent for more than five days before ovulation, but not to do it immediately before either, or it would lower Sam's sperm count. It took the spontaneity out of their sex life, but they enjoyed each other anyway, and Sam had been a terrifically good sport about their efforts in pursuit of a baby. He had also been told not to drink excessively right before she ovulated, and never to use a hot tub or a sauna. Heat killed sperm, and he teased her sometimes about wearing ice packs in his shorts, which he knew couples with fertility problems sometimes did. But they didn't have a 'problem,' there was nothing wrong with them. Alex was forty-two years old, and it was taking time to get pregnant.

'So, are my services needed tonight?' he asked good-humoredly as she sat down next to him on the couch in the study.

'Not yet,' she said, feeling silly. It was hard not to with all the testing, figuring, discussing, hoping. But it still seemed worth it to both of them, so they hadn't thrown the towel in yet. Far from it. 'I still think it'll be this weekend.'

'I can think of worse things to do on a Saturday afternoon,' he said happily as he put an arm around her. Carmen came in for half days on Saturdays so they could sleep in at least once a week, but she was a good sport about staying later too. She was really the ideal person for them, and they loved the fact that

48

she adored their baby, and Annabelle loved her too. They relied on her completely.

Alex told Sam about her trial the following week, and the deposition she'd sat in on that day, without telling him anything confidential. And he told her about an extraordinary new client in Bahrain, and a prospective new partner his two other partners had introduced him to. He was English and had a tremendous reputation in the financial world for making Olympian deals, but Sam had met him several times, and still wasn't crazy about him, and wasn't sure they should let him into the partnership. He thought he was too showy.

'What's his appeal?' Alex asked, she was always intrigued by his business. And he bounced a lot of ideas off her to see what she thought of them. He respected her opinions and her sharp sense about some of the risks that were inherent in his business.

'He's got a hell of a lot of money, and some tremendous international contacts. I don't know . . . I just think he has a very real potential to become an asshole. He's so damn full of himself. He was married to Lady Something-or-other, she's the daughter of some very high-up British lord, but it's all so much talk and bullshit. I don't know. Larry and Tom think he's a walking gold mine.'

'Does he check out? Have you made inquiries?'

'Sure. And he checks out like a Swiss clock. He made his first fortune in Iran, he was very close to the Shah before he fell, obviously. And he married his second. And I guess he's been making money ever since. Lots of it. He's had some very exotic deals in Bahrain, he still has very strong ties in the Middle East, and he kind of alludes to the fact that he feels he could "get closer to the Sultan of Brunei." Frankly,

I don't believe it. But Tom and Larry do. That's about as far up there as you get in the stratosphere, before you just break up and explode with power and money.'

'Maybe you should take him on provisionally. Try working with him for six months, and see what you think about him then.'

'I suggested that to Larry and Tom, but they think it's insulting to someone of his stature. Simon isn't exactly someone you can put on probation, I suppose. But I don't know that I'm ready to make a full commitment to him.'

'Then follow your instincts. They've never served you wrong yet. I'm a great believer in that.'

'I'm a great believer in you,' he said softly as he leaned over to kiss her. He had been crazy about her for so long, and he was always torn between admiring her mind and being totally enamored with her body. It was an unbeatable combination. 'What do you say we go to bed early tonight, and do some practicing for the weekend?'

'That has a lot of appeal,' she said, kissing his neck. They both knew they could still afford the luxury of making love now. There were still two or three more days ahead of them until she'd ovulate. Making love the next day would be too close and might diminish their chances of getting pregnant. It was complicated at best, but Alex was determined to overcome that, and their attempt to get pregnant wouldn't last forever. Eventually, she'd either get pregnant, or they'd stop trying and go back to making love anytime they wanted.

Sam turned off the lights in the study and the living room, and Alex followed him into the bedroom, and slowly took off her jeans, trying not to remember the briefcase she had set down in the corner. It sat glaring at her, and sensing her thoughts, Sam saw it too, and wondered if she should be working. He asked her gently as he unzipped his jeans and took his sweater off, and she shrugged. He was a lot more important to her at the moment.

They slipped into bed, between the Pratesi sheets she bought on Madison Avenue, and felt their cool smoothness on their skin, and as Sam wrapped his arms around her powerfully, she forgot anything but him as he made love to her. And even her longing for a baby was suddenly forgotten. All she could think of was him, as he held her in his arms and plunged slowly into her. They hung lost in space for an indeterminable time, aching with pleasure, and then returned slowly to earth, drifting back to reality again, as he purred softly in her arms, and drifted off to sleep contentedly as she held him.

'I love you,' she whispered into his hair, as he snored softly beside her. She lay there holding him for a long time, and then ever so gently, she shifted his weight, and settled him on the bed, as she went to find her briefcase. She knew she still had work to do, and she couldn't just lie in bed and not do it. She sat quietly in the room's big comfortable chair, poring over files, and making notes for the next two hours. Sam never stirred, and Annabelle woke up once, and Alex went to her and got her a drink of water. She lay next to her for a little while, and held her close to her, until she went back to sleep and Alex could go back to her own room, and continue working.

She worked until one o'clock, and then she stretched and yawned, and put the files back in her briefcase. She was used to doing this. She got a lot of her work done at night, when it didn't interfere with anyone, and she could concentrate in the silent apartment.

Sam only stirred for an instant as she climbed back into bed next to him. He had never known she was gone, and when she turned off the light, she lay next to him, thinking about him, and about Annabelle, and about her trial the following week, and the new client she'd seen that day, whom she'd decided to decline, and the English prospective partner Sam had talked to her about. There was so much to think about, and to do, sometimes she almost thought it was a shame they had to waste time sleeping. She needed every hour she could get to do all that she had to do. She couldn't afford to give up a moment. But finally, in spite of everything on her mind, she drifted off to sleep beside Sam, and she was still dead to the world when the alarm went off the next morning.

Chapter 3

Her day began, as it always did, with Sam waking her up, usually with a pat and a kiss, the radio was always on, and like most mornings, she was exhausted. Each day seemed to spill over into the following one, and she was usually tired from the endless demands on her, and the relentless stresses at the office.

She got up slowly, and went to wake Annabelle, who sometimes woke before they did, but this time she hadn't. She stretched sleepily when Alex kissed her awake, and Alex slipped into bed with her, and they giggled and talked until Annabelle was willing to get up. And then Alex took her to the bathroom and washed her face and brushed her hair, and her teeth, and then they went back to Annabelle's bedroom to pick up something for her to wear to nursery school. This morning's selection was a little outfit Sam had picked up on his last trip to Paris, it was denim with pink gingham trim, with pants, a little pink gingham shirt, and a matching jacket. It looked adorable on her with little pink high-top sneakers.

'Boy, you look cute today, Princess,' her father said admiringly, as Alex dropped her off in the kitchen for breakfast. Sam was already sitting there, shaved, showered, and dressed in a dark gray suit and a white shirt and navy Hermès tie, reading the *Wall Street Journal,* his bible.

'Thank you, Daddy.' He gave her cereal and milk, and put some toast on for her, while Alex went to shower and dress. They had the routine fairly well organized and were both flexible. When Alex had an early meeting, Sam did it all, and vice versa. This morning, they both had time, and Alex had already volunteered to take Annabelle to school. It was only a few blocks away, and she wanted to make up for the frenzy of the following week when she knew she couldn't.

Alex joined them in the kitchen forty-five minutes later, just in time to grab a cup of coffee and a piece of leftover toast. By then Sam was explaining the principles of electricity to Annabelle and why it was dangerous for her to stick a wet fork in the toaster.

'Right, Mommy?' Sam looked to her for reinforcement and she nodded and concurred as she glanced at the *New York Times* and saw that Congress had slapped the President on the wrist, and one of her least favorite superior court judges had just retired.

'At least I won't have to worry about him next week,' she said cryptically, with toast in her mouth, and Sam laughed at her. She had never been at her most coherent in the morning, though she made an enormous effort for their daughter.

'What are you up to today?' Sam asked her casually. He had a couple of important meetings with clients, and a lunch at '21' with the Englishman, which might shed a little more light on the situation.

'Nothing much. Friday's my short day,' she reminded him, but he knew. 'I'm meeting with one of the associates to prepare for my trial next week.

And then I've got a routine checkup at Anderson's, and then I'll pick Annabelle up and we're off to Miss Tilly's.' Annabelle's favorite day of the week was when she went to ballet school at Miss Tilly's. It was adorable, and Alex loved taking her, which was one of the reasons why she left her office early on Fridays, to be with her.

'Why Anderson? Something happening I should know about?' He looked concerned, but she didn't. Anderson was her gynecologist, and he was shepherding her through their attempts to have another baby.

'No big deal. I'm due for a Pap smear, no biggie. And I wanted to discuss the Serophene with him. It's a little hard to preserve my sanity, and my career, and still take the doses he's recommending. I was wondering if I should take less, or more, or what, or give it a rest for a while. I don't know. I'll let you know what he says.'

'Be sure to do that.' He smiled at her, touched that she was willing to go to such lengths to have his baby. 'And good luck with the trial prep.'

'Good luck with Simon. I hope he either trips himself up, or makes you feel more confident about him.'

'So do I,' Sam said with a sigh, 'that would certainly make life simpler. I just don't know what to make of him, or whether to trust my gut, or his pedigree, or my partners' instincts. Maybe I'm losing it, and I'm just getting paranoid in my old age.' He was turning fifty that year, and very impressed by it, but Alex did not think he was paranoid by any means, and he had always had brilliant instincts.

'I told you. Trust your gut. It's never let you down yet.'

'Thanks for the vote of confidence.' They both picked up their coats, and Alex helped Annabelle into

55

hers, and the three of them turned off the lights, locked the door, and waited for the elevator to take them to their busy days. Sam kissed them both on the street and then hailed a cab, and Alex walked Annabelle to school on Lexington, as Annabelle chattered to her, and they laughed and joked all the way there. Annabelle scampered into school easily, and Alex hailed a cab and headed downtown a moment later.

Brock was already waiting in her office for her, with all the pertinent files spread out, and there were five messages waiting on her desk, all unrelated to the Schultz case. Two of them were from the previous day's prospective client, and she jotted a note to herself to call him before she left the office.

As usual, Brock was extremely organized, and his notes on the case were extremely helpful. She thanked him, and praised him for his hard work, as they finished their work around eleven-thirty. There were still half a dozen things she needed to do before she left, but her doctor's appointment was uptown at noon, and she only had time to make a few phone calls.

'Anything else I can do to help?' he asked in his usual casual style, and she glanced at the notes on her desk, feeling frantic. She could come back to work, of course, that afternoon, and let Carmen take Annabelle to ballet, but she knew Annabelle would be disappointed. But she always seemed to be late or rushed, or trying to do too many things. Her life always felt like a relay race, with no one to pass the baton to. She certainly couldn't pass it to Sam, he had his own life to lead, and his own business headaches to attend to. At least she had Brock to help at the office. And as she thought of it, she handed him two of her messages, and asked him to return the calls for her.

'That would really help.' She smiled gratefully at him.

'Happy to do it. Anything else?' He looked at her warmly. He liked working with her, he always had, their styles were amazingly similar. It was like dancing with the perfect partner.

'You could go to my doctor for me for a checkup.'

'Happy to do that too,' he grinned, and she laughed in exasperation.

'I wish you could.' It almost seemed like a waste of time now. She was fine, and she knew it. She had never felt better. And she could talk to him on the phone about the Serophene. And as she thought of that, she glanced at her watch and made a quick decision. She dialed his number from memory, and was going to postpone the appointment, but the line was busy, and she didn't want to be rude and just not show up. He was good at what he did, and he had been very attentive to her. He had delivered Annabelle, and had been part of the three-year pursuit of pregnancy since then. It didn't seem right to just stand him up. She tried again, found the line still busy, and stood up and grabbed her coat, in spite of her irritation.

'I guess I'd better go, he probably has his phone off the hook,' she joked, 'so he doesn't lose business. Call me if you think of anything we missed on the Schultz case. I'll be home all weekend.'

'Don't worry about it. I'll call if I need to. Why don't you just forget about it. Everything is really ready for him. And we can review it all on Monday. Enjoy your weekend.'

'You sound like my husband. And what are you going to do?' she asked as she shrugged into her coat and picked up her briefcase.

'Work here all weekend of course. What do you think?' He laughed.

'Great. So don't make me any speeches. *You* enjoy *your* weekend too.' She wagged a finger at him, but she was glad that he was so conscientious, and he knew it. 'Thanks for everything. I really appreciate it.'

'Just forget it. It's going to go perfectly on Wednesday.'

'Thanks, Brock.' She flew out the door then with a wave at Liz, and five minutes later she was in a cab on her way to Park and Seventy-second. She felt a little stupid going to him, she had nothing new to report, and her complaints about the effects of the Serophene weren't new to him either. But she needed a Pap smear anyway, and it always soothed her to discuss her reproductive problems with him. John Anderson was an old friend, and he listened to her worries and complaints with concern and interest. And he was deeply sympathetic to her fear that she wouldn't get pregnant again. He reminded her that there was nothing wrong with either of them, but there was no denying that she hadn't gotten pregnant in three years. There was no specific medical reason for it, but her job was stressful certainly, and she was just that much older. They discussed the Pergonal shots again, their advantages and risks, and the possibility of in vitro fertilization, though at forty-two she was not thought to be an excellent candidate for it. They discussed ZIFT, and GIFT, and the newer technologies like donor eggs, which did not appeal to her at all. And in the end, they decided to stay with the Serophene, and he talked to her about trying artificial insemination with Sam's sperm the following month, if he'd agree, to give the egg and the sperm a better chance to 'meet up,' as he put it. He made it all seem very simple, and a lot less upsetting than it could be.

And then he did a routine exam, and the Pap smear, and, after looking at her chart, asked her when she'd last had a mammogram, because he didn't see the results for any the previous year, and she admitted she hadn't had one.

'I haven't had one in two years.' But she'd never had a lump or problem, and there was no history of it in her family. It was one of those things she just didn't worry about, although she was religious about getting annual Pap smears. And there were a variety of theories about mammograms at her age anyway, about whether to have one every year, or every other.

'You really ought to get one every year,' he scolded. 'After forty, that's important.' He was of the 'every year' school of thinking. He palpated her breasts, and found nothing there. She was small-busted, and had nursed Annabelle, all of which were supposedly good news against breast cancer, and she'd already been told that the hormones she was taking did not increase the risk of cancer, which she had found reassuring. 'When are you ovulating again?' he asked offhandedly, glancing at her chart.

'Tomorrow or the next day,' she said matter-of-factly.

'Then I think you ought to get a mammogram today. If you get pregnant tomorrow, it could be two years before you have one. You won't want to get one while you're pregnant, and they're inaccurate while you're nursing. I really want you to get one today, and then it's done with, and we don't have to think about it for another year. How about it?'

She glanced at her watch, feeling mildly exasperated.

She wanted to pick Annabelle up at school, and take her home to lunch, and then to Miss Tilly's. 'I really shouldn't. I've got things to do.'

'This is important, Alex. I think you should make time for it.' He sounded unusually firm, which worried her, and she looked at him with a sudden question.

'Do you feel something that warrants it?' He had palpated her breasts very carefully, but he always did that. And he shook his head no in answer to her question.

'Not at all. But I don't want you to have a problem later. You don't want to be careless about mammograms, Alex. They're just too important. Please. I think you should do it.' He was so insistent that she didn't have the heart to ignore him, and he was right, if she got pregnant that weekend, however unlikely it might seem, she wouldn't be able to get a mammogram for a year or two, so it was probably a good idea to do it.

'Where do I have to go?' He jotted down an address that was only five blocks away. She could easily walk it.

'The entire procedure will take five minutes.'

'Will they give me the results right there?'

'Probably not. They collect the films for the doctor to look at, when he comes in, and he might not be there. He'll call me next week, and give me the results. And of course I'll call you if there's a problem, but I'm very sure there won't be. This is just good medicine, Alex. It's wise to do this.'

'I know, John.' She appreciated how careful he was, it was just annoying to have to make time, but she knew it was worth it.

She called Carmen from his secretary's desk and asked her to pick up Annabelle at school. She said she'd be home for lunch, and she would take her to ballet. She just had an errand to do on the way home. And Carmen said it was no problem.

Alex left Dr Anderson's office then and walked briskly down Park Avenue to Sixty-eighth Street between Lexington and Park, and into what looked like a very busy office. A dozen women were sitting in the waiting room, and several technicians appeared frequently in the doorway to call their names and keep them moving. Alex gave her name to the receptionist, and hoped it wouldn't take too long, as two more women arrived. They seemed to be doing a booming business, and she noticed that with the exception of only one fairly young girl, most of the women were her age or older.

She glanced absently at a magazine, looked at her watch several times, and ten minutes after she'd arrived, a woman in a white coat came to the doorway of the waiting room and called her name. There was something very loud and impersonal about the way she said it, but Alex followed her without a word. There was something strangely invasive about having people search you for disease, as though you were carrying a concealed weapon. There was an implication of guilt just by being here, and as Alex unbuttoned her blouse she realized that she felt both angry and frightened. It was terrifying. What if there was something there? What if they found something? But as her mind started to play tricks on her and convince her she was doomed, she forced herself to realize that this was just routine. It was no more ominous than her Pap smear. The only difference was that it was being performed by strangers instead of by people she knew, but other than that, there was no difference.

The woman in the white coat stood by while she

undressed, and she offered her a gown, and told her to leave it open down the front, but other than that, there was no conversation. She pointed to a sink and some towels and told Alex to wipe off any deodorant or perfume, and then pointed to a machine standing in a corner. It looked like a large X-ray machine, and had a plastic tray and some shields somewhere in the middle. Having washed while the other woman watched, Alex walked to the machine, anxious to get it over with, and the technician rested Alex's breast on the plastic tray, and then proceeded to slowly lower the upper part of the machine down on her breast and squeeze it. The technician tightened the machine as much as possible, draped Alex's arm awkwardly, told her to hold her breath, and then took two pictures, and repeated the same procedure on the other side, and told her it was over. It was actually very simple and it was more uncomfortable than truly painful. It would have been nice to know the results then and there, but Alex felt confident that they would be fine when they called her doctor on Monday.

She left the office as quickly as she had come, grabbed a cab home, and was there in time to watch Annabelle finish her lunch and dress her for ballet. And for some odd reason, it felt better than ever to be there. One couldn't totally ignore the statistics that forced women to have mammograms each year. One in eight or one in nine women would be struck with breast cancer in their lifetime, depending on the source of the statistics. Even having been near them, having been tested for it, made one shudder a little, and be grateful for the simple blessings in one's life, like taking a child to a ballet class. And Alex couldn't help but think how lucky she was, as she stooped to kiss Annabelle's bright red curls as they left for Miss Tilly's.

'Why didn't you pick me up at school?' Annabelle asked plaintively. Alex picking her up at school on Fridays was a ritual she was used to and loved, and she resented any deviation from it.

'I had to go to the doctor for a checkup, and he took longer than I thought, sweetheart. I'm sorry.'

'Are you sick?' She looked suddenly worried and protective of her mother.

'Of course not.' Alex smiled. 'But everybody has to get checkups, even mommies and daddies.'

'Did he give you a shot?' She looked intrigued, and Alex laughed as she shook her head.

'No,' but they squeezed my boob flat as a pancake . . . 'I didn't need one.'

'Good.' Annabelle looked relieved as she skipped along beside her mother.

They proceeded to Miss Tilly's uneventfully after that, and after class they went out for ice cream, and then walked home slowly, talking about what they were going to do over the weekend. Annabelle wasn't too excited about going to the zoo. She wanted to go to the beach to swim, and Alex was explaining to her that it was too cold now to do that.

When they got home, Alex put on a video for her, and they lay down on Alex's bed and relaxed together. It seemed as though it had been a long day, preparing for the trial, and having the mammogram had left her feeling drained, and she was happy to stay home and relax with her daughter.

Carmen went home early on Friday afternoons, and Alex had dinner ready when Sam got home, later than usual, at seven. She had already fed Annabelle by then, and he opted to wait to eat until Annabelle

63

went to bed, which sounded good to Alex too. And at eight-fifteen, they were sitting in the kitchen eating fish and baked potatoes and salad, and he was telling her about his lunch with the Englishman, who had impressed him a lot more this time.

'You know, I'm actually feeling very positive about him. I think I was just worrying unduly. Larry and Tom are right. The guy is a whiz, and he could bring us some fantastic business from the Middle East. You can't ignore that, even if he is a little flashy.'

'And if he doesn't bring in business from the Middle East?' she asked cautiously.

'He will. You should hear his client list from Saudi alone.'

'And will they follow him here?' Alex was playing devil's advocate, but Sam didn't mind it. He felt comfortable now about the new man, and he had green-lighted the decision to take him in as a fourth partner. 'Are you sure, Sam? You were so worried about him yesterday. Maybe you ought to trust that.'

'I think I was being hysterical. Honestly, Alex, I talked to the guy for three hours today . . . he's the real thing. I know it. We're going to make billions,' he said confidently.

'Don't be greedy,' she scolded with a grin. 'Does this mean we can buy a château in the South of France?'

'No, but possibly a town house in New York, and an estate on Long Island.'

'We don't need that,' she said easily, and he smiled. He didn't need it either but he liked being the whiz kid of the financial world. It meant a lot to him. He liked the acclaim he had gotten from being brilliant with venture capital. His reputation and his success meant a lot to him, as well as his profits, which was why she thought he should be very careful about their new partner. But she trusted his judgment. And if the Englishman had convinced him, she was prepared to accept that.

'How did your meetings go this morning?' he asked her. 'All set for your trial next week?' He took a strong interest in her work too. Until Annabelle had come along, it was what had energized their life together.

'As much as I'm going to be. I think we'll be OK. I hope so. My client really deserves to win this one.'

'He will, with you defending him,' Sam said confidently, and she leaned over and kissed him. He looked handsome in a red sweater and jeans. He always looked good to her, better and better lately.

'What did Anderson say, by the way?'

'Not much. We ran through all the possibilities again. Pergonal still scares me, Serophene still makes me nuts, and no one wants to do in vitro on a forty-two-year-old woman, although he said some will. We talked about donor eggs, which don't appeal to me at all, and he said we might want to try artificial insemination of your sperm next month. He says sometimes that makes all the difference. I didn't know how you'd feel about it,' she said it almost shyly, and he smiled.

'I can live with it if I have to. I can think of better ways to have fun than playing with myself and reading dirty magazines, but if that'll do the trick, let's try it.'

'You're amazing. I really love you.' She kissed him, and he kissed her hard. But the test still hadn't been blue that afternoon, so they couldn't go too far.

'What about this weekend?'

'He said go for it, whenever it turns blue. It hasn't

65

yet, but I'm pretty sure it will tomorrow. It was almost there today. And he made me have a mammogram, just in case I get pregnant. Because he said that if I get pregnant, I wouldn't be having one for another year or two. It was a pain in the neck, and I had to have Carmen pick Annabelle up at school, but it was no big deal. It just seems so weird, and suddenly you realize that people do get bad results, and that scared the hell out of me.'

'But the results were fine, right?' He looked suddenly uncomfortable, and she smiled reassuringly.

'I'm sure they were. They don't tell you right there. They'll call him next week. They can only tell you if the radiologist is around, and he wasn't. But he had checked me for lumps and I didn't have any. It was just routine. High maintenance, as they call it.'

'Does it hurt?' He sounded curious, and somewhat horrified.

'Not really. They squash your boob in a machine, as flat as they can, and take pictures of it. There's something vaguely degrading about it, but I'm not sure why. You feel kind of vulnerable and stupid. I couldn't wait to leave. I'd never been so happy to see Annabelle in my life. I guess it's a reminder that things do go wrong, those things do happen to someone, and you're damn lucky when it's not you. The reminders of that are pretty scary.'

'Forget about it. Nothing like that is going to happen to you,' he said decisively, and helped her clear the table. They had a little wine, watched a movie on TV, and went to bed earlier than usual. They'd both had a hard week, and she wanted to get some rest before she became fertile over the weekend. And just as she had thought, she discovered that the kit had turned blue the next day. She knew before noon, and she whispered it to Sam over a late breakfast. Carmen took Annabelle to the park, and Sam and Alex went back to bed and made love. And she stayed in bed for over an hour after that, with her bottom propped up on pillows. She had read somewhere that that might help, and was willing to try almost anything. But she was still looking sleepy and satisfied when Sam came back for a cuddle with her just before lunchtime.

'You going to stay in bed all day?' he teased her, nuzzling her neck with his lips, and sending another thrill through her.

'With that kind of incentive, I just might.'

'When do we get to play again?' He was as fervent about it as she was.

'Anytime tomorrow.'

'Can we try again this afternoon?' he asked huskily, and she laughed as he kissed her. 'I think we need more practice.' But they both knew that they weren't 'supposed' to do it again until the next day. 'Anyway, just concentrate on making a baby,' Sam whispered to her, and then went off to shower and dress, while she dozed off again for a few minutes.

Ten minutes later, she joined him in the shower, and he was startled and aroused to feel her just behind him. It was agony forcing themselves not to make love again. The temptation was great, and they had always enjoyed each other's bodies. It was hard to restrain themselves now sometimes, just for the sake of maintaining his 'sperm count.'

'Maybe we should forget all this and just become sex fiends again . . .' he breathed into her ear, as he held her close to him in the shower, feeling the warm water pelt down on them, as little rivers of it snuck into their mouths as he kissed her. 'I love you so much . . .'

'Me too . . .' she said hungrily, as she felt him throbbing against her stomach. 'Sam . . . I want you . . .'

'No . . . no . . . no . . .' he said, teasing her, in a hoarse voice, as he turned the cold water on full force on both of them, and she screamed in astonishment as it hit her, and then she laughed as they both leapt out of the shower.

They were wearing jeans and sitting sedately in the kitchen drinking coffee and reading the paper when Carmen and Annabelle came home. Carmen made them all lunch, and Sam and Alex took Annabelle to the park that afternoon, and they all went to dinner at J. G. Melon that night. It was fun doing that sometimes on the weekends. And on Sunday, they rode their bicycles in the park, and Sam put Annabelle in the little seat on the back of his, as they rode around the reservoir. It was a beautiful warm day, and on Sunday night they all agreed that it had been the perfect weekend.

As soon as they put Annabelle to bed, and they knew she was asleep, Sam locked the door to their bedroom, and slowly peeled away Alex's clothes until she stood before him like a long, elegant flower, one perfect, exquisite lily. He made love to her as he had before, with all the force of his need, and his lust, and his passion. She was a woman who brought many things out in him, all things that only made him love and want her more. Sometimes he felt as though he couldn't love her more, but there was always a surge, a moment, a floodgate that opened somewhere and drowned them both with his feelings.

'Wow . . . if I don't get pregnant after that, I give up . . .' she whispered weakly afterwards, as she lay with her head on his chest, and he gently stroked one of her breasts with enticing fingers.

'I love you, Alex . . .' he said softly, turning over to look at her. She was so beautiful. So perfect. She always had been.

'I love you too, Sam . . . I love you more . . .' she teased, and he smiled and shook his head.

'You couldn't.'

They kissed again, and lay entwined on their bed, not even sure anymore if it mattered if they made a baby.

Chapter 4

On Monday morning, Alex got up before Annabelle or Sam, and she was dressed when she woke them both up, and breakfast was already on the table, and in the oven. She helped Annabelle dress, as usual, but Sam had promised to take her to school. Alex wanted to get to the office early. She had a mountain of things to do, and final details to prepare for the trial on Wednesday. And she had also scheduled a meeting with Matthew Billings to discuss several cases. Brock Stevens was going to be working with her all day, along with both of their paralegals.

'I'll probably be home late,' she explained to Sam, and he understood, although Annabelle looked sad when her mother told her.

'Why?' she asked, with her huge green eyes turned up to her mother's. She hated it when Alex came home late, and Alex didn't seem to like it either.

'I have a trial to get ready for, sweetheart. You know, when I go to court and talk to the judge.'

'Can't you just call him on the phone?' Annabelle looked very unhappy, and Alex smiled at her, and gave her a kiss and a hug, and promised to come home as early as she could manage.

'I'll call you when you come home from school. Have a good day, sweetheart, and have fun in school. Promise?' She touched her chin and turned the sweet little face up to her, and Annabelle nodded, her huge eyes looking into her mother's. 'What about my Halloween costume?'

'I'll check it out today, I promise.' She felt so torn, so pulled sometimes, between her family life and her career. It made her wonder how she would manage two children instead of one, but other people seemed to do it.

She put on her coat and slipped out of the apartment quietly, it was only seven-thirty in the morning. And the cab ride down Park was speedy at that hour. She was in her office by a quarter to eight, and she felt a little tug at her heart as she thought of Annabelle and Sam having breakfast without her. But by eight o'clock, she was hard at work, and Brock Stevens had just brought her coffee. And by ten-thirty she was reassured, they really were fairly well prepared for Jack Schultz's defense on Wednesday.

'What about everything else?' she asked Brock distractedly, as she went down a list of other projects she needed him to work on. He had already taken care of most of them, but she had had a number of new ideas over the weekend. And she was just outlining them to him when Elizabeth Hascomb hesitantly opened the door to her office, and peeked in at them. But the moment Alex saw her, she shook her head and put up a hand to stop her. She didn't want any interruptions. Her phone was turned off and she had already told Liz not to come in or interrupt her.

Liz hesitated at the door, in spite of Alex's stern look, and Brock turned to see what was distracting Alex.

71

'Something wrong?' Maybe it was an emergency, but Alex looked very annoyed at the interruption.

'Liz, I asked you not to interrupt us.' Her tone was sharper than usual, but the pressure on her was enormous.

'I know . . . I . . . I'm terribly sorry but . . .' She spoke to Alex apologetically from the doorway.

'Did something happen to Annabelle or Sam?' For a moment, Alex looked terrified, but Liz was quick to shake her head and reassure her. 'Then I don't want to hear it.' Alex turned away again, fully prepared to ignore her.

'Dr Anderson called. Twice. He asked me to interrupt you.'

'Anderson? For heaven's sake . . .' Now Alex looked really annoyed. He had told her he would call her either way about the mammogram, and he was probably calling to reassure her. But asking to interrupt her was a real imposition. 'He can wait. I'll call him when we break for lunch, if we do. Otherwise, I'll call him later.'

'He said he wanted to talk to you this morning. Before noon.' It was already eleven-thirty, and Liz was being a nuisance. But Dr Anderson had insisted that it was very important, and well worth annoying Alex. So Liz had taken him at his word, and remained steadfast in her delivery of his message. But Alex looked anything but pleased. She felt sure that the call was just routine, and it wasn't worth throwing everyone into a tizzy for. For an instant, as she looked at Liz, she wondered if it could be bad news, but the idea of that was so inconceivable that she went back to being irritated instead of worried.

'I'll call him when I can. Thank you, Liz,' she said pointedly, and went back to the list she was explaining

72

to Brock, but now he was looking distracted.

'Why don't you call him, Alex? It must be important for him to ask Liz to interrupt you.'

'Don't be silly. We have work to do.'

'I could use another cup of coffee anyway. I'll get you one too, while you call him. I'm sure it'll only take you a couple of minutes.' She was prepared to resist, but it was clear now that Liz had so unnerved everyone that none of them would get back to work until she called her doctor.

'Oh for heaven's sake. This is ridiculous. Okay . . . get me a fresh cup, please. I'll see everyone back here in five minutes.' It was eleven thirty-five, and eleven-forty by the time he and the paralegals cleared the room. They were wasting precious minutes. They had work to do. She watched them close the door behind them as they left, and she quickly called her doctor, anxious to get the conversation over quickly.

His receptionist answered the phone, and promised to put her right through to the doctor. The wait seemed interminable, as much because she had other things to do as because she was suddenly nervous. What if it *was* bad news? She felt foolish for even thinking it, but it was possible. Lightning had certainly struck others before her.

'Alex?' Dr Anderson was on the line, and he sounded as busy as she did.

'Hi, John. What's so important?'

'I'd like you to stop by at lunchtime, if you could.' His voice gave away nothing.

'That's impossible. I'm going to trial in two days, and I have a stack of things to do. I've been in my office since seven forty-five this morning, and I probably won't leave here till ten o'clock tonight. Can we discuss it on the phone?'

'I'd rather not. I really think you should come in to see me.' Shit. What did this mean? She found that suddenly her hand was shaking.

'Is something wrong?' She couldn't bring herself to say the word, but she finally knew she had to. 'Is it the mammogram?' She didn't have any lumps, so how could it be? But he hesitated for a long time before he answered.

'I'd like to discuss it with you.' It was obvious that he didn't want to do this over the phone, and she was suddenly afraid to force him.

'How much time do you need?' She was glancing at her watch, and trying to assess how much time she could afford. At lunchtime, even the traffic would be against her.

'Half an hour? I'd like to spend a little time talking to you. Could you come right now? I just saw my last patient of the morning. I've got a woman at the hospital, and I have a patient in early labor. This would probably be as good a time as any.'

'I'll be there in five or ten minutes,' she said tersely, standing as she prepared to hang up. Her heart was suddenly racing. This couldn't be good. But now she wanted to know, whatever it was. Maybe they had confused her results with someone else's.

'Thank you, Alex. I'll be as quick as I can.'

'I'll be right over.'

Alex sped past Liz, carying her handbag and her coat, Brock and the others weren't even back yet. 'Tell them to get something to eat, I'll be back in forty-five minutes.' She was halfway to the elevator by then, and Liz shouted after her down the hallway.

'Are you all right?'

'I'm fine. Order me a turkey sandwich.' And as Liz watched her disappear down the hall, she wondered if

74

she might be pregnant. She knew they wanted more kids, and John Anderson was her obstetrician.

But Alex knew full well that it wasn't that, as she rode uptown in a cab, agonizing over why he had called her. It had to be the mammogram, and then suddenly she thought of it. It wasn't the mammogram, it was the Pap smear. Shit. She had cancer of the cervix. How would she get pregnant now? Although she had a number of friends who had had treatments using freezing techniques or laser beams applied to precancerous conditions, and had still managed to get pregnant. Maybe it wasn't as bad as she feared, all she wanted to know was that her life wasn't in danger and she could still get pregnant.

The cab reached his office in record time, and she hurried inside to the empty waiting room. They were expecting her and they waved her straight through to his office. He was wearing a suit, instead of his white coat, and he looked unexpectedly serious when he saw her.

'Hi, John, how are you?' She was a little out of breath from hurrying and from the anticipation of seeing him, and she sat down in a chair with her coat on.

'Thank you for coming. But I really thought you should. I wanted to talk to you myself, in person.'

'Was it the Pap smear?' she asked, feeling her heart speed up again. And the palms of her hands were damp as she clutched her handbag. But he was shaking his head.

'No, it isn't. It's the mammogram.' But it couldn't be. She had no lumps, no bumps, no problems. He reached down then and put a piece of film on the light box behind him. He pointed to a frontal view, and then put another film up with a side view. It all

75

looked very mysterious to her, like a weather map of Atlanta. He turned then to look at her, with a look of painful importance. 'There's a mass there,' he pointed to it, and only because he showed her where it was could she see it. 'It's very large and quite deep. It could be a number of things, but the radiologist and I are very worried.'

'What do you mean, it could be a number of things?' She was suddenly totally confused by what he was saying. It was as though all of a sudden she couldn't hear him. Why was there a mass deep inside her breast? What was it and how did it get there?

'There are several possibilities, but a mass of this size, at this depth, in this particular area, is never a good thing, Alex. We think you have a tumor.'

'Oh Jesus.' No wonder he didn't want to tell her on the phone, and insisted that Liz interrupt her. 'What does that mean? What happens now?' Her voice was thin and her face pale, and for a moment she thought she might faint, but she forced herself not to.

'You need a biopsy, as quickly as possible. Within the next week ideally.'

'I'm going into trial in two days. I can't until after the trial is over.' It was as though she hoped it would go away by then, but they both knew it wouldn't.

'You can't do that.'

'I can't let my client down. Are you telling me a few days will make that much difference?' She was horrified. What was he saying to her? That she was dying? The thought and the terror of it made her tremble.

'A few days won't necessarily make that much difference,' he admitted cautiously, 'but you can't afford to drag your heels on this. You need to choose a surgeon and get the biopsy done as soon as possible, and then you'll have to see what he recommends, based on the pathologist's findings.' Oh God. It was all so complicated and frightening, and so ugly.

'Can't you do the biopsy?' She sounded suddenly desperate and very frightened. She felt as vulnerable as she had feared she would when she went to the mammography lab and began to panic. And now, the worst had happened, or almost. It was happening. It was rolling out in front of her like a terrifying movie.

'I don't do biopsies. You need a surgeon.' He picked up a piece of paper from his desk then, and she noticed that she had already been there for half an hour, but suddenly her whole life had changed, and she wasn't ready to leave yet. 'I wrote down the names of a few very good people, a woman and two men. You should talk to them, and see who you like best. They're all excellent surgeons.' *Surgeons!*

'I don't have time for this.' She started to cry in spite of herself, it was all so horrifying, and she felt uncharacteristically overwhelmed and astonishingly helpless. She was torn between anger and terror. 'I don't have time to go shopping for a doctor. I have a trial, I can't suddenly back out of it. I have responsibilities.' She sounded hysterical even to her own ears, but she couldn't help it. And then she looked up at him in genuine terror. 'Do you think it's malignant?'

'Possibly.' He wanted to be honest with her. On the film, it didn't look good. 'It could very well be. Or it could be fooling us into thinking it is. We won't know till you get the biopsy, but it's important that you do that quickly, so you can decide on a plan of action.'

'What does that mean?'

'It means that if the biopsy is positive, you'll have to make some decisions about the course of treatment. Your surgeon will advise you, of course, but some of the decisions will have to be yours.'

'You mean like whether or not to take my breast off?' She looked appalled and her voice was shrill as she asked him.

'Let's not get ahead of ourselves here. We don't know anything yet, do we?' He was trying to be gentle with her, but it was making it worse. She wanted to face it now, she wanted him to swear to her it wouldn't be malignant. But he couldn't do that.

'We know I have a mass deep in my breast, and you're worried about it. That could mean I'll lose a breast, couldn't it?' She had him on the witness stand and she was relentless.

'Yes, it could,' he said quietly. He was deeply sorry for her. He had always liked her, and this was a terrible blow for any woman.

'And then what? That's it? The breast is off, no more problems?'

'Possibly, but not necessarily. It's not as simple as all that. I wish it were, but it isn't. It will depend on the type of tumor you have, the extent of its malignancy, if there is any, and the nature of the involvement. It will depend on whether or not your lymph nodes are involved, how many, and whether or not it has spread to other parts of your body. Alex, there are no simple answers. You may need extensive surgery, you may need a lumpectomy, you could need a course of chemotherapy, or radiation. I just don't know. I can't tell you anything until you have a biopsy. And I don't care how busy you are, make time to talk to these surgeons. You *have* to.'

'How soon?'

'Do your trial if you have to, if it's really only a week or two, but plan to have the biopsy in two weeks, no matter what. And we'll take it from there after you do that.'

'Who do you like best on this list?' She handed it back to him, and he glanced at it, and then handed it back to her quietly.

'They're all excellent, but I like Peter Herman. He's a very good man, and a nice one. He cares about more than just surgery and biopsies. He's a human being, for a surgeon.'

'Fine,' she nodded, still looking stunned. 'I'll call him tomorrow.'

'Why not this afternoon?' He was pushing her, but he wanted to, he didn't want her to use her work as an excuse, or get caught up in denial.

'I'll call him later.' And then she had a sobering thought, as she glanced at him again. She felt as though she had a ten-thousand pound weight on her shoulders. 'What if I got pregnant this weekend? What if I'm pregnant and have a malignant tumor?'

'We'll cross that bridge when we come to it. You'll know if you're pregnant around the same time you have the biopsy.'

'What if I have cancer and I'm pregnant?' Her voice was nervous and strident. What if she had gotten pregnant and she had to sacrifice her baby?

'We'll have to establish priorities, you're the most important.'

'Oh God.' She dropped her face in her hands, and then looked up at him again a moment later. 'Do you think the hormones I'm taking have anything to do with this?' The thought of it terrified her even more. What if she had killed herself trying to get pregnant?

'I honestly don't think so. Call Peter Herman. See him as soon as possible, talk to him, and let's do the biopsy as soon as you can, within reason.' It seemed a reasonable course of action. And now she had to go home and tell Sam there was a mass on

79

her mammogram. She still couldn't believe it. But it was there. She could see it on the film, and in the expression in John Anderson's eyes. He looked devastated, as she stood up and looked at him. She had been with him for almost an hour.

'I'm so sorry, Alex. If there's anything I can do right now, don't hesitate to call me. Tell me which surgeon you settle on, and I'll take it from there.'

'I'll start with Peter Herman.'

He handed her the films from the mammogram, so she could show them to whichever surgeon she chose. Just the word 'surgeon' seemed ominous, and as she walked out into the October air, she felt as though she'd just been hit with a two-by-four to her stomach. She couldn't believe what she'd heard, or what had happened.

She picked up her arm and hailed a cab, trying not to remember everything she'd ever heard about mastectomies and lumpectomies, and women who could no longer raise their arms, and other women who had died from cancer. Everything he had said to her was suddenly jumbled in her head, and as she rode back to the office, she didn't even cry. She just sat and stared straight ahead, unable to believe what he had told her.

And when she got back to her office, the whole team was sitting there, Liz and Brock, the law clerk, and the two paralegals. They were waiting for her, and Liz had ordered her turkey sandwich on whole wheat bread, but she just couldn't eat it. She stood and stared at them, and Brock noticed that her face was deadly white, but no one said anything. They went straight to work, and went right through to six o'clock. It was only after that, when they were summing up, after everyone had left, that Brock even dared to ask her.

'Are you all right?' he asked cautiously. She had looked terrible to him all day, and her face had been deathly pale ever since she came back from the doctor's. And more than once, he had noticed that her hands were shaking when she passed him papers.

'I'm fine. Why?' She tried to look nonchalant, but she failed dismally. He was smarter than that, but he didn't want to press her.

'You look tired. Maybe you're burning the candle at too many ends, Mrs Parker. What did the doctor say?'

'Oh, nothing. It was a waste of time. He just needed to give me the results of some tests, and they never do it over the phone. It was ridiculous really. He could have mailed it to me, and saved us all time.' He didn't believe a word she said, but it seemed to be important to her to say it. He just hoped it was nothing serious. If it was, going to trial in two days certainly wasn't going to help her. He would do all he could for her, but she was still the attorney of record and had to take all the heat and the pressure, and do all the arguing and much of the preparation. He didn't dare ask her if she was up to doing the case, he knew that she would have taken the question as an insult.

'Are you going home?' He hoped for her sake that she was. He still had work to do for her, for the trial, but he could see a pile of files on her desk too and that didn't bode well for an early evening.

'I've still got a few things to do, for other clients.' She had managed to return all her phone calls late that afternoon, but she hadn't had time to call Peter Herman, or so she told herself when she thought of it. She was planning to call him the following morning.

'Can I do anything to help? You ought to go home

and get some rest,' he urged, but she was determined to stay and finish.

He went back to his own office after that, and she called Annabelle at home, who was upset that Alex hadn't called her at lunchtime.

'You said you would,' she said, making Alex feel instantly guilty. She had completely forgotten after her unexpected trip to the doctor.

'I know, sweetheart. I meant to, but I got stuck in a meeting with a lot of people and I couldn't call.'

'That's okay, Mommy.' She went on to tell her then everything she'd done that afternoon with Carmen. And listening to her excited little tales made Alex feel almost jealous. She hated even more having to tell her she was going to work late. Suddenly, not being with her seemed all the more poignant.

'Can I wait up for you?' Annabelle said hopefully, as Alex sighed, praying that the shadows in her breast would not turn out to be cancer.

'I'll be too late. But I'll kiss you. I promise. And I'll wake you up tomorrow morning. This is just for this week and next, and then we'll be back to having lunch and dinner together.'

'Are you taking me to ballet this week?' Annabelle was really putting it to her, and Alex was wondering where Sam was.

'I can't. Remember? We talked about it. I'm going to be talking to the judge this week and next. I can't come to ballet.'

'Can't you ask the judge to let you come?'

'No, sweetheart. I wish I could. Where's Daddy? Is he home yet?'

'He's asleep.'

'At this hour?' It was seven o'clock. How could he be asleep?

82

'He was watching TV and he fell asleep. Carmen says she'll wait for you.'

'Let me talk to her. And Annabelle. . .' Her eyes suddenly filled with tears as she thought of her, that incredible little pixie face with big green eyes and the freckles and the red hair. What if Alex died? What if Annabelle lost her mother? The thought of it choked her so badly she couldn't speak for a moment and then she whispered the words. 'I love you, Annabelle . . .'

'I love you too, Mommy. See you later.'

'Sweet dreams.' And then Carmen came on the phone, and Alex told her that she could leave as soon as Annabelle was in bed. All she had to do was wake Sam and tell him she was going.

'I feel bad waking him, Mrs Parker. I stay till you come home.'

'I won't be home for hours, Carmen. Honestly, just tell him when you want to go. He'll wake up.'

'Okay, okay. When you comin' home?'

'Probably not till around ten o'clock. I have a lot to do in the office.' But when she hung up, she just sat staring at the phone, thinking of all of them, feeling as though she had already lost them. It was as though a shadow had come between her and them today. They were alive, and she might be dying. It wasn't impossible. It was incredible. She still believed there had to be a mistake. She wasn't sick, she didn't have a lump. All she had was a gray shadow on an X-ray. But a gray shadow that John Anderson had admitted could kill her, if it was malignant. It was unbelievable. Yesterday she had been trying to get pregnant, and today her own life was in danger. And the hormones she had taken the week before made it all the more difficult now to maintain her composure. They made everything seem more upsetting, and more alarming, and she tried to tell herself that the terror she was feeling wasn't real, it was just the hormones.

Brock checked back with her at nine o'clock, and he noticed that she still hadn't eaten the sandwich that had been on her desk since lunchtime. She had been drinking coffee all day, and now she was drinking a big glass of water.

'You're going to get sick if you don't eat,' he scolded her with a look of concern. She looked even worse than she had before. She was almost gray now.

'I wasn't hungry . . . actually, I just forgot to eat. I was too busy.'

'That's a lousy excuse. You're not going to do Jack Schultz any good if you get sick before his trial date, or in the middle of it.'

'Yeah, that's a thought,' she said vaguely, and then she looked up at him with worried eyes, 'I guess you could take over for me, Brock, if you had to.'

'I wouldn't think of it. You're the attorney they want. You're what he's paid for.' It was exactly what she had said to her doctor that afternoon, when she said she couldn't do the biopsy until after the trial. People were depending on her . . . and then she thought of Annabelle and Sam and had to fight back tears again. Her engine was running low, and she was suddenly overwhelmed by everything that had happened. The mammogram films were in an envelope on her desk, but what she had seen there was emblazoned in her mind forever.

'Why don't you go home?' he asked gently. 'I'll finish up. You've got everything a lot more in control than you think. Trust me.' He was gentle and kind, and half an hour later, she decided to go home. She was just too tired to make sense anymore, or do intelligent work. She felt as though she'd been run over by a semi. And for the first time in years, she didn't even take her briefcase. Brock noticed it, but he didn't remind her. And as he watched her go, he felt sorry for her. It was obvious that something was wrong. She had never looked worse, but he didn't know her well enough to ask her, or offer to help her.

She laid her head back against the seat of the cab, and she felt as though it were a bowling ball, and it was just too heavy to hold up anymore. She just couldn't do it. And when she got home, she paid the cab, and walked into the building, feeling like a thousand-year-old woman. She rode up in the elevator, wondering what she was going to say to Sam. This would be terrible news for him too, for all of them. A bad mammogram was nothing to take lightly, and statistics about breast cancer kept leaping into her head, and none of them were good news. She couldn't even begin to imagine how she would tell him.

He was watching TV in the living room when she walked in, and he looked up at her with a smile when he saw her. He was wearing jeans and his white shirt from work. His tie was still lying on the table.

'Hi, how was your day?' he asked cheerfully, reaching out to her, and she sat down heavily on the couch beside him. She suddenly had to fight back tears again, just seeing him had brought all the terror back to her. She just couldn't bear it. 'Wow . . . looks like a rough day . . .' And then he remembered the hormones she'd been taking. 'Oh poor baby, those damn pills making you emotional again? Maybe you shouldn't take them.' Between that and the trial, she really had a lot to cope with. He pulled her into his arms, and she clung to him as though she were drowning.

'You look worn out,' he said sympathetically when she looked up at him and dried her eyes. He was right.

The pills were making this even harder than it should be. Or were they? 'You must be going crazy before the trial.'

'I am. It was a hellish day,' she admitted, as she lay back on the couch next to him, exhausted.

'I hate to say it, but you look it. Did you eat?'

She shook her head. 'I wasn't hungry.'

'Great. How do you think you're going to get pregnant if you starve yourself. Come on.' He pulled her to her feet, or tried to, 'I'll make you an omelet.'

'I couldn't eat. Honest. I'm beat. Why don't we just go to bed?' That was all she wanted. She wanted to see Annabelle, and lie next to him, for as long as she could. Forever.

'Something wrong?' He suddenly wondered why she looked the way she did. She looked worse than usual, even before a trial, and she didn't answer him as she tiptoed into Annabelle's bedroom. She stood there for a long time, watching her, and then knelt down next to her, and kissed her. And then she walked into their own room. He was watching her, concerned, and she started undressing, and left her clothes on the chair as she put on her nightgown. She didn't even have the energy to take a shower or brush her hair. She brushed her teeth, and climbed into bed and lay there with her eyes closed, knowing she had to tell him.

'Baby,' he tried again, as he lay down next to her, 'what's wrong? Did something happen at the office?' She took her work very seriously, and if she'd done something that had injured a client she would have tormented herself just as she seemed to be doing now. But she was quick to shake her head and deny it.

'Anderson called me again today,' she said in a low voice, and he watched her.

'And?'

86

'I went to see him at lunchtime.'

'What about? You can't have figured out already that you're pregnant?' It had only been two days, and he smiled at her. She was so anxious to have a baby.

She hesitated for a long time, torturing both of them, but she hated to say the words, to tell him and make it real. She hated to do it to all of them. But she knew she had to.

'There was a shadow on my mammogram.' She said it like a death knell, but Sam seemed a lot less impressed than she was.

'So?'

'It could mean that I have a tumor.'

' "Could." That means they don't know squat. And Martians could land on Park Avenue at midnight. But will they? Not likely. Probably just as likely as your "shadow" being a tumor.' She liked the way he thought about it. It restored her faith in her own body, which, in the past twelve hours, seemed to have betrayed her. But maybe it hadn't. Maybe Sam was right. Maybe she was just overreacting. 'They don't know anything. It's probably just what it appears to be, and nothing more than that. A shadow.'

'Anderson wants me to see a surgeon and have a biopsy. He gave me three names to call, but I don't have any time before the trial. I thought I'd call one tomorrow, and see if he could see me at lunchtime. Otherwise, I'll have to wait till after the trial,' she said, looking worried.

'Did he think that would make a big difference?'

'Not really,' she admitted, feeling better than she had all day, 'but he said I should get to it soon.'

'Obviously, but there's no need to panic. Half the time these guys are protecting themselves, they don't want to get sued, so they tell you the absolute worst, just in case, so you can't ever say they didn't warn you. And then if it's good news, everyone's happy. They never take into account the damage they cause by scaring you to death. For chrissake, Alex, you're a lawyer, you should know that. Don't let these bozos scare you!' She looked up at him with a grin, suddenly feeling both relieved and foolish, and he was smiling at her. He wasn't panicking. He didn't think she was going to die. He wasn't clinging to her, or being melodramatic. He had put the matter completely into perspective. And she suddenly realized that he was right. Even John Anderson wouldn't want to leave himself open to a lawsuit.

'What do you think I should do?'

'Get through your trial, have the biopsy in your own sweet time, but stay calm, and don't let these clowns scare the pants off you. And I'll bet you the profit on my next deal that your shadow is just that . . . and nothing more. Look at you, you're the healthiest woman I know. Or at least you would be if you ate occasionally and got some sleep.' But just talking to him now she felt better, and so relieved. He was intelligent, he kept a cool head, and he was probably right. It was probably just a scare, and not a tumor.

She felt immeasurably better when they turned off the lights that night, and only slightly worried again when she woke up the next morning. For an instant, she remembered that something terrible had happened the day before and she had that feeling of foreboding you get when you're in the midst of disaster. But as soon as she woke up she reminded herself of everything Sam had said and she felt better again. And she made a point of waking Annabelle up and having her sit in the kitchen with her while she made breakfast. She even had a list of possible costumes for her. Liz had researched it the day before. They had a pumpkin, a princess, a ballerina, and a nurse, all in Annabelle's size, who opted instantly for the princess. It was exactly what she had dreamed of. 'Oh Mommy, I love you!' she said, throwing her arms around her mother's waist.

'Me too,' Alex said, giving her a one-handed squeeze with a smile, as she flipped pancakes for her. She suddenly felt like celebrating. It was as though she had already been relieved of a terrible burden. Annabelle was happy, and Sam had convinced her that the shadow the doctors had seen was surely a false alarm. She wanted with her entire being to believe him. And this time, when Alex left for work, she swore and crossed her heart that she would call Annabelle at lunchtime.

She left her with Sam again, and kissed him fervently before she left, thanking him for his reassurances of the night before.

'You should have called me at the office. I'd have told you then.'

'I know. I guess I overreacted. It was stupid.' But anyone would have.

She kissed them both good-bye, and hurried out to the office. Brock was already waiting for her again, along with the rest of the team. She met with Matthew Billings, and it was eleven-fifteen before she remembered to call the surgeon Dr Anderson had recommended.

A nurse asked why she was calling him, and Alex explained that it was about a biopsy, as Brock came back into her office for a file, and she prayed that he would take it quickly. He did and then disappeared again, as she wished she had locked the door. But maybe, if Sam was right, it really wouldn't matter.

89

Eventually, Dr Peter Herman came on the line, and he sounded serious to her, and not terribly friendly. She explained about the shadow on the film, and that Dr Anderson was concerned and felt that she should see him.

'I've already spoken to him,' Peter Herman explained. 'He called me this morning. You're going to need a biopsy, Mrs Parker. As soon as possible, I believe Dr Anderson explained that.'

'Yes, he did.' She tried to maintain the calm that Sam had given her the night before, but it was more difficult with a stranger. She felt threatened by him, and everything he represented. 'But I'm a trial attorney, and I start a trial tomorrow. I really can't do anything for the next week or ten days. I was hoping to come and see you after that.'

'That would be a very foolish decision,' he said bluntly, denying everything Sam had said to her, or perhaps confirming it. Maybe he was just protecting himself from malpractice, she told herself. This way, he had warned her. 'Why don't you come and see me today, and then we'll know where we stand. And if we need to, we can set the biopsy up for a week from next Monday. Would that suit you?'

'I . . . yes . . . it would . . . but . . . I'm very busy today. My trial starts tomorrow.' She had already told him that, but she was feeling desperate again, and very frightened.

'Two o'clock this afternoon?' He was relentless, and she found herself incapable of arguing with him. She nodded her head silently at first, and then agreed to come to his office at two p.m. Fortunately, his office wasn't far from hers. 'Would you like to bring a friend?' The question surprised her.

'Why would I do that?' Was he planning to hurt her,

or render her somehow unable to take care of herself? Why would she take a friend to meet a doctor?

'I find that women very often get confused when confronted with difficult situations and large amounts of information.'

'Are you serious?' If it weren't so shocking, she would have laughed. 'I'm a trial lawyer. I deal with difficult situations every day, and probably more "information" than you deal with in a year.' She was not amused by his comment.

'The information you deal with normally is not about your own health. Even physicians find facing malignancies of their own difficult and upsetting.'

'We don't know that I have a malignancy yet, do we?'

'You're quite right, we don't. Will I see you at two o'clock?' She wanted to say no, but she knew that she shouldn't.

'I'll see you then,' she said, and hung up, furious with him. Part of her reaction was the hormones and part of it was that he was the potential bearer of bad news and she feared him deeply. And as soon as she hung up, she called one of her paralegals in, and gave her an unusual project. She gave her all three names Dr Anderson had given her, and told her to find out about their reputations. 'I want to know everything about them, any dirt, any good stuff, what do other doctors think. I'm not sure who you should call, but call everyone, Sloan-Kettering, Columbia Presbyterian, the medical schools where they teach. Call everyone you have to. And please don't tell anyone you're doing this for me. Is that clear?'

'Yes, Mrs Parker,' the paralegal said meekly, but she was the most industrious worker assigned to Alex and she knew she would get her the information.

And two hours later, she already had the scoop on Peter Herman. Alex was about to leave when the girl came hurrying in and told Alex that he had a reputation of being cold to his patients, but he was the best there was surgically, and there was something to be said for that. One of the hospitals she'd called, and the most illustrious, said he was extremely conservative but one of the best breast surgeons in the country. And the early reports on the other two were that they were almost as good, but not quite, and even more unpleasant to their patients than Peter Herman. Both of them were supposedly prima donnas. And Herman supposedly liked dealing with doctors and not patients, which was probably why John Anderson liked him.

'At least he knows what he's doing, even if he's no Prince Charming,' Alex commented as she thanked her paralegal, and asked her to continue to follow up on the others. And as she took a cab to his office, she wondered what he would say to her about the gray mass on the mammogram. She had had a range of views now, Sam's optimistic one, and John Anderson's far more ominous one, which Sam said was probably nonsense. She liked Sam's view of it a lot better.

But unfortunately, Peter Herman did not share Sam's assessment of the situation. He told her that the shadowy area they saw was clearly a tumor deep in her breast in an area, and of a shape that almost always indicated a malignancy. Naturally, they couldn't be sure until they did the biopsy, but in his experience what they were going to find would be a tumor, and not a good one. After that, it would depend on the stage it was in, the degree to which it had infiltrated, whether it was hormone receptor negative or positive, and if there was metastasis. He was cold and matter-of-fact, and he painted anything but a pretty picture.

'What will all of that mean?'

'I won't know till we get in there. At best, a lumpectomy. If not, you may want to follow a more extreme course, which would mean a modified radical mastectomy. It's the one sure way of being certain that you've eliminated the disease, depending on the stage of the tumor, of course, and the extent of the involvement.' He showed her a chart that meant absolutely nothing to her, which had letters and numbers on it and covered a variety of contingencies, all of them completely confusing.

'Is a mastectomy the only way to wipe out the disease?' she said in a strangled voice, realizing that he'd been right. She was completely confused, and felt utterly stupid. She was no longer the trial lawyer, she was merely the woman.

'Not necessarily,' he answered her, 'we may want to add radiation or chemotherapy. Again, this will depend on other factors at the time, and the extent of the involvement.' Radiation or chemotherapy? *And* a modified radical mastectomy? Why didn't they just kill her? It wasn't that she was so enamored with her breasts, but the idea of being completely disfigured *and* desperately ill from chemo or radiation made her want to vomit just thinking about it. Where was Sam now with his cheerful prognosis, and warnings about surgeons fearing malpractice? She couldn't even remember it now. What Herman said was so much more real, and so utterly terrifying, she could hardly think straight.

'What exactly would the procedure be?'

'We'll schedule you for a biopsy. I would prefer to do it under general anesthesia since the mass is so deep in your breast. And after that, you'll have to make the decision.'

'*I* will?'

'Presumably. You're going to have to make some informed choices. There are a number of options in this area of medicine. You'll have to make some of the decisions, they don't all rest with me here.'

'Why not? You're the doctor.'

'Because there are choices to be made, involving more or less risk, and more or less discomfort. It's your body and your life, in the final analysis, and you must make the decisions too. But with early detections such as these, I almost always suggest a mastectomy. It's a great deal wiser and surer. You can always have reconstructive surgery within a few months to restore the appearance of the breast, if you wish to.'

He made it sound like having a fender put back on a car, and not a breast on her body. And she didn't know it, but his preference for mastectomies as the surer cure was what had earned him his conservative reputation.

'Would you do the biopsy and the mastectomy on the same day?'

'Normally not. But if you prefer it that way, we can. You seem to be a very busy woman, and it would save you time, if you're prepared to entrust me with that decision. We can work that out beforehand, in the event of certain findings. We would have to plan that carefully.' Of course, she thought of Sam, to avoid a lawsuit. And then she thought of something else.

'What if I turn out to be pregnant in the next few weeks?'

'Is that possible?' He seemed surprised, and she felt faintly insulted. Did he think she was too old to have babies, just tumors?

94

'I've been taking Serophene and trying to get pregnant.'

'Then I would think you'd want to abort, if you were, and proceed with treatment. You can't afford to let something like this go for eight or nine months. Your husband and family need you, Mrs Parker, more than they need another baby.' It was all so coldblooded and so simple, like the razor-sharp edge of a scalpel. She still couldn't believe what she was hearing. 'I'd like to suggest that we schedule your biopsy for a week from next Monday and you come in to see me before that to discuss the options.'

'There don't seem to be very many of those, or am I missing something?'

'I'm afraid not, at this point anyway. First we have to see what you've got there. And then we can decide what to do about it. But you should know that my preference is almost always mastectomy in the case of early cancers. I want to save your life, Mrs Parker, more than your breast. It's a question of priorities. And if you have a malignancy that deep in your breast, you may be a lot safer, and better off, without the breast now. Later, it may be too late. It's a conservative stance, but it's one that has proven to be reliable over the years. Some of the newer, riskier views can be disastrous. Doing a mastectomy early on could well be a great deal safer. And if indicated after the surgery, I'd want to start an aggressive course of chemotherapy four weeks after the surgery. This may sound frightening to you now, but six or seven months from now, you'll be free of the disease, hopefully forever. Of course, I can't recommend that to you now. We'll have to see what the biopsy tells us.'

'Would I still be able to . . .' She could hardly bring herself to say it, but she knew she had to. She wanted to know, since he had been so free about suggesting an abortion if she were pregnant, '. . . would I be able to conceive afterwards?'

He hesitated, but not for long. He had been asked this question before, though usually by younger women. At forty-two, most women were more interested in saving their own lives than in having babies. 'It's possible. There's about a fifty percent sterility rate after chemotherapy. But it's a risk we'd have to take, of course. It could do you grave harm not to have it.' Grave harm? What did that mean? That it would kill her not to have chemo? It was a nightmare. 'You'll have time to think about all this, during your trial. And I'd like you to make an appointment whenever possible. I'll try to accommodate your schedule as best I can. I understand from John Anderson that you're a very busy attorney.' He almost cracked a smile, but not quite, and Alex wondered if this was the 'human' side John Anderson had referred to. If so, it was very small in comparison to the cold-blooded technician and scientist he was the rest of the time, when he was not being 'human.'

He scared her to death with his icy factual explanations, but she also knew of his excellent reputation. What she needed was an excellent surgeon, if it turned out that she had a tumor and it was malignant. And she could have Sam to boost her spirits.

'Is there anything else I should explain to you?' he asked, and surprised her with the question. But all she could do was shake her head. It was worse than what she'd heard the day before, and he had completely overwhelmed her. She could already imagine herself without her left breast, and undergoing chemotherapy. Did that mean she would also lose her hair? She couldn't bring herself to ask him. But she had known women who had been through it, and worn wigs, or had the shortest of short haircuts. She knew what everyone did, that if you had chemotherapy, you lost your hair. It was just one more affront to a rapidly growing list of terrors.

She left his office in a daze, and when she got back to her own office, she wasn't even sure what the doctor looked like. She knew she had spent an hour with him, but suddenly his face was blank, along with almost everything he had said except the words tumor and malignancy, mastectomy and chemotherapy. The rest was an indistinguishable blur of sounds and noises.

'Are you okay?' Brock walked into her office almost as soon as she got back, and he was shocked at how she looked again, and very worried. 'You're not getting sick, are you?' She already was sick, probably, according to her doctors. It seemed incredible. She felt perfect, nothing hurt, she wasn't ill, and they were telling her she probably had cancer. Cancer. She still couldn't bring herself to believe it. Nor could Sam.

She told him that night, when she got home, everything Dr Herman had said, and Sam just brushed all of it off again, with the same calm, easy insistence.

'I'm telling you, Alex, these guys are protecting themselves against malpractice.'

'But what if they're not? What if they're right? This guy is the biggest breast surgeon in his field, why would he lie to me just to cover his own ass?'

'Maybe he has a big mortgage on his house, maybe he needs to take so many boobs off every year to cover it. What do I know? You've gone to a surgeon, he's not going to tell you to go home and take an aspirin. Hell, no, he's going to tell you that you need to take your boob off. And if nothing else, he's going to scare the hell out of you, to cover himself, just in case you do have something there, which I don't believe for a minute.'

'Are you telling me he's lying to me? That he'd do a mastectomy even if I didn't have cancer?' Cancer. They were saying it now like 'Kleenex,' or 'microwave,' or 'nosebleed.' It was a dreaded word that had become part of her daily vocabulary, and she hated hearing it, especially when she said it. 'Do you think this guy is a complete charlatan?' She didn't know what to think now, and Sam's attitude was making her crazy.

'Probably not. He's probably basically responsible, or Anderson wouldn't be recommending him to you, but you can't trust anyone, not doctors anyway.'

'That's what they say about lawyers,' she said glumly.

'Baby, stop worrying. It's probably nothing. He'll make a little cut in your breast and find out there's whipped cream in there, sew it up, and tell you to forget it. Don't put yourself through this in the meantime.' He was so purposely blithe about it that in some ways it made her even more nervous.

'But what if he was right? He said that masses like this, this deep in the breast, are more often malignancies. What if it is?' She kept trying to make him see what was happening, but he just wouldn't.

'It won't be a malignancy,' Sam insisted doggedly. 'Trust me.' He absolutely refused to hear what she was saying. He seemed to be shielding himself from the realities with optimism and good humor. His insistence that nothing would happen to her made her feel suddenly lonely, and although she desperately wanted to, she didn't entirely believe him. All he had done was shake her faith in both Dr Anderson and Dr

98

Herman. So much so that on the second day of the trial, she used a brief recess to call one of the other doctors Anderson had recommended.

She was younger and had published fewer articles, but she was just as respected, and reputed to be just as conservative as Dr Peter Herman. Her name was Frederica Wallerstrom, and she agreed to meet Alex before court the next day, at seven-thirty in the morning. And when Alex met with her, she wanted Dr Wallerstrom to be the solution to all her problems. She wanted her to be nurturing and warm, tell her that her fears were in vain, and that more than likely the tumor would be benign, and none of the horrors she had heard would apply to her. But Wallerstrom looked extremely stern, said nothing at all as she examined first Alex, and then the films, and when she spoke, her eyes were cold and her face entirely without emotion.

'I'd say Dr Herman was being quite accurate in his assessment. You can never tell of course, at this stage. But my guess would be that it's probably malignant.' She didn't mince her words, and she seemed unconcerned with Alex's reaction. As she listened to the woman with the cropped gray hair and powerful hands like a man's, Alex felt her own palms grow damp and her legs start to tremble. 'We could be wrong of course, but you develop a sense of these things,' she said coolly.

'And what would you recommend if it is malignant, Dr Wallerstrom?' Alex asked, trying to remind herself that she was the consumer here, that she was auditioning this woman, and she still had options and choices. But she felt like a child, helpless and without knowledge or control, as the other woman eyed her with dispassion.

'There are the advocates of lumpectomies, of course, in almost all circumstances, but, personally, I think the risks they take too often prove them wrong, and a decision like that can be disastrous later on. A mastectomy is the surest way of assuring that you have eliminated the disease, coupled with chemotherapy in most instances, of course. I'm a conservative,' she said firmly, discarding the other school without hesitation, no matter how respected or valid their theories. 'I'm a proponent of mastectomies. You can do other things. You can opt for a lumpectomy and radiation, but you're a busy woman, and how realistic is that? You won't have the time, and you may regret it later. Sparing the breast now could prove to be an enormous mistake later. You can risk it of course. It's your choice. But, personally, I completely concur with Dr Herman.' Not only did she agree with him, but she seemed to have nothing to add, no warmth, no kindness, no compassion for Alex as a woman. If anything, she was even colder than Dr Herman. And although Alex had wanted to like her, because she was a woman, if nothing else, she liked her even less, and could hardly wait to rush out of her office and take a breath of air. She felt as though she were suffocating from everything Dr Wallerstrom had told her.

Alex arrived at the courthouse at a quarter after eight, and she was shocked to realize how little time the doctor had actually spent with her on such a serious matter, or maybe it was only serious to Alex. To everyone else, it seemed like a very ordinary occurrence. An easy choice. Get rid of the breast, and the problem. It was all so simple, as long as they were the doctors, and not the patient. To them, it was a matter of theories and statistics. To Alex, it was her life, her breast, and her future. And none of the choices were easy.

She was disappointed to realize that having gotten a second opinion, she was no more certain of what would happen to her, no more reassured about the outcome or the options. She had somehow hoped that Dr Wallerstrom would allay all her fears, and tell her that everyone else was overreacting and being foolish. Instead, she had only heightened Alex's fears, and made her feel even more frightened and lonely. The biopsy would still have to be done, the situation and the tumor analyzed, and the ultimate decision would have to be hers, and her surgeon's. There was still the chance, of course, that the tumor would be benign, but after everything they had said to her in the past few days, it seemed less and less likely.

Even Sam's cheerful refusal to believe the worst seemed patently absurd now. And with his adamant refusal to discuss the possibilities with her, the pressures of the trial, and the fertility medication she knew she was still reacting to, she felt as though she was barely clinging to sanity during the entire week. She felt as though she were walking underwater.

The only thing that kept her from losing her mind completely was incredibly solid support from Brock as they worked their way through the trial, and it seemed like a miracle when the jury absolved Jack Schultz of absolutely everything the plaintiff wanted. They denied the plaintiff everything, and Jack must have thanked her a thousand times. The trial only took six days, as it turned out, and they were finished at four o'clock on Wednesday. Winning had been the only good thing that had happened.

She sat in the courtroom, feeling drained, but looking pleased, and she thanked Brock for all his help. It had been the hardest ten days of her life, harder than anyone knew, and they had done some extraordinary teamwork.

'I couldn't have done it without you,' she said graciously, and really meant it. The last few days had worn her down more than even he suspected.

'You were the one who did it.' He looked at her admiringly. 'You're a pleasure to watch in the courtroom. It's like great ballet, or fine surgery. You don't miss a stitch, or a step, or an incision, or a suture.'

'Thank you,' she was packing up their files, with his help, and his words had reminded her that she had to call Peter Herman. She dreaded seeing him again, and the biopsy was only five days away now. She knew nothing more than she had before, except that her visit to Dr Wallerstrom had confirmed Peter Herman's assessment. And Sam had literally refused to discuss any of it with her again. He said it was a big fuss about something that would never happen. She hoped he was right, but, for the moment, he seemed to be the only one who thought so.

She tried to feel victorious about the trial, and Jack Schultz sent her a magnum of champagne, which she took home with her, but she wasn't in the mood to celebrate. She was nervous and depressed, and very frightened about Monday.

The day after the trial ended, she went back to see Peter Herman, and this time he didn't pull any punches. He told her in no uncertain terms that if a tumor that big and that deep turned out to be malignant, she would have to have a modified radical mastectomy, and extensive chemotherapy, and it was best to face it. He explained that she had two choices. She could have the biopsy, under general of course, and then discuss the options with him again afterwards. Or she could sign a permission slip before the biopsy, which would allow him to do whatever he felt was necessary, after he'd done the biopsy. It would mean being put under general anesthesia once instead of twice, and trusting him completely. It was unusual, he explained, to do the procedures in one step rather than two, but he also correctly sensed that Alex wanted to get it over with in a single operation. The only complication would be if she was pregnant. And he said that, whether she was or not, he'd understand perfectly if she preferred doing the procedures in two stages.

But, as with the lumpectomy versus the mastectomy, she had to be the one to make the decision. She had to choose if she wanted to do the biopsy by itself, or in tandem with the actual operation. To Alex, as she discussed it with him, it seemed simpler to deal with it all at once, rather than prolong the agony, and go back to the hospital again for a mastectomy, if the tumor was malignant. She trusted Dr Herman to make the right decision once he biopsied the tumor. And she had already made the most difficult choice of all since seeing Dr Wallerstrom. Although the prospect of doing only a lumpectomy was very tempting to save her breast, even the vaguest hint of greater safety by eliminating the entire breast won her over. Both views were heatedly debated by equally respected surgeons, and yet it was clear to her which Peter Herman preferred, and much as she ached at the prospect, she decided to follow his thinking. She had already agreed to the modified radical mastectomy he had described to her, if the tumor proved to be malignant. And to chemotherapy, if he felt it was needed. But they would make that decision later.

But the real agony for her was what she would do if she was pregnant. She knew what she owed Sam and Annabelle, but she also knew how difficult, if not impossible, it would be to give up an unborn baby. Dr Herman explained very clearly as she stared at him that in the first trimester of pregnancy, mastectomies were always performed rather than lumpectomies, because of the inadvisability of doing radiation. Having a lumpectomy automatically meant the necessity for radiation. But in the case of a mastectomy, if chemotherapy was advised, it would almost certainly cause a spontaneous abortion. It would do the same in the second trimester as well, so if chemotherapy was necessary, it would more than likely kill her baby. It was only in the third trimester that they felt they could afford to wait, and treat the cancer after the baby was delivered.

He said very honestly that he thought there was almost no chance at all that her mass would prove to be benign. He had just seen tumors like it too often. What he was hoping for her was that it would not have infiltrated, or metastasized, and that there would be minimal node involvement. And he also hoped, of course, that it would be nothing more than a Stage I tumor. She felt herself blanking out on him again, and forced herself to listen and understand what he was saying. She wished Sam were there with her but he was so busy denying that there was even going to be a problem, she hadn't even thought to ask him.

'What about the pregnancy?' Dr Herman asked her before she left. 'How real a possibility is that?' It could affect some of their decisions.

'I don't know,' she said sadly, 'for the moment.' She wouldn't know for sure until that weekend.

'Would you like to have some counseling, before the biopsy?' he asked, showing his 'human' side again, which was very small, and very seldom seen, but at least he was trying. 'Particularly, if you might want to make this a one-time procedure in the event of a malignancy, you might like to speak to a therapist, or some other women who've been through it. Normally, we recommend peer groups, but that usually isn't until later. They're extraordinarily helpful.'

She looked at him ruefully and shook her head. 'I don't have time. Particularly if I'm liable to be out of the office for several weeks.' She had to cover all possibilities, and she had already asked Matt Billings to cover for her, and she had given a lot of her work to Brock. She knew he would take good care of it. But she hadn't told either of them where she was going. She had intimated only that she had a medical problem that needed to be worked out, and it could take anywhere from two days to two weeks, but they were prepared to accept that and help her out as much as possible. Brock said he hoped it was nothing serious, and Matthew didn't even think of it, and wondered if she was going to have a nose job, or her eyes done. His wife had done it the year before and he didn't think Alex needed anything of the sort, but he also believed that all women were a little crazy about their looks, and Alex looked so healthy, it never dawned on him that she might have a serious problem.

'How soon do you really think I'll be able to go back to work?' she asked the doctor honestly.

'Possibly in two or three weeks, depending on how you do. And then of course it'll depend on how you do with the chemo. We'd be starting that approximately four weeks after surgery. Some women do very well, others have more problems.' To him it was already a foregone conclusion. She had cancer, the breast was coming off, and she was going to have chemo. Maybe Sam was right and it was just a factory that lopped off boobs to pay the rent, but it was hard to believe that. From what Peter Herman said, it was a lot easier to believe she had a serious problem.

He wanted her to go to the hospital that weekend for blood tests and a chest X-ray, and they had discussed the impossibility of her giving her own blood on such short notice. But he had told her that even radical mastectomies rarely required transfusions, and if need be, after the surgery, he would call her office to organize donor-specific blood, and other than that, there was nothing left to say, until Monday. He told her that he wanted to hear from her over the weekend if she discovered she wasn't pregnant, and she agreed to call him. And eventually, she left his office feeling wooden.

She went back to her office for the rest of the afternoon, and home to Annabelle and Sam for dinner that night, and only Carmen noticed how quiet and withdrawn she was. Alex didn't say anything to Sam about her visit to Dr Herman, until later that night, but when she did, he was already half asleep, and he didn't even answer her, as she explained what the doctor had said to her. And when she looked over at Sam again, he was snoring softly.

She cleared her desk on Friday morning before noon, and Brock came by to pick up some files, and wish her luck the following week.

'I hope whatever it is works out, the way you want it.' He suspected what it might be, he had heard the word 'biopsy' in one of her conversations. It was a word that struck fear in his heart, but he hoped that hers wouldn't be serious, and that she'd be back in the office quickly. She said a hasty good-bye to him, and then gave Liz her final instructions. She said she'd be calling in for messages, and she could send work to the house in a few days, if Alex wasn't back yet.

'Take care of yourself,' Liz said quietly, and then hugged her as Alex fought back tears, and then turned away so Liz wouldn't see them.

'You take care too, Liz. I'll see you soon,' she said, exuding a confidence she didn't feel, and then she cried all the way uptown in a cab, to pick up Annabelle at school. It was Friday and they had ballet to go to.

She took Annabelle out to lunch at Serendipity, and then they went straight to Miss Tilly's. Annabelle had never been happier. She was pleased that Alex was around again, and not 'busy with the judge' anymore. Annabelle told her in no uncertain terms, over a hot fudge sundae, that she really didn't like that.

'I'll try not to do it more often than I have to.' Alex hadn't said anything to her about her trip to the hospital on Monday, and on Saturday she tried to talk to Sam about what they should say to her about it. She thought a business trip was the best idea, explaining that she was going to the hospital would be much too threatening.

'Don't even think of it,' Sam said, looking annoyed at her, 'you'll be back by that afternoon, for heaven's sake.' As he said it, he looked edgy and sounded angry.

'I might not be,' she said quietly, upset that he was continuing to refuse to face the problem. He was cling-ing to denial. 'I could end up there for a week if they do a mastectomy,' she said, trying to force herself, as well as Sam, to accept it, but he refused to hear it.

'Will you stop it? You're driving me crazy. What is this? Do you want sympathy, or what?' She had never seen him quite so frantic. It was as though she had touched a nerve, and she wondered suddenly if his anxiety had anything to do with his own memories about his mother. But whatever his reasons for avoiding her, he was making Alex even more nervous.

'Actually,' she finally turned on him, angry for the first time since it had all happened, 'I want some support from you. This crazy routine of refusing to believe anything is happening isn't making it easier for me. Has it ever occurred to you that I need your help with this? This isn't easy for me. I might lose a breast in two days, and you're insisting it couldn't happen.' Tears filled her eyes as she said it.

'Nothing's going to happen,' he said gruffly, and then turned away to hide his own tears. But he never spoke of it to her again, and by Sunday she understood that he wasn't going to. He couldn't. It scared him too much, it was all too reminiscent of his own mother. But whatever the reason, it left Alex with no support at all. She had plenty of acquaintances, and some friends she knew well, but she seldom saw them, except the ones she worked with. She never had time to see friends, she was always working. Sam was her best friend, and right now he just couldn't face the threat of what could be happening to her, or make himself help her. And she was embarrassed to call anyone else. 'Hi . . . this is Alex Parker, and I'm having a breast biopsy tomorrow, want to come by? . . . actually, I might even be having a mastectomy, if it turns out to be a malignancy, but Sam says we're really just doing it to buy the doctor a Mercedes . . . anything for a good cause.' It was too hard for her to call anyone, harder still to admit that Sam was letting her down. But he was. Terribly. And that night she explained to Annabelle that in the morning she had to go away for a few days on business. Annabelle looked disappointed but she said she understood, and Alex promised to call her, and told her that Daddy would take good care of her, and she had to fight back tears as she said it. Annabelle hugged her tight and told her how much she would miss her, which made it even harder for Alex.

'Will you be back in time for Miss Tilly's on Friday?' she asked with huge green eyes, as Alex fought to maintain her composure.

'I'll try, sweetheart, I promise,' she said hoarsely, clinging to her little girl and praying nothing terrible would happen. Maybe Dr Herman was wrong, and she'd be lucky. Being with Annabelle made her feel so vulnerable and so frightened. 'Will you be a good girl and have a nice time with Daddy and Carmen? I'm really going to miss you.' More than she'd ever know, Alex thought, choking on tears, but she was doing this to save her life, both the biopsy and whatever came later. She wanted to be there for Annabelle for a long time. For ever.

'Why are you going, Mommy?' Annabelle asked sadly. It was as though she sensed that there was more than Alex was saying.

'Because I have to. For work.' But even to her own ears, she didn't sound convincing.

'You work too much,' Annabelle said softly. 'I'll take care of you when I'm big, Mommy. I promise.' She was so sweet, and Alex didn't want to leave her. She couldn't bear the thought of leaving her the next morning and she clung to her for a long time before finally turning off the light, and going to make dinner for herself and Sam.

But she was so nervous, she was nauseous. All she could think of was what she was about to go through. And Sam stayed well away from the subject all through dinner. He went to read some reports afterwards and Alex went back to check on Annabelle. She lay next to the sleeping child for a little while, she just wanted to feel her curls against her cheek, and feel her breathing softly before she left her. And then she stood watching her from the doorway. She looked like a little angel, asleep in her bed, and Alex walked back into her own bedroom, praying for a miracle at the hospital the next morning. All she wanted was her life, even if it cost her a breast to keep it.

Sam was asleep in front of the TV when she slipped into their bed. He had had a hard week too, with a large group of Arab investors visiting from Saudi. But he had scarcely said a word, and certainly not a kind or encouraging one, to Alex about the morning. It was impossible not to be angry at him. She lay next to him for an hour, wanting to talk to him, but when he finally stirred, he just pulled off his jeans and his T-shirt, and slipped into bed, without really waking.

'Sam? . . .' she said softly, wanting to wake him, to talk to him, to be near him, even to make love to him, but he was a million miles away now, and oblivious to her problem.

'Hmmm . . . ?'

'Are you sleeping?' It was obvious that he was, but she didn't want him to. But he was beyond rousing. 'I love you,' she said, as she lay looking at him. But he didn't hear her. He didn't hear anything. He was far away, in his own world. Too much so to help his wife, or to accept what was happening to her. He was just too afraid to deal with it, and she knew that. But she had never felt as lonely in her life. In his own way, he had deserted her completely.

And when she went to the bathroom before she went to sleep, she discovered what she had prayed wouldn't happen. She had gotten her period, in spite of their attempts two weeks before, and the hormones she had taken. There would be only a biopsy, and possibly surgery. There would be no baby.

Chapter 5

Alex woke at six the next day, and prowled around the house for a little while, wishing it were a different morning. She started a pot of coffee for Sam, set out the breakfast things, and looked at Annabelle, sleeping soundly. Sam was still asleep too, and it was so odd looking at both of them, knowing she'd be gone soon, for a few hours, or a few days, to win or lose a battle that could take her away from them forever. It was unthinkable, as she stood staring into Annabelle's room. How could she ever leave her little girl? What would happen to them? She couldn't begin to fathom what was about to happen to her that morning.

She was careful not to eat or drink anything, although she longed for a cup of coffee, and as she brushed her teeth, she suddenly found she had to fight back tears. There was an overwhelming urge to run away, to hide from all of it, but there was no hiding now from the treachery of her own body. Instead, she stood up and looked at herself, with tears running down her cheeks, her toothbrush in her hand, as she stared into the mirror. She set the toothbrush down and dropped the straps on her nightgown. The silky gown fell easily to the floor without a sound, and she stood looking at herself, the small firm breasts that she had always taken for granted. The left was a fraction larger than the right, and she remembered suddenly with a smile that Annabelle had always preferred it to the other when she nursed her. She couldn't help but appreciate the symmetry of her breasts, and the long, graceful lines of her body. She had long legs, a small waist, she had always had a good figure and never thought much about it. And what would happen now? Who would she be, if she lost the breast today? Would she be someone else? Would she be so hideously deformed that Sam would no longer want her? She had wanted to talk about it with him, to hear him say that he didn't care if she had one breast or two. She needed to hear the words, but he hadn't been able to face even the idea of it, and he had told her all week that nothing was wrong with her and she was being morbid.

And now, she stood looking at herself, and she cried as she realized what might happen to her. She couldn't even imagine it. A breast was a small price to pay for a life, if it came to that, but she didn't want to lose it either. She didn't want to be deformed, or look like a man, or have reconstructive surgery. She didn't want any of it. And most of all, she didn't want to lose her breast, or have cancer.

'Hi,' Sam said sleepily, as he walked past her to the shower. She hadn't seen him come in, and he didn't seem to notice that she was crying. She turned away from him self-consciously, as though there were already something ugly about her, and covered herself with a towel. 'You're up early.' What a surprise. Fancy that! The way he said it made her want to hit him. All the understanding he had ever had for her seemed to have vanished in less than two weeks of total denial.

'I'm having surgery today,' she reminded him in a constricted voice, as he turned on the shower.

'You're having a biopsy. Let's not get too dramatic.'

'When are you going to wake up?' she snapped at him. 'When are you going to face this thing? After I lose the breast, or not even then? Is this so goddamn threatening that you can't reach out to me for a single moment?' He needed to hear it from her, needed to know how badly he was letting her down, but he couldn't face that either. He stepped into the shower without looking at her, and said something she couldn't hear as she stared at him in renewed amazement. She took two long steps over to him, and yanked back the shower curtain, until they were both soaking wet and she looked at him in complete fury. 'What did you just say to me?'

'I said you're being melodramatic.' He looked both embarrassed and annoyed at her, as she stood there looking very wet and very beautiful and his body acknowledged her with an erection. But they hadn't made love once since she'd had the results of the mammogram. They had done nothing at all since 'blue day.' First, she'd had the trial, and now she was dealing with the trauma of possibly having cancer. And he had made no overtures to her either. He was trying to avoid her.

'I think you're being a sonofabitch, Sam Parker. I don't give a damn if you're having trouble coping with this, so am I. And it's happening to me, not you. You could at least be there for me. Is that so much to ask? Is that so difficult for you, Mr Important, Mr Venture Capitalist, Mr So Fucking Scared He Can't Face What's Happening?' She was so furious she wanted to hit him, but he pulled the shower curtain away from her, and turned to continue his shower.

'Why don't you go easy on both of us, Al? It'll all be over by this afternoon, and you'll feel a lot better.' They both knew that the Serophene she'd taken four weeks before didn't help her ability to cope, or her disposition, but this was also not about hormones. This was about real life, and a threat to her very survival and existence. It was a threat to everything she was, her health, her life, her looks, her femininity, even her ability to have children. What else was there? Many things perhaps, but she had not yet come to see them. Neither had Sam. He had his head in the sand and was seeing nothing.

Carmen arrived just as Annabelle woke up, and Alex went to talk to them while Annabelle got dressed, and Carmen noticed that she was extremely nervous. Alex hadn't said anything different to her than she had to Annabelle, only that she had to go away on business for a few days, and needed Carmen to stay at the apartment.

'Is everything okay, Mrs Parker?' Carmen said suspiciously, she had never seen Alex look quite that way, and, for a minute, Alex was tempted to tell her. But it made it too real to confide in her. It was easier just to pretend that she was going away on business.

'Everything's fine, Carmen, thanks.' But Carmen was suspicious again when Alex came back dressed in jeans and a white sweater. She never wore clothes like that when she went away, she didn't even have stockings on, just bare feet in loafers, and she was wearing no makeup. Carmen frowned as she looked at her, and then glanced at Sam, who was drinking coffee, eating eggs, and reading the morning paper. He was dressed normally, in a business suit, and when he put the paper down to talk to them, he seemed unusually cheerful. He didn't say anything to his wife, but he was particularly funny with Annabelle and Carmen. And she didn't know what was happening, but something in her gut told her she didn't like it. But Annabelle was aware of nothing.

At seven-fifteen, Alex reminded him that they had to leave, and he picked up his briefcase and Alex's bag, and promised Annabelle he'd be home for dinner. He kissed her, rumpled her curls, and then he went to ring for the elevator, while Alex stood there and held her baby.

'I'm going to miss you a lot,' Alex said huskily, feeling herself shake as she held her. She didn't want to give away too much, but she wanted more than anything to hold her for as long as she could. But the elevator had already come and Sam was calling her. 'I love you, baby, I'll see you soon . . . I love you . . .' she called over her shoulder, as tears streamed from her eyes, and she ran for the elevator as Carmen watched her. Annabelle was already watching cartoons on TV by then, but Carmen was haunted by the look on her employer's face, as she put Sam's dishes into the sink, and then she remembered that Alex hadn't eaten anything, she hadn't even had a glass of juice or a cup of coffee. Something was very wrong. She just knew it.

By then, Alex and Sam were in a cab, on the way to the hospital, and he was making easy conversation, while she wished he wouldn't. It was almost worse than talking about what was happening, and all she could think of was Annabelle's sweet little face when she left her, or the way she had felt in her arms when she'd kissed her goodbye. It was almost beyond bearing.

'We have another group of Arabs coming in today, and some people from the Netherlands. I must say,

Simon knows some extraordinary people. I was really wrong about him.' He chatted on as they headed east to New York Hospital, where they were going to meet Dr Peter Herman.

'I'm glad to hear it,' Alex snapped at him, indifferent to Simon's virtues, or their potential clients. 'Are you going to stick around for this, or are you going to the office?' Nothing would have surprised her, but he also knew she wanted him to be there.

'I told you I'd stay, and I will. I had Janet call the doctor and he said what with the anesthetic, the procedure will take about half an hour, forty-five minutes if they get delayed. You'll be down shortly after that, and you can sleep it off until the afternoon. I thought I'd hang around till ten-thirty or eleven, you'll be awake by then, or you'll have woken up and gone back to sleep in your room. And then I'll come back this afternoon and get you.'

There was a long silence as she nodded and stared out the window. 'I wish I shared your optimism.' She had already told him that she had opted for a 'one-stop' procedure. She was going to sign a permission form that would allow the doctor to do whatever he had to once he got there. So that if the biopsy brought bad news, he would perform all the needed surgery that day. She didn't want to come back again after an agonizing wait, knowing that she had to lose the breast anyway. Whatever was going to happen, was going to happen today, biopsy, mastectomy, or lumpectomy if the problem was minimal enough to warrant taking out only the lump. But she already knew Dr Herman's thoughts on that subject. She wouldn't know what he'd done to her until she woke up. But at least she only had to face the terror once. Sam still thought she was crazy.

'You really trust this guy that much?' he asked again, as they crossed York Avenue and the hospital loomed ahead like a dinosaur ready to devour her.

'His reputation's excellent. I checked him out thoroughly. And I got a second opinion.' She had never even told him. 'The second doctor completely agreed with what he'd said, Sam. It's pretty clear, but not very pretty.'

'I still wouldn't give him too much leeway. Take it one step at a time.' But she didn't agree with him, and when she'd called John Anderson to discuss it with him, he had thought she was doing the right thing. He told her to trust Peter Herman completely.

The cab stopped in front of the hospital, and Sam paid for it and grabbed her small tote bag. She had brought only a few things, in the hope that Sam would be right, and it wouldn't be a long stay. And he could bring her the rest of what she'd need if she had to stay longer. But packing her tote had reminded her of when she'd gone to the hospital to have Annabelle. It was a happier time, and it seemed only moments ago, although she was almost four years old now.

They followed the arrows to the registration desk, but Alex had preregistered, when she'd gone in for her blood work and chest X-ray the day she saw Dr Herman. They gave her a slip to take upstairs, and gave her a room number on the sixth floor, and a little plastic tub that held a toothbrush and a cup, soap, and toothpaste, and just holding it depressed her. She felt suddenly like an inmate in a prison.

They went silently upstairs, amid the hubbub of the hospital, and Sam looked uncomfortable and pale, and Alex looked terrified as they got off the elevator, and walked past two people with IVs, asleep on gurneys. The nurses at the nurses' station told her where to go, and they walked into a small ugly room, painted in pale blue, with a poster on the wall, and a hospital bed that seemed to eat up the entire room. Nothing about it was pretty, but at least she was alone and didn't have to talk to anyone, except Sam, who was making idle chitchat about the view, and how incredibly expensive hospitals were getting, and how socialized medicine wasn't working at all for Canada or the U.K. She wanted to scream at him, but she knew he was making a frantic effort to cope, even if he wasn't helping. He was too unnerved himself just from being there even to try to help her.

A nurse hurried in to make sure she'd had nothing by mouth since midnight the night before, and an orderly shoved an IV pole into the room, and tossed a gown on the bed for her, and said he'd be back in a minute, and suddenly as she stood there, Alex started to cry helplessly. This was awful. And Sam took her in his arms and held her there, wanting to tell her he was sorry.

'It'll all be over soon. Just try to forget about it. Think about Annabelle, about going to the beach next summer . . . or Halloween . . . and before you know it, it'll be over.' She laughed at what he said, but even the thought of Halloween with Annabelle wasn't enough to block out the terror she was feeling.

'I'm so scared,' she whispered as he held her.

'I know . . . but you're going to be OK . . . I promise.' But he couldn't promise that, no one could. It was up to God. And she wasn't sure what He had planned for her. But for the moment she was scared stiff, and she looked it.

'It's so weird . . . we're both so powerful in our own ways. We're strong people, with good jobs, we move a lot of people around, make a lot of decisions that affect money and people and corporations . . . and then you get hit with something like this, and you're powerless. You're suddenly at the mercy of everyone, people you don't even know, and fate, and your own body.' She felt like a child, totally helpless to stop the nightmare in which she was living.

The nurse appeared at the door again, told her to undress and put on the gown, and someone would come in to start her IV in a minute. There was no time, no sympathy, no interest.

'Is that supposed to be good news?' Sam teased. 'Like they're coming back with a four-course breakfast?'

'Nothing about this is good news,' Alex said, drying her eyes again, wishing she weren't there, or that she'd decided to ignore the shadow on her mammogram, but she knew she couldn't. Maybe Sam was right. Maybe it all was a lot of nonsense to keep the medical profession in business. She hoped so.

The nurse came back into the room then, while Alex changed, and she had her lie down so she could start the IV. It was just saline solution so she wouldn't be dehydrated. 'And then we've got a line in, in case we need to give you anything else. You're going to be having a general today,' she said, like a stewardess announcing that they were going to be flying over St Louis.

'I know,' Alex said, trying to sound like she was in control again, like she was part of it, and had made the decision, but this woman didn't care. That wasn't the issue for her, who had decided what or why. This was a body factory, a warehouse for bodies in disrepair, and she had to get them moving as fast as they could, to make room for the next ones.

The IV burned as it went into Alex's arm, but the nurse said that it would stop in a few minutes. She took Alex's blood pressure, listened to her heart, made a notation on a chart, and flipped a switch that turned a light on in the hallway. 'They'll know you're ready to go now. I'll call upstairs. They should be taking you to the O.R. in a few minutes.' It was already eight-thirty, and her biopsy was scheduled for nine. She had been there since seven-thirty.

'Any calls you want me to make while I'm waiting for you here?' Sam asked casually as she lay there, watching her IV and looking unhappy, as a nurse came in with a clipboard.

'No, thanks. I think I've got everything pretty much taken care of at the office,' she said as she glanced at the paper the nurse handed her to look at and sign. Alex had spent the whole week before, preparing to be away for the next two weeks, just in case, and there was nothing left to do now. The paper the nurse had handed her was the consent form she had already discussed with Dr Herman. She only read a few lines, which explained that anything up to and including a radical mastectomy might be performed, though he had already told her that he rarely did anything more than modified radicals anymore, which meant that he took, along with the breast, the tissue high up in the arm, the minor pectoral muscles, and not the majors. The major ones made reconstructive surgery impossible. With only the minor pectorals gone, you could still do reconstructive work, and add implants, and there was no greater danger to the patient in leaving the major pectorals intact. She couldn't bear reading any further. She signed and looked up at Sam with tears in her eyes, trying not to think of what was going to happen to her, as she handed the nurse back her clipboard.

'Then don't forget to call Annabelle at lunchtime, in case I'm still asleep,'. . . or still in surgery, please God, no . . . she said, wiping her tears from her cheeks with trembling fingers, as he took one of her hands in his own.

'I'll call her. I'm having lunch at La Grenouille with Simon's Arabs and his assistant from London. He's got some woman with an Oxford econ degree coming in. He says our Harvard B School guys don't hold a candle to the kids from Oxford.' He smiled at the snobbism, trying to distract her, just as two orderlies appeared in the doorway, like black angels with a gurney between them. They wore green pajamas and blue gowns, with shower caps on their heads, and what looked like shower caps on their shoes, and it was obvious that they had come for Alex.

'Alexandra Parker?'

She wanted to say no, but she knew that wouldn't help as she nodded. She was too choked to speak, and she started to cry again once she lay on the gurney and looked up at Sam. Why had this ever happened?

'Hang in there, kiddo. I'll be right here. And to-night we'll do something to celebrate. Take it easy.' He leaned down to kiss her and she spoke in a strangled whisper through her tears.

'I just want to go home with you and Annabelle, and watch TV.'

'That's a deal. Now go get this thing over with, so we can forget all about it.' He tweaked her boob then, and she laughed. She wanted desperately for this to be over. And maybe he was right not to get excited about it, but for her, it was impossible not to. And she tried not to remember that he had never told her he would love her, even with her breast off.

They rolled her inexorably down the hall, and into a large elevator where people stepped aside and stared at her, wondering what was wrong with her, and why she was there, and pretended not to look at her. Her bright red hair lay across the pillow, and two men glanced at her, thinking that she was very pretty.

They reached the surgical floor then, and there was an overwhelming smell of antiseptics, and electric doors snapped open and closed, until suddenly she found herself in a small room that was filled with chrome and machinery and bright lights, and she recognized Peter Herman.

'Good morning, Mrs Parker.' He didn't ask her how she was, he knew, as he touched her hand and tried to reassure her.

'We'll have you asleep very shortly, Mrs Parker,' he said gently, which surprised her. He seemed right in his element here, and he seemed kinder to her than he had before. Or was it only that he had won, and he was doing what he wanted? Was Sam right? Was she wrong? Were they all crazy? Were they lying to her? Would she die? Where was Sam? . . . and Annabelle . . . her head was reeling as they stuck another needle in her other arm, and she thought she tasted garlic and then peanuts, and someone told her to count backwards from one hundred. She only reached ninety-nine, and then everything went black around her.

Chapter 6

Sam paced around the small claustrophobic blue room for almost an hour, until nine-thirty. He called his secretary, returned some calls, confirmed his lunch date with Simon. They had meetings with their attorneys that afternoon too. Simon was joining their partnership, bringing with him all his important connections, and very little money. His would be a limited partnership, and he would have a smaller percentage in the firm than Sam, Tom, or Larry. But he seemed satisfied with that for now. He said he could always buy in for more later, once he'd proven himself, and the business had grown as a result of his connections.

Sam walked down the hall after that, and bought a cup of vile coffee from a machine, which he only took two sips of. It made him ill just being here, with the smells, and the people hobbling down the halls, in wheelchairs, or on gurneys. He still had a dread of hospitals even if the last time he had been there was when Annabelle was born, but Alex needed him then. This time he felt both useless and helpless. She was somewhere else, asleep, unaware of who was there with her, and who wasn't. He could have been anywhere. And by ten-thirty, he wished he had been. She should have been back to the room by then, or someone should have called to say when she'd come down. He didn't want to leave without seeing her, or at least talking to her doctor. But he wanted to be at his office by eleven. And he was serving no purpose at all sitting there, and he knew it. He felt like the forgotten man in the tiny blue room.

He called his office again, and then strode purposefully out of the room to the nurses' station.

'I'd like to check on Mrs Alexandra Parker,' he said curtly. 'She was scheduled for a breast biopsy at nine. They said she'd be finished before ten. It's almost eleven now. Could you call and check if there's been a delay. I can't wait around here forever.' She raised an eyebrow at him, but didn't say anything. He looked important and well dressed, and he was very good-looking. And he had an aura of command about him, which even she responded to, though she had no idea who he was, or why he shouldn't have to wait like everyone else in the world. But she called upstairs anyway, and they told her that everything was running late. After all, this was Monday. They had all the leftover surgeries from the weekend, arms and legs and hips that had waited to be set since the night before, and appendectomies that hadn't been too hot to wait through the weekend.

He was reminded again of checking on flights, and waiting interminably at the airport. That had happened to them once when she had promised to meet him in Washington for a party, while they were dating. There had been a storm in New York, and he had waited six hours for her at the airport. This was beginning to feel like that. And he was truly exasperated by eleven-thirty.

'This is ridiculous. She's been up there long enough for open-heart surgery. They took her up three hours ago. They could at least let us know how late they're running.'

'I'm sorry, sir. There could have been an emergency that had to be put ahead of your wife's case. We can't help that.'

'Can you at least find out where she is and what's happening?'

'She's probably in the recovery room by now, unless everything went haywire and they bumped her. I'll call. Why don't you have a cup of coffee and wait in her room, and I'll come in as soon as I hear something.'

'Thanks very much.' He smiled at her, and she decided he was difficult but worth it. She called the surgical floor for him again then, and got very little information, except that Alexandra Parker was still in the O.R. They started late, and the nurse on the phone had no idea when they'd be finished.

The nurse walked back to Alex's room and found Sam and relayed the message, and he called his office again, apologizing for the eleven o'clock partners' meeting he was missing. He told them he'd catch up with them when he could, maybe even as late as one o'clock at La Grenouille. He just didn't feel right leaving without knowing what had happened.

It was finally twelve-thirty when they told him Alex was in the recovery room, four hours after she'd gone upstairs. The delays were ridiculous, he complained. And the nurse told him that Dr Herman would be down to speak to him in a few minutes.

It was ten to one when he arrived, and Sam looked like a caged lion pacing the room, as he waited. He had been there for long enough with their dismal decor, and their antiseptic smells, and their endless waits designed for people who had nothing else to do with their lives. He had a business to run, and he couldn't sit around all day cooling his heels waiting to talk to some damn doctor.

'Mr Parker?' Dr Herman entered the room in his operating gown, with his mask still around his neck, and what looked like socks over his shoes. He extended a hand and shook Sam's, and very little showed in his eyes as Sam watched him.

'How's my wife?' He didn't waste any time, he assumed she was fine, and he was almost late for lunch with Simon, his assistant, and their new clients, after waiting for an entire morning.

'She's doing as well as we can expect right now. She lost very little blood, and we didn't have to give her any transfusions.' That was important to everyone these days, and he assumed it would be to Sam, but he looked unimpressed and a little confused when he heard it.

'Transfusions for a biopsy?' There was a long moment's silence. 'Isn't that a little unusual?'

'Mr Parker, as I suspected, your wife had a large mass deep in her breast, involving mainly the ducts, but it has infiltrated the surrounding tissue, although the margins of the tumor were clear. We'll have to wait another two or three days to tell us about possible lymph node involvement. But there was no question that it was a malignancy, and I believe it was a stage two cancer.' Sam's head suddenly reeled as he listened. It was not unlike what Alex had felt when she'd first heard that she had a shadow on her mammogram. All the information after that was just a jumble of sounds and noises.

'We're hoping that we got all of it,' Herman went on, 'but I had already discussed with your wife the danger of a recurrence. Recurrences of breast cancer are more often than not fatal. And the important thing in successful treatment of cancers such as these is removing all of it, while it is still encapsulated, before it has spread to any other part of the system. To that end, we try to espouse extremely aggressive measures. With luck, if her lymph nodes are not excessively involved, I think we got it.'

'Just exactly what does that mean?' Sam asked, feeling sick, just asking him the question. 'You took the mass out of her breast?'

'Obviously. We took the breast too, of course. It's the only way you can be absolutely sure there won't be a local recurrence. You can't have a recurrence in a breast that isn't there. It could recur in the chest wall, or travel elsewhere, of course, or metastasize, but that will depend on how advanced the tumor is, and how many lymph nodes are involved. But eliminating the breast solves a lot of problems.' Alex had understood that.

'Why didn't you just kill her? Wouldn't that solve the problem too? What kind of barbarian bullshit is that to just chop off her breast so it wouldn't spread? What kind of medicine do you people practice?' Sam was livid, and shouting.

'Cautious medicine, Mr Parker. We endorse aggressive attacks against cancer. We don't want to lose our patients. And just so you understand, we did some auxillary dissection too, which means we removed her underarm nodes, but I'm hoping she doesn't have a lot of nodular involvement. That will be confirmed by pathology in the next few days, and we'll have the results of her hormone receptor tests in about two weeks, and then we'll have a better idea how to treat her.'

'How to *treat* her? What else are you going to do?' He was still shouting at him. With one stupid move, they had butchered poor Alex.

'Depending on the lymph node involvement, we're probably going to have to do some fairly aggressive chemotherapy, just to make sure that there won't be a recurrence. There could be an issue of hormone therapy too, but we don't know that yet. And at her age, it's doubtful. Since we took the breast, there's no need for radiation. We won't be starting chemo for a few weeks. She'll need time to get on her feet, and we need time to assess her situation. Our tumor board will be meeting to discuss her case, of course, once we have all the pathology reports. I can assure you that your wife's treatment will be given very serious consideration.'

'Just like you gave her breast?' How could they do that to her? He still couldn't believe it.

'I promise you, Mr Parker, there was no choice,' Peter Herman said quietly, he had dealt with outraged husbands before, and frightened ones, and those who just couldn't cope with the reality, like this one. The husbands were no different than the patients. But he had a feeling that Alex Parker had understood all the dangers better than he had. 'We did a modified radical mastectomy on her, which means that we took the entire breast, and breast tissue, extending toward the breastbone, collarbone, and ribs, and her minor pectoral muscle. This means that she'll be able to have reconstructive surgery in a few months, if that's her wish, and if she's up to it during the chemo. If not, she can wait, and wear a prosthesis.' He made it all sound so simple, and even Sam knew it wasn't. Dr

Peter Herman had changed everything with a single stroke of his scalpel. And just listening to him now made her sound like a mutant.

'I can't understand how you could do this.' Sam stared at him in uncomprehending horror, and Peter Herman realized that it was just too soon for him to absorb it.

'Your wife has cancer, Mr Parker. We want to cure her.' That said it all, and there were tears in Sam's eyes as he nodded.

'How good do you think her chances are for survival?' It was a question Dr Herman hated to answer. He wasn't God. He was a man. He didn't know. He wished he could give them all guarantees of long life, but he couldn't.

'That's hard to know right now. The tumor was deep and large, but the whole purpose of radical surgeries, and aggressive treatment afterwards, is to wipe out the *entire* cancer. If we even leave point zero one percent, it could eventually do her grave harm. That's why we can't afford to leave the breast once it's diseased to the extent that hers was. And sometimes finding it early enough, and attacking it radically, can mean the difference between success and failure. We hope that we got all of hers, that it was contained, that it has not infiltrated, and that her nodes are not too excessively involved. We hope that, for her, radical surgery was the answer, and chemotherapy will be the additional guarantee she needs. But only time will tell us if we've been truly successful. You're both going to have to be very strong, and very patient.' She was going to die then, Sam decided as he listened. They were going to butcher her piece by piece, cut off one breast, then the other, scoop her insides out, and boil her guts with the poisons in the chemo, and then she'd die anyway.

He was going to lose her. He couldn't stand it. And he was not going to hang around and watch her die, just as he had his mother.

'I don't suppose I should bother asking what your success rate is with these kinds of cancers?'

'Sometimes excellent. We just have to be as aggressive as your wife can tolerate. But she's in good health, which is in her favor, and she's a strong woman.' But not a lucky one. At forty-two, she was going to have to fight for her life. And there was a good chance that she wouldn't win it. He just couldn't believe it. It was like one of those bad movies where the heroine dies, and the husband is left alone with the children. Just like his father, and it had killed him. But Sam already knew he wasn't going to let this kill him. He couldn't let her do that to him. His eyes filled with tears as he forced himself not to think of her body the way it had been, and the way it would look now. The words were all so ugly . . . reconstructive surgery . . . prosthesis . . . he didn't even want to see it.

'Your wife will be in the recovery room for the rest of the afternoon, I'd say. I think she should be back here by about six or seven. I think she might do well with private nurses for the first few days. Would you like me to arrange that?'

'That would be fine.' Sam looked at him coldly. The man had destroyed his life in a single moment. It was impossible for Sam to accept the fact that the doctor hadn't given her the cancer, he had tried to cure it. 'How long will she have to be here?'

'I'd say until Friday. Possibly sooner, if she does well. A lot will depend on her attitude, and her recovery. It's actually a fairly simple operation, and there's less pain than one would expect, especially in a case like hers where the involvement was mainly ductal. That's more the "plumbing" of the breast, and there aren't a great many nerves there.' Sam felt sick hearing about it. He'd already heard a lot more than he wanted.

'Get her round-the-clock nurses, please. When can I see her?'

'Not until she comes back from the recovery room, early this evening.'

'I'll be back then.' He stood looking at the doctor for a long moment, unable to thank him for what he'd done. He might as well have killed her. 'Will you be seeing Alex again today?'

'This evening, when she's a little more awake. If there's any problem before that, we'll call you. But I don't anticipate any complications. The operation went remarkably smoothly.' Sam's stomach turned over as he heard the words. To him, the only thing that was remarkable was that they had butchered Alex.

The doctor left the room then, well aware of Sam's hostility, and Sam left his office number and the number at La Grenouille at the nursing desk, and then he hurried out of the hospital, feeling frantic. He needed air, he needed room, he needed to see people who hadn't lost anything, who weren't sick, or dying of cancer. He couldn't stand being there for one more moment. He felt like a drowning man as he gulped the cool October air, and by the time he found a cab, he felt slightly more human.

He gave the driver the address of La Grenouille, and tried not to think of anything Peter Herman had said about Alex, about how little they knew, and how much they hoped, and nodes, and tumors, and tests and biopsies, and metastasis, and chemo. He didn't want to hear another word about it. Ever.

The lunch crowd at La Grenouille was in full swing, and it was almost two o'clock when he got there. He felt as though he had just returned from another planet.

'Sam, my boy, where *have* you been? We got drunk as skunks waiting for you, and finally, just so we didn't fall out of our chairs, we had to order.' Generally, their Arab clients didn't drink, but there were a few less religious, more sophisticated Moslems who did when they weren't in Arab countries. The men Simon had brought with him today were all dramatic-looking, handsome men, who had lived in Paris and London for years, and had enormous oil fortunes they'd invested in the world markets. Simon himself was roughly Sam's age, though heavier built, with wavy blond hair, blue eyes, and if you were tall enough you could see that he was slightly balding. But he had a very aristocratic British air, he was given to tweeds, handmade shoes, and impeccably starched shirts, and remarkably important clients. Sam had finally even decided that he liked him. He had a great sense of humor, and he was anxious to become friends. He had a wife he'd left 'at home,' they were separated, though they vacationed together frequently and seemed to have an interestingly open arrangement. And he had three kids, all boys, at Eton.

And sitting next to him was the young woman he had mentioned to Sam. The Oxford graduate in economics. Her name was Daphne. She was a striking-looking young woman in her late twenties. She had long, straight dark hair almost the color of Sam's, and it shone as it hung almost to her waist. She was tall and lithe, with creamy English skin, and dark eyes that danced as she looked at Sam. She seemed always about to crack a joke, or to say something unbearably funny. And he saw when she went to the ladies' room after a little while that she was not only very tall, but she had an incredibly good figure, and her skirt barely covered her bottom. She had an Hermès Kelly bag slung over one arm, and she was wearing a short black wool dress, silky black stockings, and a string of pearls. She reeked of sex and class and youth, and it was obvious that every man at La Grenouille thought she was gorgeous.

'Pretty girl, eh?' Simon smiled at him after he saw Sam watch her cross the room with a look of admiration.

'I'll say. You certainly know how to hire your assistants,' Sam teased him, wondering briefly if he had slept with her.

'Smart too,' Simon added softly as she returned. 'You should see her in a bathing suit, and she's dynamite on the dance floor.' Sam saw a glance pass between Daphne and Simon and wasn't quite sure what it was, camaraderie or cohabitation, or maybe just desire on Simon's part. Daphne seemed very cool in the company of half a dozen men, and he overheard her having a very intelligent conversation about oil prices with one of the Arabs.

For Sam, it was a blessed afternoon, a huge relief to be in the midst of busy, healthy, living people, after his hellish morning at New York Hospital. But he knew he still had to go back and face her. As a result, he drank a little too much wine, and made a few too many overtures to the Arabs, but they didn't seem to mind. They were very excited about Sam's firm, had heard good things about them from friends and associates, and they seemed pleased that Simon was becoming a partner.

It was only after Sam got back to the office and had met with their attorneys, that he started to come down, and think of what lay ahead of them, as he thought of Alex. He was staring into space, thinking about it, and the shock of knowing that she had cancer.

'Bad time?' He hadn't seen anyone come into the room, and he started when he heard her voice almost next to him. It was Daphne.

'Not at all. Sorry. I was spacing out. What can I do for you?'

'You looked a little ragged when you got to the restaurant,' she said, looking honestly at him, as her long, shapely legs couldn't help but catch his attention. But she could carry it off, and with brains too, it made for an interesting combination. It was difficult not to be bowled over by her, but Sam was also aware that she could be someone's girlfriend. He had never cheated on Alex, but Daphne was certainly young and appealing. 'Bad day?' she asked, slipping into a chair, and watching him.

You could say that. 'Not really. Just complicated. Some days are like that. A deal I was working on went a little wild. But things are in control,' he explained, not wanting to tell her, or anyone, about Alex. He wasn't sure why, but there seemed something wrong about it, as though they had done something terrible, as though she had something to hide now. An ugly secret called cancer.

'Some deals are like that,' she said coolly, appraising him. She crossed, and then uncrossed her legs, and he tried not to watch her. 'I wanted to thank you for letting me join you. I know Simon is new here, and he's a bit brash about putting his own people forward sometimes. I didn't want you to feel that you had to put up with me, because of Simon.'

'Have you known him for a long time?' She seemed awfully young to have been involved with anyone for long, but Simon had told him she was twenty-nine. But she laughed in answer.

'Very long. Twenty-nine years actually. He's my cousin.'

'Simon?' Sam looked amused, he had assumed a much racier relationship than that one, although anything was still possible, but it seemed a little more unlikely. 'How lucky for him.'

'I'm not sure about that. He's actually quite close to my brother. He's always said that I'm a terrible brat. He's only been impressed with me since I went to Oxford. My brother's fifteen years older than I, and he and Simon are quite keen on going hunting. Not my thing, I'm afraid.' She smiled at him, and Sam tried to pretend he didn't notice how beautiful she was as she uncrossed her legs again. There was something very unsettling about her, and he was wondering if it was going to be a good idea to have her around the office. Simon was hoping to have her work with him for a year, and then she wanted to go back to England, and go to law school. And in some odd ways, she reminded Simon a little bit of Alex. She had the same fire, the same bright, alive look she had had when he met her.

'Do you like it here? In New York, I mean. I suppose it's not terribly different from London.'

Big cities were fun and busy, and alive. Like Daphne. 'I like it very much, though I don't know anyone, except Simon. He's taken me to some clubs, and he's dear about letting me tag along. I suppose it's a great bore for him, but he's very patient.'

'I'm sure it's not a bore for him at all, he must love it.'

'Well, he's very kind. And so are you. Thank you very much for letting me be here.'

'I'm sure you'll be an asset to the firm,' he said formally, they exchanged a smile, and he watched her admiringly as she left his office.

Five o'clock came all too soon, and then six, and he couldn't decide whether to go home to Annabelle, or back to the hospital to see Alex. He didn't want to call and wake her, and the doctor had said she probably wouldn't even be in her room until seven. So he went home first to see Annabelle, ate dinner sitting next to her, watching television, and then put her to bed with a story. Carmen asked if he'd heard from Mrs Parker, and Annabelle complained that Mommy hadn't called her. And Sam explained that she was probably in meetings all day, and couldn't call them, but he looked unusually somber as he said it. And Carmen was watching him with a look of suspicion. She just knew something was wrong. She had noticed the small tote bag too, and the absence of a real suitcase.

At eight o'clock he changed into jeans, and seemed to hesitate before going back to the hospital. He knew he had to go, but suddenly he didn't want to see Alex. She would be woozy and sick, and probably in a lot of pain, in spite of what the surgeon had said about 'ductal' tumors being less painful. They had lopped off her breast after all, how good could that feel? It made him feel sick again as he thought of facing her. Who was going to give her the news? Or would she just know? Could she feel it?

He looked grim when he got to the hospital, and went up to the small, ugly blue room, and much to his chagrin, she was wide awake when he saw her. She was lying in bed, with an IV pole next to her, and an elderly nurse reading a magazine in the light of the single lamp that was lit in the room. Alex was crying softly and staring at the ceiling. But he wasn't sure if she was in pain or if she knew about her breast, and he could hardly ask her.

The nurse looked up as he came in, and Alex explained that he was her husband, and then the nurse nodded and left the room as discreetly as she could, and took her magazine with her. She said she'd be just outside in the hallway.

Sam walked slowly to her bedside, and stood looking down at her. She looked as beautiful as ever, but very tired and pale, a little the way she had looked right after Annabelle was born, but this time she looked anything but happy. He took her right hand in his own, and he could see that her left side and her whole upper body were heavily bandaged.

'Hi, kiddo, how are you?' He looked uncomfortable, and she did nothing to hide her tears. There was reproach in her eyes when they met his.

'Why weren't you here when I got back to the room?' She couldn't have been there long. They had said around seven.

'They told me you wouldn't come back here until tonight. And I wanted to be with Annabelle, I thought that's what you'd want.' It was partially true, and partially he just hadn't wanted to come back here. And she knew that.

'I came back to the room at four. Where were you?' She was relentless in her anguish.

'I was at the office, and then I went home to see Annabelle. I just put her to bed, and then I came back here.' He made it sound innocent and easy, and as though he couldn't have come back a moment sooner.

'Why didn't you call me?'

'I thought you were sleeping,' he said, looking nervous.

And then she looked at him and the floodgates opened. She cried as though she would never stop. Peter Herman had seen her when she came back from the recovery room, and he had told her everything, about the tumor, the mastectomy, the risks, the dangers, the nodes he had taken too, the fact that he thought, and hoped, that the tumor had clean margins and hadn't spread beyond them, which he thought looked very hopeful, and the fact that most likely in four weeks they would be starting chemo. From where Alex was looking at it, she thought her life was over. She had lost a breast, and she could still lose her life. She was disfigured now, and for the next six months she was going to be desperately ill on chemo. She would very probably lose her hair, and just as possibly be permanently sterile after the treatment. Right now, it seemed like there was nothing left, not even her marriage. Sam hadn't even been there for her when she woke up. He hadn't been there when the doctor had told her the devastating news. Herman hadn't wanted to wait to tell her any of it, he didn't want her worrying or guessing, or discovering that the breast was gone, or hearing it from the nurses. He was a firm believer in telling his patients everything, and he had. Alex felt as though he'd killed her. And Sam had done nothing to stop it, or help her.

'I lost my breast,' she kept saying over and over as she cried. 'I have cancer . . .' Sam listened without saying a word, he just held her, and cried along with her. It was much more than he could cope with.

'I'm so sorry . . . it's going to be all right. He said he thinks they got it.'

'But he doesn't *know*,' Alex sobbed uncontrollably, 'and I probably have to have chemo. I don't want it. I want to die.'

'No, you don't,' he said sharply. 'Don't even say that.'

'Why not? How are you going to feel when you look at my body?'

'Sad,' he said honestly, which only made her cry more. 'I'm very sad for you.' He said it as though it was her problem, and not his. He was very sorry for her, but he didn't want this to become his problem. He didn't want it to kill him, as it had his father, once his mother had cancer. In his mind the two deaths were linked and he was fighting now for his own survival.

'You'll never want to make love to me again,' she sobbed, concerned with lesser problems than he was.

'Don't be stupid. What about blue day?' He tried to make her smile, but he only made her feel worse as she looked up at him in anguish.

'There won't be any more blue days. I have a fifty percent chance of being sterile after the chemo. I'm not supposed to get pregnant for five years, or it could cause a recurrence. And five years from now, I'll be too old to have a baby.'

'Stop thinking the worst about everything. Why don't you just relax and try to look at the bright side?' he said, trying to show an optimism he didn't feel. But Alex wasn't buying.

'What *bright* side? Are you crazy?'

'He says that losing the breast could mean saving your life. That's goddamn important,' Sam said firmly.

'How would you like to lose one of your testicles? How would that be?'

'It would be miserable, just like this is. I didn't want this to happen, neither did you. But we have to make the best of it.' He was trying, but she didn't want to hear it.

'There is no "best of it," there's me too sick to move for the next six or seven months, disfigured for the rest of my life, and unable to have more children. And then maybe too there's a recurrence.'

'Is there anything else you can think of to depress yourself? How about hemorrhoids and prostate? For chrissake, Alex, I know this is terrible, but don't make it worse than it is.'

'It couldn't be much worse. And don't tell me how to look at it. You're going to walk out of here and go home tonight. You're going to be with Annabelle, and I'm not. You're going to feel fine all year, and when you look in the mirror tomorrow morning nothing will be different. Everything in my life has changed. So don't tell me how to look at anything. You don't understand it.' She was shouting at him, and he had never seen her as miserable or as angry.

'I know. But you still have me, and Annabelle, and you're still beautiful. And you still have your career, and everything that matters. Okay, so you lost a breast. You could have had an accident too. You could be crippled. You can't let this destroy you. You can't do that.'

'I can do anything I damn well want. Don't make me speeches.'

'Then what do you want from me?' he asked, exasperated finally. He didn't know what to say to her. This was not his forte, or the place he wanted to be, or the situation he wanted to be in.

'I want some reality, some sympathy. You wouldn't even listen to me for the last two weeks when I told you this could happen. You didn't want to know how I feel, you don't want to know how scared I am of everything that's going to happen to me. You just want to mouth a lot of platitudes and feed me a lot of bullshit. You weren't even here for chrissake when they told me what had happened to me. You were at your office, making deals, and at home, watching fucking TV with our daughter, so don't tell me how to feel. You don't know shit about what I'm feeling.'

'I guess not,' he said quietly, stunned by her venom. She was furious, at anyone, and everything, and him, because nothing would change this. 'I don't know what to say to you, Al. I wish I could change it, but I can't. And I'm sorry I wasn't here.'

'Me too,' she said, and started to cry again. She felt so alone, and so scared, so vulnerable, and so helpless. 'What am I going to do?' She looked at him pathetically. 'How am I going to work, or be a wife to you, or take care of Annabelle?'

'You just have to do what you can, and let the rest slide for a while. Do you want me to call your office?'

'No.' She glared at him miserably. 'I'll call them myself in a few days. Dr Herman says I might be able to work when I'm on chemo, it'll just depend on how I feel. Some people do, but I don't think they're trial lawyers. Maybe I can do some work at home.' She just couldn't imagine how she was going to manage. Six months of chemo seemed like an eternity to Alex.

'It's too soon to think about all this. You've just had surgery. Why don't you take it easy?'

'And do what? Go to a support group?' The doctor had told her about those too, and she refused even to consider it. She wasn't going to sit around with a lot of other misfits.

'Why don't you just relax?' he said as Alex bristled, and the nurse suddenly appeared and offered Alex a shot for the pain, and some sleeping medicine. The doctor had left orders for both, and Sam told Alex he thought she should take it.

'Why?' She glared at him. 'So I stop yelling at you?' She looked like a kid to him and he bent down and kissed her on the forehead.

'Yeah. So you'll shut up for a while, and get some sleep, before you drive yourself crazy.' Everything she had feared had happened to her, in a single morning. And now she had to learn to live with it.

She had a rough road ahead of her, and she knew it. She understood perfectly what lay ahead. Unlike Sam, who still wanted to deny it. 'I love you, Alex,' he said gently after the nurse gave her the shot, but Alex didn't answer. She wasn't sleepy yet, but she was too miserable to tell him she loved him. And then, a few minutes later, she started to doze off. She didn't speak to him again, she just fell asleep, holding his hand, and he stood there and cried as he watched her. She looked so tired and so sad, and so broken, all covered in bandages, her beautiful hair like flame, and her body so badly injured.

He tiptoed quietly from the room once she was asleep, and signaled to the nurse that he was leaving. And as he rode down the elevator, he thought of what Alex had said to him. That he could walk away from this, and go home. It wasn't happening to him, just to her. And as he walked slowly home, he couldn't deny it. He was still whole, he wasn't in danger. He had nothing to fear, except losing her, which was so intensely frightening, he couldn't face it. He looked at himself in a store window on the way home, and saw the same man he had always been. Nothing had changed, except that he knew he had lost part of himself that afternoon, the part that was irretrievably bound to Alex. She was leaving him, bit by bit, just as his parents had left him, and he wasn't going to let her take him down with her. She had no right to do that to him, to expect him to die with her. And as he thought of it, he walked home as briskly as he could, as though there were muggers running after him, or demons.

Chapter 7

When Alex woke up the next day, there was a woman sitting in the chair, waiting for her, and the nurse was changing her intravenous. There was relatively little pain, just as Dr Herman had said, but there was a weight on her heart the size of Hoover Dam as she remembered what had happened.

The woman smiled at her, she was wearing a flowered dress and she had gray hair, and Alex had no idea who she was as she watched her.

'Hi, I'm Alice Ayres. I thought I'd come to see how you're doing.' She had a warm smile and lively blue eyes and she looked old enough to be Alex's mother. Alex tried to sit up, but that was hard, and instead the nurse raised her bed, so she could talk to the woman who'd come to see her.

'Are you a nurse?'

'No, just a friend. I'm a volunteer. I know just what you're going through, Mrs Parker. Or may I call you Alexandra?'

'Alex.' She stared at her, unable to comprehend what the woman was doing there. Alex's breakfast arrived then, but she told the nurse she didn't want it. It was all soft diet after surgery but all she wanted was a cup of coffee.

'I wouldn't do that if I were you,' Mrs Ayres said to her as Alex waved her breakfast tray away. 'You need your strength and plenty of nutrition.' She was a little like the Fairy Godmother in 'Cinderella.' 'How about some oatmeal?'

'I hate hot cereal,' Alex said, sounding belligerent, and staring at the older woman. 'Who are you and why are you here?' It was all very surrealistic.

'I'm here because I've had the same operation that you did. I know what it's like, and how you feel, probably better than most people do, maybe even your husband. I know how angry you are and how scared you are, and how shocked, and how you feel about the way you'll look. I've had reconstructive surgery,' she explained, handing Alex her cup of coffee. 'I'd be happy to show it to you, if you like. It looks pretty good, in fact, it's very good. I don't think most people would know I'd had a breast removed. Would you like to see it?' Alex thought that sounded disgusting.

'I'd rather not, thanks.' Dr Herman had already explained that she could have an implant put in, and her remaining nipple either 'shared' with the other breast, or an artificial one tattooed on the implant. The whole thing sounded horrible, and not worth the trouble. She was wrecked anyway. Why not just leave it? 'Why did you come and see me? Who asked you to?'

'Your surgeon put you on the list for visits from our support group. Eventually, you might want to join us for a group, or talk to some of the women about their experiences. It can be very helpful.'

'I don't think so.' Alex glared at her, wishing she would leave, but not wanting to say it. 'I'd rather not discuss this with strangers.'

'I understand.' Alice Ayres stood up, smiling gently. 'It's not an easy time. And I'm sure you're worried about chemo. We can answer some of those questions too, but so can your doctor. We have a men's group too, if your husband is interested.' She put a little booklet next to Alex's bed, and Alex ignored it.

'I don't think my husband is interested either.' Sam go to a group of husbands of women who lost their breasts to cancer? Not likely. 'Thanks anyway.'

'You take care, Alex. I'll be thinking about you,' she said gently, as she touched a foot under the covers, and then left the room. She reported to the nurses that it had been a classic first visit. Alexandra Parker was angry and depressed, completely to be expected. They planned to visit her again on a regular basis, and Alice Ayres made a note to the parent group to send out someone younger. She thought a woman Alex's own age might be more helpful to her. Their youngest group member was twenty-five and she visited most of the younger women. But there were plenty of women Alex's age to draw from.

'What was that all about?' Alex barked at the nurse who had just come on duty for her.

'I think it's fairly routine. They're good people, and they help a lot of women,' her nurse explained as Alex predictably dropped their brochure in the garbage. 'Now how would you like a little sponge bath?' Alex glared at her in answer, but she had no choice but to live within the hospital routine. They 'bathed' her and she brushed her teeth. She stared out the window from her bed, and then lunch came. More soft, bland food. She didn't touch any of it, and just after that, her surgeon came, and looked at the dressing and the drain. Alex was afraid to look at herself yet, and she looked up at the ceiling, wanting to scream while he changed it. And as soon as he left, Sam called. He was at the office, and planning to come by later that afternoon, he had thought it would do her good to rest and get some sleep. Annabelle was fine, and he said he couldn't wait to see her, and Alex didn't believe him. If he was so anxious to see her why hadn't he come by that morning, or at lunch? He explained that he was going to the Four Seasons with one of his oldest clients. He wanted to introduce Simon and his assistant to some of his clients too. But he was going to drop by and see her on his way home, he promised.

She wanted to hang up on him, but she didn't. She called Annabelle instead, and they had a nice chat about school, and her 'trip,' and Alex promised her she'd be home by the weekend. And after that she had a shot for the pain, but she had to admit there wasn't much. But it was easier to drift in and out of sleep and drugs than to contemplate her future, and the absence of her husband. And when she woke up, she called her office. Matt Billings was out, as was Brock, but Elizabeth Hascomb told her that everything was in good control. There had been no emergencies since she'd been gone, and they all missed her.

'Are you all right?' she asked, sounding concerned, but Alex's voice was strong and she sounded a lot better than she had even that morning.

'I'm fine. I'll be back as soon as I can.'

'We'll be waiting.'

That afternoon, Dr Herman told her that she could eat regular meals now and leave as early as the next day, or she could wait until she felt a little stronger. But the incision was healing nicely.

'I'd rather stay,' she said quietly, and surprised him. He had figured her for someone who'd want to rush out in two days. It would have been possible for her, but he always recommended staying just a little bit longer.

'I thought you'd be anxious to leave us.' He smiled, not unaware of the trauma she had gone through.

'I have a three-year-old at home. I'd rather be in better shape when I go back to her, so I don't have so much to explain.'

'I'd say you'll be in pretty good shape by the weekend, and the drain can come out by then, which will leave only the dressing. You've had major surgery, so you'll be tired, but I don't think you'll be in pain. We can handle that with some medication if it's a problem. All you have to do after that is get your strength back. And then in three or four weeks, depending on the rest of your tests, we'll begin treatment.' 'Treatment.' Such a benign word for chemotherapy. Just thinking about it made her heart ache.

'What about work?'

'I'd say give it another week. Until the dressings are off, and you're stronger. And then, of course, once you start chemotherapy, you'll have to see how well you're able to cope with work, but if we adjust the doses correctly, you should be able to handle a moderate workload.' When was the last time her workload had been moderate? Maybe the day she'd had Annabelle, and never before or since then. But at least he wasn't saying she couldn't work. He was saying she'd have to try it. That was something.

He left her then, and she sat quietly in a chair staring out the window. She had gone for a walk down the hall, and found that she felt weak and dizzy and oddly out of balance. Her dressings hampered her, and she couldn't move her left arm, but at least she wasn't left-handed.

She was alone in her room when Sam arrived at five o'clock, carrying a big bunch of red roses. And he hesitated in the doorway when he saw her. The

look on her face was one of such despair that he
didn't even know what to say to her. She'd been
sitting there, contemplating her fate and her future.
And for just an instant, he had remembered a terrifying image of his dying mother, and wanted to
run out of the room, screaming.

'Hi, how are you feeling?' he asked, trying to sound
casual, as he set the flowers down, and she only
shrugged and didn't answer. How would he feel? But
she didn't see that he was shaking.

'I'm okay.' She sounded anything but convincing.
Her chest was throbbing a little bit, and the drain
annoyed her, but that was to be expected. 'Thanks for
the flowers.' She tried to sound enthused, but didn't
quite make it. 'Dr Herman says I can go back to work
after next week.' That was something anyway. And
Sam smiled when he heard it, and felt better.

'Well, that ought to cheer you up. When are you
coming home?'

'Maybe Friday.' She sounded anything but pleased,
and she was worrying about taking care of Annabelle,
and what she would tell her about the dressing. 'Will
you ask Carmen to spend the weekend? I know she
needs a day off, but I don't think I can manage yet
without her.'

'Sure. And I can take care of Annabelle. She's no
problem.' Alex nodded, missing her terribly, and
then she looked up at Sam, wondering what their
life would be like now. They had spent so much
time and energy trying to have another child, and
making love on schedule, what would life be like
now without that? What would it be like without a
breast? How would he look at her? What would it
look like? Dr Herman had showed her photographs
so she would be prepared, and they had terrified

her. It was just a clean flat slab of flesh, with no nipple, and a diagonal scar where the breast had been. She couldn't even imagine how Sam would react to that when they finally took off her dressing. Dr Herman had told her she could shower once the drain was removed. The sutures would take longer to dissolve, and after that, she would be left with the same flat, scarred chest she had seen in the pictures.

'Why don't we do something this weekend?' Sam suggested casually, and she stared at him. He was acting as though nothing had happened. 'Why don't we call someone and have dinner with friends, or go to a movie, if we have Carmen.' Alex stared at him in disbelief. How could he?

'I don't want to see anyone. What would I say? Gee, I just lost my breast so we thought we'd go out to dinner to celebrate, before I start chemotherapy? For chrissake, Sam, have a little sensitivity. This isn't easy.'

'I'm sure it's not, but you don't have to sit around feeling sorry for yourself either after this. There is life after breasts, you know. You weren't that big anyway, for heaven's sake, so what's the big deal?' He tried to joke with her, but it was a very big deal to her. She had lost a part of her self-image and her self-confidence, and her life was at stake now. That was about as big a deal as you get, no matter how small your breasts were. She hadn't wanted to lose one.

'How are you going to feel about me now?' she asked him honestly, facing him from across the small room. She wanted to hear it, since he had never reassured her about it before the operation. But he felt that the fact that he was there told her everything. To Alex, it didn't. He was passing through once a day for an hour, between office and home, and the rest of his busy life. That was a little too easy.

'What does that mean?' He looked annoyed at the question.

'I'm asking you if it's going to gross you out to see me the way I am now.' She hadn't even seen it herself yet, so she wasn't sure what she was talking about, but she was desperate for reassurance.

'How do I know what I'm going to feel? I can't imagine it makes that much difference. Why don't we cross that bridge when we come to it?'

'Like when? Next week? Tomorrow? Now?' There were tears in her eyes again, he wasn't saying what she needed to hear, or what she wanted. And he looked faintly panicked by her question. 'Do you want me to show it to you, or would you rather see a picture first, so you're forewarned? Dr Herman has some great ones, very clear, very graphic. It just looks like a flat piece of meat with no nipple.' Alex saw him go pale and he looked suddenly angry.

'Why are you doing this? Do you want to scare me, or just turn me off before we even start? What's the deal here, Al? Are you mad at me, or just pissed off at life? Maybe you better reconstruct your attitude, before you start worrying about getting your breast back.'

'Who said I was trying to get my breast back?' She looked surprised at what he'd said to her.

'Dr Herman said you could have reconstructive surgery in a few months, if you were up to it. That sounds like a good idea to me.'

'Would you rather I stay hidden till then?' she asked nastily, and he threw up his hands in obvious irritation.

'You're being a real bitch about this. I'm sorry you

lost your breast. I'm sorry you've been "disfigured."
I don't know how I'm going to feel when I see it.
Okay? I'll let you know. All right?'

'Be sure you do that.' But he had said none of
the right things for her. There was no reassurance
that it didn't matter to him, that she was beautiful
anyway. He just wanted to go on with their life, and
pretend it hadn't happened. Dinner and a movie with
friends sounded fine to him. He refused to realize how
distraught she was over what had happened. And she
was making no effort yet to get out of her depression,
and he certainly wasn't helping.

'Why don't you just concentrate on getting your
strength back and getting home? You'll feel a lot
better once you're home with Annabelle, and you can
go back to work, and get your life back to normal.'

'How normal do you think it's going to be while
I'm on chemotherapy, Sam?' she asked him bluntly.

'As normal as you're willing to let it be,' he said
brutally, but not really understanding what was in
store for her either. 'You don't have to make such a
big deal of this, you don't have to punish us too. It's
going to be hard on Annabelle if you stay angry like
this. You're going to have to make your peace with
what happened.' It had only been a day though. 'I'm
not even sure anymore I know how to help you.'

'Apparently not,' she said unhappily, 'you seem to
be a little too busy with your own life to be incon-
venienced by all this, from what I can tell. You seem
to be awfully busy at the moment with Simon and his
new clients.'

'I have a busy professional life, so do you. If this
were happening to me, you wouldn't be staying home
from work, or canceling trials or meetings with your
clients either. Try to be realistic. The whole world

didn't come to a shrieking stop yesterday because of what happened to you.'

'That's reassuring.'

'I'm sorry,' he said unhappily. 'I feel like everything I say just makes you madder.'

'You could try saying it doesn't matter to you, that you love me anyway, with one breast or two, if that's the case. And if not, then I guess you're saying what's true for you. Maybe that's all that matters.'

'How do I know what I'm going to feel? How do you? Maybe you'll never want to have sex with me again after this. What the hell do I know?' He was being painfully honest with her and she wasn't ready for it. Her doctor could have told him that, or any therapist, or even Alex herself, but he wouldn't have listened. He was telling her the truth, as he knew it. And she didn't want to hear it.

'I know that I would love you, no matter what happened to you, no matter how disfigured you were, even if you lost your face, or your balls, or your hair, or had to spend the rest of your life in a wheelchair.'

'That's very noble of you,' he said coolly, 'but it's also a lot of bullshit. How do you know what you would feel if something like that happened to me? You don't know zip until you get there. It's very easy for you to pretend it wouldn't affect you, but maybe it would. Maybe it would turn you off, even if that wasn't the politically correct thing for you to be feeling.'

'Are you saying it will turn you off?'

'I'm saying I don't know, and that's honest. I can't tell you it won't scare me, or make me a little nervous at first. Hell, it's a big change. But at least we can make an effort not to let it rock us to the core. This doesn't have to be the big deal you're making of it.

Besides, there's more to life than just breasts and sex and bodies. We're friends too, not just lovers.'

'But I don't want to be just friends,' she said plaintively, starting to cry again, while he tried to hide his exasperation.

'Neither do I, so give it a rest, Al. Just let it be for a while. Let us both get used to this, and see what happens.' Why couldn't he lie to her? Why couldn't he tell her he loved her anyway? Because that wasn't Sam. She had always loved his honesty and integrity, even when it hurt her. And it was hurting her now, terribly. 'What I don't understand is how your whole identity can be wrapped up in one breast, and not even a very big one at that. I mean for chrissake, you weren't a topless queen, or a go-go dancer. What's the big deal? You're an attorney. You don't need boobs. You're an intelligent woman. You lost your breast, not your brain, so what's all this craziness about?' It was about losing her life, and a part of her identity, and possibly her sex life. She no longer even felt like the same person.

'I just lost a breast, which even if it was small, I'm still vain enough to not want to be scarred for life . . . I may lose my hair . . . my ability to have children . . . everything's changed, and you're even telling me you're not sure how you're going to feel about me physically. How could I not be freaked out by this, Sam? I'd have to be dead not to feel it.'

'Maybe I just don't get it. If I found out I was sterile next week, I'd be sorry, but I'd be happy we had Annabelle, and let it go at that. Stop making such a big deal out of everything. Your identity is your brain and your life and your career, and everything you are and do and represent, not one boob or two. Who cares?'

'Maybe you do,' she said honestly.

'Yeah. Maybe so. So what? So screw me. Learn to live with it yourself, then maybe I'll feel better about it. But I'm not going to sit around and wring my hands with you, it would drive us both crazy if I did.'

'So what are you saying to me?'

'I'm telling you to stop feeling sorry for yourself, and forget it.' There was something positive in what he said, and yet there was another part of him that was being deeply insensitive to what she was feeling. 'I don't want to think about your having cancer all the time. I can't do it.' That was more honest than she knew.

'What do you mean, "all the time"?' She looked shocked as she looked at him. 'This happened yesterday, and I've seen you twice in two days for less than an hour each time, I wouldn't say we've spent a lot of time on this.'

'I don't think "we" should have to. It's something *you're* going to have to deal with and work out.'

'Thanks for your help.'

'I can't help you, Alex. You have to help yourself.'

'I'll remember that.'

'I'm sorry you're so angry,' he said quietly, which only made her madder.

'So am I.' They sat quietly for a few more minutes and then Sam stood up, and looked at her uncomfortably.

'I guess I should go home to Annabelle. It's getting late, and I promised her I'd come home for dinner.' Alex felt him slipping out of her grasp, and it panicked her. She had said none of the right things to him to elicit his sympathy, and he hadn't said anything right either. She was angry at him for not being there for her. He hadn't been there when she woke up from the surgery, or when they'd told her she'd lost her breast and had cancer, and he hadn't been there all day today. He'd been out with Simon and his clients, at fancy restaurants, making deals and being important. And he didn't seem to understand any of what she was feeling. He didn't understand how shaky she was, or how scared, how unsure of herself suddenly, or of his love for her. And it was too easy for him to just say that one breast or two was unimportant. It was important to her. She cared about how she looked to him, and she cared desperately about whether or not he loved her, and he wasn't saying anything to convince her that he would love her no matter what. In fact, he was reserving judgment to see how it affected him when he saw what it looked like. She was still furious when he left, and she noticed that he kissed her on the forehead again, instead of the lips, as though he was suddenly afraid to touch her.

She sat in her room and cried again that night. She didn't even bother walking down the hall, or calling Annabelle, and she didn't call Sam either. She just wanted to be left alone, and she had her back to the door, when it opened and she heard someone come in. She assumed it was the nurse, and she didn't turn to see. She just sat in her chair and kept on crying.

She felt a hand on her shoulder then, and, for a wild moment, she thought it might be Sam, but when she looked up, she was startled to see Elizabeth Hascomb. 'Did you come to visit me?' Alex asked her, surprised to see her.

'Yes, I did,' she explained, 'but I didn't know it was you until tonight,' suddenly feeling as though she was intruding, but that was just what she needed to do, and she knew it. 'I work for the breast surgery support group here, twice a week, and you were on the visiting list tonight when I got here. The card said A. Parker

. . . I couldn't believe it. I asked to be assigned to see if it was you. I hope you don't mind, Alex,' she said gently, and then she put her arms around her like a mother and brought tears to her employer's eyes. 'Oh Alex . . . I'm so sorry . . .' Alex couldn't even speak for a while, she just sat in Liz's arms and sobbed. She couldn't hold up anymore, there were so many fears and terrors and disappointments to deal with. 'I know . . . I know . . . just cry . . . you'll feel better.'

'I'm never going to feel better again,' Alex said miserably, looking at her through her tears, and Liz smiled.

'Yes, you will. It's hard to believe now, but you will. We've all been through it.'

'You too?' Alex was surprised, she didn't know that about Liz.

'I've had both breasts removed,' she explained, 'years ago. I wear a prosthesis. But they do wonderful reconstructive work now. At your age you should think about that. Not yet though,' she said gently. She seemed so wise and loving, and Alex was so relieved that Liz had come to see her.

'I have to have chemotherapy.' Alex started to cry harder again and Liz sat and held her hand, grateful she had found her. She had never suspected what Alex was going through, although she realized now that she should have.

'I had chemo. And hormone therapy too. I've had it all, but that was seventeen years ago, and I'm fine. You will be too, if you do everything they tell you to do. You have a wonderful doctor.' And then she looked at her more pointedly. Alex was in bad shape and she could see it. 'How's Sam taking all this?'

'First he wouldn't even acknowledge it was happening, he kept telling me they wouldn't find anything.

And now he's annoyed that I'm upset. He thinks I'm making too much of it, and losing a breast is "no big deal," but at the same time he's saying it might bother him, and he just doesn't know how he feels about it, he'll let me know when he sees it.'

'He's scared, Alex. It's frightening for him, too. That's small consolation for you, but some men just can't cope with the threat of their wife having cancer.'

'His mother died of cancer when he was a kid, and I think this reminds him of it. Either that, or he's just being a bastard.'

'Maybe a little of both. What you need to do now is concentrate on *you*. Never mind him. Sam can take care of himself, especially if he's not going to take care of you. What you need to do is get as strong as you can, and stay that way. You have to fight the disease. You can worry about everything else later.'

'But what if he's disgusted by me, if my body frightens him?' That was terrifying her, as Liz looked at her calmly. All her sympathy was for Alex, not Sam. She knew. She'd been through it, and it hadn't been easy for her either. Her husband had had a hard time coping at first, but eventually he had come around, and been a big support to Liz. But she knew, better than anyone, that with or without Sam, Alex had to survive this.

'He'll have to grow up, won't he? He's a big boy, he can figure it out. He knows what you need now, but if he can't provide it, then you have to get it from friends, or family, or a support group. We're here for you. I'm here, anytime you need me.' Alex started to cry again then, and Liz took her in her motherly arms and held her.

She gave Alex a few exercises to do, and told her some things to think about, and she didn't leave her any booklets. She knew Alex too well to do that. Alex had no patience with brochures or superficial information. She got right to the heart of things. And for her, the heart of things right now was survival.

'When are you going home?'

'Probably Friday.'

'Fine. Get strong, sleep a lot, take the medications, if you're in pain. Eat regularly, get as healthy as you can before you start chemo. You're going to need all your energy for that,' she said wisely.

'I'm coming back to the office after next week.' She said it tentatively as though asking Liz's opinion. It was suddenly very comforting to have someone to talk to who'd been there. And Liz had survived it.

'A lot of women go back to work, even during chemo. You'll just have to figure what works best for you, when to rest, when to stay home, when to take the most advantage of your energy. It's a little bit like waging a war. All you want to do is win. Never forget that. And no matter how miserable it is, chemo will help you win this.'

'I wish I believed that.'

'Don't listen to the horror stories, and just keep your focus on the goal. Win, win, win. Don't even let Sam distract you from that. If he can't help you, forget him for now.' Alex laughed at the vehemence with which Liz said it.

'You make me feel better.' And then she looked at her secretary sheepishly, amazed at this other life she'd known nothing about. It was incredible how there were things about people no one knew, and that were so important. Just as no one had known she was coming to have a biopsy, and possibly surgery, while she was away from the office.

'I think I was very rude this morning to some

160

woman from your support group. Alice something,' Alex said apologetically, and Liz smiled at her.

'Ayres. She's used to it. Maybe one day you'll do something like this. It means a lot to a lot of people.'

'Thank you, Liz,' she said, and meant every word of it.

'May I come back and see you tomorrow? Maybe at lunchtime?'

'I'd love that. Just don't tell anyone at the office. I don't want them to know. Although eventually, I'll have to tell Matthew, probably once I start the chemo.'

'That's up to you. I won't say anything.'

They embraced again, and Liz left, and when Alex went to bed that night, she felt better than she had in days, and surprisingly less angry. She lay in bed thinking about everything, and she decided to call Sam and tell him she loved him.

But the phone rang for a long time, and eventually Carmen answered. It was ten o'clock by then, and she sounded as though she'd been sleeping. 'I'm sorry, Carmen. Is Mr Parker there?'

Carmen hesitated for a moment, and then answered with a yawn. She could see their bedroom door open at the end of the hall, and no light on.

'No, sorry, Mrs Parker. He's not here. How are you?'

'I'm fine,' she said, sounding a little more convincing than she had that afternoon. 'Did he go to a movie?'

'I don't know. He went out after Annabelle had dinner. He didn't eat with her, so maybe he went out with friends. He didn't tell me, and I think he forgot to leave me a number.' It was always Alex who remembered to leave the number where they could be reached when they went out for the evening.

She wondered where Sam had gone, but he'd probably been upset after their conversation at the hospital, and he'd gone out for something to eat, and a walk. He did that sometimes when he was troubled. Sam needed to be alone to resolve his problems.

'Well, just tell him I called.' She hesitated again, and then, 'And tell him I love him. And kiss Annabelle for me in the morning.'

'I will, Mrs Parker. Good night . . . and God bless you.'

'God bless you too, Carmen . . . Thank you.' She wasn't sure if He had blessed her lately or not, but at least she was alive, and in three days she'd be back home with her daughter. And three weeks after that, the fight would begin in earnest. But after talking to Liz, she was determined to win it.

She sat in her hospital bed that night for a long time, thinking of Liz, and Sam, and Annabelle, and all the good things in her life she was going to have to concentrate on if she was going to win the war. . . Annabelle, she reminded herself, as she drifted off to sleep after a shot . . . Annabelle . . . Sam . . . Annabelle, and, as she thought of her, she remembered holding her in her arms, and nursing her as a baby.

Chapter 8

After he'd left the hospital, the phone had rung as soon as Sam sat down to dinner with Annabelle. It was Simon. He had arranged an impromptu dinner with some clients from London. Did Sam want to join them? He explained that he was just about to have dinner with his daughter.

'Well, stop eating, man. They're a grand bunch, Sam. You'll like them. And I think they're important. They represent the biggest textile mills in Britain, and they're aching to make investments over here. They're good men, you really should meet them. And I've got Daphne with me.' Was that supposed to be an incentive? Sam wasn't sure, and he argued for a little while. After haranguing with Alex for over an hour, he was exhausted. But he was also depressed, and the prospect of sitting around alone at home after Annabelle went to bed depressed him further.

'I really shouldn't.'

'That's nonsense.' Simon held firm. 'Your wife's out of town, isn't she? Why don't you give your tot a little kiss, and come out with us? We're meeting at Le Cirque at eight, and then Daphne has found some ridiculous place downtown to take them dancing. You know the Brits, they've got to party while they're away or they feel they've been cheated. They're worse than the Italians, because it's so fucking boring in England. Come on, man, stop whining. We'll expect you at eight. Done?'

'Done. I'll be there. I might be there five minutes late, but I'll come.' He wanted to put Annabelle to bed and read her a story.

He went back to the kitchen then and sat with her, until bedtime. And after he'd read *Goodnight Moon* to her again, and turned off all but the night-light, he went to his bedroom and changed his shirt and shaved, and thought about Alex. It had been a rough couple of days for both of them, and he was beginning to wonder just how rough it would be when she got home on Friday. She was making a real issue of the surgery and the missing breast. And the truth was that it frightened him more than a little. Who wouldn't be worried about seeing that? There was no way it could be anything but very ugly. But he didn't want to tell her that. He wished she wouldn't push him about it. He remembered his mother asking him again and again if he loved her, before she died, and he had to close his eyes and force her voice out of his head, as he thought of Alex.

He brushed his hair, washed his face, and splashed on some after-shave, and by the time he left, he looked as though he had just stepped off the cover of *GQ* in a dark gray suit, and a white shirt. He looked like just what he was, one of the most exciting businessmen in New York, and heads turned, as they always did, when he got to Le Cirque. Half the people there knew who he was, and had read about him, the others wondered who he was because he was so good-looking, mostly the women. He was so used to it, he never paid attention to it anymore, and it was usually Alex who teased him about it. She accused him of leaving his fly open in the hope that women would watch him. And he thought of that now as he made his way across the restaurant and smiled, thinking of his wife. But when he thought of her, it was as she had been before, not as she was now, deformed and angry, at New York Hospital.

'Glad you could make it, Sam!' Simon stood up and greeted him the moment he arrived, and introduced him to everyone. There were four Englishmen, and three American girls that someone had introduced to them. They were all very pretty, two were models, and one was an actress. And then there was Daphne, which left only Sam and Simon unescorted. They were a large group in a small restaurant, and the noise was deafening. Sam managed to have an intelligent conversation nonetheless with one of the Englishmen, and on his other side was Daphne, who spent a lot of time talking to one of the models. They finally got to talk to each other over dessert, while the others drank and chatted.

'I hear your wife is a very important attorney,' she said conversationally to him, and he nodded. Somehow, right now, talking about Alex seemed painful, and it was easier not to.

'She's a litigator with a firm called Bartlett and Paskin.'

'She must be very intelligent, and very powerful.'

'She is.' He nodded, but something in the way he said it told Daphne that this wasn't a comfortable subject.

'Do you have children?'

'A little girl named Annabelle,' he smiled at that one, 'she's three and a half and adorable.'

'I have a four-year-old son in England,' she said easily.

'You do?' He looked startled. Somehow she seemed too young for a husband or children, although he knew she was twenty-nine, but still it surprised him. Everything about her suggested she was single.

'Don't look so shocked,' she laughed at him, 'I'm divorced. Didn't Simon tell you?'

'No, he didn't.'

'I was married to a shocking rotter at twenty-one. He finally ran off with someone else and we got divorced, which was why everyone in the family thought it would do me good to get away for a year. Therapy, I think you call it here. We call it a bit of a holiday,' she smiled at him.

'And what about your son?'

'He's very happy with my mother,' she said matter-of-factly.

'You must miss him.'

'I do. But we're not quite as sentimental about children in England as you are over here. We ship them off to boarding school at seven, you know. He'll be away at school in three years, and eventually at Eton. And I think it'll do him good to get a bit detached from Mummy in the meantime.' It was not the kind of thing he could imagine himself doing. He would have been heartbroken without Annabelle, but Daphne was very cool, and very aware of what she wanted. 'Does that shock you?' She could see in his eyes that it surprised him.

'A little,' he said honestly, with a smile. 'It's not exactly the image we have of motherhood over here.' But on the other hand she didn't look like a motherly type, and maybe she wanted some freedom before she was any older.

'I think as a nation we're a bit more cold-blooded than you are. Americans seem to get terribly wound up about what they ought to be doing, and what's expected of them, and what they *should* be feeling. Britons just *do* it. It's rather simple.'

'And a little self-centered.' He liked talking to her, very much in fact. She was smart and honest and totally open about who she was and what she wanted.

'It's terribly simple, you go after what you want, when you want it, without apologizing, or pretending that you're doing anything other than what you are. I rather like it. Things seem a bit more exaggerated here. Everyone's always apologizing for what they're doing, or not doing, or not feeling.' She laughed, and Sam liked the sound of it. It was an unbridled sound of almost sensual amusement, and he could imagine her easily with her clothes off and totally unembarrassed. 'Have you ever been divorced?' she asked bluntly, and he laughed at the question.

'No, I haven't.'

'Most Americans have, or at least that's the impression they give me.'

'Was your divorce very traumatic?' It was an oddly personal conversation between two strangers, but he was enjoying it. There was something totally open and abandoned about her.

'Not at all. It was a great relief. He was a complete bastard. For the life of me, I can't imagine how we stayed married for so long, seven years. It was quite dreadful, I assure you.'

'Who did he run off with?' He liked being somewhat forward with her. It was fun playing the game of discovering things about her.

'A barmaid, naturally. Quite a pretty one though.

167

He's already left her. And he's living in Paris with some girl who says she's an artist. He's quite mad, but fortunately he takes good care of Andrew, our son, so I don't need to panic.' She seemed anything but panicked, she seemed completely in control of any situation. And more than one of the Englishmen were eyeing her with interest. She looked as though she could have had anyone she wanted.

'Were you in love with him?' Sam asked her, feeling brazen.

'Probably. For a while anyway. At twenty-one, it's awfully difficult to tell the difference between love and good sex. I'm not sure I ever figured out which one it was.' She smiled cheekily at him, and as he looked at her, he wished suddenly that he were young enough to have her. She was terrific. But then he thought of Alex. And it was as though Daphne saw that.

'And what about you? Are you in love with your wife? I hear she's very pretty.' She was, for forty-two, for any age. But she was not quite as outrageous or even as striking as Daphne and he knew it.

'Yes, I love her,' he answered firmly, as Daphne watched him intently.

'That's not what I asked you, is it? I asked if you were *in* love with her. There's a difference,' she said, raising an eyebrow.

'Is there? We've been married for more than seventeen years. That's a long time, you get very attached to someone by then. I love her very much,' he said, as though trying to convince himself, but he still hadn't answered Daphne's question.

'Are you telling me you don't know if you're still in love with her? Were you ever?' she persisted, playing cat and mouse with him, but he didn't mind it.

'Of course I was.' He sounded shocked at the

question, and Simon was amused by the intense look on their faces from across the table. They were huddled together, as though solving all of life's greatest problems.

'Then when did it change? When did you stop loving her?' Daphne accused, sounding like a lawyer, and Sam wagged a finger at her.

'I never said that. That's a terrible thing to say.' Especially now. But all he could think about as he looked at her was Daphne.

'I didn't say it. You did. You said you *were* in love with her, but you don't seem to be able to tell me if you are now,' she said, looking incredibly sexy as she persisted.

'Sometimes marriage is like that. There are dead spots in the water sometimes, when you kind of run dry and get stale, and none of the right things seem to happen.'

'Is this one of those times?' she asked, her voice a velvet purr that tore at his insides.

'Maybe. It's hard to say.'

'For any particular reason? Did anything happen?'

'That's a long story,' he said almost sadly.

'Have you had affairs?' she asked bluntly, and this time he laughed at her.

'Has anyone ever told you that you're outrageous?' And beautiful . . . and sensual . . . and have skin like velvet. . .

'Completely.' She smiled dazzlingly at him. 'Actually, I pride myself on it.'

'Well, maybe you shouldn't,' he tried to chide her unsuccessfully.

'At my age, I can do almost anything I want. I'm not quite old enough to be held seriously accountable, and old enough to know what I'm doing. I hate really young girls, don't you?' She leapt from one subject to another, as she flipped her long black hair over her bare shoulders, and she was incredibly alluring. In some ways, she was so much like Alex, and in others she was very different. She was much bolder, more outrageous, yet she had that razor-sharp mind, and the same long, lanky body. But she was much more overtly sexual than Alex had ever been, and Sam was embarrassed to admit that he liked it, but he hoped that no one knew it. She made him constantly want to tease her back, to play with her, to play a game that neither of them could lose. But he also knew full well that he was not free to play it. She knew that too. But it didn't seem to stop her from playing.

'What about you?' he teased her in answer to her question about young girls. 'Do you like young men, or old ones?'

'I like all men,' she said naughtily, 'but I prefer men your age,' she said smoothly.

'Shame on you,' he scolded softly, 'that was pretty obvious.'

'I'm always obvious, Sam. I hate wasting time.'

'Me too. I'm married.'

'Is that a problem?' Her eyes bore straight into his, and he knew he had to be fair here.

'I think so. I don't do this.'

'That's too bad. It could be amusing.'

'I want more in life than "amusing." That's a dangerous sport. I haven't played it in years. That's a game for a single man. The lucky devils.' He laughed right into her eyes, wishing for just an instant that he were younger and free again. She made him feel good, even if just for a minute. It was like eating cream puffs.

'I like you,' she said honestly. She liked the way he

170

played fair and square and she thought his wife was a lucky woman.

'I like you too, Daphne. You're a terrific girl. You almost make me wish I were single.'

'Will you come to the discotheque with us after dinner?'

'I probably shouldn't. But I might.' He smiled at her, thinking about how much he'd have liked to dance with her, but how dangerous it might be, particularly right now, with Alex in the state she was in, and the tension between them.

But after they left the restaurant, the limousine was just standing there, and Daphne took his hand and pulled him in with the others, and he didn't have the heart to resist her. They went all the way downtown, to a place in SoHo he'd never heard of, and there was a wonderful blues band wailing away, and it seemed inevitable that they wound up in each other's arms, dancing in the dark nightclub, as he felt her body pressed against his, and he had to force himself repeatedly to think of Alex.

'I should go,' he said finally. It was very late, and there was a growing feeling of duplicity to what they were doing. There was no fooling himself now. He was married and she wasn't. No matter how attractive she was, he couldn't do this.

'Are you angry at me?' she asked softly, as he paid for their drinks, and he prepared to leave her with Simon.

'Of course not. Why should I be?' He was surprised by her question.

'I've made a shocking play for you tonight. I didn't mean to make you uncomfortable.' She was apologizing for her behavior.

'You didn't. You flattered me. I'm twenty years

older than you are, and believe me, if I could, I'd be after you in a flash, but I can't.'

'You flatter me,' she said demurely, looking at him with eyes that tore his heart out.

'No, but I'd like to.' And then he volunteered something he hadn't meant to. 'My wife is very sick.' He looked away as he said it, trying not to think of everything that had happened in the last two days, or the words that had passed between them. 'It made things a little difficult. I'm not sure what's going to happen.'

'*Very* sick?' She didn't want to say the word 'cancer,' but he understood what she was asking.

'*Very* sick,' he confirmed to her with a look of sorrow.

'I'm sorry.'

'Me too. That's not easy for her, or for me. And it makes things a little confusing.'

'I didn't mean to add to the confusion,' she said, sitting so close to him that he could see down her dress and he loved what he saw there.

'You didn't add to the confusion at all. Don't apologize. This is the most fun I've had in years . . . and I need it, very badly.' He looked at her again and something came between them just then that surprised him, there was an exchange of real feelings. This wasn't playtime anymore, this was a person he could talk to, and suddenly he didn't want to leave her. 'Shall we have a last dance?' It was not what he had intended at all, and he was annoyed at himself for a moment, and then overwhelmed with tenderness and desire for her as they danced cheek to cheek to the music. Her body molded against his, it was as though he'd been made for her and she for him, and they danced through two more songs, and finally he forced himself to leave her. He walked her back to

172

Simon, regretfully, like a borrowed jewel he hated to return, but knew he had to.

'You two seem to be having a good time,' he said pointedly. He could see what had been happening, and he was intrigued by it. Sam didn't seem the type for extramarital adventures, but he was sure coming on to his cousin. Then again maybe he was all talk, he was going home, wasn't he? 'She's a little vixen, isn't she?' Simon teased.

'Take good care of her,' Sam said seriously, and then left them. He was lost in thought all the way home in the cab, remembering what it had been like dancing with her. It was a memory he wouldn't soon forget, and as he walked into the apartment, he felt guilty toward Alex. And even more so, when he walked into his bedroom and saw Carmen's message from her on his pillow. But that night it wasn't Alex's face he saw as he drifted off to sleep. It was Daphne's.

Chapter 9

He called Alex the next morning when he got up, but the nurse said she was in therapy, and wouldn't be back for half an hour. And by then, he was on his way downtown to the office. He had a client waiting for him, and a thousand phone calls to make, and he didn't have a chance to call her again. And after his clients left, he ran into Daphne in the hallway. Her face lit up like spring the moment she saw him, but she was extremely polite and businesslike as they chatted for a few minutes, and then she walked slowly back to his office with him and said that she hoped she hadn't made a nuisance of herself the night before. She had gotten carried away, and from now on, it would be strictly business, she promised.

'How disappointing,' he laughed at her. 'I think I was the nuisance.'

'Not at all.' Her voice was a caress, but her behavior was completely proper, and very English. 'I don't usually make a habit of chasing married men. You're just so attractive, Sam, you really should be sprayed with dark paint, or have a bag over your head before you go out with strangers. You're really quite dangerous.' She flattered him and she played, and he loved it.

'I suppose I should have stayed home,' he said unconvincingly, 'but I had an awfully good time, particularly at the nightclub.'

'So did I,' she said hauntingly, and suddenly they both realized they were flirting.

'What do we do about this?' He acknowledged it with a smile before she did.

'I'm not sure yet. Cold showers, I suppose. I've never tried that.'

'Maybe we should try them together,' he said, and then regretted it. He couldn't seem to handle being anywhere near her, all he wanted was to be with her, and charm and seduce her. This had never happened to him before, and he had no idea what to do to stop it. They were like matchsticks near a flame, and the conflagration was instant. 'We're just going to have to behave,' he said finally and firmly.

'Yes, sir,' she saluted him with a smile, and then disappeared down the hall to her office next to Simon. But as she went, he stood there watching her, unable to keep his eyes off her figure.

'Watch out!' Larry, his old partner, said as he passed him in the hall. 'She's dangerous . . . English girls are,' he whispered.

'Why has no one ever warned me?' Sam pretended to moan as he went back to his own office. And as though to clear his head, he called Alex.

'Where were you last night?' she asked plaintively. 'I called you.'

'I know. I'm sorry. I was out with Simon and some new clients from London. He called after I got home and talked me into it. We went to Le Cirque for dinner.' He suddenly felt as though he was saying too much and owed her an explanation. 'How are you feeling today?'

175

'Okay,' she said, still sounding depressed. 'I saw Liz Hascomb last night, it turns out she's a volunteer here for one of the support groups.'

'That's nice,' he said, feeling alienated from her. All she talked about was her illness and the things that related to it. 'Do you think she'll tell people at your office?' He knew how much she wanted to keep this private, but she sounded confident when she answered.

'I don't think so. Liz is very discreet. But she was pretty surprised when she saw me . . . and very helpful.'

'I'm glad.'

'How's Annabelle?'

'Great. She's getting all excited about Halloween. She keeps trying on her costume.' Tears sprang to Alex's eyes as she listened.

'Are you coming up today?' She said it hesitantly, as though she wasn't sure if she could count on him anymore, and hearing that in her voice hurt him.

'Of course I am. I'll stop by on my way home.' She'd been hoping he'd come for lunch, but she didn't want to press him. He told her he was staying in, and trying to get some work done.

But when he tried to concentrate, all he found he could think of was Daphne. It was nightmarish. He had a sick wife, a young child, and a load of responsibilities, and all he could think of was Simon's hot little cousin from Britain. It put him in a rotten mood by the time he saw Alex. He was feeling guilty and on edge and he was sorry he'd ever met Daphne. He didn't need any more complications in his life, but he was suddenly obsessed with her, like a drug he had to have and had never tasted.

'What's up? You're all wound up.' Alex spotted it immediately, which annoyed him even more. It was like a neon sign someone had hung around his neck and it kept flashing the word 'Daphne.'

'Don't be silly,' he snapped at her, without meaning to, 'I'm just worried about you. We can't wait for you to come home on Friday.'

'Have you said anything to Annabelle yet?'

'Of course not.'

'I think we ought to tell her I had a little accident on my trip.'

'Why say anything?'

There it was. Denial again. It never ceased to amaze Alex. 'I'm wearing a bandage. I'm going to have a scar, my breast is gone. I'm not feeling well. She can't jump all over me. How do you think we'd get away with not telling her anything, Sam? She's not stupid.'

'You don't have to parade around naked in front of her.'

'For the rest of my life? She takes baths with me, she watches me get dressed. I've never hidden my body from her. Besides, in a few weeks I'm going to be sick, and apparently very tired, from the chemotherapy. She needs to know that.'

'Why do you have to keep making so much about this thing? Why does it have to be Annabelle's problem, and mine? Why can't you just live with it quietly? I don't understand it.'

'Neither do I. I don't understand how you can keep pretending this isn't happening. It's not just happening to me, it is happening to all of us, at least to the extent that you both have to understand it.'

'She's three and a half years old for chrissake. What do you want from her? Sympathy? Is that it? Alex, this is sick.'

'I think you're crazy.'

'Stop whining about everything, stop turning it into a nightmare for everyone. Talk to a therapist, do something, go to a group, but don't put it on me and Annabelle like a lead weight. Don't punish us for your misfortunes.' She turned her back on him then and looked out the window.

'I'd like you to go now.' Her tone was icy.

'That would be a pleasure.' He stormed out of her hospital room and he never called her that night. Nor did she call him. She called Annabelle and kissed her good night, but she didn't ask to speak to Sam, which only Carmen noticed.

He stayed home alone that night, thinking of what lay ahead of them, and he didn't like it. She was going to make a big deal about everything, her scar, her missing breast, her health, and eventually her 'treatment,' her chemotherapy, and then they were going to have to hear about her hair, or the lack of it, and how sick she was, and then months and years of waiting to hear if her tests were all right, if it had recurred, if she was going to live another year. He just couldn't take it. It was just like his mother. And this was not how he wanted to spend the rest of his days, listening to her daily reports about her cancer. Suddenly he saw her as a tragic figure trying to swallow him alive and ruin his life. The Alex he had known and loved had disappeared, and in her place was this angry, frightened, depressing woman.

They spoke twice on Thursday about Annabelle, but they agreed it was better if he didn't come to see her. But Liz Hascomb did. She had come every day since discovering that Alex was there, and what had happened.

And on Friday, Sam came at noon to take her home from the hospital. It was the first time he had seen her in two days, and she looked suddenly very fragile when he saw her. She was wearing a dress she had asked him to bring her. It was a loose knit that fit easily over her bandage, and for the most part concealed it. And he had brought her a bright blue coat to wear over it. She hadn't bothered to put any makeup on, but she looked tall and thin, her hair was clean, and falling generously over her shoulders. She looked better than he had expected her to, but she also looked very frightened. Her eyes seemed huge, and her face pale, and he saw that her hands shook, as she put her nightgown away in her tote bag.

'Are you feeling all right, Alex? Are you in pain?' He was surprised by how unnerved she looked. She had actually looked better to him on Tuesday and Wednesday, and he wondered if she had had some kind of surgical setback. It made him feel guilty again for not seeing her the day before, but he just couldn't take the pressure. But now she looked so upset and so nervous.

'I'm okay,' she said a little hoarsely. 'It's just kind of scary going home. No nurses, no help with my dressings, no volunteers from the support group. Suddenly, I have to go out in the world again, and everything is different, or at least I am. And what do I say to Annabelle when I see her?' Her eyes filled with tears as she thought of it, she had cried about it with Liz Hascomb the night before, and Liz kept reassuring her that everything Alex was feeling was completely normal.

'Then why does Sam keep acting like I'm crazy?' she had asked her.

'Because he's scared too. And that's normal too. The only problem with Sam is that he doesn't admit it.'

And he didn't look afraid now, as he put an arm around Alex and picked up her tote bag. He looked completely in control, and very calm, as they rode downstairs in the elevator and got into a limousine he had hired for the occasion.

The car drove them home, and the apartment was quiet when they got there. Carmen had picked Annabelle up at school, and taken her straight to ballet. Alex wanted to settle in before she got home, and change into a dressing gown, but she was amazed at how exhausted she was by the time she got there. She was drained by all her emotions. And it depressed Sam to see her change into her nightgown. She had her back to him, and she put her dressing gown on before she turned around, so all he saw was pink satin when she turned to face him.

'Why don't you stay dressed? It might worry Annabelle to see you in your nightgown.'

'I'm really tired. I thought I'd lie down.'

'You can lie down in your dress,' he reproached her. He thought she was playing invalid again, and she knew it. But he didn't know how tired she was, or how worn out, or how afraid of seeing their little girl and what she would say. It was all very upsetting and desperately scary. And as she lay on their bed and turned on the TV, she saw Sam put his coat on. He had brought her the lunch that Carmen had left for them and now suddenly, he was disappearing.

'Where are you going?' She was afraid to be alone. She was suddenly afraid of everything, and she was sorry she had come home, but eventually she had to.

'I'm going back to the office,' he explained. 'I'll

try and come home early this afternoon. I've got a meeting with Larry and Tom I just couldn't cancel. Call me if you need me.' She nodded and he blew her a kiss, but she noticed that he didn't come near her. He hadn't kissed her properly since her surgery, and she wondered how long it would be before he would come near her again.

The last thing she wanted to do was pressure him, but she felt so lonely while he kept his distance.

Alex lay quietly on their bed for a long time, waiting for Annabelle to come home, thinking about what to say to her. She thought of many things, but the moment she saw her, everything she'd planned to say to her was suddenly forgotten. All she could think of was how adorable she was, how much she loved her, and how much she had missed her.

Annabelle gave a huge squeal when she saw Alex standing there, waiting for her, in the doorway to her bedroom. Alex had heard the elevator, and then Carmen's key in the front door, and her whole body was shaking as she waited.

'Mommy!' she screamed, and then hurled herself into Alex's arms, as Alex tried to protect herself from the blow, but she couldn't. She winced painfully, and Carmen saw it. But Annabelle only saw that her mother was home, and she was quick to step back and look up at her impishly.

'What did you bring me from your trip?'

Suddenly Alex realized that she had completely forgotten, as Annabelle's face fell. 'You know what? They didn't have anything good at all, not even at the airport. I think maybe you and I will have to go to F.A.O. Schwarz next week, and see what we can find there. How does that sound?'

'Wow!' Annabelle clapped her hands, instantly

forgetting her disappointment. She loved going to F.A.O. Schwarz with her mother. And then she looked surprised when she saw Alex was in her nightgown.

'Why are you in your nightie?' she questioned her suspiciously just as Sam had said she would. In many ways, she was a lot like Alex. She saw everything, and wanted to know why things happened.

'I was taking a nap before you came home, and I had kind of a little accident in Chicago.'

'You did?' Annabelle looked impressed, and then very worried. 'Did you get hurt?' She looked as though she was about to cry, and Alex quickly kissed her to reassure her.

'Kind of.' She was still working on her story.

'Did you get a Band-Aid?' Alex nodded. 'Can I see it?' She opened her dressing gown with trembling hands, and Carmen gasped when she saw the enormous dressing. She knew instantly that something terrible had happened, and her eyes flew to those of her employer. 'Does it hurt?' Annabelle asked, still fascinated by the size and location of her bandage.

'A little bit,' Alex said honestly, 'we have to be a little bit careful we don't bump it.'

'Did you cry?' She nodded, and instinctively looked up at Carmen, whose eyes filled with tears when she saw her. She reached out and gently touched Alex's arm, and the gesture touched Alex deeply. Annabelle ran to her room then to get her doll, and Carmen scolded her.

'Why didn't you tell me, Mrs Parker? Are you okay?'

'I will be,' she said flatly. It was clearly her breast, but Carmen still didn't know the full extent of the damage, although she had already guessed it from the shape of Alex's profile.

Annabelle came bounding back into the room, carrying three dolls and a book, and she was full of tales from ballet and school, and she had made a drawing for her, and could hardly wait for Halloween. There was going to be a parade at school, and Katie Lowenstein was giving a party. She had a thousand news items to share, and Alex suddenly wondered how she had survived five whole days without her. Just seeing her brought her back to life, and gave her something to fight for.

'Are you all right, Mrs Parker?' Carmen asked her repeatedly while the two played on Alex's bed, and she brought her a cup of tea and a chicken sandwich, and urged her to eat it. And although she wasn't hungry, she remembered Liz's words about building up her strength, and she forced herself to eat it. Liz called that afternoon, to see how she was doing at home, and she was happy to hear Alex sounding so much better. Annabelle had improved her spirits immeasurably, but later, when she took off her dressing gown because she was warm, she noticed that Annabelle shied away from her a little bit. The dressing scared her. Quietly, Alex put her dressing gown back on and reminded herself not to let Annabelle see the bandage more than she had to. In some ways, Sam was right. She didn't have to make it their problem, and she didn't intend to. She needed their love and their support, but the one thing she didn't want was their pity, or to scare them. In some ways, Sam was just as skittish as their daughter.

Late that afternoon, Carmen came to take Annabelle for her bath, and she asked to bathe with her mother instead, in the marble tub, with her Mommy's fancy bubbles.

'You can take a bath in my tub, sweetheart, with

my bubbles. But I can't get my big Band-Aid wet till next week.' In the hospital, they had been putting a big garbage bag over it when she took a shower. 'You go ahead and take a bath without me. Okay?' Annabelle agreed, as Alex glanced at the clock. It was five, and she had thought that Sam said he would come home early. But Alex knew Friday afternoons were always long for him. It was always hard, wrapping up all the loose ends before the weekend.

As it turned out, Sam was at his office taking care of the details of his latest deal, but he was also stalling.

'Still hard at work?' Daphne asked casually as she glanced into his office at five-fifteen. She was just leaving for the weekend herself. She and Simon were going to Vermont with friends from England. Everyone had told them about the remarkable turning of the leaves, and Daphne had insisted she wanted to see it.

'It's beautiful,' Sam confirmed, wishing he were going with her. He ran a hand through his hair, and looked somewhat grim. He knew it was time to go home, but he'd been dreading it. The tension with Alex was palpable, and even Annabelle wouldn't ease it.

'What about you? Are you doing something fun?' she asked, hating to leave him. He looked so sad and so alone, as though he had no place to go, and didn't want to leave the office.

'Not really. My wife just came home from the hospital. I think we'll be taking it pretty easy.'

'I'm sorry, Sam,' she said softly, as their eyes met dangerously again and he smiled gently.

'Thanks, Daphne. Have fun. I'll see you on Monday.' She nodded, wanting to walk across the room and put her arms around him, but he looked so serious she didn't dare. Instead, she just watched him for a moment, and then blew him a kiss and left the room, wishing she could spend the weekend with him and not Simon and their friends from England.

And at five-thirty, he ran out of excuses. He put on his coat, and went downstairs, and walked a few blocks before taking a cab home. He was home before six, and Alex looked up at him in surprise when she saw him. She had been playing with Annabelle and reading her a story. Carmen was making dinner for them, and she had insisted that she wanted to stay for the weekend.

'Hi. How was your day?' She tried to sound casual, but he looked awkward with her, and when he answered, he sounded like a stranger.

'Fine. Sorry I'm late, it was a crazy afternoon.'

'No problem. I kept busy with Annabelle. We had a great time.'

They all had dinner at the table in the kitchen, and Annabelle talked more than either of them. And much to Alex's surprise, she didn't seem to sense the tension between her parents. She was so happy to have her mother home, she was flying high and full of funny stories and jokes and new songs, and unintelligible tales about her friends. It was a lively dinner. And then they put her to bed, and Carmen cleaned up the kitchen. But when Alex and Sam went to their own room, suddenly the conversation ran dry and she didn't know what to say to him, and he seemed to have nothing at all to say to her. He looked tired and distracted.

'Everything okay at work?' she asked, wondering why he was so nervous.

'Fine.' But he couldn't ask her the same thing. She hadn't been to her office all week. Everything she knew was about her illness.

He turned on the television, and sought refuge in it, and eventually he fell asleep, as Alex watched him. She was drained from the emotions of coming home to them, but she was glad she was here. She just didn't know what to do with Sam. But Liz had reassured her again, when she called her that afternoon, and told her to be patient. She said she'd had the same problems with her husband at first too, the awkwardness, the fears about her illness, the resentment too, but eventually he had adjusted.

Sam woke up after the late news, stirred, and looked up at her, as though surprised to see her there next to him, and then, without a word, he went to change into his pajamas. She had already bathed as best she could, and changed her nightgown again, and then she'd put on a bed jacket so the dressing wouldn't upset him. But when he came back to her after he'd showered, which seemed an eternity to her, he seemed to hesitate before coming back to bed again.

He was suddenly afraid of her, as though she might taint him with her problem. She wanted so much from him, and he just didn't know how much he had to give her. His own inadequacy frightened him more than anything. It was easier not to be around her.

'Is something wrong?' She looked at him, confused. It was as though he wasn't sure if he should sleep with her. But with Carmen in the guest room, there were no other options.

'I . . . would it be . . . will I hurt you if I sleep here?' Suddenly she couldn't help smiling at him. He looked so uncomfortable in his own skin, and so ill at ease with her. It was tragic in a way, except that it had made her feel both sad and angry. And yet she felt for him too. He looked so awkward.

186

'You won't hurt me unless you hit me over the head with your shoe. Why?' She tried to pretend that everything was normal, but they both knew it wasn't.

'I just thought maybe . . . if I rolled over . . . or touched you . . .' He was treating her like a piece of glass instead of a woman, and he seemed to go from one extreme to the other. One minute he wanted to pretend there was no problem at all, and the next he wanted to go to the ends of the earth to avoid her. It was more than a little distressing.

'You won't hurt me, Sam,' she said quietly, trying to reassure him. But he slipped into bed as though there were a land mine on her side of it and he was afraid to set it off. He lay there stiffly on the edge of the bed, keeping as far away from her as he could. And doing that made her feel like a pariah.

'Are you all right?' he asked her nervously before he turned out the light. 'Do you want anything?'

'I'm fine.' Or at least she wished she were, and she was certainly fine enough to sleep beside him. But it was obvious that he didn't want to. Eventually, he fell asleep clinging to the edge of the bed, as Alex watched him. It was as though, with the absence of one breast, overnight they had become strangers. And once he was asleep, she lay in bed and cried, pining for her husband.

He woke up on Saturday long before she stirred, and by the time she got up, and changed her bed jacket for the dressing gown again, he and Annabelle were dressed and talking about going to Central Park to fly a new kite he had bought her.

'Want to come?' he asked hesitantly, but she shook her head. She was still very tired, and it would be easier to wait for them at the apartment.

187

'I'll wait here. Maybe Annabelle and I can make cookies when you come home,' she said, trying to be entertaining.

'Yum!' Annabelle announced. She liked both plans. The cookies and the kite. And she and Sam went out half an hour later, with their kite, in high spirits. He had hardly spoken to Alex since she got up, it was as though now that she was back in the apartment, she was a real threat to him. He was even less communicative than he had been when she was in the hospital. It was very unnerving.

They came home for lunch, and Alex made them soup and sandwiches. Carmen had gone home for a few hours, and Alex insisted she didn't need her, but she said she'd come back anyway. She wanted to be there to help Alex.

Annabelle explained excitedly that they had flown the kite really high for a while, near the model-boat pond, and then it had flown into a tree, and Daddy had to climb way up to get it.

'Well, not as "way up" as all that,' he confessed, looking amused. They'd had a good time. And they'd bought chestnuts and pretzels.

Alex had done her hair while they were gone, and she had dressed. She was wearing a full sweater and jeans, and you almost couldn't see anything of what had happened to her. You barely saw the swell of either breast in the oversized sweater. But Annabelle noticed it later when she was sitting on Alex's lap and leaning against her.

'Your hurt boobie has gotten smaller, Mommy,' she said, staring at her chest as though she was surprised. 'Did it fall off when you got bumped?'

'Kind of.' She smiled, trying to retain her composure. It had to be discussed eventually and now

188

was as good a time as any. Better sooner than later. Sam was in the other room, and he looked a little startled when he came back and heard what they were saying.

'Will it look different when you take the bandage off? Is it all gone?' Annabelle looked amazed that a part of her mother had actually disappeared. She looked more than puzzled.

'Maybe. I haven't looked yet.'

'Could it just fall off?'

She didn't want to frighten her or mislead her. 'No, it couldn't. But it got pretty hurt. That's why they gave me the big bandage.'

'How did it happen?' Annabelle looked surprised at what had happened to her mother on her trip, but Sam looked annoyed at her. Fortunately, Annabelle left the room to get a game, and forgot to listen to the answer to her question, for which Alex was very grateful, because she didn't have one. 'How did it happen?' was one question she didn't want to answer.

But Sam had been listening and he didn't like the subject of their conversation.

'Why did you have to explain it to her? Why does this have to be a topic of conversation with her? She's three and a half years old for chrissake. She doesn't need this.' Neither did he, and he was almost fifty.

'Neither do I, Sam, but we're stuck with it anyway. And she asked me. She was sitting on my lap, and she felt the difference.'

'Don't sit her on your lap then. There are plenty of ways around it.'

'So I've noticed. You seem to be finding all of them.' He was avoiding her at every turn, and later that afternoon, he said that he had to go to the office, which surprised Alex. He rarely ever went there on the weekend. But she knew why he was doing it now. He just couldn't stand being near her.

Alex and Annabelle stayed home, making cookies and watching *Peter Pan* and *The Little Mermaid*. It was three o'clock by the time he left and the atmosphere between them was so tense that Alex thought it was just as well he'd gone out for a while. She really couldn't stand the tension. The air between them was electric.

'Why is Daddy mad at you?' Annabelle asked as they cut cookie dough, and Alex was astonished at the question.

'What makes you think Daddy's mad at me?' she asked, intrigued by the little girl's perception.

'He's not talking to you. Unless he has to.'

'Maybe he's just tired,' Alex explained, rolling out some more dough while Annabelle picked up big chunks and ate them.

'He missed you while you were away. So did I,' she said gravely. 'Maybe he's mad at you for going.'

'Maybe so,' Alex agreed, unwilling to bring their daughter into their problems. 'I'll bet he'll be fine when he comes home.' She kissed the tip of her freckled nose, and handed her another lump of cookie dough to munch on.

But sitting in his office downtown, Sam was looking glum. He had very little work to do. His work required people and clients, and deals to make. He didn't have the kind of avalanche of paperwork that Alex constantly lived with. And he had come to the office merely to escape, and now that he was here he felt stupid. He was running away from her, and he knew it. But he was afraid to see her body now, or her pain, afraid that he couldn't live up to what she wanted. It was so much easier to be angry at her, and hard on her, and avoid her.

'What are you doing here?' He heard a voice from across the room and jumped a foot as he looked up. He had been absolutely certain there was no one else in the office. The alarm had been on, and the watchman downstairs didn't tell him anyone was there. She must have just come in. It was Daphne. She was wearing a tight black jersey shirt and a pair of black leggings that made her legs seem endless. Her hair was in a long braid, and she was wearing little black suede boots that looked very English.

'I thought you were in Vermont,' he said, still looking very startled.

'I was supposed to be. But Simon got the flu, and his friends didn't want to go without him, so we stayed here. And I thought I'd use the opportunity to catch up on some work. I hope you don't mind, Sam. I didn't mean to intrude. You looked a million miles away when I saw you.' She said it sympathetically, and she looked very young and very sexy as she stood in the middle of his office. 'How are things going?'

'Not so great, I guess, or I wouldn't be here,' he said honestly, as he stretched his legs out under his desk and played with a pencil. It was odd how he could say anything to her, and nothing to Alex. He stood up and walked over to her then. 'I don't even know why I came in.' He looked at her unhappily, and then he smiled. 'Maybe I just had a sixth sense you'd be here.'

'That's not worthy of you,' she teased, 'but I'll accept it anyway. Can I make you a cup of coffee?'

'Sure, I'd like that.' He followed her into their pantry, faintly aware of her perfume. It smelled musky and warm and sexy. 'I'm sorry,' he said suddenly as she turned to look at him, 'I've been acting like a lunatic this week. I don't know if I'm up or down or sideways. It's been hell, and I have no right to take it out on you.'

'If having dinner with me at Le Cirque, and taking me dancing downtown is "taking it out on me," then please feel free to do so anytime you'd like, Sam.' She smiled at him enticingly, but there was more than just sex appeal to her, there was something very warm and sympathetic. She was mischievous and playful, but she seemed very caring too, and he liked that about her. There were so many things about her that reminded him of the best of Alex. And then she turned his stomach over with the bluntness of her next question. Her voice was very soft as she looked at him, but he wasn't prepared for what she asked him. 'Is your wife dying, Sam?'

For a long moment he wasn't sure how to answer her. 'She could be. I don't know. She's very sick, I suppose, although I don't completely understand it.'

'Is it cancer?'

He nodded. 'She had a breast removed this week, and she's about to start chemotherapy.'

'How difficult for you, and your little girl.' All her sympathies were with them, and not with Alex.

'I suppose it is . . . or it will be . . . Chemotherapy sounds like a nightmare. I'm not sure I'd do it.'

'That's what we all say, until we're faced with it, and then we fight like dogs and try anything we can, to cure it. My father died last year, and he tried everything including some sort of magic pills he got in Jamaica that were nothing but voodoo. I can't blame her for trying. But it's hell on you. Poor Sam.' They were standing in the small airless room while the coffee brewed, and her voice was barely more than a whisper.

'You shouldn't feel sorry for me,' he whispered back, not sure why they were speaking so softly, they were the only people there, but all he wanted to do was get closer to her and speak softer still. 'I'm fine . . .'

'Aren't you though,' she replied, and then he was completely unprepared for what happened next. She put her arms around his neck, ran her fingers down the back of his neck until he had chills, and kissed him. And he felt his whole body respond with a surge that almost frightened him, it was so beyond his control. He wanted to tear her leggings off and lay her on the floor next to him, but he didn't dare do more than kiss her, and allow his hands to drift hungrily down her body. She was all muscles, and tight stomach, and splendid little behind. She was built like a ballerina, and her breasts filled both his hands. Their mouths and tongues were relentless. It was Daphne who broke away first, breathlessly. She had started an avalanche that she herself could no longer control, it was so exquisite, it was almost beyond bearing. 'Oh God, Sam . . . I can't . . . oh God . . . how I want you . . .'

'I want you too,' he whispered back, devouring her neck and her breasts with his lips, and then he was kneeling next to her, and nuzzling her where her thighs met. She let out a long, soft moan, and as he pulled her closer to him, he suddenly came to his senses. He couldn't do it.

'Daphne . . . we can't . . .' He stood next to her again, holding her close to him, feeling guiltier than ever toward Alex. But he was consumed with desire for Daphne. 'I can't. I have no right to complicate your life like this . . . or do this to my wife.'

'I don't care,' Daphne said hoarsely. 'I'm a grown woman, I have a right to make my own decisions.'

'It won't go anywhere . . . you deserve more than

this. I'm half out of my mind with wanting you. I have been ever since we met, but what does that give you?'

'A leg over, I hope.' She laughed suddenly at him, using the English expression for a piece of ass. But fortunately, he knew it.

'I'd like to give you something better than that, but I don't have it to give. Not now.' Not yet. And maybe never.

'It would do for a start,' she said playfully. 'I don't ask for much.'

'You should. You deserve it.' And then without saying more, their lips met again, and he held her and felt her next to him for what seemed like hours until neither of them could stand it any longer. 'We're going to have to do something about this, if it keeps up.' And with that, they both laughed at his very obvious erection. She was stroking it through his jeans, and the touch of her hand was driving him crazy.

'I was suggesting something like that.' She smiled and kissed him again, and then bent to nibble at the lump in his blue jeans.

'Stop it,' he said unconvincingly, '. . . no, don't . . . oh God . . . Daphne . . . I'm going to profess undying love in a few minutes if you don't stop.' She was driving him into a frenzy, and he loved the sensation.

'I was hoping you would.' She smiled mischievously at him, and then she stood up and poured him a cup of coffee.

'How can I do this?' he asked, thinking of both his wife and daughter.

'Things happen sometimes. Those are the realities of life. It doesn't always work out just as we planned. In fact, I'm not sure it ever does. My life certainly doesn't.'

'Mine is a disaster at the moment.'

194

'Are you close to her?' she asked, as they sipped their coffee, and tried briefly to forget each other's bodies.

'I thought I was. Now we can't seem to talk about anything. The only thing there is, is her disease. It's all she can think about, all she's interested in, all she knows. I can't stand it.'

'I'm not sure I blame her. But it's a lot to expect of you, though, isn't it?'

'I suppose I owe her that.' And then he confessed his darkest secret. 'My mother died of cancer when I was fourteen. I hated her for it. It's all I remember about her, how sick she was, how she talked about it all the time, and had endless operations. They chopped her up in little bits, until they finally killed her. And her dying killed my father. I felt like she tried to kill all of us. She would have killed me too, except I wouldn't let her. I wouldn't let her poison me like she did him. I refused to become a part of her tragedy. That's how I feel now about Alex. It's as though I have to keep away in order to save myself.' It was a terrible confession, but he felt better once he said it. And she seemed to understand exactly what he meant, and in a way that Alex hadn't understood yet. She was too wrapped in herself to see his terror clearly.

'You can't do it alone though, can you?' Daphne said in the husky voice that drove him to distraction.

'I'm not sure,' he said. 'I think I probably should try. But you're not making it any easier.'

'Actually,' she said, touching the bulge in his jeans again until it grew in her hand and he closed his eyes in pleasure, 'I rather thought I was making it harder.'

'You certainly are.' He kissed her, wanting her desperately, but firm in his resolve not to have her. He owed that much to Alex. He wouldn't let her have his soul. But at least he owed it to her to be faithful. It was just bad luck that Daphne had crossed his path at that particular moment. Or maybe it was meant to be that way. Maybe this was his reward for what he was losing.

They stood there together in the pantry for a long time, and it was dark when they looked outside. He felt as though days had passed since he had come there. His voice was ragged with desire for her, as he held her for a last time, and then they put their coffee cups in the sink, and she washed them and put them away, and she followed him back to his office.

'Are you going to stay?' he asked. He hated to leave, but he knew he had to. He had to get home. And he had done absolutely nothing except paw Daphne.

'I'll take my work home,' she said easily. He went to her office with her while she got it, and then he kissed her there too. She fell backwards against the desk in his arms, and the temptation to take her right there was almost irresistible, but again he forced himself to remember that he was married. The leggings she wore didn't make it any easier for him. It was like holding her with no clothes on. He could feel every inch of her beneath his hands, and there was nothing that she tried to keep from him. Eventually, he freed her breasts from the shirt she wore, and they were so beautiful he almost cried. They were perfect and round with pink nipples that stood erect in his fingers, begging for him, and she asked for him as he played with her relentlessly and kissed her.

It was another half hour before she put her shirt on again, and they finally left the office. It was almost seven o'clock by then, and Sam felt like a kid as they got into a cab, and he told her he'd drop her off and then started necking with her in the backseat while she giggled.

'You'd better start locking your office door,' he

warned. 'I'm not sure I can control myself when I see you.' It certainly didn't seem like it, but Daphne didn't appear to mind.

He dropped her off on East Fifty-third where she'd rented an apartment in an old town house. It had been owned by a movie star, and there was still quite a bit of furniture there, but Daphne said it was pretty shabby.

'Want to come up?' she invited him, standing outside the cab in her outrageously appealing leggings, but he shook his head.

'I don't trust myself to behave.'

'Neither do I,' she laughed, and then looked suddenly serious as she reached into the cab and took his hand in hers. 'Come back whenever you want to. Even if you just want to talk. I'm here for you, Sam. And crazy as it sounds at this point . . . I think I love you.'

'Please . . . don't . . . I can't . . . but thank you.' He kissed her gently again, and she waved and stepped back, as he made a mental note of her address and knew he shouldn't.

He was home by seven-fifteen, and Alex looked anything but pleased when she saw him. But she didn't say anything. She had guessed correctly that he was avoiding her, but she would have been even more upset if she'd known what he'd been doing. For a moment, he thought he smelled Daphne's perfume on him, and he went to wash his hands, and change his sweater.

'You must have had a lot of work,' she said cautiously after Annabelle went to bed. Carmen had finished the dishes and had already disappeared into the guest room.

'I did.'

'Business must be very good. You've never had to do that.'

'Simon's bringing in a lot of new clients. He's really terrific.'

'Are you watching how he's handling things? His style may not be yours or Tom and Larry's. You don't want some shiny flash in the pan screwing up your business.'

'He won't. He had a great reputation in London for bringing in business, and big money.'

'Clean money?'

'Obviously.' He looked annoyed again. She was always questioning everything. She was a true attorney in that she was always suspicious. He had been leery of Simon at first too, but he was convinced by now that Simon was going to do great things for their business. And he had brought Daphne with him . . . what more could he want? Sam found himself thinking of her again as he sat down to dinner with Alex.

'So what were you working on?' she asked, looking interested in what had kept him at the office all afternoon, and he almost choked on his salad when he heard the question.

'Nothing much . . . just a few things . . . some housekeeping.'

'Since when do you do that?' she asked. She seemed skeptical but not suspicious. It was obvious to her that he was simply staying away so he didn't have to see her, which was true. What she had no way of knowing, fortunately, was what he'd been doing with Daphne.

Their dinner together was anything but warm, or even interesting. They seemed to be groping for subjects of mutual interest, which was unusual for them, but at least they were together and she was home. The worst had already happened, or almost, and now all she had to do was hang in and survive the treatment. Their marriage would fall into place again after that. She was sure of it. It was just rough now, as they both adjusted to a new situation.

But he was just as cautious about lying next to her that night as he had been the night before. He was solicitous and polite, but he made no attempt at all to come near her. And once again, when he fell asleep, she lay on her side of the bed and cried. Just a little kiss or a hug would have meant so much to her, even if he was afraid of what lay beneath her nightgown.

The strain between them was so great, it was a relief to both of them when the weekend ended. Sam left for work at eight o'clock on Monday morning. And she took Annabelle to school for the first time since her operation. And at nine o'clock, she had an appointment with Dr Peter Herman. He was going to check her sutures and her dressing. She was desperately afraid of what she would see when he changed it. But she would have been even more afraid if she could have seen what Sam had waiting for him when he got in. Daphne was wearing a little navy blue Chanel suit, with a miniskirt and her long, sexy legs, and she only wanted to confirm to him that Saturday had been no mistake, and she had no regrets. She wanted Sam more than she'd wanted any man in years, and she said so.

'I just want you to know,' she whispered as she closed the door to his very luxurious office, 'that I'm in love with you. You don't have to do anything. You don't even have to want me. But I'm here for you, anytime, any way that works for you. I accept who you are and your responsibilities. But I love you, Sam. And

I'm yours, whenever you want me.' Daphne Belrose was the ultimate temptation.

He kissed her then, longingly, with all the anguish and hunger he felt, and she returned it, and then stood back, smiling at him, and let herself quietly out of his office.

Chapter 10

Alex only had to wait for half an hour in the waiting room, and then Dr Herman took her into his office and asked her how she was doing. She told him she was still tired after the surgery, but had very little pain, and he was very pleased at what he saw when he took off her dressing. He said it was very clean, and the sutures were healing nicely. In fact, she was doing even better than he'd hoped. And he'd had the final results of her tests. They had been pretty much as he'd expected, four of her lymph nodes were involved, the tumor was hormone receptor negative, and she was the perfect candidate for chemo. In a little more than two weeks, he was going to start her on chemotherapy, as soon as she was stronger.

To Alex, it was not good news, but it was also not unexpected. And he had already explained the process to her. She had a minimum of nodular involvement, which was a good sign, in spite of her Stage II tumor. 'The wound is very clean,' he explained, 'if you decide to go ahead with reconstruction later on, your plastic surgeon will be very pleased.' He seemed quite happy with everything, and Alex wanted to be too, but the fact was that she had lost a breast the week before, and had been told she had cancer. These were hardly causes for celebration. And now she knew for sure that she had to face chemo.

And then the doctor turned to her with curiosity, wondering how she was doing. She seemed a little more somber than usual, but that was also to be expected. 'Have you looked at the wound yet yourself?' She shook her head at him, looking frightened.

'Perhaps you should. You have to prepare yourself. And what about your husband?'

'He hasn't seen it either.' She had the suspicion that he was terrified, and she was right of course. But she couldn't blame him, she didn't want to see it either.

'I urge you to look at it. You'll be bathing again soon, and of course you'll see yourself, but a good look in the mirror won't hurt. It's time to face it.' But nothing he had said to her prepared her for what she saw, when she went home and slowly removed the bandage to shower. She had taken off her dress, and the bra she'd worn, and then slowly pulled off her dressing, and with a determined look, she walked over to the mirror. She tried to keep her eyes on her face, but slowly, she let them drift down, until she screamed, and took a step backwards from the mirror. It wasn't possible. It was hideous beyond belief it was so ugly. Where her breast had been, there was a flat slab of flesh. It was pink now, but it would be white one day, and across it was a red scar where they had made the incision, cut away her breast, and its skin and even its nipple, and then sewed it together. She thought it was the ugliest thing she'd ever seen, and even knowing that it might have saved her life did nothing to console her. She felt sick after looking at it, and she sat down on the carpet on the bathroom floor and hugged her knees as she sobbed. It was almost an hour later when Carmen heard her. She was still sitting there, crying like a child, hiccuping and sobbing.

'Oh Mrs Parker . . . Mrs Parker . . . what happened? . . . are you hurt? Should I call the doctor? . . . Mrs Parker?' Alex couldn't stop crying. All she could do was shake her head, as she cried and clutched her knees close to her single bosom.

'Go away . . . go away . . .' she cried, sounding like Annabelle, and Carmen got down on her knees next to her, crying for her as she would for an injured child.

'Don't cry . . . don't cry . . . we all love you . . .' she said, as she put her arms around her.

But Alex could only shake her head and cry louder. 'He hates me . . . I'm so ugly . . . he hates me . . .'

'I will call him,' she said reassuringly, and Alex let out a scream, and dropped her head down on her knees, begging Carmen not to call him.

'Just leave me.' Carmen tried to hold her but Alex wouldn't let her, and eventually Carmen didn't know what else to do, and went back to the kitchen. She sat there listening to her cry, dabbing at her own eyes, until finally Alex stopped. 'Will you please pick Annabelle up?' Alex said to Carmen in an exhausted voice that was completely devoid of emotion.

'Why don't you do it, Mrs Parker? She will love to see you.'

'I can't,' she said in a voice that sounded more dead than alive. They had killed her.

'Yes, you can. If you want, I will go with you. Come . . . we go together . . .' She led Alex back to her little dressing room, and took out a loosely knit dress and held it out to her. 'Annabelle likes this.'

'I can't, Carmen. I can't do it.' She started to sob again, but this time Carmen clung to her shoulders and held her.

'Yes, you can.' They were both crying by then. 'I will help you.'

'Why?' Alex wanted to give up and die, but Carmen was holding her and wouldn't let her.

'Because we love you. We are going to help you until you are strong again. You will be fine very soon,' she said confidently, trying to give Alex courage. But Alex only shook her head as she stepped into the knit dress Carmen held for her.

'I won't be fine. They're going to give me chemotherapy.'

'Ah no . . .' She looked horrified, and then, 'All right . . . we will get through it.' Carmen was determined to help Alex. She was a good woman, and a good employer, and she didn't deserve this. She had a husband who loved her, and a little girl. She had to live for them, and Carmen was going to help her do it. 'We go to pick up Annabelle, and then we have lunch. And then you take a nap, and I will take Annabelle to the park.' She was speaking to her like a child, and Alex responded to it from the depths of her anguish. She had never seen anything as ugly as what the surgeon had left her.

But she went with Carmen to Annabelle's school, and then they walked home quietly. Alex was silent, but Annabelle didn't seem to notice. And once they were home, Carmen gave them homemade tomato soup, and a turkey sandwich for each of them. And then she tucked Alex into bed, and told Annabelle that her mother needed a nap, which Annabelle thought was a game. She helped Carmen tuck her Mommy into bed, and then they went to the park and played.

She told her Daddy about it late that afternoon, and he wondered if Alex had been playing invalid again, as he put it.

'What's up?' he asked casually, after Annabelle went to bed. 'You sleeping all afternoon?' In his voice was a barely concealed tone of disapproval. He didn't want her languishing in front of Annabelle, he had lived with that as a boy, and the memory of it still drove him crazy. Even as an adult now, he had an almost phobic hatred of illness.

'I just took a nap. I was very tired. I went to see Dr Herman.' Her voice was lifeless as she looked at him, and her eyes gave away nothing.

'Are the results of the pathology reports in?'

'Yes. Four of my nodes are involved. I need chemo,' she said in a dead voice. And then, 'He took off my dressing.'

'Great. That's a step forward at least. That should have cheered you up.' He spoke enthusiastically, as though to spur her on, ignoring the fact that she needed chemo, and she looked at him as though he came from another planet.

'Not exactly.'

'Why not? Was there a problem?'

'Not really.' Only a small one . . . my breast seems to have fallen off with the dressing . . .

'So what's the big deal? Why are you so tired?'

'What do you want from me?' she snapped at him. 'Polaroids? Can't you figure it out for yourself for chrissake? I lost a breast. It's a big deal, to me, if not to you, and I don't buy the idea that it's no big deal to you either. You've been acting like I have leprosy ever since I got home, standing halfway across the room from me. I get the message. You don't think this is so cute either.'

'I never said it was. But it doesn't have to be the tragedy you make it.'

'Maybe not, pal. But let me tell you one thing, it sure ain't pretty.' She looked venomously at him, filled with all the horror of what she had seen in the mirror.

'Don't make it such a big deal. He told you, you can have it rebuilt eventually.'

'Sure, if I want to go through another very painful operation and a bunch of skin grafts and tattoos, and silicone implants, which are dangerous. This is not exactly the tea party you make it out to be.'

'Fine. But don't be such a crybaby for God's sake. Losing a breast is not the worst thing that could happen.'

'What is?'

'Dying,' he said bluntly.

'Give me time, I might do that too. But in the meantime, I seem to have misplaced a few things I was rather fond of. One of them is my left breast, and the other one is my husband. You seem to have gone right out the window with my tit, or hadn't you noticed? Because I have. I'm sick and tired of your disappearing act, of your acting like I don't exist, because you can't cope with what happened.'

'That's not true,' he said angrily, all the more so because it was and he knew it.

'The hell it isn't. You haven't been here for me once since I got the news, and ever since the surgery, you've been treating me like your maiden aunt and not your wife. How long is that going to go on, Sam?

206

How long do I have to do penance for the sin of losing a boob? Until I get it reconstructed so I don't scare you to death when I take my clothes off, or are we shot for good? It might be helpful to know so I don't hang around annoying you, or make you sick sometime when I take a shower.'

'You make me sick with your analysis and accusations. You couldn't make me half as sick if they took both your breasts off.'

'Really? Wanna make a bet? You have no idea how ugly this is. It's a lot worse than you think.'

'It's as bad as you make it. You're the one turning this into an agony. You're the one who can't accept what happened.'

'Are you sure?' She was suddenly unable to control herself a moment longer, and as she stood in front of him she unbuttoned her nightgown. He felt his heart pound as he watched her, but it was too late to stop her, and he knew he had goaded her into it. She slipped it brusquely off one shoulder and then the other, and then she let it drop to the floor without a sound, except a gasp from him. She hadn't bothered to replace the dressing, and he saw everything she had seen that morning. The angry scar, the missing breast, the bright pink flesh. Just as she knew, it was shocking, and his face showed how he felt about it. There was no way on earth he would have touched her. 'Pretty, isn't it, Sam?' She was crying now, and gulping air as she sobbed, but he didn't come near her.

'I'm sorry, Alex.' He walked across the room to her then, and held her nightgown out to her. 'I'm sorry,' he said softly, and pulled her into his arms, as they both cried. It was just too awful.

'I can't live with this, Sam,' she cried, wanting her breast back, wanting her life to be what it had been only a few weeks before. It was impossible to understand why any of this had happened.

'It'll be OK . . . you'll get used to it. We both will,' he said softly, praying it was true.

'Will we?' she asked sadly. 'Do you want me to get it fixed?'

'It's too soon anyway, why don't you see how you feel about it later.'

'I hate it, and I hate myself,' she admitted as she slipped on her nightgown, and he helped her when she got it tangled. He wanted to help her cover it up as soon as possible, so neither of them had to see it. 'I'm sorry I'm angry at you all the time. I just don't know how to handle it.'

'Neither do I,' he admitted. 'I guess we just have to give it time.'

'Yeah,' she said sadly, looking at him, unable to believe he would ever resume their sex life. 'Maybe.'

'You'll feel better when you go back to work next week,' he said encouragingly as he turned the TV on, anything so they didn't have to talk to each other.

'Maybe I will,' she said, unconvinced, but she would much rather have had her husband than her job back. And all he could think of as they watched TV was what he'd just seen. He wasn't sure that he could ever touch her again. It made the agony of wanting Daphne even more painful. And he felt guiltier than ever remembering how exquisite her breasts had been when he'd touched them, and he remembered exactly how they'd looked when he took off her shirt and freed them. She was so young and inviting and alive, and her body was so perfect.

'I don't feel like a woman anymore,' Alex said sadly as he turned off the light at midnight.

'Don't be silly, Alex. A breast doesn't make you who you are. Losing it doesn't change anything. You're as much a woman as you ever were.' But nothing he did confirmed it. And as he lay in bed all that night, keeping well away from her, the only thing he could think of was Daphne.

Chapter 11

The only thing that brought Alex and Sam together at all was trick-or-treating with Annabelle the following weekend. She went as the princess, as planned, and she looked adorable in her pink velvet costume with sparkles and rhinestones. She wore a little silver crown, and carried a wand, and she had a great time trick-or-treating in their building. Alex usually dressed up too, but she hadn't put together a costume this year, and at the last minute she dressed as Cruella De Vil in a black and white wig and an old fur coat, and Annabelle loved it. And Sam brought out the Dracula costume he wore every year, and Alex did his makeup.

'You look good with black and white hair,' he mused as he looked at her. She was wearing a slinky red knit dress. She was wearing a prosthesis now in her bra, which was heavy but looked surprisingly realistic. And Sam couldn't help but admire her figure. Even without the missing breast, she still had sensational legs, and the body of a model. He seemed to be noticing things like that more and more these days, especially on Daphne.

He and Daphne had been behaving themselves admirably, though not without enormous effort. Only once, he had given in to the urge to kiss her when they were alone in his office. But otherwise, they had done nothing they shouldn't have, in spite of a number of meetings and business lunches together with clients. She was very helpful on some of their new deals, and remarkably knowledgeable about international finance. Interestingly, he had never mentioned her to Alex. Instinctively, he knew he couldn't. Alex would have sensed instinctively that there was something to this. His partners had wondered about it too, but no one had dared to ask, only Simon continued to make a crack now and then about how appealing English girls were, particularly his cousin. Sam always agreed with him but no one except Daphne knew how infatuated he was with her, or how desperately horny she made him.

'You look pretty good,' Alex said as she put the last of his Dracula makeup on him. Standing in front of him in the bathroom under the lights was the longest they had been close to each other since her operation. It would have been the perfect opportunity for him to say something to her, or put his arms around her, or even kiss her, but he just couldn't bring himself to do it. He was too scared of what would happen after that, what she might expect from him, and he might not be able to deliver. Nothing about her turned him on right now. She was intrinsically too ill, her body had changed too much, there was too much fear and too many bad memories for him even to want to try it.

She handed him his Dracula teeth, and Annabelle gave a squeal of happy terror when she saw him. 'Oh Daddy, I love you!' she said, and then she giggled. He laughed, and Alex grinned. It was the happiest they'd been in a month, and the rest of the evening was just as pleasant. They stopped and visited friends, shared a glass of wine with them, ate candy with the kids, and by the time they got home, Annabelle was half asleep, and her parents were both in very good humor.

'That was fun,' Alex said happily. It always was. Halloween had been magical ever since they'd had Annabelle. Before that, it had meant nothing. Thinking about it made Alex sad again, knowing that she would probably never have more children. It was just too unlikely now, with the statistics of sterility after chemo and the importance of not getting pregnant for the next five years. And by then, she'd be forty-seven. The prospect of another baby was over.

She also knew that, at forty-two, she would probably go through menopause, as a consequence of having chemo. It was still difficult to understand the words, to absorb them, to make them hers, mastectomy, malignancy, chemotherapy, nodular involvement, metastasis. It was incredible. Her entire vocabulary had changed in a month, and with it her life and her marriage. There was no hiding from what it had done to them, and to her relationship with Sam. He was completely removed from her now, in all the ways that mattered. But he wouldn't admit to it, of course. He was completely committed to pretending nothing had happened, which made it even harder. How could you fix something no-one would admit was broken?

'Are you going to bed?' She looked surprised when he got undressed and got into bed after they'd gone trick-or-treating. It was only ten o'clock and neither of them seemed tired when they got home at nine-thirty.

'There's nothing else to do,' he said as she looked at him. 'I thought I'd turn in early.' In the old days, that would have meant a little romance, but now she knew he'd be asleep, or pretending to be, before she got out of the bathroom, as indeed he was twenty minutes later. He just couldn't face her, or bear to deal with his 'obligations.' And that was the last thing she wanted anyway. If he didn't want her, she'd rather do without, forever if she had to.

She read late into the night, she was feeling better by then. And she was going back to work on the Monday following the Halloween weekend. She had a lot of work to catch up on and a lot of organizing to do. She had two weeks until she began chemotherapy, two weeks in which to feel pretty good and do all the work she could, two weeks to get her office in order before her life turned upside down again. It was a lot to deal with.

And on Monday when she left for work, and dropped Annabelle off at school, she almost felt like her old self again, except that Sam barely spoke to her at breakfast. He never even took his nose out of the *Wall Street Journal* to kiss her good-bye, but she was getting used to it. And at least now she'd have her work to keep her busy, and her colleagues to talk to. The last two weeks had been the loneliest in her life, and she couldn't imagine anything worse than what had happened.

'Is Daddy still mad at you?' Annabelle asked, as they walked to school. And Alex looked down at her with interest. It surprised her that even she had noticed.

'I don't know. I don't think so, why?'

'He seems different. He doesn't talk to you much, and he never kisses you, and he looks mad when he comes home from work.'

'Maybe he's just tired.'

'Grown-ups always say they're tired when they're mad. But they're mad. Just like Daddy. I think he is. You'd better ask him.'

'Okay, Princess, I will. You were great on Halloween. Best princess in town.'

'Thank you, Mommy.' She threw her arms around her mother's neck, and Alex nearly melted as she watched her run into school with the others. And with that she hailed a cab with her right arm, and hopped into it and headed downtown. Her left side was still a little sensitive, but she felt alive again for the first time in two weeks. It had been exactly two weeks to the day, almost to the hour, since her mastectomy, and she already felt better. Comparatively, she felt great. The only trouble was she hadn't yet started chemo.

'Well, look who's here.' Liz Hascomb beamed at her as soon as she saw her, and came around her desk to give Alex a warm hug.

And when Alex walked into her office, she found flowers on her desk from Liz, and neat stacks of the files Brock had worked on and completed.

'Wow! It looks like you guys did just fine without me.'

'Don't believe that for a minute,' Liz reassured her. There was a list of messages an arm long, most of them with the information as to how the matters had been resolved, some had been passed to Matt, some to other partners, and Brock had handled all of the details and research. There was a handful of names who had chosen to wait the two weeks for Alex, and she sat down and read the names and information, as Liz went to get her a cup of coffee.

She looked up when Liz came back in, and smiled. It felt great to be back in her chair, to be here among friends, and to feel useful. She felt up to it again, although she was still a little bit tired. But it was like getting an important part of her identity back again. It was only half of it, but it made a difference.

'How're you feeling?' Liz asked quietly as she set down the cup of coffee.

'Fine. Great actually. I'm really surprised. I just get tired.'

'Give it time. Don't rush anything.' She went back to her own desk then, and Alex just sat there, looking around, savoring being back in her office. It was wonderful just being there. She sat back in her chair with a smile and took a sip of the hot coffee. And just as she did, Brock Stevens poked his head in.

'Welcome back,' he beamed.

'Thank you,' she smiled warmly in answer. He looked more than ever like a big blond kid. He was wearing glasses, and a lock of hair hung over his eyes, and there was a constant look of mischief about him. 'It looks like you did all my work while I was gone. Maybe I should just go on permanent vacation.'

'Not a chance. I've been saving all the hard stuff for you. Jack Schultz called about two hundred times, by the way, just to thank you.'

'I'm glad we won,' she smiled. 'He deserved it.'

'So did you.' He'd never seen anyone work as hard as she did to win his case, and it couldn't have been easy for her. He knew now that she'd been sick when she did it. Sick or in some kind of trouble. He knew she'd been out for surgery, though he still didn't know exactly what had happened. But something about Liz's eyes when he asked about her told him that this was no small matter. 'What are you going to do today?' He thought she looked thin and a little tired but very pretty.

'Catch up on my files, read what you've done, try and figure out what's left for me to do now.'

'Oh, just a few things here and there. We have two new clients, who are being sued by former employees. There are about four new cases that came in, there's a hot libel suit that came in from some movie star. Matt knows more about it.'

'Lucky man. Maybe I'll just let him keep it.' She looked more relaxed than usual, she hadn't hit her stride yet, she was mostly savoring the moment.

'Are you all right now, Alex?' he asked gently. 'I know you've been sick. I hope it's not anything to worry about.' It certainly hadn't hurt her looks. And for a moment, she was about to tell him she was fine, and then she decided not to. She was going to need his help in the coming months, and there was no reason not to tell him. She had to start somewhere.

'I'm fine now. And I will be eventually, I hope. But I've got some rough spots to go through.' She hesitated, staring into her coffee cup, searching for the right words. This was new to her, humbling herself, asking someone to help her. And then she looked up and their eyes met, and she was surprised by the kindness she saw there. He looked so gentle, so concerned, she knew she could trust him. 'I'm going to start chemotherapy in two weeks,' she said with a sigh, and she thought she heard his breath catch. His eyes bore deep into hers with silent questions.

'I'm sorry to hear that.'

'So am I. I'm going to keep on working if I can, but I'm not quite sure what that means yet. They say that if it's done right, you can manage, except for extreme fatigue. I'll just have to see how far I get once they start it.' He nodded, understanding.

'I'll do everything I can to help you.'

216

'I know that, Brock,' she said, feeling her voice tremble as she said it. It was touching to know that she had friends, and even to know that people she scarcely knew, but only worked with, were there to help her. 'I appreciate everything you've already done. I couldn't have managed without you. That trial was pretty rough, with surgery hanging over my head. At least that's behind me.' He looked at her, but didn't ask where they'd found the cancer. And she'd worn a heavy black and white tweed suit that showed nothing.

'I'm so sorry you have to go through this. But you'll do fine,' he said confidently, as though trying to convince her.

'I hope so. It's a whole new world out there.' She set down her coffee cup and looked at him pensively. He was nice to talk to. 'It's so odd, I'm in control of things so much of the time. It's very strange to be in the throes of something I have so little control of. I can't do anything, except follow the dotted lines, and hope I wind up in the right place. But there are no guarantees on this one. The odds aren't even all that impressive. I think they found it early enough, at least I hope so. But who knows . . .' Her voice trailed off, and he reached across the desk and squeezed her hand. His touch brought her back, and their eyes met.

'You have to want to make it. You have to decide, right now, that you're going to, no matter what. No matter how bad it gets, or how rotten you feel, or how much it hurts, or how scary. It's like a contest, like a trial. No matter what the other side throws at you, you've got to throw it right back. Don't drop that ball for one second!' He said it with a vehemence that startled her, and made her wonder if he'd been there. Maybe someone in his family had, or maybe there was more to Brock than his easy going ways suggested. 'Don't ever forget that.' He pulled his hand away from hers then, and nodded. 'If I can do anything to help today, yell.' He stood up then, and looked down at her with a smile. 'It's good to have you back. I'll check in with you later.'

'Thanks, Brock. For everything.' She watched him go, and went back to the work on her desk, but his words, and the warmth behind them, had impressed her.

Matt Billings took her to lunch, and told her about the new cases that had come in, particularly the movie star with the libel suit. He had passed it on to another partner, which was what Alex would have done. Although she liked doing libel occasionally, this one was too hot to handle. The woman claimed that one of the most respectable magazines in the country had libeled her. It was not going to be easy to prove, given the limited rights of celebrities in the press, and the magazine's powerful reputation. They were going to scream long and hard about First Amendment rights. Alex was just as happy not to have that hot potato to handle. And Matt had already admitted to her that the plaintiff in this case was no sweetheart.

'Lucky Harvey.' She referred to their partner who had taken the case.

'Yeah. I kind of thought you'd be glad you missed that one.'

He also told her about a big industrial suit that had come in, and some other minor matters that involved the business dealings of the law firm. He brought her up-to-date on everything, and then he looked at her and asked her pointedly how her health was.

'Better, I guess,' she said carefully, 'not that I was ever sick. I had what they called a "gray area," a mass that turned up on a mammogram a month ago, just before I tried the Schultz case. I tried it anyway,' which he knew, 'and then I took care of business. But business, in this case, is not quite taken care of.' He raised an eyebrow and listened. He had always been fond of her, and didn't like hearing that she was in trouble. When she'd left for the two weeks she'd told him she had some minor surgery that was 'nothing.' This did not sound like 'nothing' to Matthew.

'What's happening now?' He looked suddenly worried.

She took a breath. She knew she'd have to say the words one day, and maybe it was time to try it. He was an old friend, and a respected colleague. 'I had a mastectomy.' The word was harder to say than she thought, but she did it, and he looked shocked instantly. 'And I have to start chemotherapy in two weeks. I want to keep working, but I have no idea what kind of shape I'm going to be in. After that, they claim I'll be fine. They think they got it all, and the chemo is just for insurance. It'll take six months but I want to go on working.' The chemo was a kind of insurance she would have preferred to do without, but with her lymph nodes involved and a Stage II tumor, she knew she had no option.

Listening to her had left Matt stunned. He couldn't believe it. She was so beautiful and so young, and she looked so well. He had never suspected the serious nature of her problem. He had hoped it was nothing. But a mastectomy? And chemotherapy? That was a lot to swallow.

'Wouldn't you rather just take the six months off?' he asked kindly, while wondering at the same time how they would manage without her.

'No, I wouldn't,' she said bluntly, a little frightened that he might force her to do that. She didn't want to stay home and feel sorry for herself. Sam was right about that much. She wanted to work, and distract herself, and do the best job she could at the moment. 'I'd rather be working. I'll do the best I can. If I get too sick, I'll tell you. I have a couch in my office. If I really have to, I can lock the door and lie down for half an hour. I can rest at lunchtime if I need to. But I don't want to stay home, Matt. It would kill me.' He didn't like to hear her say that word, and he was impressed that she was determined to keep working.

'Are you sure?'

'Yes, I am. If I feel differently about it once I start, I'll tell you. But for right now, I want to stay here. It's only six months. Some women get sick as dogs when they're pregnant. I was lucky, I didn't. But others do, and they keep right on working. No one expects them to stay home. I don't want to stay home either.'

'This isn't the same thing, and you know it. What does your doctor say?'

'He thinks I can do it.' Though he had told her to minimize the stress and exhaustion. He had said that he didn't think she should go to trial during that time, but she could probably handle everything else, and she said as much to Matt now. 'I can just limit my trial work during that time. My associate is very good, and maybe some of the other partners can do the trial work. I'll do everything else, all the preparation, all the setup and research. I can sit in for the courtroom stuff, and make all the motions. I'd just need backup for the actual trial so all the responsibility didn't rest on me at the final moment. That wouldn't be fair to the client.'

'This doesn't sound fair to you.' He was devastated to hear what she had told him. But he could also see that she was determined to work through it. 'Are you sure?'

'Totally.' She was amazing. He respected her enormously, and as they left the restaurant, he put an arm around her shoulders.

Everyone was being so kind to her that it brought tears to Alex's eyes frequently. Everyone wanted to help her, except Sam, who just couldn't. It was odd how life worked sometimes. The one person she needed most couldn't be there for her. But at least she had the others.

'What can I do to make this easier for you?' he asked as they strolled back to the office. It was a cold day, and the wind chilled her to the bone even with a coat and a tweed suit on.

'You're doing everything you can already. I'll let you know how I'm doing. And Matt,' she looked up at him pleadingly, 'please don't tell more people than you have to. I don't want to be the object of curiosity, or pity. If someone needs to know because they're being asked to share my workload, or work on a case with me, fine, but let's not take out billboards.'

'I understand.' And he thought he was discreet. But within a week it seemed as though everyone in the law firm knew something about her problem. Word spread like wildfire among secretaries, partners, associates, paralegals, even one of her clients. But much to her surprise, although it embarrassed her, everyone was supportive. They sent her notes, stopped in to say hi, offered to do things for her. At first, she found it irritating in the extreme, but eventually she came to understand that these people cared, they wanted to help her, they wanted to do everything they could to help her make it. Their regard for her professionally translated instantly into how much they cared about her as a person.

By the following week, her office was filled with flowers, notes, letters, and homemade baked goods. She had cookies, brownies, baklava, and some fabulous apple strudel.

'Oh for heaven's sake,' she groaned as Liz came in with a German chocolate cake, while she was working on a brief with Brock Stevens. 'I'm going to weigh two hundred pounds when this is all over.' But people had been so sweet to her. She hadn't stopped writing thank-you notes since she'd come back to work. And she'd been secretly giving Liz and Brock her goodies to take home with them. She'd already taken as much as she felt she could home to Sam and Annabelle, and Carmen.

'Would you like something to eat?' she asked Brock with a grin when they stopped for a cup of coffee. 'It's like running a restaurant.'

'It's good for you. It reminds you that everyone loves you.' He had heard the news again and again . . . had a breast removed . . . mastectomy . . . chemotherapy . . . Alex Parker . . . she could be dying . . . By now, he knew a lot more than she'd told him. But Matt Billings had been so upset he'd told his secretary and four other partners right after his lunch with Alex. And they had told their secretaries, who told associates, who had told other partners, who had told their paralegals, who had told . . . it was limitless. But so was their affection.

'It sounds a little crazy to say right now, but I'm very lucky.'

'Yes, you are. And you're going to stay that way,' he said firmly. He was always very definite with her now about the future, and it made her wonder if he was religious.

At home, things were no different than they'd been. Sam had gone to Hong Kong for three days to meet a connection of Simon's, and he had made an extraordinary deal that had made the front page of the *Wall Street Journal*. Sam's professional life had always been faintly Hollywood anyway, filled with financial stars and enormous hits, but with the arrival of Simon it was suddenly even more so. It seemed as though none of their deals could miss, and he was busier than ever. But his three days away from her seemed to have put even more distance between them. And he had told her nothing about the deal until she'd read about it herself in the paper. And the night he got home, she couldn't help telling him how she felt about it.

'Why didn't you say anything?' she asked, hurt that he hadn't told her himself about a deal that was that important.

'I forgot. You've been busy too. I hardly saw you all week.' But she knew as well as he did that a deal like that hadn't happened in a few days. He had to have been working on it for a month, or longer. He had just closed up all the routes of communication between them. And for days after the Hong Kong trip, he had gone to bed right after dinner and insisted he was jet-lagged.

'What are you afraid of, Sam?' she asked finally, as he went to get undressed right after dinner. His game now was to be sound asleep before she got to bed. She was staying up to work, catching up on cases that had come in while she was out for two weeks, and trying to get ahead of her work load before she started chemo. 'I'm not going to jump you if you stay up past eight o'clock. You might like to stay up sometime to see

223

more than *Sesame Street* and the six o'clock news on TV, not to mention a little adult conversation.'

'I told you, it's been a rough week. I'm jet-lagged.'

'Tell that to the judge,' she said ironically, and he snapped at her instantly.

'What's that supposed to mean?'

'Nothing, for chrissake. I was kidding. I'm a lawyer, remember? For heaven's sake, what's happening to you?' He was completely humorless with her. They never talked, they never laughed, they never relaxed, they never cuddled. Overnight, they had become angry strangers. All because she'd had a mastectomy. He acted as though it were the ultimate betrayal.

'I don't think that was amusing.' He actually managed to look insulted. 'It was tasteless.'

'Oh for chrissake. What do you think is amusing anymore? Surely not me. You haven't said more than five words to me since I went to the hospital, or maybe since I told you about the mammogram.' It had been six weeks since the nightmare had begun, and it was beginning to seem endless. 'What's it going to be like, Sam, when I start chemo?'

'How do I know?'

'Well, let's see,' she pretended to be figuring it all out as they chatted, 'if you got really annoyed at me about the mammogram, and the biopsy, and then seriously pissed off at me once I had surgery, and have hardly spoken to me since I came home from the hospital, what do you do when I get chemo? Maybe walk out on me? Or just ignore me completely? What exactly do I have to look forward to, and when is this going to end? When it's all over, or when I just give up, and concede that our marriage is over? Give me a clue here.'

'Okay, okay.' He walked slowly back to where she stood, cleaning up their dinner in the kitchen. Annabelle had gone to bed an hour before and they knew she was asleep so she couldn't hear them. 'So it's been a rough six weeks. That doesn't have to mean everything is finished. I still love you.' He looked sheepish and awkward and unhappy as he looked at her. He knew how bad things were, he just didn't know how to fix them. He loved her but the pressure of wanting Daphne made it all the harder. Moving toward Alex again would have meant giving up something with Daphne. But getting closer to her meant betraying his wife. And for the moment, he was just standing in the middle, panicking, getting closer to neither. But he also knew that while he agonized over it, he was destroying his relationship with Alex. He knew he had to say or do something to make things better with her, but he just couldn't. He couldn't even bring himself to look at her body. The only body he wanted now was Daphne's. It was a frightening situation.

'I just need time, Al. I'm sorry.' He stood looking at her, wanting to make it up to her, and yet not wanting to make an effort. He wanted time out, and there was no way to get it without hurting her. He didn't want to do that, but he also didn't want to give up dreaming of Daphne and he still wasn't ready to support Alex through her illness.

'I just think this is a rough time for you to go through change of life, Sam. I'm going to need your help while I'm going through the chemo. And to be honest,' which she always was, painfully so, 'you haven't helped yet. That doesn't exactly give me much hope for the future.' She was becoming strangely calm about it, and a little less angry.

'I'll do my best. I'm just not real great around sickness.'

'So I noticed.' She smiled ruefully. 'Anyway, I just thought I'd mention it. I'm scared,' she said in a gentler tone. 'I don't know what it's going to be like.'

'I'm sure it's not as bad as it's cracked up to be. It's like the horror stories you hear about childbirth. Most of them are bullshit.'

'I hope so,' she said, because she had heard some bad ones when she joined Liz a few times at the support group. She went to please Liz but it helped her too. And a few of them had done well with chemo. But most people admitted that chemotherapy was rough. It made you feel worse than anything you could imagine. 'Anyway, I'm glad business is going so well for you these days. It looks like Simon really is an asset. I guess we were both wrong.'

'We sure were. You wouldn't believe the people he put me in touch with in Hong Kong. They are fabulously wealthy. Rich Chinese, in the shipping industry. They make the Arabs look like paupers.'

'How much are they investing with you?' she asked as she put the dishes in the dishwasher. She had always been very interested in his business, and that was still a safe subject between them.

He smiled at her now, proud of himself, as well he should be. 'Sixty million.' She was hurt though that he hadn't told her about it sooner, it was only now when she pressed him.

'That's a nice chunk of change for a boy from New York,' she praised.

'Cute, huh?' he grinned, looking like the man she'd fallen in love with.

'Very. I'm proud of you.' It was a funny thing to say to a man who wouldn't come any closer to her than to stand across the room, a man who had hurt her as badly as he had. But she was willing to give him his due. A sixty-million-dollar deal in Hong Kong was a real coup. 'It must feel pretty good.' It did. And he had had Daphne with him. But more to his own amazement, they had continued to abstain even in Hong Kong. It had driven them both crazy, but he still didn't want to cheat on Alex, no matter how great the temptation. But he also didn't want to sleep with Alex now, he couldn't. The only one he wanted physically was Daphne, and he refused to let himself have her.

He went back to their bedroom then, and watched TV for a while, but as usual, by the time she went in half an hour later, he was asleep, and she shook her head as she looked at him. He was hopeless. He was so afraid of getting close to her again that he would have done anything to avoid it.

'Maybe he's narcoleptic,' she whispered to herself as she picked up her briefcase and went back to the study. Whatever he needed to warm up to her again, he was definitely not getting it, and she was just going to have to be patient. A woman in the group had had similar problems with her husband, and they had even separated for a year. He just couldn't face her raw need, and the fear of her dying, so he had shut her out. And she had left him. But now they were back together. And she had been free of the disease for six years. They had been back together for four of them. Hearing those stories gave Alex hope. But it still didn't make it any easier to deal with Sam. And the next day they had a huge fight after Annabelle's bedtime.

Just before dinner, Alex had explained to Annabelle that the next day she was going to the doctor and they were going to give her some medicine. And it was going to make her pretty sick. Eventually, it might even make her hair fall out. It was pretty bad stuff, but it was kind of like vaccinations. Taking it was going to make her sick for a while, but then strong again, and it would keep her from getting bad sicknesses. But Annabelle was going to have to be kind of patient with her, because sometimes she'd be okay, but sometimes she'd feel sick, and sometimes she'd be very tired. It was the best she could do, and when she was finished, Annabelle looked very worried.

'Will you still take me to ballet?'

'Sometimes. If I can. If I'm too tired, Carmen will take you.'

'But I want *you* to take me,' Annabelle whined. She was good about Alex's being tired most of the time, but sometimes it really scared her.

'I want to take you to ballet too, but we have to see how I'll feel. I don't know yet.'

'Will you wear a wig if your hair falls out?' She was intrigued by that, and Alex smiled.

'Maybe. We'll see.'

'That would be really ugly. Will it grow back?'

'Yes.'

'But it wouldn't be long anymore. Would it?'

'Nope. It would be short like yours. We could be twins.'

And then suddenly Annabelle looked terrified. 'Will my hair fall out too?'

Alex was quick to put her arms around her and reassure her. 'Of course not.'

But after she'd gone to bed, Sam was furious and went after Alex with a vengeance. 'That was the most disgusting thing I've ever heard. You scared her to death.' His eyes were blazing at Alex, and as always, she was hurt by his complete lack of compassion.

'I did not. She was fine when she went to bed. I even got her a book about it. It's called *Mommy's Getting Better.*'

'That's disgusting. Did you see the look on her face when you told her about your hair?'

'Look Goddammit, she has to be prepared. If I'm going to be too sick to do things for her while I'm on chemotherapy, she has to know it.'

'Why can't you suffer quietly? You're always making it her problem, and mine. Jesus, have a little dignity for chrissake.'

'You sonofabitch!' She grabbed at his shirt and it tore in her hand, which surprised both of them. She had never done anything like that, but he was driving her to distraction. She had lost her husband, her breast, her sex life, her sense of her own femininity, her own sense of well-being and immortality, her ability to have more kids. She had done nothing but lose things that were really important to her in the last six weeks, and he had done nothing but criticize her for it. 'God damn you! All I do is struggle with what's happening to me, and try and manage it so it doesn't inconvenience you, doesn't hurt her, doesn't overburden my partners at the law firm, and all you ever do is bitch at me and treat me like a pariah. Well, fuck you, Sam Parker. Fuck you if you can't take it.' All her anguish of the last six weeks came spewing out of her like a volcano. But he had so much pain of his own that he still refused to hear it.

'Stop congratulating yourself for how noble and long-suffering you are. All you do is whine about your goddamn breast, which wasn't such hot stuff in the first place. I mean, who even notices that it's gone, and the only other thing you do is 'prepare' us for chemotherapy. Get it over with for chrissake, do it, don't beat us to death with it. She's three and a half years old, why does she have to go through it with you?'

'Because I'm her mother and she cares about me, and my feeling sick is going to affect her.'

'You're making *me* sick, and that's affecting me. I can't live like this, with the daily cancer bulletins from Sloan-Kettering. Why don't you just take out billboards?'

'You shit! You didn't even ask about the pathology reports when I got them.' It was the day he had first seen her scarred breast and his horror had superseded his interest.

'What difference does it make? They cut your breast off anyway.'

'It might make a difference if I live or die, if that still matters to you, or maybe that's like the breast you care so little about. Maybe if I disappear too, you won't even notice. I don't see how you could. You don't even bother to talk to me anymore, let alone touch me.'

'What's to talk about, Alex? Chemotherapy? Lymph nodes? Pathology? I can't stand it anymore.'

'Then why don't you get out and leave me to it? You're certainly not helping.'

'I'm not leaving my daughter. I'm not going any-where,' he spat at her, and then stormed out of the apartment. He stood on the street after that, aching to take a cab to Fifty-third Street, to Daphne, but he didn't do it. He wouldn't let himself. He called her from a pay phone instead and burst into tears. He said he was starting to hate his wife, and himself. He explained that she was starting chemotherapy the next day, and he just couldn't take it. And Daphne sympathized completely. She asked if he wanted to come over for a little while, but he said he really didn't think he should.

He knew he was too vulnerable now, he needed her too much. And he couldn't let her be the excuse for ending his marriage. He had to work this thing out, and see it through. He had to do something, but he didn't know what. He didn't understand it, but he hated Alex suddenly. The poor woman was sick, and he hated her for what she was doing to his life. She had brought sickness into it, and fear. She was going to abandon him. She was destroying everything. Without knowing it, she was keeping him from Daphne.

He walked all the way to the East River and back again. And all the while, Alex lay on their bed, staring at the ceiling. She was too angry to even cry, too hurt to ever forgive him. He had abandoned her. He had failed her completely. In six weeks he had negated everything they'd ever shared, denied anything they'd ever felt, and destroyed all the hope and respect they had built in seventeen years together. And the promise of 'for better or worse, in sickness and in health' had been completely forgotten.

It was two hours later when he came in, and she was still lying there. But he never came to see her. He said not a word to her. She lay there, awake, all night, and Sam slept on the couch in the study.

Chapter 12

The oncologist Dr Herman had referred her to was located on Fifty-seventh Street, and was a woman. Alex had been told to expect to spend an hour and a half with her the first time, and forty-five minutes to an hour and a half thereafter. There would be two visits a month, unless of course there were any problems, in which case she would see her more often.

Alex had scheduled the appointment at noon, and was expecting to be back in the office at one-thirty.

Both Brock and Liz knew that she was starting chemotherapy on that day, and of course Sam did too. He had left for the office, after their massive argument the night before, without even bothering to have breakfast. And he never called her in the morning to tell her he was sorry, or wish her luck with the chemo, let alone offer to go with her. She had already figured out one thing, she was going to have to get through this without him.

The building was a modern one, off Third Avenue, and the waiting room was well decorated and had an open, airy feeling. It was warmly lit, and decorated in soft yellow, and everything about it was deceptively cheerful. If they had led Alex into a dark tomb, it would have seemed much more appropriate. And for some reason, she was relieved to see that the woman she'd been referred to was her own age. She seemed quiet and capable, her name was Jean Webber. And Alex was pleased to see, from her diploma on the wall, that she had gone to Harvard Med School.

They talked in her office for a while at first, and the doctor discussed the pathology reports with her, and what they meant. It was a relief to be treated like an intelligent human being. She explained that the cytotoxic drugs they would use were not 'poisonous,' contrary to common belief, but that their purpose was to destroy bad cells and spare good ones. She explained also that Alex's tumor had been Stage II, which was not great news, but that other than the four lymph nodes involved, there had been no further infiltration. It had gone no further. The prognosis, as far as Dr Webber was concerned, was good. And like the other doctors involved, she felt absolutely sure that chemotherapy was necessary to obtain a complete cure. They couldn't take the risk of leaving even a fraction of a cell to divide and spread. Only a hundred-percent cure was acceptable, and would assure Alex that she would remain free of cancer. Because of the mastectomy, radiation was not necessary. And because of the nature of her cancer, hormone therapy would not be necessary either. The final results of the tests had indicated that it would not be useful. A chromosomal test had been done too, to examine the DNA of the cells involved, to see if there was a normal or abnormal number of chromosomes, and they had found that Alex's cells were diploid, which meant that they had the normal two copies of each chromosome. She had had the optimum outcome. It was a relief hearing about it, except that even with the good news

233

came bad news. The bad news was that she had had cancer at all, and she had six months of chemotherapy ahead of her now, which profoundly depressed her.

When they talked about it, Dr Webber understood. She was a small woman with dark brown hair flecked with gray, which she wore pulled back neatly, and she wore no makeup. She had a sympathetic face, and small, neat-looking, immaculate hands, which moved to emphasize what she was saying.

She tried to explain to Alex that while the side effects of chemotherapy could be disagreeable, they were not as fearsome as people believed, and with proper treatment they could be managed. And she assured Alex that none of the side effects caused permanent damage. Dr Webber said she wanted to hear from her if she was having any problems. And the side effects to be expected, and discussed, were loss of hair, nausea, body pain, fatigue, and weight gain. She might also experience sore throats, colds, and problems with elimination. She could expect to stop menstruating immediately, but she told her that it was not impossible that she would menstruate again after chemotherapy. The eventual sterility rate was fifty percent, but that gave her an even chance of still having a baby, if she still had a husband, Alex thought to herself, as she forced herself to listen to the doctor. And Dr Webber went on to reassure her that there was no evidence of birth defects afterwards.

There were potential, but remote, problems with bone marrow, though, and her white count getting too low, but these were less than likely. And bladder irritations were not uncommon. Only the weight gain surprised Alex, it would have seemed that with the nausea and vomiting she would lose weight and not gain it, but the doctor explained it just seemed to be an unavoidable factor, like the hair loss. She suggested that Alex go out and select a wig she liked immediately, even several of them. Given the drugs she would be taking, it was almost certain she would lose all or most of her luxurious red hair. But it would grow back afterwards, the doctor reassured her.

The doctor was as informative and as reassuring as she could be, and Alex tried to pretend to herself that she was listening to a new client, and had to hear all the evidence before reacting. It was a good system for her and it worked for a while, but as she continued to listen, what she began to hear couldn't help but overwhelm her. The nausea, the vomiting, the loss of hair, the relentlessness of it made her feel breathless.

The doctor explained that she would have a physical exam each time she came, a blood test, and regular scans and X-rays, all of which could be performed in her office. They had the latest state-of-the-art equipment. She told her that she would be taking an oral drug, Cytoxan, for the first fourteen days of every four-week month, and then she would be coming in for methotrexate and fluorouracil intravenously on the first and eighth days of that same four-week month. After the intravenous drugs were administered, she could go back to her office. She wanted Alex to be careful to rest more than usual on the day before they were given to make sure that she minimized the problems and didn't lower her white count.

'I know it all sounds very confusing at first, but you'll get used to it,' she smiled. Alex was startled to realize they had been talking for almost an hour when the doctor led her into the next room for the examination.

Alex undressed carefully, folding her clothes on a chair, as though each moment, each gesture mattered, and she found she couldn't control her shaking. Her hands were shaking like leaves, while the doctor looked at the surgical site and nodded approval.

'Have you picked out your plastic surgeon yet?' she asked, but Alex only shook her head. She hadn't made that decision. She didn't know if she even wanted reconstructive surgery. The way things were going she wasn't sure she cared. And thinking about that brought tears to her eyes, as the doctor pricked her finger for her blood count. Suddenly, there was a catch in her throat for everything, and as the doctor set up the IV, Alex suddenly found herself sobbing and apologizing for it.

'It's all right,' the doctor said quietly, 'go ahead and cry. I know how frightening this is. It won't ever be as scary as the first time. We are very, very careful with these drugs.' Alex knew that that was why it was so important to have selected an excellent and board-certified oncologist. She had heard horror stories of people who had been killed by improperly administered chemo. And she couldn't help thinking about that now. What if she had a reaction? What if she died? What if she never saw Annabelle again? Or Sam? . . . even after the awful fight they'd had the night before. It didn't bear thinking.

Dr Webber began an IV infusion of dextrose and water first, and then she added the drug to it, but the IV kept backing up, and her vein collapsed just after they started. It was painful, and Dr Webber immediately took the IV out, and looked at Alex's other arm, and then her hands, which were still shaking.

'I generally prefer the dextrose and water first but your veins aren't looking so great today. I'm going to do a "direct push," and then we'll try this way again next time. I'm going to inject the undiluted

236

medication right into your vein. It stings a little bit, but it's faster, and I think for today you'll be happier if we get this over with quickly.' Alex couldn't disagree with her, but the 'direct push' sounded very scary.

Her neat small hands took Alex's hand, and she carefully examined the vein at the top of it, and then injected the medication into it, while Alex tried not to pass out from the sheer emotions. And as soon as she was finished she asked Alex to press hard on the vein for a full five minutes, during which time she wrote out a prescription for the Cytoxan, and went to get out a single pill and a glass of water. She handed it to Alex, and watched her take it.

'Fine,' she said, satisfied. 'You've now had your first dose of chemotherapy. I'd like to see you back here exactly a week from today, and I want to hear from you if you think you're having any problems. Don't be shy, don't hesitate, don't tell yourself you're being a nuisance. If anything seems unusual to you at all, or you just feel rotten, call me. We can see what we can do to help you.' She handed Alex a printed sheet of side effects that were normal, and those that weren't. 'I'm on call twenty-four hours a day, and I don't mind hearing from my patients.' She smiled warmly and stood up. She was a lot smaller than Alex and she seemed very dynamic. She was lucky, Alex thought, as she looked at her, she was doing her job. It was just like the people who came to her, with terrible legal problems, and frightening lawsuits. She could take care of them, she could do her best for them. But the problem and the anguish were theirs, not hers. Suddenly, she envied the doctor.

Alex was stunned to realize as she left that she had been at the oncologist's for two hours. It was just after two o'clock, and her hand was still sore as she hailed a cab. There was a Band-Aid over where the doctor had injected the medications. Alex was beginning to learn all the terms and phrases. It was information she would have been happier not knowing, and she felt enormously relieved as she rode back to the office. She didn't feel sick, she hadn't died, nothing terrible had happened to her. At least the doctor knew what she was doing. She thought about buying a wig as they drove down Lexington Avenue. It seemed depressing to be thinking about it now. But the doctor was probably right. It would be less upsetting to have one on hand when she needed it, rather than going to stores, hiding her balding head with a scarf on. The thought of it was far from cheering.

She paid the cab and went up to her office, and Liz was away from her desk when she got in. Alex answered her calls from the messages on her desk, and she started to relax finally a little while later. The sky had not fallen in. So far, she had survived it. Maybe this wouldn't be so bad after all, she told herself, as Brock came in, in his shirtsleeves, with a stack of papers. It was four o'clock, and she'd been busy for the past two hours.

'How'd it go?' he asked with a look of concern. There was always something very nice about the way he asked her. It wasn't cloying and intrusive, it was just very obvious that he cared, and that touched her. He was almost like a younger brother.

'So far so good. It was scary as hell though.' She didn't know him well enough to tell him she'd cried, that she'd been to hell and back, waiting for the injection to kill her.

'You're a good kid,' he said, 'do you want a cup of coffee?'

'I'd love one.'

He was back in five minutes and they worked for an hour, and she left promptly at five o'clock, so she could go home to Annabelle. It had been a pretty good day, but a tiring one, all things considered.

'Thanks for all the help,' she said to Brock before she left. They were starting a case together for a small employer who was being sued in a bogus discrimination case. This time the woman had cancer, and claimed she was passed over for a promotion. Her employer had done everything he possibly could to help her. He even had set up a room for the employee at work, so she could rest as much as she needed to, and he had given her three days a week off while she was having chemo, and held her job for her. But she was still suing. She claimed she wasn't promoted because of her cancer. What the woman wanted was to make some money, sit at home, and be able to pay for all her treatments and then some with what she made on the lawsuit. The cancer appeared to have been cured, and she didn't even want to work anymore. But she still had a lot of leftover debts from her treatments. And there was no doubt, Alex had discovered herself, that most insurance plans paid only minimum amounts for cancer treatment. If you couldn't afford the very expensive treatments that saved lives, you were in big trouble. Alex's own insurance was picking up very little of her expenses. But still, the plaintiff in her case had no right to take that out on her ex-employer. He had even offered to help her, a fact that she had later denied, and that he had no proof of. As usual, Alex felt very sorry for the defendant. She hated the injustice of people who thought they ought to clean up just because someone else had money and they didn't. And it was also a good time for her to be taking the case, because she had a lot of very useful firsthand information about cancer.

'I'll see you tomorrow, Brock,' she said as she got ready to leave.

'Take care of yourself. Bundle up. And eat a good dinner.'

'Yes, Mom,' she teased, but they were all things Liz had told her too. She had to keep warm, and make sure she kept her strength up. She wasn't looking forward to the weight Dr Webber said she might gain. She hated being overweight, although she seldom was, and she knew Sam hated heavy women.

'Thanks again.' She left, and went home, thinking of how nice they all were, and how relieved she was that her first treatment was over. It had been even more traumatic than she'd expected, and she'd been even more undone by it, and yet it had gone pretty smoothly. She wasn't looking forward to going back in a week, but maybe it would be better this time, and after that she had a three-week break before the next one. Liz had filled her prescription for the pills, and she had them in her handbag. It was like being on the pill again, which she hadn't been in years. You couldn't allow yourself to forget them.

Annabelle was in the bathtub when she got home, and she and Carmen were singing. It was a song from *Sesame Street,* and Alex joined them as she put her briefcase down and walked into the bathroom.

'And how was your day?' Alex asked as she bent down to kiss her after the song was over.

'Okay. How did you hurt your hand?'

'I didn't . . . oh, that.' It was her Band-Aid from the chemo. 'At the office.'

'Does it hurt?'

'Nope.'

'I got a Snoopy Band-Aid at school,' Annabelle said proudly, and Carmen told Alex that Sam had called and said he wouldn't be home for dinner. Alex hadn't heard from him all day and she assumed that he was still furious about the night before. But now she couldn't even tell him that the chemo had gone smoothly. She thought of calling him at work, but after all the ugliness they'd exchanged the night before, she thought it was better to wait until she saw him. She noticed too that he was going out a lot more with clients at night than he used to. Maybe it was another one of his ways of avoiding dealing with her, and it was certainly working. She felt as though she never saw him.

She had dinner with Annabelle, and decided to try and wait up for him. But she was so exhausted that she fell asleep at nine o'clock, in bed, with the light on. It had been the hardest day of her life, harder even than the surgery, and she was totally exhausted.

And as she slept, Sam was having a quiet dinner with Daphne, in a small restaurant in the East Sixties.

He looked agonized and she was sympathetic as she listened. She never made demands on him, never pressed him, never reproached him for what he didn't give her.

'I don't know what's happening to me,' he said, his steak untouched and getting cold, as she held his hand and listened. 'I feel so sorry for her, I know what kind of need she's in, but all I ever feel for her anymore is anger. Rage at what's happened to our life. It seems like it's all her fault, except I know it isn't. But it's not my fault either. It's just rotten luck, and now she's starting chemotherapy and I just can't face it. I can't look at her anymore, I don't want to see what's happening to her. It's terrifying to look at, and I'm just not good with things like that. My God,' he was near tears, 'I feel like a monster.'

'Of course you're not,' Daphne said gently, still holding his hand, 'you're only human. Those things are terribly upsetting. You're not a nurse, for heaven's sake. Surely she can't expect you to take care of her . . . or even to be able to stomach . . .' she groped for words, '. . . looking at it. It must be quite awful.'

'It is,' he said honestly. 'It's barbaric. It's like they just took a knife and sliced it off. It made me cry the first time I saw it.'

'How awful for you, Sam,' Daphne said warmly, thinking entirely of him and not Alex. 'Don't you think she understood? She's an intelligent woman. She can't possibly expect it not to affect you.'

'She expects me to be there for her, to hold her hand, to go to treatments with her, and talk about it with our little girl. I just can't stand it. I want my life back.'

'You have a right to it,' Daphne said soothingly, she was the most understanding, least demanding woman he'd ever met. All she wanted was to be with him, under any circumstances, in spite of all the limitations he'd imposed on their relationship. He'd finally agreed to have dinner alone with her occasionally, as long as she understood he couldn't sleep with her. He couldn't do that to Alex. He'd never been unfaithful to her, and he didn't want to start now, no matter how great the temptation, although everyone in the office already thought he was having an affair with Daphne. And Daphne had made it very clear to him that she was so in love with him she would accept any conditions, as long as he just saw her.

'I love you so much,' she said softly, as he looked at her, consumed with conflicting emotions.

'I love you too . . . that's the craziness of all this . . . I love you, and I love her too. I love both of you. I want you but my obligations are to her. But all we have left now are obligations.'

'It's not much of a life for you, Sam,' Daphne said sadly.

'I know. Maybe this thing will resolve itself eventually. It can't be happy for her either. Eventually she's going to hate me. I think she does already.'

'Then she's a fool. You're the kindest man that ever lived,' Daphne said staunchly, but Sam knew better, and so did Alex.

'I'm the fool here,' he said, smiling at her. 'I should grab you and run before you come to your senses, and find someone your own age with a less complicated life.' He'd never been as smitten with anyone since his boyhood, maybe not even with Alex.

'Where would you run to?' she asked innocently, as they finally both began eating their dinner. Whenever they were together, they talked for hours and forgot everything around them.

'Maybe Brazil . . . or an island near Tahiti . . . someplace hot and sensual where I could have you all to myself, with tropical flowers and smells,' and as he described it, he felt her hand go to him under the table. It made him smile, and her fingers were deft and artful. 'You're a bad girl, Daphne Belrose.'

'Perhaps you ought to prove that to yourself one of these days. I'm beginning to feel like a virgin,' she teased him, and he actually blushed.

'I'm sorry.' He wasn't making life easy for anyone, but he felt so guilty.

'Don't be sorry,' she said seriously. 'It'll make it all the more worthwhile when you finally do work it

243

out.' She was certain he would, it was just a question of time. But she could wait. He was well worth waiting for. He was one of the most desirable men in New York, and one of the most successful. Even here, in an out-of-the-way restaurant, people recognized him, and nodded recognition, and the headwaiter had considered it a real coup when he saw them. Sam Parker was one of the biggest fish on Wall Street.

'Why are you so patient with me?' he asked, as they ordered dessert and he ordered the restaurant's only bottle of Château d'Yquem at two hundred and fifty dollars a bottle.

'I told you,' she lowered her voice conspiratorially, 'because I love you.'

'You're crazy,' he said, as he leaned over and kissed her. And then he toasted her with the Yquem. 'To Simon's little cousin,' he said harmlessly, but what he wanted to say was 'To the love of my life,' but he didn't. It would have been too disloyal to Alex. How could this happen to him? How could Alex get cancer and he fall in love with someone else all at once? It never dawned on him that the two events were related.

'I'm going to be very grateful to Simon one day,' he said conspiratorially, and she laughed.

'Or very angry. That's the bad thing about all this foreplay. You're building up an awful lot of expectations about me. I might turn out to be very disappointing.'

'Not likely,' he said confidently, aching to make love to her right then. Every moment they spent together was a tantalizing caress that tortured his body.

He walked her all the way home afterwards, but, as always, he refused to go upstairs with her. They lingered forever, kissing on the doorstep, with her caressing him, and his hands covering every inch of her body.

'We might as well go upstairs, you know,' she tried to entice him with her lips and her hands, and he was about to burst with desire. 'I think it might be a great relief to the neighbors.'

'It would be a great relief to me, I can promise you. I'm not sure how much longer I can stand this,' he said, kissing her again in desperation.

'Not long, I hope, sweet Sam,' she whispered in his ear, as her hands gripped his buttocks and pressed him to her. His body found her hot and throbbing against him, and he shuddered with desire when he realized she wasn't wearing any underwear, even in the cold November wind of a New York winter. It took all the strength he had to resist her.

'You're killing me,' he said, laughing hoarsely with the delicious agony of it. 'And you'll catch pneumonia.'

'Then you'd better keep me warm, Sam.'

'Oh God, how I want to.' He closed his eyes and pressed her against him.

He finally managed to tear himself away from her, though with ever greater difficulty, and he walked the twenty-five blocks home to regain his senses. It was nearly midnight by then, and Alex was dead to the world with the light on. He stood looking at her for a long time, silently apologizing to her, but his heart longed for Daphne, not Alex. He quietly turned off the light, and went to bed. And it was six o'clock in the morning when he woke to a strange grating sound. It was rasping and mechanical, and it went on and on and on, and no attempt to ignore it would keep him asleep. At first he thought it was a machine, and then he thought it might be the alarm, and then some crazy sense told him the elevator might be broken. But no matter what, the sound wouldn't stop, and when he finally woke up and turned over, he realized that it was Alex, vomiting and retching uncontrollably in the bathroom.

He lay there for a little while, not sure if he should bother her or not, and then finally, he got up, and stood in the doorway.

'Are you all right?' For a long time she didn't answer, and then finally, she nodded.

'Great, thanks.' She hadn't lost her sense of humor, but she still couldn't stop retching.

'Is it something you ate?' Even now, he still had denial.

'I think it's the chemo.'

'Call the doctor.'

She nodded and went on vomiting, and he went to shower in the guest bathroom. He came back half an hour later, and she had stopped and was lying on the bathroom floor with a cold cloth on her head, and her eyes closed.

'You're not pregnant, are you?'

She kept her eyes closed and shook her head. She didn't even have the energy to insult him. She had gotten her period before the surgery. Another 'blue day' had come and gone since, and he wasn't even speaking to her, let alone making babies. How did he think she could be pregnant? And she was having chemotherapy. How could he be so stupid? For a smart guy, he was a real jerk when it came to cancer.

She finally got enough energy to crawl across the bedroom on her hands and knees and call Dr Webber. The answering service put her through immediately, and the doctor told her that it wasn't an unusual reaction to the first treatment, though she was sorry to hear it. She suggested that she eat carefully, but a little food might actually help to settle her stomach, and she had to take her pill today, no matter how sick she felt, or how much she vomited. She could not miss it. She also offered her additional medication for the vomiting, which might help, but Alex was afraid to put any more chemicals into her system, and the additional medications had their own side effects as well.

'Thank you,' Alex rasped, and went to vomit again, but this time it was all over in a few minutes. There was nothing left but bile anyway. Her whole body felt as though it had been turned inside out. It took her forever to dress and she was green by the time she went to the kitchen to watch Sam and Annabelle having breakfast. He had helped her dress, and had kept her away from Alex.

'Are you sick, Mommy?' Annabelle asked, looking worried.

'Sort of. Remember the medicine I told you about? Well, I took some yesterday and it made me kind of sick.'

'It must be very bad medicine,' Annabelle said loyally.

'It's going to make me better,' Alex said firmly, and forced herself to nibble a piece of toast, in spite of all her inclinations not to touch it. She noticed then that Sam was looking over his paper at her in acute annoyance. It was bad enough to wake him up vomiting, but she knew how he hated her explanations to Annabelle. 'Sorry,' she said pointedly at him, in less than pleasant tones, and he went back to his paper.

She hung back while he left to take Annabelle to school, and he made no further mention of her vomiting that morning. But as soon as they were gone, Alex threw up again, and thought about not going to the office. She sat down on her bed, and cried, and decided to call Liz, and then something made her stop. She wasn't going to give in. She was going to go to work if it killed her.

She washed her face again, and brushed her teeth, and put another cold cloth on her head, and then with a look of determination she put on her coat and picked up her briefcase. She had to sit down in the hall again, and her stomach turned, but she made it to the elevator and down to the street, and felt better. The cold air helped, but the cab ride didn't. She felt desperately sick again by the time she got to work, and she barely made it to the ladies' room, where she was violently sick again. She looked awful by the time she got to her office, where Brock and Liz happened to be talking. She was almost a shiny green, which really shocked them. They both followed her inside and looked at her with obvious concern, as Alex collapsed into her desk chair with a look of exhaustion.

'Are you all right?' Liz asked worriedly as Brock stared at her, frowning.

'Not really. It's been a rough morning.' She closed her eyes, as she felt a wave of nausea come over her again, but she refused to give in to it, and it passed. She opened her eyes again to see Brock and not Liz. He looked very worried.

'She went to get you a cup of tea. Do you want to lie down?'

'I don't think I'd ever get up again,' she said honestly. 'Why don't we get to work,' she said bravely.

'Are you up to it?'

'Don't ask,' she said grimly, and shaking his head, he went to get his papers. As always, he was working in his shirtsleeves, with his horn-rims pushed high on his head when he didn't need them. He had pencils in his pocket, a pen in his teeth, and a foot-high stack of papers when he came back to her office, with a box of Saltines for Alex.

'Try these.' He dropped them on her desk, and sat down with the work they were sharing. And as they made their way through it, he watched her carefully. She looked awful, but she seemed to feel a little better while she was working. It distracted her from her miseries. And Liz kept her well supplied with tea, and she nibbled at the crackers Brock had brought her.

'Why don't you lie down for a while during lunch?' he suggested, but she shook her head, she didn't want to break their momentum. They were doing some very detailed work on one of her new cases. And they ordered chicken sandwiches instead, which Alex actually felt well enough to eat by lunchtime.

It was fully an hour later when the food caught up with her, and suddenly she looked panicked, as she felt it rising. She had a tiny bathroom adjacent to her office, and without a word to Brock, she disappeared, and vomited horribly and then retched for half an hour while he couldn't help but hear it. It was agonizing listening to her, and after a while he went out, and came back with a cold damp cloth, an ice pack, and a pillow. Without knocking or saying anything, he opened the door, which she hadn't locked fortunately, and she suddenly felt his strong arms behind her, as she knelt huddled over the bowl, and slumped against the wall. For a moment, he was afraid she had fainted but she hadn't.

'Lean against me, Alex,' he said quietly, 'just let yourself go.' She didn't argue, she didn't say a word, she was just too sick and too grateful for the help, from

249

any quarter. She slumped back into his arms, as he sat on the floor holding her, the bathroom was barely big enough for both of them with their long legs, but they just made it. He put the ice pack on the back of her neck, and the wet cloth on her forehead. And for an instant, she opened her eyes and looked up at him, but she didn't speak. She couldn't.

He flushed the toilet for her, and put the lid down, and after a little while, he laid her down on the pillow, and covered her with a blanket. She was grateful for all of it, and he sat with her the entire time, watching her, holding her hand, and saying nothing.

It was almost an hour later when she finally spoke to him, in a soft voice. She was completely drained, and even talking was an effort. 'I think I can get up now.'

'Why don't you lie here for a while?' he said softly, and then he had a better idea. 'I'm going to move you, Alex. Don't do anything. Just let yourself go.' She had stopped vomiting long enough to be moved to the other room, and with no effort at all, he scooped her up, surprised at how light she was for her size, and laid her down on the gray leather couch in her office. It felt wonderful to her, and he put the pillow under her head and the blanket over her. She was mildly ashamed of herself for giving up so completely, but she didn't really care. She was just grateful that he was there to help her.

'Lock the door,' she whispered to him as he stood next to her, like a mother watching her baby.

'Why?'

'I don't want anyone to walk in and see me.' She had assured everyone that she was going to be able to work during chemotherapy, and this was hardly an auspicious beginning.

He did what she asked, and then came to sit in a chair next to her. He didn't want to leave her alone, but she did look a little better.

'Do you want me to take you home?' he asked cautiously, but she shook her head in answer to the question.

'I'm staying.'

'Do you want to sleep for a while?'

'I'll just lie here. You work. I'll get up in a few minutes.'

'Are you serious?' He was amazed at her. He had never admired her more than at this moment. She refused to give up or to be beaten. She was a real trouper.

'Yes,' she answered him. 'You work . . . and Brock? . . .' She was whispering and so was he. 'Thank you.'

'Never mind. That's what friends are for.' It only saddened her to know that Sam couldn't do this.

Brock turned off some of the lights, and she lay there for a while with her eyes closed, and then half an hour later, she got up and joined him at her desk. She looked a little rumpled and her hair was mussed, and her voice was hoarse, but she was ready to go back to work, and neither of them mentioned what had happened.

He remembered to unlock the door, and Liz came in with tea and coffee and a snack, and no one was any the wiser. And at five o'clock Brock walked her to the elevator, and carried her briefcase.

'I'll catch a cab for you, and then come back up,' he said matter-of-factly.

'Don't you have anything else to do than help old ladies across the street?' she teased, but they had become friends that afternoon, and she knew she

251

wouldn't forget it for a lifetime. She didn't know what she had done to deserve that kind of friendship from him, but it had made an enormous impression. 'You must have been a Boy Scout.'

'Matter of fact, I was. There was nothing else to do in Illinois. Besides, I've always had a soft spot for old ladies.'

'Apparently,' she grinned at him. She felt about a thousand years old at that moment, but he thought she was remarkable.

It took him a few minutes to catch a cab, and he told her to wait inside while he did. She was about to argue with him, but he didn't hang around to discuss it with her, and he was very firm in his directions. He had already paid the taxi for her, so no one else would hijack it, when he came back inside to get her.

'All set.' He put her in and waved as she drove off, still amazed at all he'd done for her. She wondered how she would ever thank him. And by the time she got home to Annabelle, she felt like a dishrag. She would have liked to have a warm bath with her, but Annabelle still hadn't seen her scar, and she had no intention of letting her see it. So she had a bath by herself with her bathroom door locked, and sat at dinner with Annabelle, but ate nothing. She said she was going to eat later, with Daddy.

He came home at seven o'clock just before Annabelle went to bed, and read her a story. And then he and Alex sat down to the dinner Carmen had left them. But Alex only picked at her food. In spite of making an effort to eat it, she just couldn't.

'Did things get better today?' he asked, as solicitously as he could, although Alex clearly had the feeling he didn't really want to discuss it.

'I was fine,' she said, eliminating totally the report that she had spent an hour on the bathroom floor of her office, and another half hour on the couch, with Brock Stevens holding her ice pack. 'I have a lot of new cases.' It was what he wanted to hear, even if it was only part of the story.

'So do we,' he smiled, trying to forget their argument of the night before and all the ugly things they had said to each other. 'We have an awful lot of new clients, thanks to Simon.'

'You don't suppose there's any hanky-panky there, do you, Sam?' she said suspiciously, a lot of new clients of that magnitude almost made her a little nervous.

'Stop looking for problems in everything. Don't be such an attorney,' he chided her, none too gently.

'Occupational hazard.' She smiled weakly at him, feeling nauseous again, just from the smell of his dinner.

She cleaned up alone afterwards, but by the time she was through the little she had eaten had come back to haunt her. She wound up on her bathroom floor again, retching horribly, and this time there was no Brock Stevens with a pillow and an ice pack.

'What's wrong with you?' Sam finally asked as he came to look at her. He had to admit, she looked awful. 'Maybe it's not just the chemotherapy. Maybe you have appendicitis or something.' It was hard for him to believe the chemo would actually do that.

'It's the chemo,' she said, sounding like the voice out of *The Exorcist*, and vomiting instantly again, and he left, unable to watch it.

Eventually, she made it to their bed, and collapsed exhausted, while he glanced over at her in annoyance. 'I know this is unsympathetic of me, but why is it that

253

you were fine at work all day, and you get sick the minute you see me? Is this a bid for sympathy, or do I have this effect on you?' he asked, not realizing what she'd been through all day, and she didn't want to tell him she'd lied about what had happened at the office.

'Very funny.'

'Do you think you're reacting to this emotionally, or maybe you're allergic to this stuff?' He just couldn't understand it or believe it. He had never seen anyone throw up that violently or that often.

'Trust me, it's the chemo,' she said again. 'I have a sheet that tells you what to expect. Would you like to read it?'

'Not really,' he said honestly, 'I'll take your word for it.' And then, as though he were still trying to explain it, 'You were never like this when you were pregnant.'

'I didn't have cancer, and I wasn't having chemo-therapy,' she said dryly, still trying to recover from the onslaught. 'Maybe that made a difference.'

'I think this is psychological. I really think you should call your doctor.'

'I did. She said this is unfortunate, but normal.'

'It doesn't seem normal to me.' He didn't want to understand it. He had complete denial.

In the end, they went to sleep, and when she awoke the next morning, she was nauseous again, but she didn't vomit. They both went to work normally, and she took Annabelle to school, which made her feel better. Every little step toward normalcy was a victory suddenly, and she managed to get through an entire morning at work without feeling sick or being distracted.

It was only that afternoon, working with Brock again, that her turkey sandwich got the better of her and she wound up back on her bathroom floor feeling like she was dying. He didn't hesitate to come in this time, and she was shocked to realize that he was holding her head and her shoulders while she vomited and she didn't even care. In fact, it was less frightening not to be alone and have him with her. She was ashamed for feeling that way, but when she lay against him afterwards, she looked up at him, wondering why he did it.

'You should have been a doctor.' She grinned foolishly at him. This was certainly one way to establish a friendship.

'I hate the sight of blood,' he confessed.

'But not the sight of vomit? What is it with you, you like women who throw up?'

'I love 'em,' he laughed. 'I ended a lot of dates like this in high school and college. I got pretty good at it. Things are supposed to be a little more sophisticated in New York, but maybe not, huh?'

'You're crazy,' she was still too weak to move, and they were sitting on her bathroom floor again, as she leaned against him. 'But I'm beginning to like you.' It was kind of like being married. There was no embarrassment, just her need, and his willingness to fill it. For a moment, she wondered if God had sent her just the right friend at just the right moment.

And then Brock sounded more serious, when he spoke to her again. 'My sister went through this.' He sounded very sad when he said it.

'Chemotherapy?' She sounded surprised, as though no one had ever been through it before her.

'Yeah. Breast cancer just like you. She almost gave up the treatment plenty of times. I was a junior in college, and I went home to take care of her. She was ten years older than I was.'

'Was?' Alex asked nervously, and he smiled.

'Is. She got through it. You'll get through it too. But you have to do the chemo, no matter how bad it gets, or how terrible it is, or how much you hate it. You've *got* to do it.'

'I know. It scares the hell out of me. Six months seems like forever.'

'It isn't,' he said, sounding older than he was. 'Dead is forever.'

'I get it. Honest.'

'You can't screw around, Alex. You have to take the pills, no matter how sick they make you, and go for the treatments. I'll go with you if you want. I went with her. She hated them, and she was afraid of needles.'

'I can't say I loved it either, but it didn't seem so bad, until I started puking my brains out. But then again, it's one way to meet friends.' She smiled up at him and he grinned. He wasn't wearing his glasses and his tie was askew. He had a blond boyish look, but at the same time, his eyes said he was much wiser. At thirty-two, he had seen a lot more than she knew. He had an old soul, and a good heart, and he really liked her.

'Shall we go back to work?' she asked after a little while, and Liz was just putting some mail on her desk, and was surprised to see them both come out of the bathroom.

'Hi,' Alex said casually, 'we were having a meeting.'

Liz laughed, and had no idea what they were doing in there, but it seemed funny to her as she went back to her desk.

'People are going to think we're shooting up or snorting cocaine if we keep this up,' Alex laughed, 'or having sex in the bathroom.'

'I can think of worse rumors than that.' He laughed easily, and sat down across the desk from her. She was looking better.

'Yeah. Me too.' She hadn't made love with Sam in almost two months and they weren't likely to be doing it again soon, from the look of things between them. But sex didn't seem much of an issue. Survival was more to the point. That was the only issue at the moment. They worked together all afternoon, and at the end of the day, he got her a cab again, although she insisted she felt fine. And on Friday, she managed to take Annabelle to ballet. Remarkably, she was doing everything she needed to. And she wasn't feeling great, but she wasn't totally out of commission either. And she was beginning to think that maybe, just maybe, she'd survive it. Whether or not her marriage would was another thing. She thought that a great deal less likely.

Chapter 13

Dr Webber was very pleased with Alex's progress the following Monday. 'You're doing fine,' she complimented her. Her blood count was good. And they were able to do the intravenous treatment, preceded by dextrose and water, which was a little less traumatic for Alex, now that she knew what to expect from the treatment.

This time she got just as sick, but it didn't come as big a surprise to her. And Brock continued to nurse her, and Liz to watch her like a guardian angel.

'I'm starting to feel guilty about this,' she said to Brock, as they sat on her bathroom floor again the day after her second treatment.

'Why?' He looked puzzled.

'Because you're not having chemotherapy, I am. Why should you have to go through all this? You're not married to me. This is my nightmare, not yours. You don't have to do this.' She couldn't understand why he was so kind to her. There was no reason for it, though it certainly helped her. He was the only person who was really there for her at the moment.

'Why not share it?' he said simply. 'Why not let someone else help you? It could happen to any of us.

258

Lightning can strike any one of us at any moment. No-one's exempt. And if I'm here for you, maybe someone will be there for me one day, if it ever happens.'

'I will,' she said gently. 'I'll be there for you, Brock. I'll never forget this.' And they both knew she meant it.

'I'm actually doing this for a raise,' he said laughingly, as he helped her up. They had been there for an hour. It had been a very rough morning.

'I figured you had to have an ulterior motive,' she grinned. She was a lot more tired this week after the treatment. And Thanksgiving was in two days. It exhausted her just thinking about doing the turkey. 'Why not take my job?' she said jokingly as they sat down again. 'You'd be great at it.'

'I'd rather work with you.' He looked at her as he said it, and for an odd moment she felt something different between them. She wasn't sure what it meant, or if she should acknowledge it. But she looked away, embarrassed for a moment. She was so open with him now, so free, and she wondered if maybe she shouldn't. Maybe they were getting too close. After all, she was a married woman. But he was also just a kid, as she reminded herself, he was ten years younger than she was.

'I like working with you too, Brock,' she said kindly, treating him like her junior again, and then she laughed at herself, which was one of the things he loved about her, 'when I'm not throwing up all over you.'

'I'm very careful to stand behind you,' he said in the way that only people who had been through what they had together could get away with.

'You're disgusting.'

They talked about their Thanksgiving plans late that afternoon. He was going to friends in Connecticut,

259

and she was staying home with Annabelle and Sam. She confessed to him then that she wasn't enthusiastic about doing the cooking.

'Why doesn't he do it then? Can he cook?'

'Well enough, but Thanksgiving is my specialty.' And then she admitted something she hadn't told anyone else. 'I feel like I have to prove something to him. He's very angry about all this. Sometimes I think he hates me for it. I need to show him that I can still do everything I used to, that nothing's changed.' It sounded so pathetic when she said it, but he seemed to understand perfectly. Better than Sam did.

'It's only changed temporarily. Can't he understand that? Even if you can't do it now, you will later.'

'He's still too angry to see that.'

'That's rough on you.'

'Yeah, tell me about it.'

'How's your little one holding up?'

'She's doing okay. She gets worried when I'm sick, and I try to keep it away from her as much as possible. None of this is easy.'

'You need good friends to help you through it,' he said warmly.

'I'm lucky to have you.' She smiled at him. And the night before Thanksgiving, she gave him a hug and told him that she was thankful for him this year. They went downstairs together, and for an odd instant, she felt sad when she left him. She could be so honest and outspoken with him. While she sat throwing up next to him, she had come to rely on him, and on being able to tell him her feelings. Suddenly a four-day holiday without talking to him seemed very lonely.

And when she got home, she saw the turkey in the refrigerator, and thought of all the work she had to do the next day, making stuffing and yams, and popovers, and vegetables and mashed potatoes. And Sam always liked both pumpkin and mince pie, and Annabelle liked apple. And she had promised to make pureed chestnuts this year, and homemade cranberry sauce. It made her feel ill just thinking about it, but she knew that this year, more than any year, she really had to. She felt as though her relationship with Sam was resting on it, and how much she could prove to him that she could still do it.

He had had his own tender partings at the office too. Daphne was going to Washington, D.C., that night to visit friends, and he felt an ache of loneliness when he took her to the train and watched her leave. He was getting more and more attached to her, and more and more unhappy whenever he didn't see her. It frightened him to know he would be alone with Alex for four days, but he acknowledged that maybe it would do them good. But as soon as he got home that night, he realized that it wasn't going to be easy to pretend that things were the way they always had been.

She was lying on their bed with an ice pack on her head, and she had just thrown up, Annabelle told him.

'Mommy's sick,' she said quietly, 'will we still have turkey?'

'Of course we will,' he reassured her, and put her to bed, and then came back to look at his wife, stretched out miserably on their bed. 'Do you want to go to a restaurant tomorrow and just forget it?' he asked, with a tone of accusation.

'Don't be silly,' Alex said, wishing they could forget the whole thing, but of course they couldn't. 'I'll be fine.'

'You don't look fine.' He was always torn between thinking she was exaggerating, and it was really psychological, and feeling sorry for her. It was hard for him to know what to think. 'Can I get you anything? Ginger ale? Coke? Something to settle your stomach?' She was guzzling whole bottles of Maalox these days, but nothing helped her.

She got up again after a little while, and went to do what she could in the kitchen. She set the table for the next day, and as she did, she realized that each step was an agony. She felt crushed by exhaustion. Her whole body ached, and she wondered if she was coming down with the flu, or just having more side effects from the chemo. Her bladder bothered her too that night, and by the time she got to bed, Sam was asleep and she felt like death and she looked it. He had promised to help her in the morning.

She set her alarm clock for six-fifteen, so she could put the turkey in the oven. It was a big bird, and it would take a long time to cook. They ate their Thanksgiving dinner at noon usually. But when she got up, she was too sick to move, and she lost an hour throwing up as quietly as she could in the bathroom.

But by the time Annabelle got up, she was putting the turkey in, and a little while later Sam joined them. Annabelle wanted to go to the Macy's Thanksgiving Day parade, and Alex didn't have the heart to ask him not to and help her cook dinner.

They left around nine o'clock, and Alex was doing the best she could in the kitchen. She had made the stuffing, done the vegetables, and was about to start on the potatoes. They had bought the pies fortunately, but she still hadn't tackled the popovers or the chestnuts.

And the moment they left, Alex was seized with a bout of vomiting that left her choking and breathless. She was so frightened she almost called 911, and suddenly longed for Brock to be there to help her. She got an ice pack for herself, and finally stood in the shower, throwing up, thinking that might help. She was still in her nightgown, looking gray, when they came back at eleven-thirty.

'Didn't you get dressed?' He looked shocked when he looked at her. She hadn't even combed her hair, which told him she hadn't even bothered to make the effort. But the turkey smelled good, and everything was either in the oven or on the stove. 'What time do we eat?' he asked, as Annabelle went to her room to play and he flipped on the television to watch football.

'Not till one. I started the turkey a little late.' It was a miracle, considering how sick she'd been that morning.

'Do you need help?' he asked casually, as he put his feet up. It was more than a little late, and she didn't say anything. She had managed to do all of it, which amazed no one more than it did her. Sam had no idea what she'd been battling to do it.

She went to get out of her nightgown then, and put on a white dress and comb her hair. But she didn't have time or feel well enough to put on makeup. She was almost the color of the dress when they finally sat down to eat. And Sam glanced at her, as he carved, irritated that she hadn't made the effort to put on makeup. Did she want to look sick? Did she want them to feel sorry for her? Using a little blush certainly wouldn't have killed her.

But Alex had no idea how bad she looked, although she certainly felt it. She felt as though her whole body were dipped in lead, and she could scarcely move as she served their dinner.

Sam said the same grace they always did, and

Annabelle told her mother all about the parade. And five minutes after they'd started to eat, Alex had to make a wild dash from the table. The work, and the heat in the kitchen, and the smells had just been too much for her. She couldn't do it. She did everything she could to stop throwing up, but she couldn't.

'For God's sake,' Sam came to snarl at her, desperate to keep up the appearance of normalcy for Annabelle, and himself, 'can't you at least make the effort to sit there?'

'I can't,' she said, between retching and tears, 'I can't stop.'

'Force yourself, for chrissake. She deserves a better Thanksgiving than this. We all do.'

'Stop it!' she screamed at him, sobbing openly, shouting so loud they both knew Annabelle could hear them, 'stop doing this to me, you bastard! I can't help it!'

'The hell you can't, dragging around all day in your nightgown, wearing that goddamn white face like a ghost so it scares everyone. You don't even try anymore, except to go to work. But for us, you let it all hang out and puke all over yourself whenever it suits you.'

'Go fuck yourself,' she moaned, and then threw up all over again. Maybe he was right. Maybe it was emotional. Maybe she just couldn't take any more shit from him. But whatever it was, she couldn't stop it. She didn't get back to the table until dessert, and poor little Annabelle looked quiet and sad when she saw her mother.

'Do you feel better, Mommy?' she asked in a small voice, with big, unhappy eyes. 'I'm sorry you're sick.' Maybe he was right. Maybe they all felt responsible. Maybe she was making everyone miserable. Maybe it would be better if she died. She didn't know what to think anymore, or what had happened to him. He was a complete stranger, everything he had ever meant to her, all the gentleness and love he had shown her for years, had totally vanished.

'I'm okay, sweetheart. I feel better now,' she said to Annabelle, and ignored Sam. And after dinner, Annabelle lay on the couch with her, and Alex told her stories. She let Sam do all the cleaning up, and he looked furious when he was finished. Annabelle had just gone to her room to get a video, when he came out of the kitchen and saw Alex.

'Thanks for a great Thanksgiving,' he said sarcastically, 'remind me to go somewhere else next year.'

'Be my guest.' He hadn't said a word to thank her for all the work she'd done, or all the effort.

'You had to ruin it for her, didn't you? You couldn't even sit there for an hour, just so she'd be sure to know how sick you are.'

'When did you turn into a complete prick, Sam?' Alex asked casually, as she looked up at him. 'You know, I never realized what a miserable human being you were before. I guess I was too busy.'

'Maybe we both were,' he muttered, and stalked into the study to watch football. He'd had other Thanksgivings like this before. Years when his mother had been too sick even to come out of her room, or cook a turkey. His father usually got drunk. And once he was at school, he hadn't even bothered to come home for Thanksgiving. The holidays meant a lot to him, and it meant a lot to him to have Alex make the effort. She always had before. But now, she was just like his mother, and all it did was make him hate her.

After the football game, he went out alone that afternoon. He went for a long walk in the park, by himself, and when he came back, they ate leftovers, and Alex seemed to be in better spirits. Having ruined their Thanksgiving meal, she was free to perk up now, and feel better. Or at least that was his perception of it.

Annabelle still seemed subdued, and she had asked her mother why she and Daddy shouted all the time, and why they were angry at each other. Alex told her it didn't mean anything, grown-ups just did that sometimes. But Annabelle still looked worried.

Sam put Annabelle to bed himself that night, and made a point of saying to Alex that she was probably too sick to do it, and remembering what Annabelle had said about their arguing, Alex said nothing to him.

She went to their room, after kissing Annabelle good night, and lay on her bed, thinking of how miserable their life was. How bitter it all had become. It was hard to believe things would ever get any better.

And she surprised Sam with what she said when he came back from putting Annabelle to bed. Alex looked over at him with a look of resignation. Maybe she had to finally accept it, that things were never going to be the same again, and it was all over.

'You don't have to be here, you know. I'm not holding you hostage.'

'What's that supposed to mean?' He looked more than a little startled, and she suddenly wondered if he'd been waiting for this. Maybe he just didn't have the guts to tell her he wanted out, and he had been waiting for her to end it. He seemed to be looking for excuses lately to hate her.

'It means that you seem to be pretty unhappy these days, and you don't seem to want to be here. Anytime you want out, Sam, the door is open.' They were the hardest words she'd ever said, but she knew they needed saying. And after all she'd been through in the past two months, nothing was as hard as it had once been. She was fighting for her life. And her marriage.

'Are you telling me to get out?' he asked, almost hopefully, she thought.

'No, I'm not. I'm telling you that I love you, and I want to stay married to you, but if that's not reciprocal, if you don't want to be married to me anymore, you can leave anytime you want to.'

'Why are you saying that?' he asked suspiciously. What did she know? What had someone told her? Was she a mind reader? Or had she been listening to gossip about Daphne?

'I'm saying that because I'm beginning to feel like you hate me.'

'I don't hate you,' he said sadly, and then he looked at her cautiously, afraid to say too much, but he knew he had to be honest. 'I just don't know what I feel anymore. I'm angry about what happened to us. It's like lightning struck us two months ago, and nothing's been the same since.' They were the same words Brock had used only that week about his sister. Lightning. 'I'm angry, I'm scared, I'm sad. You don't seem the same to me anymore. Neither do I. And I can't stand all this constant talk of sickness and treatment.' They hardly ever talked about it, but just the reality of it was too much for him, and Alex knew that.

'I think I remind you of your mother now,' Alex said honestly, 'and that's too much for you to deal with. Maybe you're afraid I'm going to die and abandon you the way she did.' She had tears in her eyes when she said it, but it didn't bring him any closer. 'I'm afraid of that, too. But I'm doing everything I can to keep that from happening.'

'Maybe you're right. Maybe it's all a lot more complicated than it appears. But I think it's a lot simpler. I think we've both changed, something snapped between us.'

'And? Now what?'

'That's what I haven't figured out yet.'

'Let me know when you do. Do you want to see a therapist with me?' she asked. 'Lots of people going through what I am see therapists, ours isn't the first marriage that's been on the line because of one partner or the other having cancer.'

'Christ, why do you have to blame it all on that?' Just her saying the word seemed to make him nervous. 'What does that have to do with it?'

'That's when everything started, Sam. Everything was fine before that.'

'Maybe not. Maybe this just brought it to a head. Maybe three years of sex on schedule and hormones and trying to have another baby did us in.' It had never seemed to bother him before, but anything was possible.

'Do you want counseling?' she asked again, but he shook his head in answer.

'No, I don't.' All he wanted now was Daphne. That was his cure, his escape, his freedom. 'I want to work this out myself.'

'I don't think you can, Sam. I don't think either of us can. Are you moving out?' she asked nervously, afraid he might, but seeing no other answer.

'I don't think we should do that to Annabelle, particularly before Christmas, and her birthday.' Alex wanted to scream 'what about me?' But she didn't. 'What I want is more freedom. I think we should go our own ways, without owing each other any explanations. Let's talk about it again in a couple of months, maybe after Annabelle's birthday.'

'What'll we say to her?' Alex felt devastated, but tried not to show it.

'That's up to you. As long as we're both living here, I doubt if she'll even notice.'

'Don't be so sure. She asked me today why we shout at each other all the time now. She knows, Sam. She's not stupid.'

'Then it's up to us to behave better in front of her,' he said in a voice filled with reproach that made her want to hit him. He was no longer the man she married and loved. But for Annabelle's sake she had to make the new arrangement work.

'I think this is going to be harder than you think,' Alex said honestly as she looked at him across their bedroom. After nearly seventeen years of marriage, it was going to be impossible to live together like roommates.

'It'll be as easy as we make it. Besides, I have a lot of traveling to do in the next few months.'

'Your business seems to be changing dramatically,' she commented, trying not to think of their shattered personal life, 'what's that all about?'

'Simon has really opened things up for us.'

'I still think you should be leery of him, Sam. Maybe your instincts were correct right from the beginning.'

'I think you're paranoid, and I'm not going to discuss it with you.'

'I see. What do we do now? Just say good morning and good evening in the halls? Do we eat dinner with each other anymore?'

'If it works out with our schedules. I don't see why things have to change that much from the way they are now, at least as far as Annabelle is concerned. But I'll move into the guest room.'

'How will you explain that to her?' Alex asked with interest. He seemed to have it all figured out, and she wondered if he'd already planned it, and she'd walked right into it for him. She didn't trust him anymore either, any more than she did his new partner, Simon. She had drawn up the partnership papers for him, and she just didn't like Simon, or any of the things he'd asked for.

'With you so sick,' Sam said sarcastically, as though she were faking it, 'I'm sure she'll understand that I don't want to disturb you.'

'That's big of you,' Alex said coolly, concealing all the hurt and disappointment she felt, 'this is certainly going to be interesting.'

'I think it's the only solution for right now. It's a good compromise.'

'Between what and what? Walking out on me because I lost a breast, and just ditching me because you're tired of me? What compromise are we making? What effort have you made since all of this happened?' She was angry at him, and hurt, and devastated by everything that had happened. He was right. It was like being hit by lightning, and she knew now that they would be scarred forever.

'I'm sorry you see it that way. But at least we're trying, for Annabelle's sake.'

'We're not trying,' she corrected him, 'we're faking it. We're covering up for her. Who do you think you're kidding, Sam? This marriage is over.'

'I'm not ready to divorce you,' he announced patronizingly, and once again she wanted to get up off the bed and hit him.

'That's big of you. Why not? Do you think it would

look bad? Poor Alex gets her boob lopped off and you can't just walk out and divorce her? It looks a lot better to wait a few months. Actually, technically, you could wait the full six months of the chemo, and then everyone would think you'd stuck by me. Christ, Sam, you stink. You're the biggest fraud in town, and I don't give a damn who you hide it from. I know it. And you know it. And that's enough. Go do whatever the hell you want. We're finished.'

'How can you be so sure? I wish I were,' he said honestly. He wanted to be free, but another part of him wasn't ready to leave her. He wanted all his options open with no responsibilities. He wanted it all. Daphne, and the possibility of coming back to Alex, maybe a year later. He didn't want to give up Alex forever.

'You've convinced me,' she said, in answer to his question. 'You've been a complete shit to me ever since my mastectomy. The only excuse I've been able to make for you is that you couldn't handle it, but you know what? That's getting old, Sam. I'm getting tired of making excuses. He's tired . . . he's freaked out . . . this is hard for him . . . this reminds him of his mother . . . he doesn't get it . . . it's too threatening for him . . . You're a miserable excuse for a human being.' There were tears in her eyes as she said it, and tears in his while he listened.

'I'm sorry, Alex.' He turned away from her then, and she started to cry softly. What a rotten time they had had ever since they'd discovered the shadow on the mammogram. It wasn't fair, but it still had to be dealt with. 'I'm sorry,' he said again, this time looking at her, but he made no move to approach her, or console her, he just couldn't.

He walked out of the room, and she heard him in

the study then, and half an hour later, she heard the front door close. He never said another word to her, he went out and walked for hours, to the river, and then slowly south, until he finally found himself on Fifty-third Street. He knew what he wanted, and he wondered if he had destroyed his marriage just so he could have it. But it was too late to think about that now. He had done what he had to, or what he wanted. It was too late to pick up the pieces, he was only very sorry he had had to hurt her. But she had hurt him too, even if it wasn't her fault. In an odd way, he felt as though she had betrayed him.

He stopped at a phone booth on Second Avenue, and he knew it didn't make sense. She had gone to Washington for Thanksgiving. But he wanted to call her anyway, just to hear her voice on her machine, and he wanted to leave her a message and tell her that he loved her.

She answered it on the second ring, and for an instant he was too surprised to answer.

'Daphne?'

'Yes.' Her voice was sensual and sleepy. It was after midnight, and she'd been in bed. 'Who is this?'

'It's me. What are you doing here? I thought you were in Washington for Thanksgiving.'

She laughed, and he could almost see her stretch lazily as she did it. He was freezing in the phone booth.

'I was. We gorged ourselves on an enormous lunch, and went ice-skating, and I flew home tonight. They were all going their separate ways tomorrow. It wasn't really meant to be a weekend. Where are you?' He hadn't called her at night since Alex's chemotherapy had started and Daphne only called sparingly. He was married after all, and she was *very* cautious. She

272

was too smart to do otherwise, and she respected his situation.

Suddenly he chuckled mischievously into the phone in answer to her question. 'I'm freezing my ass off in a phone booth on Fifty-third and Second. I've been walking for hours, and I wanted to call you.'

'What on earth are you doing there? Why don't you come up, at least for a cup of tea. I promise I won't bite you.'

'I'll hold you to that, you know,' and then, feeling very vulnerable and battered, it had been a rough day since he'd last seen her, 'I missed you.'

'I missed you too,' she said very softly, sounding sexier than ever. 'How was Thanksgiving?'

'Pretty grim. I don't really want to talk about it. She was sick. It was hard on everyone, Annabelle most of all . . . I don't know . . . we had a long talk tonight. I'll tell you all about it.' But just listening to him, she knew that something was different. He seemed freer suddenly, and much more open. He sounded tired, and sad, but he didn't sound as anxious or conflicted.

'Come on up, before you freeze.'

'I'll be there.'

He was less than a block away, and he ran all the way to her door. Suddenly, he knew that it was the only place he wanted to be. It was the only place he had wanted to be ever since he met her. She was so healthy and young, so beautiful, and so perfect.

He pressed the buzzer downstairs, and she buzzed him in, and he bounded up the steps like a teenager, and then stopped as he saw her standing in the doorway. Her luxurious black hair hung past her shoulders, concealing one breast, and leaving the other bare. She wore a delicate white cotton nightgown, with tiny embroideries on it, which you could see through completely. Her entire body was revealed to him as she stood there, and then without a word, he went to her, and pulled her inside, and closed the door behind them.

The apartment was cozy and warm, and he pulled the nightgown over her head, without waiting a moment, he brushed back her silky dark hair, and stood admiring her in all her splendor, the perfect breasts, the tiny waist, the long, graceful legs, and the exquisite place where they came together.

'Oh my God . . .' was all he said. There was only one small light on in the bedroom, and he laid her on the feather bed she had brought with her from England. She was beautiful beyond his dreams, sensual beyond all his expectations, experienced beyond anything he could realize and she brought him to the edge of ecstasy and back again, and felt him explode inside her half a dozen times before morning. It was the most extraordinary night of his life. He had made a fire in the fireplace, and made love to her on the floor in front of it, and then on the bed again, and then finally in the bathtub. They had made love before the dawn, and again after it, and when they awoke at noon, he couldn't believe that he wanted her again, and was still capable of doing anything about it. But she let her silky lips drift across his stomach down his thighs, and then back up between his legs until they found what they were looking for and he craved, and this time he came in her mouth with a shuddering furor.

'Oh God . . . Daphne . . . you're going to kill me . . .' he murmured happily, '. . . but what a way to die. . .' He took her in his arms and held her there, unable to believe his good fortune. They had waited months for this, and he hadn't wanted to come to her until he was free of Alex. But now he knew that he was, he had to be. There was no other woman he wanted in the world now, except Daphne.

'I love you,' he whispered as she drifted off to sleep in his arms again, with her back to him, and her perfectly round bottom pressed against him, but this time, he was truly sated.

'I love you too,' she whispered back, smiling. He had been well worth waiting for. She had always known he would be. He cupped her breasts with his hands then, and thought of how lucky he was, and he drifted off to sleep with her, trying not to let himself think of Alex.

Chapter 14

If nothing else, out of sheer politeness, Sam called Alex late Friday afternoon and told her he wouldn't be home for the rest of the weekend. He didn't say where he was and she didn't ask any questions. He said he'd call her and check in, and then he spoke to Annabelle and said he'd miss her. He wondered if Alex knew where he was, or why, but he didn't let himself think of it. After that, he and Daphne went to Bloomingdale's and he bought half a dozen shirts, some jeans, corduroy pants, a jacket, socks, some underwear, and a sweater. And then they went to the drugstore and bought a razor and all the toiletries he needed. He didn't want to go home just yet, he didn't want to see them. He wanted to be completely alone with Daphne.

He cooked dinner for Daphne that night, and she pretended to help him, but she insisted on wandering in and out of the kitchen stark naked. And in the end, he almost burned their dinner. They left it in the microwave and went to bed. And at midnight, she made him an omelet. But most of their time was spent exploring each other's bodies, and preferences. They talked long into the night and he made popcorn and they watched old movies, but they kept missing the essential parts of the plot when he made love to her again, and they kept coming back just as the film was ending.

They spent another extraordinary night in each other's arms, and by Saturday morning it was as though they had always been lovers. He knew he wanted to stay with her, and spend the rest of his life with her. All he had to do now was deal with Alex.

'What do you want to do today?' he asked as they stretched lazily, and the prospect of making love all day crossed his mind again, but he thought they should at least make an effort to do something.

'Can you ice skate?' Daphne asked, looking like a child as she sat up in bed next to him, but a very well-endowed one.

'I was on the hockey team at Harvard,' he said proudly.

'Shall we do that?'

It was like starting life all over again. She was so young and so alive. She had no responsibilities and no burdens. They went to Wollman Memorial in Central Park, and he found that she was a very good skater. They danced, and spun around, and did loops around each other. She did very pretty camel spins, and he was impressed. And then he took her to lunch at Tavern-on-the-Green, but by two o'clock they were back in bed again, feeling as though they had been separated forever.

'What are we going to do about work?' he asked as they lay side by side after making love for the second time at four-thirty. 'I'm not sure I can stay away from you long enough to get up and go to the office.' Not to mention the fact that he had told Alex that he would live at home for the next two months and talk about their relationship again in January after Annabelle's birthday. That had been before he had made love to Daphne. Now everything had changed again. But he still thought he should live by his agreement.

He had already explained it to Daphne the day before, and she thought it a very reasonable solution.

'It would be awfully hard on your little girl if you suddenly disappeared, particularly right before Christmas,' Daphne said sympathetically. He was glad that she saw it that way. It made it a lot easier for him. But she had always been very patient with him, right from the beginning.

'I can't wait for you to meet her.'

'Slowly, my darling, slowly,' she said, describing the sexual tortures she designed for him a few moments later. All thoughts of their families disappeared in an instant. But later that night she told him that she was taking her son skiing in Switzerland for a week at Christmas. It would make the choice of who to be with over the holidays a little easier for him, and he suggested he meet her after her son went back to his father. They agreed on a week in Gstaad, followed by a few days in Paris.

It was a weekend of making plans and becoming friends, and falling in love as he told himself he never had before, but that was only because he was trying to forget Alex.

And she was trying to forget him too. She spent a quiet weekend with Annabelle, trying to marshal her forces. She was still sick, but she didn't throw up quite as often. Liz called to see how she was, and a couple of friends called her too, having heard the rumors. But she didn't feel like seeing anyone, and she couldn't help wondering where Sam had gone, if he was alone, or just hiding. Annabelle seemed willing to accept the story that he had gone away on a business trip, even on Thanksgiving weekend.

Sam never came home on Sunday night, although she thought he would, but she wasn't worried about it. She was sad, but not really concerned. He had called Annabelle a couple of times over the weekend, but Alex hadn't talked to him. She had just handed the phone to her daughter, and tried not to think about her husband.

It was actually a relief when Monday rolled around, and she could go back to work and try to forget her problems.

And after she dropped Annabelle off at school, she got to the office and felt better. Everyone looked rested and happier after the long weekend. Even Alex did, although it certainly hadn't been a good one.

'How was the holiday?' Brock asked, as they worked that afternoon. He had had a great time in Connecticut with his friends, although he'd gotten a lot of bruises, he said, playing touch football.

'Honestly?' She smiled cautiously in answer to his question about the weekend. 'It stank. I think Sam and I have finally figured out that it's not going to work anymore. The party's over. I was sick as a dog on Thanksgiving, and he was mad as hell. I keep thinking it reminds him of when his mother was dying and she took them all down with her, but he won't admit it. He just gets crazy and behaves like an asshole.

'Anyway, we've agreed to go our separate ways, while living under one roof, which should be a challenge. I don't have the energy to argue about it. We're going to review the situation in seven weeks, after Annabelle's birthday.'

'That sounds very civilized.'

'I guess it is,' she said sadly. 'Actually, I think it sounds pathetic. It's amazing what two people can do to each other when they really try. I never thought this would happen to us, but I guess life is full of surprises.' She felt tired and old, and unable to fight him. She just didn't feel up to it. Although for the next two weeks she felt a lot better than she had before that. She had stopped taking the pills, according to her treatment plan, and she wasn't due for another intravenous treatment until two weeks before Christmas.

But when she started them again, she was just as sick as she had been the first time. It overwhelmed her particularly, because with all the problems in her life, she hadn't done her Christmas shopping, and suddenly she realized she just couldn't. She had the F.A.O. Schwarz catalog on her desk, and she had circled several things, but she didn't have the energy to shop for clothes or little gifts for Annabelle and Sam, or anything for her friends or colleagues.

'I feel like shit,' she admitted to Brock, as she lay on the couch in her office. He was used to seeing her that way now, and sometimes she worked with him while she lay down, and evaluated the information he gave her.

'What can I do for you?' he asked sympathetically. 'Do you want me to do some shopping?'

'Since when do you have time for that?' They were both buried in an avalanche of new cases. She had passed a couple on to Matt, but she and Brock were trying to cover the others.

'I could go at night. The stores are open late. Why don't you give me a shopping list?' But she didn't even have time to answer him. She fled to the bathroom, throwing up, and it was half an hour later before she left the bathroom and could talk again.

And the following week, she had another intravenous treatment, which left her even weaker. It was only a week before Christmas, and she still hadn't bought a single present. But by then, Liz and Brock took the matter out of her hands for her. She was so sick that she had to stay home for a day, and Liz came and picked up her list at the apartment. She was sad to see her so ill. And when she got there, she found Alex in tears. She had been standing in front of her bathroom mirror and crying. Her hair was coming out in clumps, and she had fistfuls of long red hair in her hands when she came to the door to let Liz in.

'Look what's happening to me,' she sobbed. She knew that it had been a strong possibility, but she hadn't even had time to buy the wig Dr Webber had suggested. She had spent the morning throwing up, and then gone to the mirror to see that her hair was falling out in bunches. 'I can't stand it,' she sobbed, as Liz held her in her arms, trying to console her. 'Why did this happen to me? It's not fair.' She was crying like a child, and Liz was glad she had come instead of Brock. He idolized her and it would have broken his heart to see her.

Liz led her into the living room, after Alex threw the hair away, and she sat sobbing in her bathrobe. She looked terrible, her face was pale, her eyes were red, there was a new puffiness to her face that one couldn't quite put a finger on, but something about her was different. She was still beautiful but she looked sick, very sick, and desperately unhappy.

'You have to be strong,' Liz reminded her firmly, determined not to let her wallow in self-pity.

'I have been strong,' Alex almost shouted at her, still sobbing. 'And what's it done for me? Sam is as good as gone, I never even see him anymore. He comes in at

281

midnight, or he doesn't come in at all, he lives in the guest room like a stranger, and the only time I ever see him is with my daughter. I'm sick all the time, she's scared of me now, and wait till she sees me without hair. The poor kid isn't even four years old yet, and she has a monster for a mother.'

'Stop it!' Liz snapped at her, and surprised Alex. 'You have a lot to be grateful for, and this isn't going to last forever. You have five more months of this to get through, and then, if you're lucky, it'll be all over. And if Sam is a casualty of real life, then to hell with him. You have to think of yourself now, and your daughter. No one else. Do you understand that?' Alex nodded and blew her nose, surprised by the older woman's sternness, but she knew exactly what she was talking about. She'd been through it. Her husband had been more supportive of her than Sam but it had been her fight, and no one else's, and she said as much to Alex.

'Chemotherapy is miserable, and losing a breast is a terrible thing, but you can't give up. Your hair will grow back, you won't be throwing up forever. You have to look beyond this. Think of what you want to be doing in five months. Keep your mind on that, and not this, hold something out to yourself as a goal,' she suggested wisely.

'Not throwing up anymore would be a great place to start.'

'You'll get used to it eventually. That's a terrible thing to say, but it's true. Even that you can handle.'

'I know. I find myself on the bathroom floor now, kind of expecting to be there. It doesn't surprise me anymore.' And then she looked stricken again. 'But losing my hair does. I know I should have expected it, but I guess I didn't.'

'Have you bought a wig yet?'

'I didn't have time,' Alex said, feeling sad and stupid.

'I'll get you one. A nice red one like your own hair.' Liz patted her shoulder. 'Now where's this Christmas list of yours? I'm going to do what I can today, and then Brock and I are going to divide the rest of it tonight, and see if we can't get it all taken care of. I can finish it for you this weekend.' And Carmen had already promised to stay late to wrap the gifts. They were incredible. Who would have thought three months before that the three most important people in her life would turn out to be her housekeeper, her secretary, and her associate at the law firm? But they were all godsends. And she couldn't have made it without them.

She also would never have expected Sam to fail her. He hardly ever came home, and he stayed away from her, as though he couldn't handle it at all anymore. But whenever she saw him, he looked like he was hurrying out, and he was well dressed and looked very handsome.

Brock and Liz both came by late that night, with a treasure trove of goodies. She had called Brock at work and asked him to pick out a really nice handbag for Liz at Saks. He had bought a beautiful black lizard one, and they both agreed she was going to love it. They had bought beautiful things, and after Liz left, Brock stayed for a while, and had a cup of tea with her in her kitchen.

'Thank you for doing all this. I feel like such a burden to everyone.' But she had no choice, and she knew it. She had to accept that.

'It's not such a big deal,' he said quietly. 'Going Christmas shopping for a friend is not exactly like climbing Mount Kilimanjaro, though I might do that for you too. But you'd have to give me a little warning.'

She smiled gratefully at him, he had been such a good friend, and it meant a lot to her. Staying home for a day had done her good too, and she didn't feel quite as rocky. But she was still feeling sensitive about her hair. She was wearing an Hermès scarf when they dropped by, and Liz had warned him about what had happened. She had wanted to get a wig for her, but she hadn't seen any decent ones, and Alex had said that she was going to get one the next morning.

'Are you alone here now?' Brock asked, referring to Sam, but she understood and shrugged.

'Most of the time.' In the past three weeks, he had traveled a lot and not come home much of the time. She hardly ever saw him. 'I'm getting used to it. I think it's harder on Annabelle, though she sees more of him than I do.'

Brock realized it was going to be a tough Christmas for her, with her marriage on the rocks, and her health so frail, and now losing her hair as well as a breast. He felt sorry for her, and wished he could have changed it for her. He had been planning to go skiing in Vermont between Christmas and New Year's, and wondered if he should have offered to stay in town and keep her company, but he didn't think she'd accept it. And then he had a better idea.

'This might sound a little strange, but would you like to come to Vermont with me between Christmas and New Year's?' Knowing her treatment schedule as well as he did, it was easy to figure out that she would be in the better phase, when she was taking neither pills nor IV treatments. 'You could bring Annabelle too. I'm staying in a house I borrow from friends every year, at Sugarbush. It's very rustic, but it's

284

comfortable. You could sit by the fire all day, and I could put Annabelle in ski school.'

'Actually I think Sam is taking her away with him before he goes to Europe. I think they're going to Disney World.' But she couldn't imagine going to Vermont with Brock, no matter how sympathetic he was or how well she knew him. And Brock could easily see her hesitation.

'Why don't you think about it? It'll be lonely for you here.'

'All right,' she promised, but didn't really mean it.

He stayed for a little while, and then he left, and she went to bed, thinking how lucky she was to have such good friends. And the next morning she felt surprisingly better. Until she looked in the mirror again, and saw that more hair had fallen out during the night. There were three huge locks of it in her scarf, and she had a crazy urge to save it. And when she looked in the mirror, she saw that parts of her scalp were already showing. It made her cry again. She was losing everything. She didn't even feel like a woman now, just a thing, a body that was falling apart slowly. She hastily put her scarf back on before Annabelle came in, and she was surprised to see Sam with her when she went to make her breakfast. He had already given her cornflakes.

'You look pretty, Mommy,' Annabelle said, admiring a dark green suit, and a matching scarf she had found in a drawer. She actually looked very chic and very European.

'What's that all about?' He smiled at her, amused. She looked very glamorous, which was an unusual look for her at the office. 'Going somewhere today?' he asked, purely conversationally. He was trying to be pleasant, and Alex knew it. He had no idea why she was wearing the scarf, and he wasn't sensitive enough to guess, so she didn't tell him.

'I have an appointment this morning.' She had an appointment at a wig store on Sixtieth Street where Dr Webber had sent her. She said they had great styles and varied shades, and were very helpful with her kind of problem. 'Do we need to talk about Christmas again?' Alex asked him across his paper. 'I know Annabelle is going to be here with me, and then you're taking her, was it on the twenty-sixth? For a week?'

'I'm taking her to Disney World until the first, and then I'm flying back here, and leaving for Switzerland.' He smiled at Annabelle. 'And I'll be back on her birthday.'

'Sounds like a tight schedule,' Alex said tartly, wondering where he was going. 'Are you going to be here on Christmas with us, or do you have other plans?' she asked coldly as Annabelle's face fell.

'You're not going to be here, Daddy?'

'Of course I am,' he reassured her, and looked daggers at Alex. 'We'll all be together for Christmas.' She looked immediately relieved, and Alex sat back in her chair and closed her eyes, fighting a wave of nausea. It was so exhausting being with him, and even being with Annabelle sometimes. They took so much from her. It took so much energy just giving them what they needed, and fighting for her survival and dignity with Sam. It was an uphill battle she just didn't have the strength for.

Sam took Annabelle to school, and Alex went straight downtown to the wig store. She felt hesitant when she walked in, but she was amazed at the extent of their selection. Dr Webber had been right and in a very short time, Alex had picked out two very expensive wigs that looked just like her own hair, and then a shorter pageboy she really liked, and a really short one that looked like Annabelle's curls, all in her coppery natural color. She paid for them by check, and cautiously put one on. If anything it was even more lush and a little longer than her own hair, and it was beautifully styled and very glamorous. It was a great look with her green suit, and she tied the scarf around her neck and felt human again. It was amazing the difference hair made. She realized she had been stupid not to buy them sooner.

'Wow! Look at you!' Brock whistled as she walked into her office, and Liz smiled from ear to ear. She knew where Alex had been and she was pleased to see her looking as well as she did. She was still very pale, but she looked a lot better than she had the day before. 'Did you go to the hairdresser?' Brock asked, and then suddenly felt stupid when he remembered what Liz had told him. For a moment, he'd forgotten.

'You could say that.'

'I like it,' he said admiringly, and Alex felt embarrassed suddenly at the way he looked at her. They had gotten so close over the last two months, but they were just friends. Yet once in a while she thought she saw something different in Brock's eyes, as though he was looking at her like a woman, not just a buddy, and it surprised her.

They went right to work and she got a good morning in, and then she lay down on her couch and dozed at lunchtime. Other people were going to Christmas lunches and parties with friends, but all Alex had the energy for was work, and spending time with her daughter.

She worked alone at her desk for the rest of the afternoon, and she met with two of her partners before she went home. Brock was going Christmas shopping again, and when she got home, Carmen was wrapping her presents. It made her feel useless and helpless, but she was too exhausted even to offer to help her.

Sam came home with a Christmas tree that night, and he stuck around long enough to decorate it, and then he left. And she sat alone, feeling depressed, remembering the Christmas before Annabelle was born, only four years before, and countless others. It all seemed so long ago, and like part of another world. It was incredible how much had changed since then. She sat in her bed that night, reading her mail, and trying not to think of Sam, when she noticed an invitation he had left open on the table. It was a Christmas party given by friends, and she put it aside to regret it. She didn't have the energy to go anywhere, certainly not to parties.

It took everything she could muster to take Annabelle to see Santa Claus at Macy's on Saturday, and by the time she got home, she was vomiting again, she was so exhausted. Carmen wasn't there, and after a little while Annabelle wandered into the bathroom to find her. Alex was lying there, on the floor, with her wig off, and her eyes closed. Almost all of her hair was gone now. It had fallen out in a matter of days, and the day before she had cut most of it off, there were just little tufts now, but even those were coming out daily. There was almost nothing left now.

'Mommy! Your hair fell off!' Annabelle screamed, seeing the wig on the floor next to her, and Alex jumped up with a start, she hadn't wanted her to see it. And Annabelle was crying as she looked at her, clutching her own head in terror, as Alex tried to console her.

288

'It's just a wig, sweetheart, it's okay. It's okay.' And then she saw Annabelle looking at her in horror. It wasn't a pretty sight, there was something sick about it, as the little sparse tufts stuck out here and there, and you could see her scalp all around them. Alex had almost wondered if she should shave it. 'Remember, I told you Mommy's hair might fall out. It's okay, it'll grow back.' She was on her knees, holding her, but the little girl only sobbed harder. 'I love you, please don't cry . . .' She hated the wig, and the reason for it. Everything was so wrong in her life suddenly. She wanted to blame it all on Sam but she knew she couldn't.

It took a long time to settle Annabelle down again, and when Carmen came in in the afternoon to baby-sit, she was still upset and Alex told her what had happened.

'It's all right, she'll get used to it.' Carmen patted Alex's arm. Alex had already put the wig on. She put on the shorter one that afternoon, and while Annabelle took a nap, Alex decided to get some air and go for a walk. Christmas was two days away, and she felt as though she had barely acknowledged it. Liz and Brock had done all her shopping for her, except for a beautiful dresser set she had Tiffany's send her for Sam, and an art book she'd been saving for him for ages. She hadn't been to any parties, or seen any friends. Other than their visit to Santa Claus, and the tree Sam and Annabelle had decorated, she hadn't paid any attention at all to Christmas.

'Will you be all right, going out, Mrs Parker?' Carmen asked her with a look of concern.

'I'll be fine. I just want to walk up Madison for five minutes.'

'It's very cold, wear a hat!' she called out, and Alex smiled. She was wearing one of her wigs.

'I don't need one!'

She took the elevator downstairs, and thought about Christmas Eve. Sam had said he would be with them, but she'd hardly seen him all week, and she assumed he was going to the usual parties. He hadn't asked her to join him. He knew she wasn't up to it anyway, and they weren't going anywhere together. She had even declined an invitation from their closest friends to go caroling in Greenwich Village.

She stopped and looked at the shop windows on Madison, and the windows were especially pretty at Ralph Lauren. She was standing there looking at them, when a particularly striking girl came out the door and down the steps, laughing and talking in an English accent. She was wearing a short black coat, and she had fabulous legs in tall black suede boots. And she was wearing a huge sable hat that made her look very romantic. And then she turned to someone and Alex smiled as she saw him stoop to kiss her. It reminded her of years before, and her and Sam. He even looked a little like him. He was wearing a well-cut navy blue coat, and their arms were full of packages wrapped in bright red paper with gold bows. There was something achingly bittersweet about the pair, they looked so young and so in love. They kissed again, and then Alex saw the man looking down at the girl in the hat, and as she looked, she realized who the man was. It was Sam. Her mouth opened and she stared at him, realizing suddenly what had happened. He was in love with someone else, and she couldn't help wondering how long it had gone on, and if it had happened even before she got sick. What if it was all a setup? What if he'd used her sickness as an excuse to leave her?

She wanted to tear her eyes away from them, but she couldn't bring herself to, as he tucked a hand into the woman's arm and they crossed the street to another store as Alex watched them. They had no idea she was there, and Sam had no clue that she had seen him.

They walked into another shop, and Alex felt tears rolling down her cheeks as she realized that it really was all over between them. She couldn't compete with that. The girl looked twenty-five, and even Sam looked suddenly younger. At first, looking at him, she had thought he was thirty, not fifty. She hurried back up Madison then, not hearing the carolers, or the Santa Clauses ringing bells, or seeing the people or the Christmas trees or the windows. She saw nothing except her own life, lying in shards around her.

She was back at the apartment half an hour after she'd left it, looking worse instead of better. She was deathly pale, and her hands shook violently as she hung up her coat, and walked somberly into her bedroom. She closed the door and lay down on the bed, wondering how she would ever face him again. That was why he had wanted his freedom. It had all been a sham, a game, saying that he needed time. What he had needed was a new woman. And he had one.

She walked into the bathroom then, and stood looking at herself in the mirror. To her own eyes, she looked a hundred years old, and as she slowly pulled the wig off, she saw what she had become. She was disfigured and bald. She had cancer, she had lost a breast, and her hair. She thought of the girl she had seen with him, and knew the ugliest of truths. She was no longer a woman.

Chapter 15

Sam came home to them early on Christmas Eve, after he put Daphne on a plane to London. She was going to visit her parents, and her little boy, and Sam was going to join her in Gstaad after he took Annabelle to Disney World and then brought her back to her mother.

He had given Daphne a spectacular diamond bracelet before she left, and a ruby heart pin that he had bought for her at Fred Leighton. Sam had always been generous and he had bought something pretty for Alex too, though nothing quite as important. He had bought her a very handsome Bulgari watch that he knew she'd wanted for a while, but none of the thoughtful little things that expressed his interest and affection. He didn't want to mislead her.

There was no avoiding the fact that Christmas was different this year. No matter what efforts they made, even Annabelle seemed to feel it, and she cried after they put out the cookies for Santa, and the salt and carrots for his reindeer.

'What if he doesn't bring me what I asked for?' she cried, and both Sam and Alex tried to console her. But she was inconsolable and she finally admitted that she was afraid he'd be angry at her because this year she had asked him for something a little 'harder.' 'I asked him to make my Mommy better right away so she can stop taking her medicine, and bring her hair back.' Hearing her words made Alex cry so hard she had to turn away, and even Sam had a hard time with that one.

'What did he say to you?' Sam asked hoarsely. She had asked him that when Alex had taken her to see Santa at Macy's.

'He said that was up to God, not Santa.'

'He's right, Princess,' Sam explained while Alex blew her nose and adjusted her wig. She was wearing the long one. 'But Mommy will get better anyway, and she'll get her hair back.' Sam was surprised to hear about her hair, he hadn't realized she'd lost it. Alex had never told him. It made him realize how out of touch he was. He had been so wrapped up in Daphne and their love affair for the last month, that he hadn't focused on anything else. He hadn't wanted to know what was going on at home, and he hadn't even paid serious attention to what was happening at the office.

Larry and Tom had heckled him a couple of times, and Simon seemed pleased for him. But Larry had said something to him about how sorry he and Frances were about Alex. He seemed to imply that he was sorry about 'them' too. It was obvious, because of Daphne, that they had problems in their marriage. But Sam was anything but sorry. And he figured that his partners were just jealous of him. It never occurred to him that they thought it was rotten of him to leave Alex now, when she was battling chemotherapy and cancer.

Eventually, Annabelle calmed down again, and they put her to bed together. She seemed so happy to see them that way that it tore at Alex's heart. Later

293

when they went out to the kitchen, Sam looked embarrassed.

'I didn't realize you'd lost your hair,' Sam said, as he helped himself to one of Santa's cookies. They had less of everything this year. Fewer cookies, fewer Christmas cakes, fewer presents, less cheer. Even their Christmas tree seemed smaller. With Alex sick, no one else had put in the same effort. And they hadn't sent Christmas cards either. She didn't have the energy, and she wouldn't have known how to sign them. From Alex . . . and maybe Sam . . . sort of.

'I didn't think you'd want me to announce it, about my hair,' Alex said, trying not to think of the woman she'd seen him with the day before. The hardest thing was that it was obvious that it wasn't a casual affair. When she'd seen them together, they looked married.

'It'll grow back,' he said, feeling helpless again. He always felt inadequate and uncomfortable around her.

'My hair will. Our marriage won't,' she said sadly. She knew they had agreed not to discuss it for another month, but it was difficult not to.

'Are you sure of that?' He looked her in the eye, and waited for her answer.

'Aren't you? I get the impression you've already made your mind up.' She had certainly gotten that impression watching him with the English girl outside Ralph Lauren.

'You can never be sure. It's hard not to remember the good times.'

'They don't seem that long ago to me,' she said honestly. 'Maybe you were unhappy for longer than I was.'

'I don't think unhappy's the right word. Confused. I've been confused ever since you got sick. It changed

294

you.' It wasn't ever an accusation. It was a statement. And for him, it justified his behavior and was a ticket to freedom.

'I think it changed both of us. I don't suppose things like this ever leave you where they found you. It's a long, hard road to survival.'

'It must be terrible,' he said, sympathetic for the first time. He was gentler these days, she realized now. Falling in love had mellowed him. But she didn't find that as touching as she might have. 'You've been through an awful lot.'

'With more to come,' she smiled. 'Four and a half months exactly.'

'And then what?'

'Then I wait to see if I get a recurrence. Five years seems to be the magic number. Supposedly I had the right kind of tumor for the good odds, and the chemo is supposed to give me extra insurance. I guess you just go on with your life, and try not to think about it. The women I know who've survived for a long time claim that they don't think about it anymore except when they go in once a year for routine checkups. I'd like to be there now. This is still pretty scary.' It was the first real conversation they'd had in three months, and she was amazed he was willing to talk about it. Whoever the girl was, she had almost made him human. But Alex didn't feel grateful to her, only envious and sad, and angry.

'If you get a recurrence,' he tried to sound encouraging, 'you just fight it again, I guess.'

'Not likely,' she said matter-of-factly, wishing she could take her wig off. It was very itchy. But she wouldn't have dared to let him see how she looked now. 'Except for very rare cases, you don't survive recurrences. You die. That's why they're so aggressive

295

the first time, about treatment.' He understood it better now, but he was shocked by what she had told him. He didn't think he'd heard it quite so bluntly before, or maybe he just hadn't listened. Seeing her now, after being with Daphne, tore at his heartstrings, but nothing else. For him, the rest was over. All he felt for her now was pity, and tenderness for the memories of better times.

'What are you doing while Annabelle's away?' he asked, trying to change the subject. It was getting a little heavy for him.

'Nothing. Sleep, rest, work. My social life is not exactly overactive these days. I only have so much energy. I use it on Annabelle and my cases.'

'Why don't you go away? It might do you good. Or can you do that?'

'I could. I get a two-week break from treatment every month, but I'd rather stay here.' She didn't want to go away with Brock, though he had invited her. In spite of their close working relationship, she hardly knew him. And she didn't want to go alone. There was no point. She was better off in her own apartment, her own bed, with her own things, close to her doctor, if she had a problem. She was very introverted these days, and very dependent on the familiar. There were too many frightening elements in her life now to make her open to new ones.

'I hate to think of you here alone,' he said guiltily. It was odd, now that Daphne was gone, he suddenly felt more responsible for Alex. It was like an illness, pulling him this way and that, and he didn't really like it. He was happy that he was taking Annabelle away the day after Christmas.

'I'll be fine. I really don't want to go anywhere. And I've got plenty at the office to keep me busy.'

'There's more to life than work,' he said with a smile, and she looked right at him in answer.

'Is there, Sam?'

He walked out of the kitchen then without giving her an answer. But he wondered if she had a sixth sense about Daphne, or if someone had told her. He doubted it. She was too involved with herself right now to even think there was someone else. She couldn't possibly suspect it.

All of Annabelle's presents were wrapped and hidden in a locked closet. They set them out under the tree shortly after nine, and then they retired to their own rooms, like strangers. She read for a little while, and she heard the phone ring at midnight. But she let him answer. She knew it wouldn't be for her. And she was right. It was Daphne, freshly arrived in London, and missing him already. It made him feel wonderful talking to her, and when he did, he realized again how much it depressed him to be around Alex. She wasn't exactly fun these days. She seemed to have given up on life, and everything about her seemed to be falling away and dying, her spirits, her hair, their marriage. He knew he should be more supportive, but he just couldn't.

'I miss you terribly, darling,' Daphne reassured him. 'I'm not going to be able to bear it without you. You'll have to hurry over. My God, it's cold here.' She had forgotten the miseries of the bitter London winter, and the heat in her flat wasn't working. All she had was the fireplace, she complained, and no Sam to keep her warm.

'Stop,' he said, almost wincing with the pain of missing her, 'or I'm going to get on the next Concorde.'

'I wish you would.' But they both knew he couldn't.

297

They both had to fulfill their parental duties. 'I can't bear it.'

They hung up finally, and his whole body keened for her, as he lay in bed and thought of the remarkable young woman who had changed his whole life since Thanksgiving. He had never known anyone quite like her. Even Alex, at her best, had never had that much passion.

Annabelle woke at six a.m. on Christmas Day, and it was a long, happy day for her, and a nice one for Sam and Alex. Annabelle loved all her gifts and Sam was touched by the lavishness of Alex's gift to him, and he said he loved it. She liked the watch, although she understood the message he had been giving her, that this was no longer a time for personal gifts between them, and the clarity of it hurt her feelings. But other than that, they had a very nice time together.

She managed to cook a roast beef and popovers for all of them, and to conceal how sick she felt through most of it. But it wasn't nearly as disastrous as Thanksgiving. She lay down afterwards to rest, and just for the fun of it, since they were at home, she wore her short wig, and she and Annabelle looked like twins. Sam even said he liked it.

She wore a red sweater and black suede pants, and she looked surprisingly pretty. Her face had filled out a little bit, and she had gained some weight, but not enough to object to. It was odd, given how sick she had been, but that was what Dr Webber had predicted.

They went out for a brief walk that afternoon, and Sam hailed a cab and took them to Rockefeller Center to watch the skaters. But looking at them only reminded him again of Daphne.

Alex was exhausted then, and they had to take a taxi home. It was obvious that she couldn't go a step further, and he even had to help her to her bedroom. Her joints were aching, and she was too exhausted to go another step without assistance.

'Is Mommy all right?' Annabelle asked worriedly, and he nodded, torn between sympathy for his wife, and anger over the anxiety she caused their daughter with her illness.

'She's fine,' he said firmly.

'Will she be all right when we're in Florida?'

'She'll be perfect. Carmen will be here to take care of her.' She found his answers very reassuring, and later Alex got up to pack Annabelle's suitcase. It was fun packing all her little things, but suddenly, as she did, Alex felt a wave of panic come over her. What if a day came when she could no longer take care of her, and Annabelle had to go to live with Sam? What if she lost her, too? Just thinking of it made her feel ill again, and as she sat down, her whole body was shaking. She forced herself to get up again after that, and finish packing the suitcase. She was not going to let anything like that happen, she was not going to lose her to Sam, or that woman. Fearing that made her stay up for dinner with them that night, although she was truly exhausted after all the efforts of Christmas. But she had dinner with them, and then went to bed, and slept until her alarm went off in the morning.

She helped Annabelle dress, and reminded her to have a good time, and call when she felt like it, and swim, and have a great time with Daddy. And then she pulled her close to her, and held her as though she were afraid she might never see her again. Sensing her mother's panic, Annabelle started to cry when she left her, and they clung to each other for a long time.

Annabelle knew how much her mother loved her, and instinctively felt how alone she was.

'I love you,' Alex called, with tears in her eyes, as they got in the elevator, and Sam looked at her with the familiar annoyance, as Annabelle cried softly.

'She'll be fine,' he reminded Annabelle again as they went down in the elevator with their bags, angry that he even had to reassure her. Alex had no business clinging to her and scaring her the way she did. It brought back all the same feelings of resentment he'd had since October, and ever since his own mother had died years before. For Sam it was a relief to get away from her. Just being around her was depressing, no matter how hard she tried.

They got in a cab for La Guardia, and by the time they were gone, Alex was standing alone in her bedroom, feeling lost without them. She had seen more of Sam in the last two days than she'd seen of him in the past month, and in some ways it had been pleasant, but in others it was very painful. It was like forcing herself to look at something she could no longer have, and reminding herself of all the reasons why she had loved it. Even after he had hurt her so much and failed her so badly, she still had to remind herself to stop loving him now. Caring about him was destructive and having seen him with the English girl, she knew there was no point hanging on. It was a relief now that he was gone.

After a little while, she washed the breakfast dishes and made Annabelle's bed. Carmen was not coming in. Without Annabelle, Alex had said she didn't need any help, and she had given her the day off. Alex wandered aimlessly around the apartment, and finally went to her bathroom to take a shower. She was trying to talk herself into getting dressed, and going out for a walk, so she wouldn't feel so lonely. But even thinking of it reminded her of seeing Sam with the English girl only three days before. And suddenly she didn't want to. She wanted to go back to bed, and sleep all day. She had nothing to do anyway, since she wasn't going in to the office. But a certain Spartan spirit told her to at least take a shower and get dressed. And to that end, she pulled off her wig, and happened to catch a glimpse of herself in the mirror. The last of her hair had just come out, and she was suddenly completely bald, without a single hair on her head. The last of it lay in the wig she dropped on her sink, and as she took off her dressing gown, and slipped her nightgown off, she suddenly stood staring at herself, and realized how she must look to Sam. She was bald, she was scarred. The missing breast was a slab of white flesh now, with a narrow pink scar and no nipple. She didn't even look like a man. She was even less than that. She looked like a nothing, like a mannequin, with no hair and one breast, the kind that you find lying disassembled on the floor in department stores on the day that they change the windows.

She started to cry as she saw herself, and realized that not only Sam was gone but Annabelle. She had already lost her husband, and eventually she might lose her daughter. It was as though she were being stripped of everything she had ever been or loved or wanted. The only thing left to her was her work, and she couldn't even do that the way she had once done it. She was like a broken bird, limping to earth, stripped, and dying. She felt ugly, useless, and sick. She almost wondered if it wouldn't be easier to die, to just give up now, before she lost even more than she already had. Why wait until the rest was taken from her? Until Sam told her he wanted a divorce so he could marry that girl, and Annabelle fell in love with her. Why wait for them to kill her? Or leave her all alone.

She just stood crying, staring at herself, and in the distance, she heard the phone, but she didn't bother to answer. Her stomach revolted finally from all the anguish of her illness and her realizations, and naked, she knelt on the floor and began vomiting, and eventually there was only retching. It was all too familiar now. It was what she had become, a broken machine that could only spew bile. There was nothing left of her. And when it was over, she lay on the floor and cried until finally, she went back to bed, just as she was, and lay curled under the covers. She ate nothing all day, and Sam and Annabelle never called. They were too busy having fun at Disney World. They had moved on, toward life, in a world of sunshine, while she lay alone in the dark shadows of her own winter. She lay crying in the dark, until the emptiness in her stomach made her sick again, and she went back to the bathroom. It was an endless day of vomiting and tears, and always the bald ghost she saw in the mirror. She didn't even bother to turn the lights on, but still she saw her.

And then the phone rang again late that afternoon, but she still didn't bother to answer. She was too sick, too tired, too crazy, too willing to die, even to reach out to anyone who would call her. Annabelle didn't need her now. She had Sam. No one needed her. She was nothing. No one. Not even a woman.

The phone rang incessantly, as she lay in her bed, in tears wishing it would stop ringing, but it just wouldn't. She reached out finally, and picked it up, without speaking.

'Hello?'

She knew the voice, but she wasn't thinking clearly.

'Hello, Alex?' the voice repeated.

'Yes.' Her voice sounded vague and disjointed. 'Who is this?'

'It's Brock Stevens.' It didn't sound like her, and he wondered if she had gotten a lot sicker, or gone back for additional treatment.

'Hi, Brock.' Her voice sounded dead, and he was worried. 'Where are you?' She sounded as though she didn't care, but she knew she had to say something.

'I'm in Connecticut, with friends. I wanted to ask you about Vermont again. I'm going up tomorrow.' She smiled. He was sweet. But he was also very stupid. She was dying. Why did he need a dying friend? It was a waste of time to help her.

'I can't make it. I have work to do.'

'No one's going to work this week, and we caught up on everything.'

'Okay,' she smiled weakly, overpowered by nausea again. Not eating earlier had made her sicker and she knew it. 'I'm a liar. But I can't go anyway.'

'Is your little girl there?' he asked, unwilling to let her off the hook without a fight. He wanted her to go with him. He thought it would do her good, and Liz had agreed with him when he asked her. Alex needed to get away, and the fresh air would be healthy for her as long as she didn't overdo it.

'Annabelle's in Florida,' she answered his question. 'And Sam's probably with his girlfriend,' she threw in for good measure. She was a little giddy from lack of food and water.

'Did he tell you that?' He sounded annoyed when he asked her. He thought her husband was a complete jerk, and he didn't deserve her. But even as a friend, he felt he couldn't say that.

'I saw them together, the day before Christmas Eve. She's very young, and *very* pretty.' She sounded almost drunk, and Brock got suddenly even more worried about her. 'And I'm sure she has two of everything. Sam hates anything that isn't perfect.'

'Alex, are you okay?' he asked, glancing at his watch, and wondering how long it would take him to get into the city to see her. Or he could call Liz, and she could go over. He was contemplating doing one or the other. He didn't like the way she sounded, especially since she was alone. There was always the possibility that in light of her present state of mind, she might do something crazy.

'I'm fine,' she said, lying very still with her eyes closed, so she wouldn't vomit. 'The rest of my hair fell out today. It looks a lot neater.'

'Why don't you just rest for a while. I'll give you a call in about an hour. Okay?'

'Okay,' she said sleepily. She hung up and forgot about him. She wanted to forget everything. Maybe if she just starved herself for six days until Annabelle came home, she'd be dead when they found her. It was a lot easier than dying by chemo. She drifted off to sleep, and a little while later, she heard an alarm, or a bell, or a sound. She tried to ignore it for a long time, and then she realized it was her doorbell. She couldn't imagine who it was, and she tried to ignore it some more, but it wouldn't stop. And then someone started pounding on the door, so she put her dressing gown on, and went to the door and looked through the peephole. It was Brock Stevens. She was so surprised, she opened it and they stood staring at each other, she in her beige cashmere robe and he in a heavy sweater and parka, corduroy pants, and heavy boots. There was a smell of fresh air about him, and he looked very worried when he saw her.

'I was worried sick about you,' he said as she stood there.

'Why?' She looked a little vague and she was weaving, but he knew her well enough to know she hadn't been drinking. She was just very sick and probably hadn't eaten. She stepped aside to let him in and he followed her into the living room, and then she saw herself in the mirror and realized she hadn't put on her wig. 'Shit,' she said, and looked up at him like a little kid, 'there goes that.'

'You look like Sinéad O'Connor, only better.'

'I can't sing.'

'Neither can I,' he said, still looking at her, thinking that she really looked like Audrey Hepburn. She was even beautiful without her hair, it was so simple and so unadorned. All the beauty of her face stood out like some exquisite being from another world. There was a luminousness to her that never failed to touch him. 'What happened?' he asked her. It was obvious that something had. It was as though she were trying to let go and die. And she was. But even over the phone, he had sensed it.

'I don't know. I saw myself in the mirror this morning, and Annabelle was gone, and I was sick again . . . it's just too much to fight anymore . . . Sam and his other woman . . . it's all such a mess. It's just too much trouble,' she said honestly, and he looked angry.

'So you gave up. Is that it?' He was shouting at her, and she looked startled.

'I have a right to make my own choices,' she said sadly.

'Do you? You have a little girl, and even if you didn't have her, you have an obligation to yourself,

305

not to mention the people who love you. You need to fight this, Alex. It won't go away for a while. It's not going to be easy. But you can't just lie here and die, because it's "too much trouble." '

'Why not?' she said, sounding strangely disassociated from everything. Even him.

'Because I say so. Have you eaten today?' he asked, sounding savage. And not surprisingly, she shook her head in answer. 'Go put some clothes on. I'll make something to eat.'

'I'm not hungry.'

'I don't care. I'm not going to listen to this bullshit.' He grabbed her shoulders then, and shook her gently. 'I don't give a damn what anyone has done to you, or what you think about your life right now. Stripped down to bare bones, with one breast or two, and bald as an eagle, you have an obligation to fight for your life, Alex Parker. For you. For yourself. For no one else. It's a precious commodity. And the rest of us need you. But when you look in the mirror, and you don't like what you see, you remember that that woman is you. All the trappings mean nothing. You are exactly who you were before all this happened. If anything, you're more, not less. Don't forget that.' She was in awe of him as he stood there, lecturing her, and without a sound, she walked to her bathroom. She took off her dressing gown and turned on the shower, and then she stood there for a long time, looking into the mirror, and she saw the same woman she had seen there that morning, the same broken bird, the woman with the scar where her breast had been, the woman with no hair, but as she looked at her, she knew that he was right. Not for Annabelle, not for Sam, not for him, or anyone, she had to fight. For herself, for what she had been, and could be, and always would be. She could lose a breast and her hair, but she couldn't lose herself. Sam couldn't take that away from her. She cried softly then, thinking of what Brock had just taught her, and she turned on the shower, and let it run across her head and down her shoulders, and in warm sheets across her body.

She put jeans and a sweater on, and the short wig she had left on the sink that morning, after she shook her own hair out of it. And then she walked into the kitchen barefoot.

'You don't have to wear a wig for me,' he smiled, 'unless it makes you feel better.'

'I feel weird without it,' she admitted.

He had made scrambled eggs and toast and fried potatoes. The potatoes were too much for her, but she struggled with the toast and the scrambled eggs, and managed to eat a little. But she didn't want to push her luck and spend the rest of the night sick in the bathroom. Her stomach was a disaster but she suspected that for once Sam was right, and it was due to emotions.

They sat quietly together in the kitchen for a while, and then Alex told him that Annabelle had loved all her presents.

'It was fun buying them,' he said, 'I like kids.' He smiled at her, relieved to see her eating.

'Then why aren't you married?' she asked, toying with her eggs.

'Bartlett and Paskin never gives me time,' he grinned, looking boyish and very handsome.

'We'll have to start lightening your caseload,' she teased him.

They talked for a while, about what the holidays had been like, and how difficult things had been with Sam, and then he cleared the dishes.

'You don't have to do that, Brock. I can do it later.'

'Sure, why not? Able to leap buildings in a single bound, right? So what about Vermont? I didn't come here for my health, you know. I came here for yours.' He looked her straight in the eye, and as always she was grateful to him.

'I don't think so.'

'I'm not giving up. Liz thinks it would be good for you too,' he said firmly.

'What is this? A committee?' She laughed, amused suddenly but touched too. 'Doesn't anyone care what I think?'

'Frankly, no.' He discounted her veto completely.

'Don't you have anyone real to spend this week with?'

'You look pretty real to me,' he said, with a determined look, and she shook her head and pointed at her wig.

'Don't let this piece of fluff fool you. I'm too tired to ski, I'm too old to woo, I'm too sick to be fun, and besides, I'm married.'

'Not from the sound of it, or not for long anyway.' He was being very blunt with her and she was still laughing.

'That's a nice thing to say. Well, let's say, I'm used goods.' And then she looked at him in amusement. 'Are you telling me you're asking me as your *date*?' It was obvious she didn't believe that, and he laughed too.

'No. But if it makes you feel better to think that, be my guest. I'm asking you as a buddy, a buddy who would like to see you get that pale face in some sunshine, and sit in front of a fire and keep warm and drink hot chocolate, and go to sleep at night, knowing she's with friends, and not alone in a lonely apartment in the city.'

'You make it sound pretty good, for a kid your age.'

'It is. And I have a lot of experience in the care and feeding of old bags like you. My sister was, is, ten years older than I am.'

'Give her my condolences,' she grinned. 'You sure make it difficult to refuse.'

'That's why I came to see you,' he said, looking down at her with a gentle smile, and she was reminded again of how much she liked him.

'I thought you came for a free meal,' she said, still laughing at him.

'I did, but I came to talk to you too.'

'It must have been pretty boring in Connecticut.' She was relentless with him and he was loving it. They knew each other well, and had fun together.

'It was boring in Connecticut. So are you coming, or what?'

'You mean I have a choice? I was beginning to think you were going to throw me over your shoulder and take me.'

'I might, if you don't act right.'

'You're really crazy, you know. The last thing you need, is me puking on you all the way to Vermont, and then sick as a dog when we get there.'

'I'm used to it by now,' he smiled, 'I wouldn't know what to do without it.'

'You're nuts.'

'You're cute, and this is what friends are for.'

'Is it?' she said, touched by him again. 'I thought they were only to Christmas shop, and do all your cases for you, and peel you off the bathroom floor when you're sick.' It was what husbands were supposed to be for, but hers wasn't.

'Just shut up and pack your suitcase. You're embarrassing me.'

'That's impossible.'

'I'll pick you up at eight, or is that too early?' He looked suddenly worried about her.

'It's fine. Are you sure?' she asked him again. 'What if you want to pick up girls?'

'It's a big house. I'll lock you in your room. I promise.' They were both smiling as she walked him to the door. She couldn't believe she had let him talk her into it, but she was looking forward to it suddenly. She knew she had four and a half months of sickness ahead of her, but something had happened to her. He had saved her spirit. She wanted to go with him, wanted to cling to life. But more than anything now, she wanted to make it. She knew she had to.

Chapter 16

The days in Vermont were the happiest Alex had had in ages, ever since before her sickness. She had called Sam and Annabelle to let them know she was there, and Sam sounded surprised to hear it.

'I didn't know you could still travel,' he said, sounding concerned. 'Are you sure it's all right for you to be there? Who's with you?'

'A friend from work. I'm fine. I'll see you in New York on New Year's Day.' She gave him the number, but they never called her.

The house Brock had borrowed was simple, but very cozy. There were four bedrooms, and a kind of dormitory. He gave her the biggest room upstairs, and he took a small one downstairs so he wouldn't disturb her. And they sat around together like old friends, reading and doing crossword puzzles, and having snowball fights like two children.

She went for long walks in the snow with Brock, and she even tried skiing one day, but it was too much for her. After the chemo, she just didn't have the strength. But she felt healthier than she had in weeks. She only had one really bad day. But she stayed in bed, and by evening she was better.

He found an old sled in the garage the day after they arrived and he pulled her around, so she wouldn't get too tired.

He cooked dinner for her at night, and when she told him to go out with friends, he only laughed at her and told her he was too tired. He liked staying home with her. But one night they even went to Chez Henri for dinner, where they had a lovely time, and by the end of the week, Alex was feeling a lot better again. She was at the better end of her chemo, which meant it would be time for another treatment soon, but fortunately not yet. She had never had a nicer vacation, and they became fast friends and spent a lot of their time laughing.

Another day, they met for lunch at the lodge after he skied. She kept pointing out pretty girls to him, and then she discreetly showed him a handful of attractive young skiers, whom she felt he should be with instead of her.

'They're fourteen years old for chrissake. Are you trying to get me arrested?' They were both laughing again.

'They are not! They're twenty-five if they're a day,' she said, pretending to look outraged.

'Same thing.' But even the thirty-year-olds didn't appeal to him. He was happy with Alex. But he never put the make on her, or made her feel uncomfortable. And they talked about Sam a lot. She admitted to him how much it had hurt her when she saw him with the girl at Ralph Lauren.

'I think I'd probably have killed him. Or her,' Brock said, but Alex only shook her head.

'There's no point. It's over. It's not her fault. It just happened. And I guess when I look at myself in the mirror now, I understand it.'

'That's bullshit.' He got angry when she said things like that.

'What if it had happened to him? If he'd lost an arm, or a leg, or a testicle? Would you have cashed him in?'

'No. But we're different. And I guess this . . . is a symbol of femininity. I'm not sure a lot of men weather this well. Not all husbands are like Liz's.' But she had admitted they had had their rough spots too.

'I don't think you fuck up your marriage because your wife loses a breast, or her hair, or a shoe for chrissake. How can you accept that?' Brock was outraged.

But Alex looked over at him with a wise smile. She was ten years older than he was. 'I don't have a choice at the moment. The guy's not buying, Brock. It's as simple as that. The store's closed. He's taken his business elsewhere.'

'And that's it? You give up?' He was shocked at her lack of spirit.

'What do you suggest I do? Shoot her?'

'Shoot him,' he said matter-of-factly. 'He deserves it.'

'You're a romantic,' she accused him.

'So are you,' he accused her right back.

'So what? It won't pay my rent, or keep my husband. The guy hates deformities. He hates disease. He can't even look at me. He saw me once after the surgery and almost fainted. I make him sick. This is not a great foundation for a happy marriage.'

'Face it. The guy's a coward.'

'Maybe so. But he has great taste in women. She's an awfully pretty girl, Brock. Actually, she's the right age for you. Maybe you should go sweep her off her feet, and provide some stiff competition.' He didn't

313

tell her that he'd rather have swept her off her feet. It didn't seem the right moment. And she was so at ease with him, he didn't want to spoil that.

They spent New Year's Eve at the house, watching TV, and eating popcorn, talking about their life's dreams, their careers, what they hoped to find in the years to come. She wished him a wife who would take care of him, and he wished her health and happiness in whatever form she wished it. And at midnight, they sang 'Auld Lang Syne' in perfect unison. And then she went up to bed, and thought about their friendship, and the precious rarity of good friends.

They were both sad to leave the next day, but she looked infinitely better than she had when they arrived. Something had changed subtly about her. There was more energy, more fight than there had been for a long time. She was suddenly determined to survive her cancer.

She was quiet on the drive home, thinking of seeing Sam again, even if only for one night. She knew he was leaving for Europe the next day, and she assumed she knew why. To meet his little friend there. Brock asked her from time to time if she was all right, and she said she was, but she was very pensive. He held hands with her for a while, driving on the freeway, to comfort her. He was her friend, and her colleague. They were pals.

They got home late in the afternoon, and he looked genuinely sad when he dropped her off at her apartment. She sat in the car for a minute, looking at him, and she didn't know how to even begin to thank him.

'You gave me my life back, you know. I had a great time.'

'So did I.' And then he touched her cheek gently with his fingers. 'Don't let anyone make you feel like

314

less than you. You're the greatest woman I know.'
He had tears in his eyes when he said it, and she
was touched by him again. He had a way of getting
to her heart with very little effort.

'I love you, you know. And you're very silly. The
great one around here is you. You're going to make
some lucky girl a terrific husband.'

'I'm waiting for Annabelle,' he said with a grin she
loved. The one that made him look fourteen again.

'She's a lucky girl. Thanks again, Brock.' She kissed
him on the cheek and the doorman took her bag.

And when Sam and Annabelle came home that
night, they found Alex looking infinitely better.

Annabelle was full of tales of Disney World. She
was yawning and laughing and half asleep all at the
same time. And she barely made it to her pillow, as
she kissed Alex.

'It sounds like she had a great time,' Alex said,
smiling at Sam. He could see something different
about her too. Nothing had changed but it was as
though she had made peace with herself and what
was happening.

'I had a great time too,' Sam said. 'She's good
company. I hated to bring her back.'

'I really missed her,' Alex admitted to him, but
neither of them claimed to have missed the other.
That was gone now too. The pretense that they still
had a marriage. They both knew they didn't.

He packed his bags that night, and left for London
the next morning while Annabelle and Alex had breakfast. He promised to call once he got to Switzerland,
and Annabelle reminded him to be back for her
birthday. And then she looked at Alex in surprise
after he left and pointed out that Sam had forgotten
to kiss her mother. But she didn't ask why this time.

She knew. Even Annabelle could tell the difference.

The rest of the week flew by, Alex managed to take her to ballet, and to spend a quiet weekend with her, and the following Monday the nightmare began again. It was time for another intravenous treatment. And this time she was even sicker than usual. The first one of the month always hit her hard, especially combined with the Cytoxan pills. By the time she got back to the office, she felt as though she were dying. She had had to go home early in the afternoon, and when Annabelle saw her she cried, watching her mother throw up mercilessly, and she was shocked to see her with her wig off.

Alex went to work the next day, but it was an endless day for her, and by five o'clock she crawled home. This time it was Carmen who was in tears, and all Alex could get out of her at the door was a flood of hysterical Spanish. But the moment she saw Annabelle she understood it. She had cut her beautiful red curls to the scalp, trying to look more like her mother.

'Oh baby, why did you do it?' Alex cried, sick and exhausted, wondering how she would explain it to her father.

'I want to look like you,' Annabelle cried, feeling guilty over what she'd done, and frightened over her mother's illness. And her father had been gone for a week by then, and that made her nervous too.

Alex tried to explain her illness to Annabelle again, and they read *Mommy's Getting Better*, but none of it seemed to help. Alex was too sick to put much conviction or energy into her explanations and Annabelle was just too upset to be reasonable. Even her school had just called Alex to say she was having a very hard time, and talked a lot about her mother's treatments and illness. She didn't express it, but her teacher felt that Annabelle was terrified her mother was going to die. And Alex was almost too sick and frightened to help her, and neither of them got any real support on the subject from Sam.

And worse yet, it seemed as though each month the chemotherapy made Alex more sick instead of less. And by the end of the week, she couldn't even make it to the office, but she still had to organize Annabelle's birthday party. And she knew how important that was. Annabelle needed normalcy and the reassurance of familiar goings-on. And she had looked forward to her birthday for a long time.

Once again, Liz bought most of the presents for her, and the paper goods. But when the day came, the bakery sent the wrong cake, and Alex had forgotten to call the clown. Annabelle's best friend got the flu, and so did three more of her friends, and her party slowly fell apart. The entire day was a disaster, even with Carmen's help, and Alex cried when she saw the disappointment in Annabelle's eyes.

Sam had flown in late the night before, and he was jet-lagged and cranky, and obviously not pleased to be back, and when he saw Annabelle's chopped-off hair, he went absolutely crazy.

'How could you let her do something like that? How could you? Why did you ever let her see you without the wig?' he raged.

'I was throwing up and it was on the floor, for God's sake, Sam. I can't worry about how I look every minute. I'm sick.' She didn't realize it but Annabelle was listening to them argue with frightened eyes.

'Then she shouldn't be with you,' he accused, and with a look of absolute terror, Alex hauled off and slapped him, as Annabelle began to cry out loud, but still her parents battled on.

'Don't you ever say that to me! She's not going anywhere! And don't you forget that!' Alex yelled at him and he shouted back.

'You're in no condition to take care of her,' he roared as Annabelle flew into her mother's arms.

'Oh yes, I am,' Alex snarled at him, 'and if you lay a hand on her, you sonofabitch, I'm going to hit you with the biggest fucking discrimination suit you've ever dreamed of. She's staying with me. Is that clear?' She clung to her child, shaking, as Sam glared at her in fury.

'Then keep your wig on.' He backed down only slightly in the face of Alex's threats, and his daughter's sobs. She didn't want to be taken away from her Mommy, but she also hated it whenever they fought. She knew it was probably her fault, but she was never quite sure why.

It was a rough night for all of them, and Sam left as soon as Annabelle went to bed. But the next day, he and Alex sat down and talked in earnest. This wasn't working out. It was time for him to move out, and they both knew it. Their battle in front of Annabelle the day before had shaken them both. But he absolutely amazed her by saying he didn't think he should go until she finished her treatments. As far as he was concerned, the business of Annabelle's hair seemed to prove that. He felt he needed to be there to help watch her, and keep her from getting distraught while her mother was still sick and in treatment.

'I don't need you here as a nursemaid, Sam. You can leave if you want to.'

'I'll move out in May when you're finished with your chemo,' he said firmly.

'I can't believe you're saying this to me. You're staying because of my chemo?'

'I'm staying for Annabelle's sake, in case you're too ill to take care of her. And when you're finished, I'll go.'

'I'm impressed. And then what, Sam?' She was pressing him. She wanted to know if he was going to marry his girlfriend. And who she was. But he wasn't ready to let her in on his secrets.

'I haven't figured that out yet.' But she could guess. It was pretty obvious. He was looking young and lean and very handsome. It was easy to see that he was happy and in love, and she was amazed that he was willing to hang around, even some of the time, until she finished her chemo. The end was still four months away, and nobody wanted it to be over more than Alex herself.

'Do you think you can stand it till then?' Alex asked him, pressing him again.

'I can if you can. I'm not going to be here all the time, but I'll be around and available if Annabelle needs me.'

'I appreciate it,' Alex said grudgingly, half wanting him to go, and half wanting him to stay, and not sure which was worse. It just delayed the inevitable, and she had stopped fooling herself about that. She knew that eventually, now, or in four months, he was going to leave her. And in most ways, he already had.

And when she told him the next day, Brock couldn't believe the arrangement they had come to. It made sense, for Annabelle's sake, but it was hard on everyone else, and just seemed to drag things out forever. No one was more aware of that than Daphne. She looked like a disappointed child when Sam told her what he had agreed to with

Alex, to stay at the apartment with her until May.

'I so hoped you would move in with me now.' They had had such a good time in Europe. They had made love constantly and had a great time in Gstaad and then he had taken her to Paris and bought her everything they could lay their hands on. They had gone to Cartier and Van Cleef, Hermès and Dior, Chanel and Givenchy, and every little boutique she fell in love with. But what she really wanted was Sam, even though she understood his reason for postponing moving into her apartment. It was too small for both of them anyway. And he was talking about buying a co-op for them in May, after Alex finished her treatment.

'It won't be long,' he promised her, and he certainly didn't have to sleep at their apartment every night. He was going to continue doing just what he had been, and spend most of his nights with Daphne. He wanted to introduce her to Annabelle too, but he was still afraid it would be too confusing for her, and she might tell her mother. But Daphne wasn't pressing him to meet her anyway. As she had admitted to him from the first, she was not overly sentimental about children. She was not overly sentimental about many things. But she was sexual about everything, every moment, every opportunity. They had made love absolutely everywhere in Europe, including a fitting room at Dior, and another at Givenchy. She was wild and passionate, and she made him feel young again, and totally free of his problems.

Alex caught a glimpse of them again one Saturday afternoon in February. They had just come from previewing the jewelry items at Christie's, where he'd left a bid on an emerald ring for Daphne. Sam bought her a lot of things, and seemed to be happy to spoil her. And as Alex stood watching them, she saw them stroll up Park Avenue, oblivious to anything but each other. It made her sad seeing them again. A lot of things made her sad these days. The way Annabelle looked when her father left, or when she asked about him, and Alex had to find excuses about why he didn't sleep there very often. It still made her sad to see what her body looked like, or that her hair didn't grow back. And it didn't cheer her particularly when Dr Webber suggested reconstructive surgery to her. It had been long enough since the surgery to begin thinking about it now, but she found she didn't care. She didn't like what she saw, but she was used to what she looked like. And oddly enough, it was Brock she discussed it with, and she was surprised when he thought she should have it. There was nothing she couldn't talk about with him. There was not a single sacred subject. He was the closest thing to a brother she'd ever had.

'What difference does it make, if I have one boob or two? Who gives a damn?' she said belligerently, over lunch at Le Relais during one of her better weeks without chemo.

'You give a damn, or you should. You can't live like a nun for the rest of your life.'

'Why not? I look cute in black, and I don't even have to shave my head.' She pointed to the longer, more glamorous wig she was wearing, and he made a face at her.

'You are truly disgusting. I'm serious. It'll make a difference to you one day.'

'No, it won't. I like being a freak. So what? So what, if somebody loved me, would they really care if I went to all that trouble and got an implant? I mean, hell, we're not talking about Sam. For him, I'd have to get two new ones to compete with his British bimbo.'

'Never mind.' Brock looked at her, thinking about it. 'I still think you should do it. It'll make you feel good. You won't be mad at yourself every time you look in the mirror.'

'Would you care?' she asked him bluntly. 'If you met a girl with one breast, I mean?'

'It could save a lot of time,' he said, making fun of her now, 'save you all those difficult decisions. No, I wouldn't care,' he said honestly. 'But I'm unusual, and I'm younger. Guys your age are more hung up about appearances, and perfection.'

'Yeah, like Sam. We know all about that kind, thank you very much.' She still remembered all too clearly his face when he saw her. 'Okay, so what you're telling me is that I either need reconstructive surgery, or a younger man in my life. Those are my choices.'

'That's basically it,' he responded, playing with her again. She was in good spirits. And there were things he had always wanted to say to her, and never had. He never seemed to find the right moment.

'I still think it's too much trouble. Even the doctor said it hurts like hell. And the procedure sounds disgusting. They take a little skin from here, a little from there, they make tunnels and flaps and loops and bumps, and attach implants and tattoo on nipples. Christ, why don't I just paint one on if I meet someone I like. I can do it any shape, any size, any color. You know, I could really be on to something, here,' she went on, and he laughed at her and threw his napkin at her to stop her.

'You're obsessed.'

'Can you blame me? I lost a husband with my boob, and the guy ran off and found a girl with a pair, now doesn't that tell you something? If nothing else, he was greedy.'

'I think you should do it.'

'I think I'll have a face-lift instead. Or maybe a nose job.'

'Let's go back to work before you decide to get your ears done.' He loved being with her, and working with her, and he liked Annabelle too. He had met her several times when he came by from the office with papers for Alex. Annabelle thought he was funny and she liked playing with him. He had even taken her skating one day when Alex was really sick and Carmen had the flu, and Sam had disappeared with Daphne.

They talked about their latest cases on the way back to work. Alex hadn't been to trial in four months, but there was one coming up, and she was trying to decide if she was up to doing it, if Brock helped her. She was tempted to, but she didn't want to give the client less than they deserved. It was a lot to think about while she was in the midst of chemo. And in the end, she decided to give the case to Matthew Billings.

In March, Brock invited her to Vermont again, on a weekend that Sam was taking Annabelle away. She went, and they had a lovely time. She tried skiing, and she was a little better. She was stronger, and she only had eight weeks left of chemo. She was looking forward to it desperately, but to her that meant several things. It meant Sam would move out, and move on with his life. And even though she called his friend a bimbo, she suspected that they would probably get married. He was obviously very involved with her, and he was very protective whenever Alex tried to ask him questions. He had never actually acknowledged that there was someone else, but it had become obvious that Alex knew. But he was

323

always a gentleman, and refused to discuss her with Alex.

It also meant that Alex had to get on with her life too. She had to face the fact that Sam was gone, even if he still lived in the same apartment for the moment. When the chemotherapy was over, she could go back to trial work again. But she wasn't sure what else she wanted to do. It was suddenly more than a little frightening to be on her own again, although Brock kept telling her that the worst was already over.

They were walking back from the chairlifts in Sugarbush when he said it to her again, and she looked up at him pensively, and realized that he was right. Going through chemotherapy without a husband was pretty bad, but then again she had had Brock, and he had been there for her every moment.

He had even gone to the doctor with her once so he could understand it better and see what it was like. He had held her hand through the entire procedure. There was very little he hadn't done for her in the past six months. He had become like a brother to her, and there was nothing she was afraid to tell or show him.

They started talking about reconstructive surgery again that night, after she cooked dinner for him this time, and he told her she was a pretty good cook, though not as good as he was.

'The hell I'm not. Can you make a soufflé?' she bragged. They were always like two kids together, pushing and shoving and laughing and making fun of each other, when they weren't deeply engrossed in more serious subjects.

'Yes, I can,' he lied, and she grinned at him.

'Well, neither can I,' she laughed, and they went back to discussing the surgery Dr Webber had suggested. Sometimes they played because the things they talked about were too sad. 'I don't care,' she insisted, serious at last. She really didn't want to discuss it, but Brock had brought it up.

'You should.' It was a familiar argument by now, and suddenly, she turned around and looked at him. She was completely unashamed with him. He had watched her throw up for months, and seen her bald head. She didn't see anything wrong with showing him what they were discussing. She looked at him oddly then, wondering what he would think of it. She genuinely trusted his opinion, and his kind heart.

'Do you want to see it?' she asked casually, like a kid offering to drop his pants to one of his playmates. She felt a little strange for a minute, and she laughed nervously, but he looked at her seriously and nodded.

'Yes, I would. I've always wondered what it looked like,' he said honestly. 'Somehow I could never imagine it being as bad as you described.'

'It's pretty bad,' she warned. 'It's not pretty, and there's a scar.' But even she knew that it looked better than it had in October. And then, without further ado, she pulled off her sweater and unbuttoned her blouse slowly and neatly. She took it off then, and hesitating for only a moment, she pulled off the thermal undershirt she wore with no bra. It was like a slow and very respectable striptease. She stood before him, in all her nakedness, with one breast bare, and the other missing.

He looked at her eyes first, before he looked anywhere else, and the way she looked at him gave him permission. It was a clean, simple look that passed between them. And as he looked at her, his heart went

325

out to her. She looked so sweet and so young, and so vulnerable, the one breast was still high and firm, the other looked as though it had been slashed from her body with a saber. And without thinking, he reached his arms out to her, and pulled her slowly toward him. He couldn't show her anything different than what he felt. He had loved her for too long to hide it now, with her simple, courageous gesture.

'You're so beautiful,' he said softly, into her hair. 'You're so perfect and so brave . . . and so decent, Alex.' He pulled away so he could look at her again. 'I think you're terrific.'

'With one boob or two?' she said with a small shy smile, remembering why she had shown him, but she hadn't expected his reaction. She wasn't sure what she had expected, but this sudden tenderness of his surprised her, and touched her to her very soul.

'I love you just the way you are. You were right.' He held her close to him again, feeling her warmth next to him. 'I love you just like this,' he said, bowled over by her, even more than he had been. The trust between them was immeasurable and something very special.

'You weren't supposed to say that,' she said softly. 'You were supposed to be giving me an objective opinion.' She was feeling suddenly taken with him too, and she hadn't expected that. Their relationship had been chaste for so long that she wasn't prepared for this sudden rush of sensuality and love and emotion.

'I am giving you an objective opinion,' he whispered, nuzzling her face with his lips. 'You're very, very beautiful, and I can't keep my hands off you.' And then very slowly, with a tenderness she'd never experienced before, he kissed her. And as he did, one hand gently caressed the breast she had, and the other hand tenderly touched the scar, and then her stomach and her back. And when he pulled her close to him, he held her in his strong hands, and she could almost feel the air go out of her in a rush, and then he kissed her harder.

'Brock . . . what are we doing . . .' she asked, barely able to think, and in another minute, she knew she wouldn't. 'What are we . . . what . . . ohhh . . .' she moaned softly, as he unzipped her pants, and slid a hand into them, and then pulled them down slowly. Without thinking, she stepped out of them, and his hands began to explore her legs, her hips, her thighs, and further. And as he did, she took off his clothes, and in a few minutes they stood naked in the cozy house he had brought her to for the second time, and he laid her on the couch in front of the blazing fire, and touched every inch of her with his lips. He kissed her breast, and then her scar, and then let his tongue travel slowly south as she arched beneath his touch, and he pressed himself against her. 'Oh Brock . . . oh Brock . . .' She couldn't believe what was happening. How could they be doing this? He was her friend. But suddenly he was so much more. He was a part of her world, her life, her body, as he entered her, and they each let out a long, soft moan of endless desire and anticipation. They moved together for a long time, as the fire blazed, and the sparks flew from time to time, and then suddenly he gave an astounding shout, and she gave an astonishing shudder as they came together. And then they lay silent and stunned in each other's arms. He had wanted her for so long, and she had never realized any of what he'd been feeling. They had grown slowly together like two trees, their leaves entwined, their roots slowly becoming one, until they were separate no longer.

'Oh, my God, what happened?' She smiled lazily at him, as he kissed her again, and then pulled her closer to him, as he lay still inside her.

'Would you like me to explain?' he asked. 'You don't know, you will never know, how I have longed for this. You will never know how much I have loved you, and prayed for this moment to come, if you'll pardon the pun.' He was beaming.

'Where was I when all this was going on?' she said, looking amazed, and blissfully happy. She had never been happier than at that moment. He was sensitive and kind and incredibly sexy. And they had been friends for so long that it was easy to love him now. The transition had been gentle and strong, and now she felt bound to him forever. 'How did I miss what you were feeling?' she asked again, feeling very stupid.

'You were too busy throwing up.'

'Apparently.' She smiled at him again. 'I'm glad I did something as subtle as take my clothes off.' She laughed suddenly at how naive she'd been. She'd never thought for a moment that it would come to this, but she was glad it had. She couldn't believe that she had made love to him, with her 'deformity' and her scar, without even trying to hide it from him. And now he gently slipped off her wig and tossed it aside too. They needed no artifice between them. 'I guess this means I don't get reconstructive surgery. I got the younger guy instead. Wasn't that the choice?' she smiled, and then she began to worry. 'Do you realize how old I am, you young fool? I'm *ten* years older than you. I'm practically old enough to be your mother.'

'Bullshit. You act like you're twelve. You'd be a mess without me,' he said honestly, without arrogance or pretension.

'That happens to be true. But I'm still older than you are.'

'I'm not impressed.'

'You should be. When you're ninety, I'll be a hundred.'

'I'll close my eyes when we make love,' he assured her.

'I'll lend you my wig.'

'Good.' He grabbed it then and put it on, and she laughed as he kissed her again, and she felt him rise again. And suddenly there was an urgency to his kisses, an insistence that nothing would satisfy except her body. They made love again, lying by the fire, and afterwards, afraid of exhausting her, he went and got a blanket from his bed and covered her, and they lay together as she slept in his arms. He was a happy man. And he knew he would never let her go now. He had waited too long for her to come to him, and she had drifted into his arms naked and without guile, and now he would do anything he had to, to keep her. At last, she was his now, and no longer Sam's. And Brock had every intention of holding on to her forever.

Chapter 17

Brock went to chemotherapy with her the week after they'd been to Vermont, and he sat quietly with her during the examination, followed by the intravenous treatment. All of her X-rays and scans had been coming up clear, and she only had seven more weeks now. Dr Webber was very pleased with her, and included Brock in their discussions about the treatment. She treated them very much as a couple.

'This is weird.' Alex smiled shyly at him as they took a cab back to the office. She was leaning against him and feeling the first waves of nausea begin, but she was very relaxed with him. There was no embarrassment between them.

'What's weird?' he asked, watching her to make sure she was as all right as she could be.

'We are.' Alex smiled, adjusting her wig, which had gotten crooked. 'People treat us like we're married. Did you ever notice that? Yesterday in Sugarbush, the guy in the grocery store thought you were my husband. And Dr Webber acts like you've been coming in all along. Doesn't anyone realize I'm almost old enough to be your mother?' She was surprised at how easy it all was. They had only been physically involved for three days, and it already seemed completely natural, not only to them, but to those around them.

'I guess they don't notice,' he said, kissing her nose. 'That blows that, doesn't it, Ma?'

'You should be out playing with fourteen-year-olds. *Healthy* fourteen-year-olds.'

'Mind your own business, Counselor.' The only thing they both knew they had to do was keep it a secret at work. Partners and associates were not allowed to 'fraternize,' or get married, or involved, or one of them would have to leave the firm. It was a pretty standard rule in law firms, and as the junior person to her, Brock would have lost his job, if anyone knew they were dating.

They chatted as they drove, and eventually, they got stuck in traffic. It took too long for them to get back, and the effects of the chemotherapy overcame her three blocks from their destination. They had to pull over and Brock held her gently as she vomited into the gutter on Park Avenue in front of dozens of people standing on the curb. It was terrible, and she was mortified, but she couldn't stop. Even the cabdriver felt sorry for her. It was obvious she wasn't drunk, but really sick. Brock told him to wait, and leave the meter running. It was half an hour before she could drive on again. Brock wanted to take her home, but she insisted on going back to the office with him.

'Stop being stupid, for heaven's sake. You need to go home and rest.'

'I have work to do.' And then she smiled through her misery. 'Don't think you can push me around now because I'm in love with you.'

'That would be too easy.'

He paid the cab, and took her upstairs. He had to support her as she walked, but no one who saw her thought of anything except that he was helping her. All the partners who knew them knew that Brock was her associate, and that she had been sick for months. People still felt very sorry for her.

Liz went to get her a cup of tea, and she spent another hour on the bathroom floor, with Brock alternately holding her and keeping her company. And when she felt a little better, she would talk to him about one of her cases.

'This is sick,' she said finally. 'We do more business in this bathroom than we do at my desk.'

'Not for much longer,' he reminded her, and it had been worth it. According to Dr Webber, the cancer was gone, hopefully forever.

He took her home at five o'clock, and then went back to work and stayed till nine. And before he left the office that night he called her. Sam was away again, and Brock asked if he could drop by for a few minutes to see her.

'Are you up to it?' he asked gently.

'Sure. I'd love to see you.' She was still amazed at what had happened between them over the weekend, but the brutal effects of her chemotherapy didn't allow them the time to enjoy it. But she still remembered the delicious hours they had spent in Vermont. They were like a dream, until he appeared at her apartment half an hour later. He had flowers for her, and he kissed her gently the minute he saw her. She was in a nightgown and dressing gown, and the dressing gown fell open as he kissed her and caressed her. She had put on one of her wigs before he came, and he teased her about it and reminded her that she didn't have to wear it for him.

'I think I like you better without it. It's sexier.'

'You're crazy.'

'About you,' he whispered, as he tucked her back

into bed and kissed her again. Then he went to the kitchen, and put the flowers in a vase for her. She was looking a lot better than she had that afternoon, and he sat on the edge of the bed and talked to her for a long time, running a lazy finger down her body to all the places that intrigued him. 'I'm a lucky man,' he said, watching her. He had wanted her for so long, wanted to be there for her, and to help her. He had wanted to save her from Sam, and now she had come to him, all on her own. It was Kismet.

'You're a silly boy,' she smiled at him, but it was obvious to her that he was not a boy but a man. She had to remind herself that he was actually younger than she was. He made her feel so safe, and protected, and well cared for.

'Where's Sam this time?' he asked casually, as he sat next to her on the bed at her invitation.

'London again. We hardly see him. He says he's just staying till I finish chemo. And then he's moving out. I guess he's looking for apartments. A real estate agent called him last week about a penthouse co-op on Fifth. I guess he's planning to set up housekeeping with his sweetheart.' She tried not to sound affected by it, but she was. It still hurt to think of his betrayal.

'Are you going to file?'

'Not yet. There's no rush. It doesn't make much difference. We go our separate ways now.' But it mattered to Brock. And he knew it was too soon to push her. But he wanted her to himself, he wanted a life with her. He wanted Sam out of the picture.

Brock stayed with her until eleven o'clock. And then he put her to bed, turned off the lights, and let himself out of her apartment.

The following night he cooked dinner for her and Annabelle. Afterwards he and Alex worked, and this time when he put her to bed, he had to fight to control himself. She looked so beautiful and he was aching to make love to her again, but she still wasn't feeling well, and neither of them wanted to risk waking her daughter. Annabelle had had fun playing with him, and she had no idea of what was happening. She accepted him as a friend, and there was no resistance.

By the weekend, Alex felt better again, and Carmen came in on Saturday morning, so Alex could spend the day with Brock at his apartment. They never got out of bed all day, and she had never known that making love could be like that with anyone. He was amazing. They were completely at ease in each other's arms and with each other's bodies. There was nothing to hide, or fear, or hold back. They made love for hours with total abandon.

And on Sunday, he came to spend the day with her and Annabelle. Alex told her they had to work, but they never did. They went to the zoo, and had lunch, and then they took Annabelle to the playground and watched her with the other kids, as the two of them sat like all the other Sunday parents.

'You should be with someone your age,' Alex said, but less convincingly than before, when she thought of the previous day they had spent together. It would be hard to give him up now. Everything about him, his mind, his heart, his gentleness with her, his body, were addictive. 'You should have kids.'

'Can you have more?' he asked casually. It wasn't something he worried about. He liked Annabelle, and he wouldn't have been bothered by adoption.

'I don't think so. I'd been trying to get pregnant again ever since Annabelle, with no success, though no one ever figured out why I didn't. And Dr Webber says about half the women my age become sterile after chemo. I don't know where I fall in all that, but in any case I'm not supposed to get pregnant for five years, even if I could and by then I would be too old. You deserve better, Brock.'

'I've been saying that to myself a lot,' he said, teasing her, and she shoved him.

'I mean it.'

'It doesn't bother me. I'm not sure I'd be upset if I never had kids of my own. I think adoption's a great thing. Or would you object to that?' he asked, curious. There were still things he wanted to know about her.

'I've never thought about it. But that might be nice. Don't you think though that one day you'd resent not having a child of your own blood? It's a wonderful thing,' she said, looking at Annabelle, and then at him. 'I never knew that till I had her, and realized what I'd been missing. I wish now I'd started sooner.'

'You didn't have time. Not with a career like yours. I still don't know how you do it.'

'It's a juggling act. You have to keep your priorities straight all the time, and sometimes you louse it all up. But it seems to work most of the time. She's a great kid, and I try and do as much with her as I can. Sam is pretty good with her too, when he's here.' But so far, nothing Brock had heard about Sam had impressed him.

They had dinner out with Brock that night, at a deli on Eighty-fourth Street. He told Annabelle funny stories, and did silly imitations. They were all good friends by the end of the day. And the next day he took Alex back to Dr Webber. He wouldn't let her go alone anymore, she was his now. And then it all began again, the vomiting, the fatigue, and then finally the two or three good weeks until the next time. But the time seemed to fly now.

335

They stole what time they could, at her apartment late at night, when Sam wasn't there, which was most of the time, or at his place whenever Carmen stayed. They got hungrier for each other by the day. And once they even got carried away in her office bathroom. He had gone back out with his shirt buttoned wrong and his tie askew and Alex had laughed so hard she could hardly control herself. They were like two kids, but they were having fun, and they deserved it. Alex had paid a high price for all this. And Brock had waited a long time for her. Neither of them had ever been happier, and even Annabelle really liked him, as did Carmen. She was still furious with Sam for all he hadn't done for Alex in the past six months, and it was nice to see her happy now. Even Liz had figured it out and was pleased, although, for their sakes, she still pretended not to notice.

They worked together all the time now, even more than before, and consulted each other on everything they worked on. Alex shared all her cases with him, and no one found it unusual, since she had been so sick since the fall, and relied on him so much to help her carry her workload. Everyone seemed very impressed by their system, and their results. It was the perfect relationship, and they were together constantly. There was hardly an hour of the day when they weren't, and neither of them seemed to chafe at the other's constant companionship. On the contrary, they loved it.

Even Sam noticed that she was different these days. She seemed happier and more lighthearted, and the rare times they met at breakfast, she joked with him a little bit, and didn't seem quite as angry.

It was April when she finally asked him when he was moving out, one morning when Carmen had taken

Annabelle to school, and they were both finishing their breakfast and reading the papers.

'Are you in a hurry for me to leave?' he asked, looking a little startled.

'No,' she smiled sadly, 'but the real estate agents keep calling with co-ops for you. I just figured you'd have found something by now. There can't be that many co-ops in New York.' They were calling night and day now. And Daphne was nagging him about it. She had been patient for long enough, and she wanted him to herself now. He always felt a little torn between coming home at night, not that he wanted to, but he felt guilty about Annabelle, and as though he should be there in the morning.

'I haven't found anything yet. I'll let you know,' he said coolly. 'You're not finished with your treatments yet anyway,' he reminded her. And for a minute, she got the feeling that he was dragging his feet. But she knew he didn't want to leave their daughter.

'I'll be finished in four weeks,' she said with relief in her voice. It had already been five months, the longest five months in her life, but they were almost over. She and Brock could talk of nothing else, and all the things they were going to do when she finally felt better. They were already going to movies, and had been to the opening of a play. She wanted to go to the opera with him, but she hadn't had the energy. They were talking about taking subscription seats for the following season, but that was a big commitment. 'What about you?' Alex asked Sam, trying to sound casual. 'What are you doing this summer, or haven't you figured that out yet?'

'I . . . uh . . . I don't know yet. I might go to Europe for a month or two.' He was as vague as possible, but he knew that Daphne wanted to spend

337

time in the South of France, and Simon had told him about a fabulous yacht to charter. It was all a little racier than their usual summer on Long Island and vacations in Maine, but on the other hand, he certainly could afford it, and it sounded like fun. He felt he owed some special time to Daphne after all her patience during the winter.

'Europe for a month or *two*?' Alex looked at him in surprise. 'Business must be *very* good.'

'It is. Thanks to Simon.'

'What about Annabelle? Will you be taking her with you?'

'For part of it. I think it will be fun for her.' And Daphne would have her son for a couple of weeks too, although she wasn't very excited about it. But as Alex listened, she suddenly wondered just who his girlfriend was, and how well she would care for her daughter. It was an issue that would have to be resolved before the summer.

'Annabelle doesn't know you're moving out, you know,' Alex reminded him. They had to face that, but it was still too early, and he hadn't found a place yet. 'It's going to be hard for her.' It was going to be hard for all of them, and they knew that. You didn't end seventeen years of marriage easily, even after all this preparation.

'She's going to be furious with me,' Sam said unhappily, hoping she would like Daphne and make things a little easier for him. Daphne was so young and fun and beautiful, he reminded himself practically, how could anyone not like her?

'She'll get through it.' They had gotten through a lot of tough things that year. But Annabelle seemed a little less worried about her mother lately.

338

'You seem to be doing fine,' he commented, watching her, sensing something different and more womanly about her. She had seemed so dead in those early months, and now she seemed to be coming slowly alive again. It made him feel better about leaving her, and worse at the same time. And much to his own surprise, it also made him miss her.

'I'm fine,' she reassured him. But talking to him still made her sad, and angry sometimes. It was difficult for it not to. And it was harder still not to think of the girl he was leaving her for. Alex had seen him with her again, in a restaurant, but he still didn't know it. But it had thrown her to see them.

He was still thinking about Alex when he left for work that day, and remembering how happy they had been, and some of the funny things they'd done together. She had been so wild and zany when he first met her. She was smart, and beautiful, he had always loved her directness and her honesty, her integrity, and her sense of honor. And now she was so much quieter and different. He knew it was all still there, but she felt like a stranger. He couldn't help wondering how much of it was his fault.

'You're in a sober mood today,' Daphne chided him when she saw him in his office a little while later.

'No, just working things out at home. We really have to find an apartment.' He wanted to start his new life, so he could start to forget the old one completely. Except for Annabelle of course. He knew it was time to introduce them. There wasn't much Alex could say now, even if Annabelle told her and he had sensed for a long time that Alex knew there was another woman, although he had never confessed it, and he had no idea she'd seen them. 'Have you seen anything you like this week?' he asked hopefully. But it was exasperating. They had looked at every small co-op in New York, and there was always something wrong with them. Most of them needed extensive decorating and reconstruction.

'It's so stupid really,' Daphne complained, 'there's always too many bedrooms, or not enough view, or it's too low a floor and too noisy.' They wanted fireplaces as well, and hopefully a view of the park or the river. They preferred a view of Central Park, and were looking on Fifth Avenue, and he was willing to pay over a million. He could get a mortgage on it, and with the profits from their latest deals, it was not going to be a problem.

Alex had already said she wanted nothing from him, except support for Annabelle. She was being very fair, and she had her law practice. She didn't want money from Sam. What she had wanted from him he didn't have to give her.

'Don't be such a gloomy puss,' Daphne cajoled him, as she locked the door to his office and came to sit on his lap, grinding herself slowly against him. It made him smile sheepishly, he knew he was foolish to have regrets about the past. It was over and gone. It had been good then, but this was better now. And as usual, when he slid his hand under her skirt, he found no barriers to his fingers. She wore no underwear, no pantyhose, and he loved that. Once in a while she wore a garter belt and stockings, and she had a fabulous collection of sexy bras, but underpants were something Daphne had long since dispensed with.

'Do I have any meetings on my calendar this morning, Miss Belrose?' he asked, kissing her, as she unzipped his fly for him and reached into it with nimble fingers.

'I believe not, Mr Parker,' she said in proper British

340

tones, 'oh wait a minute . . . yes . . .' she pretended to jog her memory . . . 'I just remembered one . . . ah, here it is . . .' She pulled him out of his trousers and put her lips to him, as he fell back in his chair with a groan of pleasure. Their 'meeting' didn't last long, but was extremely pleasurable, and when she left his office shortly afterwards, she wore a smile, and her skirt was slightly crooked.

Chapter 18

The needle went into Alex's vein for the last time, and then out again, on an afternoon in May, as Brock sat with her, and she cried with powerful emotions when it was over. She still had six Cytoxan tablets to take, but after that she was free. She had a final chest X-ray, a blood count, and a mammogram. She was clean. She had survived six wretched months of chemotherapy, and he had helped her do it.

She said good-bye to Dr Webber and made an appointment for a follow-up visit in six months, and even sick as she felt, she felt liberated as she left the doctor's office.

'What'll we do to celebrate?' Brock asked her as they stood on Fifty-seventh Street, looking at each other in relieved disbelief.

'I have an idea,' she said mischievously, looking at him, but they both knew that within an hour, she'd be vomiting again. But also for the last time. This would never happen to her again. She felt sure of it. She wouldn't let it.

They went back to the office, and spent a quiet afternoon. She was sick, but even that didn't seem as bad as usual. Even her body seemed to know that it had suffered the last assault, the last vicious attack on her system.

And that night, she lay in his arms, with her door locked, in case Annabelle woke up. They had finally given up their chastity in her home. And they knew that if Sam wasn't home by nine or ten, he wasn't coming, and tonight was no different.

'What'll we do now, Alex?' Brock asked her. They had been talking about Long Island again. She wanted to rent a place with him for the summer, and one of the partners had offered her his home in East Hampton, and it sounded very appealing. She just didn't want him to find out about Brock because of the fraternization rule at the law firm, but she didn't think he would. And they had such a good cover, that no one thought anything of seeing them together. 'I'd love to take a trip with you,' he said.

'Where?' She loved to dream with him. Their whole life together had been a dream so far, a promise for the future.

'Paris . . . Venice . . . Rome . . . San Francisco,' he said more realistically.

'Let's do that,' she said suddenly. She hadn't taken vacation time in a year, and although she had a lot of time coming to her, she had been out so much she felt she could go away only briefly. 'We don't have any court appearances next month, that I know of yet. Why don't we just go for a few days? It would be fun.'

'You've got a deal,' he beamed at her, and they lay there and talked about it. 'Are you going to take the house in East Hampton?'

'I think so,' she decided as they lay there. Suddenly they could make plans, they could lead a life. They could go away. She was a real person again, with hopes, and dreams, and, with luck, a future.

The next few weeks were frantic for her. She was still catching up on work, and she was taking on more responsibilities again, for future trials. She took back her full workload, and the last day of Cytoxan came and went, almost without notice. And by the first of June, she already felt stronger and more like herself again. They were going to San Francisco at the end of the month, but before that she and Sam had to deal with Annabelle, and tell her that her father was leaving.

He had finally found a penthouse that he liked. It was close to where they currently lived, and had a living room with spectacular views, a handsome dining room, three bedrooms and servants' quarters, and a kitchen that had been in *House and Garden*. It cost an arm and a leg, but Daphne absolutely adored it.

'Can we?' she begged him, like a little girl with a new doll, and he didn't have the heart to say anything but yes to her. In spite of the price, it was a beautiful apartment. They had a large master suite, a room for Annabelle, and a guest room, where Sam pointed out Daphne's son could stay when he came to visit. But she said she preferred to visit him in England. She said this was too far to drag a five-year-old alone, and his nannies were such bores she wouldn't think of bringing them with him. She always had good reasons for not bringing him over, and Sam wondered sometimes if he was a dreadful brat, or she just wasn't much of a mother. Maybe both, but he didn't worry about it. He had to focus now on Annabelle, and right before the Memorial Day weekend, Sam and Alex both came home early and told her.

'Daddy's *leaving*?' she asked, her eyes brimming with tears, and her face full of panic.

'I'm only going to be three blocks away,' he said,

344

holding her in his arms, but she fought against him in total anguish.

'Why? Why are you going?' What had she done? What had they done? Why was this happening to her? She didn't understand it. And both her parents had to fight back tears as they consoled her.

'Mommy and I just think it's better, sweetheart,' he said, trying to calm her down and explain it simply. 'I'm not here much anymore anyway. I travel a lot. And Mommy and I think . . .' How could you explain it to a four-year-old? They weren't sure they understood it themselves, how could they explain it to her now? 'Mommy and I think we'll all be happier if she has her apartment, and I have mine. You can come and visit me anytime you want, and lots on weekends. We can do lots of fun things. We can even go to Disney World again if you like.' But she was smarter than that, and her mother's girl. Bribery didn't fix it.

'I don't want to go to Disney World. I don't want to go anywhere.' And then, the killer, 'Don't you love us anymore, Daddy?'

He almost choked as he heard the words, and was quick to reassure her. 'Of course I love you.'

'Don't you love Mommy anymore? Are you still mad at her for getting sick?' The correct answer would have been yes, but he wasn't that honest.

'Of course not. Of course I'm not mad at her. And yes, I love her. But we . . .' he had to fight back tears again, as Alex held her, 'we don't want to be married anymore. Not like we used to be. We want to live in separate places.'

'Are you getting divorced?' She looked genuinely shocked. She had heard about that in school, from Libby Weinstein. Her parents were divorced, and her mommy had remarried and had twins, and Libby didn't like that.

'No, we're not getting divorced,' Sam said firmly, though Alex wasn't even sure why they weren't. What was the point of dying by inches? But neither of them seemed ready to take the final step yet, and there was no rush. So they could reassure Annabelle at least for the moment. 'We're just going to live in separate houses.'

'I don't want you to.' Annabelle glowered at him, and then with a sudden jerk she spun around in Alex's arms and glared at her mother. 'It's all your fault, for getting sick. You made him mad at us, and now he's moving out. That was mean of you! You made him hate us!' She spoke with such vehemence that neither of her parents was prepared for it, as she broke from Alex's arms and ran to her room and slammed the door, and inside, she lay sobbing on her bed, beyond consolation. They both tried talking to her, to no avail, and finally Alex decided to leave her alone for a while, and walked silently into the kitchen. Sam was already standing there, staring at her, mute with grief and guilt. He had never felt worse in his life than now as he looked at Alex.

'As usual, it's all my fault,' Alex said unhappily, and he shook his head, feeling no better than she did.

'She'll get around to hating me eventually, don't worry about it. It's neither of our faults, it's just the way it is. It's what happened.'

'She'll get over it,' Alex said, sounding unconvinced. They all would. 'She'll see that you're not that far away, and if she sees enough of you, she'll be all right about it. You're going to have to make that effort.'

346

'Obviously,' he said, annoyed at the lecture. 'I want her with me as often as you'll let me have her.'

'You can have her whenever you like,' Alex said generously, but uncomfortable with the feeling, as if they were dividing up candlesticks, and not their daughter. And then she looked at him, remembering their plans. 'What about this weekend?' He had wanted to take Annabelle to the Hamptons with him for the Memorial Day weekend. He had rented a house for four days, and he thought it would be fun for her, and Alex had agreed.

'I'd still like to take her, if she'll come.'

'She's mad at me, not you. Remember?' She and Brock were going to Fire Island for the long weekend. 'She'll be okay,' she reassured him, and then went to check on her again. Annabelle had stopped crying, and she was lying on her bed, looking like her heart was broken.

'I'm sorry, baby,' Alex said softly to her. 'I know it's hard. But Daddy still loves you, and he's going to see you all the time.'

'Will you still take me to ballet?' she asked, confused about who was going where. It was a lot for a four-year-old to absorb. At forty-three, it was a lot for Alex too. And Sam had just turned fifty.

'Of course I'll take you to ballet. Every Friday. I'm not going to be sick anymore. I finished taking my medicine.'

'All of it?' she asked suspiciously.

'*All* of it,' she confirmed.

'Will your hair come back now?'

'I think so.'

'When?'

'Soon. We can be twins again.'

'And you're not going to die?' That was the crux of it for all of them, and a hard one to promise.

'No.' It was more important to reassure her now than to be completely truthful. There were no guarantees, but there was no sign of a recurrence either. 'I'm not going to die. I'm all better.'

'Good.' She smiled at her, almost ready to forgive her for losing her father. 'Why does Daddy have to go now?' she asked plaintively. It was so hard to explain it to her.

'Because he'll be happier. And that's important for him.'

'Isn't he happy here with us?'

'Not right now. He's happy with you. But not with me.'

'I told you he was mad at you,' she chided, 'you should have listened.' Alex laughed then. They were going to be all right. They had all survived. They had made it. Bad things had happened to them, but they had managed to live through it.

She went back out to see Sam again, before he left, and she found him packing a suitcase in the guest bedroom. Most of his things were still there, but he had told her that he'd be moving in the next two weeks. He was going to stay at the Carlyle for a month until the apartment was ready. He hadn't wanted to move into Daphne's apartment, and the Carlyle seemed like a good middle ground, and a nice place for Annabelle to visit.

'She's all right. She's shaken, but she'll adjust,' Alex said sadly.

'I'll pick her up at school on Friday, and take her out to Southampton with me then. I'll bring her back on Monday night.'

'Fine,' Alex nodded, realizing that they had just

slipped into a whole new phase. Despite his comings and goings for the past six months, it had just become official. They had told Annabelle. They were getting separated, not divorced, but separated. It was a whole new world now.

'Poor little thing,' Brock said sympathetically, when Alex told him about it that night. 'It must be hard for her to understand. It's hard enough for grown-ups.'

'She blames me for it. She said that if I hadn't gotten sick, he wouldn't have gotten mad at us. There's a certain truth to that, but I guess it was all there, lurking beneath the surface. I guess I didn't have the perfect marriage I thought I did, or it wouldn't have fallen apart so quickly.'

'I think what you went through would strain a lot of relationships,' he said fairly.

She nodded, and then remembered something. 'One of these days, I want to meet your sister.' He nodded, but said nothing. And then Alex got distracted when they talked about their plans for Fire Island. It sounded like it was going to be a fun weekend. They were going to stay at a small funky old hotel in The Pines, and she knew from experience, that once you got on the ferryboat and felt the salt air on your face, you left your problems behind you. It was just what she needed.

Sam could have used a little of that kind of week-end too. He picked Annabelle up at school, with her suitcase, and took her for a quick lunch, before they picked up Daphne and headed for Southampton. He had wanted to have lunch alone with Annabelle first, so he could prepare her, but she seemed more confused than ever. The idea that there was another woman in his life seemed more than she could even vaguely imagine.

'She's coming with us for the weekend?' She looked at him blankly. 'Why?'

'Oh . . .' He groped for answers, feeling suddenly very stupid. 'To help me with you, so we have more fun.' It was a dumb answer, and he knew it.

'You mean like Carmen?' She looked confused again, and he laughed nervously.

'No, silly. Like a friend.'

'You mean like Brock?' That at least was a frame of reference she understood, and one he immediately clung to.

'Exactly. Daphne works with me at the office, just like Brock works with Mommy.' There were more similarities than he knew, but he had no suspicion of them whatsoever. 'And she's my friend, and she's coming with us for the weekend.'

'Are you going to work with her, like Mommy works with Brock?'

'Well maybe . . . but actually . . . no, we just thought we'd have fun and play with you all weekend.'

'Okay.' It seemed silly to her, but she was at least willing to meet her.

But Sam's perceptions of their weekend plans were completely different from Daphne's.

'Why on earth didn't you bring a nanny with you?' Daphne stared at him in disbelief when he picked her up at her apartment. Annabelle was downstairs in the car, he had the keys, and he was keeping an eye on her from the window. 'Or at least a maid. We won't be able to go anywhere with a child that age. We'll be bloody well stuck all weekend.' It was a side of her he'd never seen, but she was anything but amused as he picked up her suitcase.

'I'm sorry, darling,' he apologized, 'I never even thought of it.' He and Alex had always taken care of her when they went away, and it had never been a problem. But then again, she was their child, and they'd been married. 'I'll bring Carmen next time. I promise.' He kissed her and she softened a little bit. She was wearing a blue cotton sundress and he could see her breasts through it, and he already knew from experience how little was beneath it. 'You're going to love her,' he promised as they went downstairs, 'she's adorable.' But as it turned out, she was not particularly adorable to Daphne, and she was extremely suspicious.

The ride to Long Island was fraught with questions and awkward answers and minor lies, and by the time they got there, Sam was perspiring and looking very nervous. He set Daphne's things down in the room next to his, and Annabelle's in a room across the hallway. But Daphne laughed aloud as soon as she saw the arrangement.

'You're not serious, are you, Sam? She's only four years old, she can't possibly know what's going on.' And Daphne really didn't care what she told her mother. But Sam did.

'I thought you could just leave your things in there, she doesn't have to know where we're sleeping.'

'And if she has a nightmare?' He'd never even thought of it. But Daphne knew that much about children.

'We'll go in to her.' He solved the problem, and Daphne laughed at him again.

'You'll be sure and tell her not to set foot out of bed, on penalty of death, won't you, darling?'

'All right, all right.' He felt stupid and uncomfortable, and even he had to admit that Annabelle was a perfect brat all afternoon and then she ate too much candy, and spent too much time in the sun without a hat, and threw up her entire dinner all over Daphne.

'Charming,' she said, looking vastly unamused, as Sam attempted to clean it. 'My little man does that constantly too. I've tried explaining to him that it's extremely unattractive.'

'My Mommy throws up all the time,' Annabelle said defensively, glaring at her. She knew they weren't friends, and weren't going to be, no matter what her Daddy said. She wasn't like Brock at all. She was mean and nasty. And she kept touching Annabelle's Daddy and kissing him. Annabelle had seen it. 'My Mommy's very brave,' Annabelle went on, as Sam took off her dress and threw it in the sink. He felt her head for a fever, but she didn't have one. 'She got very sick, and Daddy got mad at her, and now he's moving to a new apartment.'

'I know, darling, so am I,' Daphne announced before Sam could stop her. 'I know all about it. I'm going to live there with him.'

'You *are*?' Annabelle looked horrified and ran to the room they had assigned her. And as soon as she was gone, Daphne unbuttoned the two straps at her shoulders and stepped out of her sundress, and stood in front of Sam completely naked. 'She got sick on my dress,' she explained, but he already knew.

'I'm sorry. I think this is a lot for her to stomach all at once,' he said, unaware of the pun, and Daphne smiled.

'Apparently. Don't worry about it.' She kissed him, and he couldn't keep his hands off her, but he knew he had to.

'You'd better put some clothes on. I'll go up to Annabelle.'

'Why don't you let her stew in it for a while, she's

going to have to get used to it. It's really not a good idea to mollycoddle children.' Was that how she thought of it? Mollycoddling? Was that why she'd left her son with her ex-husband in England?

'I'll be down in a minute,' he said, and went upstairs, wondering how long the war would go on. But Annabelle was crying when he got there, and she continued to cry until she fell asleep in his arms, and he felt terrible about everything that had happened. He wanted Annabelle and Daphne to love each other. They were both important to him, they were both important relationships in his life, he needed both of them, and he wanted them at least to like each other.

But when Annabelle woke the next day at six a.m., they were still in bed, and Daphne was lying naked in his arms. He had never thought of what might happen in the morning, and he had forgotten to ask her to wear a nightgown. Annabelle wandered into their room without a sound and stood staring at them, her mouth open in horror. Sam was wearing nothing either, and he suggested that Annabelle go downstairs and wait for them, but Daphne was not amused to be woken at that hour, and it put her in a bad mood all morning.

The two 'girls' went at each other tooth and nail, and Sam finally took Annabelle to the beach to get away from it, but when he came back to take Daphne to lunch, she was furious that Annabelle had to come with them.

'What do you suggest I do with her for heaven's sake? Leave her home alone?'

'It wouldn't kill her, you know. She's not an infant. I must say, you treat children in America in quite extraordinary ways. They're dreadfully spoiled and the center of everything. It's not even healthy for them. I promise you, she needs to be treated like a child,

Sam. She'd be much happier at home, with a nanny or a maid, than dragging around everywhere with you. If her mother wants to do that with her because she has a pathetic little life, then that's fine, but I'm telling you right now, I don't intend to do it. I won't inflict my son on you for more than five days a year, and don't expect me to play nursemaid to yours. I won't have it,' she said petulantly, and for the first time in six months, he was both hurt and disappointed in her, and he wondered if something in her youth had made her so disagreeable about children. It was inconceivable to him that anyone would just dislike them. But when he thought about it, he realized that she had more or less warned him right from the beginning. He only hoped that she'd be willing to change now.

The three of them went out to lunch anyway, but it was a strain. Annabelle never took her eyes off her plate, and didn't eat anything. She had heard everything that Daphne had said, and for the moment she hated her and wanted to go back to her Mommy, and after lunch she said as much to her father. But he explained unhappily that her Mommy was away for the weekend.

He managed to find a sixteen-year-old baby-sitter for that night, by asking the neighbors. And he and Daphne went to the country club at Conscience Point for an evening of dinner and dancing, and she was in better spirits when they got home, and that night he asked her to wear a nightgown. And she laughed at him, and said she didn't have one.

The next day was more of the same, and all of them were relieved when they finally drove back to the city.

Alex was already at home waiting for them, alone, when they arrived. And Daphne waited in the car downstairs while Sam took Annabelle upstairs to her mother.

'Did you have fun?' she asked, beaming, in a pair of blue jeans and a starched white shirt and red espadrilles. And Sam couldn't help noticing how pretty she looked after all these months, with a suntan.

But Annabelle's face was its own story. She raised her eyes to her mother's and they were full of tears, as Sam gently touched his daughter's shoulder.

'We had a few problems of adjustment. I guess I didn't use the best judgment. I brought a friend along, and it wasn't easy for Annabelle.' Or for Daphne. 'I'm sorry,' he apologized to both of them, and Alex looked from one to the other in dismay, wondering what had happened.

But Annabelle glanced at Sam and then at Alex and said bluntly, 'I hate her.'

'You don't hate anyone,' Alex corrected, glancing at Sam. It must have been a great weekend. She wondered what the English girl had done to get Annabelle's back up. Probably nothing except be there with Sam, Alex suspected fairly. 'You have to be nice to Daddy's friends, Annabelle. It's rude to him to be rude to his friends,' she said gently, but Annabelle wasn't so easily silenced.

'She walked around naked all the time. It was disgusting. And she slept with Daddy.' She scowled at both of them and stormed off to her bedroom without saying good-bye to her father, as Alex looked at him, a little surprised at their lack of discretion.

'Maybe you should say something to your friend. If that's true, I don't think it's suitable for her to see that.' And it worried Alex. This was no way to conduct their visits. And she was surprised that Sam had done that.

'I know,' he said miserably. 'I'm sorry. The whole thing was a nightmare. It was very awkward.' And then he looked at her ruefully. 'They were both impossible, to tell you the truth.' She should have felt sorry for him, but she didn't. It would have been funny, if she hadn't been worried about Daphne parading around naked.

'You're going to have to work something out when she visits you, if you're going to be living with her.' It was the first time Alex had acknowledged it, but Annabelle had opened up the subject. 'She's too young for that stuff.'

'I know. And I'm too old. I'll handle it. She didn't see anything she shouldn't have,' he said, looking frazzled. 'Oh, and she threw up Friday, by the way.'

'You did have fun, didn't you?' Alex laughed at him, and it reminded him of the old days for a minute. She was laughing at him, and even he had to admit there was a funny side to it. He went to kiss Annabelle then, but she was still angry at him, and refused to say good-bye to him. She was angry at the world these days, and confused about all of it. And then, after a quick kiss in the air, and a wave to his wife, Sam ran back downstairs to Daphne.

'Happy again, my love?' she asked him, moving closer to him in the car, but he was disappointed in the weekend with his daughter, and it still troubled him at times when he saw Alex. They were both haunted by the ghosts of their past life, and trying to forget them.

'I'm sorry things didn't work out a little more smoothly,' Sam said quietly, acknowledging the fiasco.

'She'll be fine,' Daphne said confidently, and started talking to him about the apartment.

But once he moved into the Carlyle in June, things were even harder. Daphne was there all the time with him, and Annabelle suddenly understood that she was a permanent intruder.

'I *hate* her!' she said adamantly every time she came home to her mother.

'No, you don't,' Alex said firmly.

'Yes, I do.'

They took her to the new apartment and she said she hated that too. The only thing she said she liked was the lemonade and chocolate cookies at the Carlyle. Sam was trying to organize their summer too, he had gotten the yacht, and a house in Cap d'Antibes, and Alex had agreed to let her go with them.

But it was Daphne who objected vehemently to Annabelle's being included. She was not having Annabelle with them in Europe, she said, not even with a nanny.

'She's my daughter, for heaven's sake.' He was horrified by her attitude and very hurt by it. This was not what he had expected from the woman he lived with. And they were going to be gone for six weeks, a long time not to see his daughter.

'Fine. Then bring her along when she's eighteen. She doesn't belong with us on a yacht, and in a house in the South of France. What if she falls overboard? I'm not going to spend my time worrying about her. I'm not bringing my son along either.' In fact, she was only seeing him for a week in London. She made it sound like the ultimate sacrifice, but Sam was beginning to know better.

They argued about it constantly, and he was not about to give in, but it was Annabelle herself who finally decided. She didn't want to go away with them, didn't want to go to Europe, and leave her Mommy.

357

They were going to spend a week in London, two in Cap d'Antibes, and three on the yacht, cruising around France and Italy and Greece. It sounded heavenly to Alex, but not to her daughter.

'Maybe she's just too young,' Alex suggested gently to Sam. 'Maybe next year.' She assumed he'd be married to the girl by then, and Annabelle would have to get along with her. It was odd, because he hadn't asked Alex for the divorce yet, but she knew it was coming, probably at the end of the summer. He probably just didn't want to look like he was pushing. She had resigned herself to it by then. Their marriage was history, it had never been as glamorous as his life with Daphne anyway. He would never have thought of going to the South of France or renting a yacht while he was married to Alex.

'What are you going to do with her?' Sam asked, worried about Annabelle, and unhappy not to have her with him for the summer.

'I've rented a house in East Hampton. I'd love having her with me. I'll ask Carmen to stay out there during the week, and I'll work a short week so I can be with her.' It sounded fine to him, and Annabelle was thrilled when they told her.

'I don't have to go with Daddy and Daphne?' she said incredulously. 'Yippee!' But her reaction really hurt him, and he was annoyed with Daphne that night when he went back to the Carlyle.

'Oh for heaven's sake, don't pout,' Daphne teased, pouring a glass of Cristal for him. 'She's only a child, she'd have hated it. And we'd have been miserable, watching her, worried all the time. It wouldn't have been a vacation.' She smiled at him, enormously relieved to have the issue disposed of. 'What do you want to do tonight? Go out or stay home?' Life was a constant party to her and if not a party, an orgy.

'Maybe I ought to do some work for a change,' he said glumly. He had been letting his partners handle everything. He and Simon were bringing in all the new deals, and Simon took care of an amazing amount of the details. Sam had been so busy traveling, and changing his life around, he felt a little guilty for not paying more attention to business.

'Oh don't work,' Daphne complained. 'Let's do something fun.' But before he could suggest anything, she had straddled him and pulled up her skirt, and there was only one thing that appealed to him. He laid her on the couch in the hotel, and took her with more force than usual. He was half angry at her and half in love with her, disappointed and hurt and so overwhelmed with passion for her that sometimes it just drove him crazy.

Chapter 19

Alex and Brock moved into their summer house at the end of June, and they both loved it. It was simple and comfortable, with blue-and-white-checked curtains and sisal on the floor. There was a big homey kitchen with Portuguese tiles, and a sweet little garden for Annabelle to play in. She thought the house was pretty too, when they took her there for the first time on the Fourth of July weekend.

She didn't seem surprised that Brock was there, and Alex was a lot more careful than Sam had been with Daphne. Brock 'officially' slept in the guest room downstairs, and he was careful to go back down again every morning before Annabelle got up, and one morning when they forgot and almost got caught, Brock slipped on his jeans and pretended to be fixing something in Alex's bathroom.

Annabelle was completely happy and at ease with him, and the three of them went everywhere together. Alex was getting her full strength back rapidly, and she was full of energy and good spirits. And in mid-July she surprised both of them by coming downstairs without her wig. Her hair was soft and short and curly.

'You look pretty, Mommy! Just like me!' Annabelle

giggled and went outside to play as Brock smiled at Alex and almost knocked her out of her seat with his next question.

'So when are we getting married, Mrs Parker?' She smiled hesitantly at him. She was very much in love with him, but she had never allowed herself to think about the future, for a variety of reasons.

'Sam hasn't even asked me for a divorce yet.'

'Why wait for him to ask? Why don't you ask him when he gets back from Europe?' It was everything Brock had hoped for.

But she looked at him seriously then, hesitating, and looking very cautious. 'It wouldn't be fair to you, Brock. I'm fine now, but what if something happens again later?' He had already proven his ability to cope with it, but that wasn't the issue. 'I don't want to do that to you. You have a right to a sure future.'

'That's bullshit,' he said, looking angry at her. 'You can't sit around for the next five years, waiting to see what happens. You have to go on with your life, and deal with whatever comes. I want to marry you, and Annabelle,' he said, taking her hand in his and kissing her from across the table. 'I don't want to wait. I want our life now. I want to live with both of you, and take care of you. I don't want this to end after the summer.'

'Neither do I,' she said honestly, but she was ten years older than he was, and she'd had cancer. 'What would your sister say to all this?' She still hadn't met her or talked to her, but she knew how much she meant to Brock. She could tell from some of the things he'd said, but generally, he spoke of her very little. 'Wouldn't she be unhappy? You should marry some nice young girl who'll give you lots of kids and no problems.'

'She would tell me to do what I think is best. And best is you. Alex . . . I mean it. I want you to ask Sam for a divorce when he comes back from Europe. And then we'll get married when it's final.'

'I love you.' She smiled softly at him from across the table, as they watched Annabelle through the picture window. She was deeply moved by his willingness to accept her under any conditions.

'I want to marry you. And I'm not going to stop bugging you till you say you will,' he said stubbornly, and she laughed at him.

'It's not as though I don't want to. What about your job?' she asked seriously. He couldn't be married to her and keep it.

'I've had two other offers this year. They were pretty good. I'd probably do better if I went elsewhere. But before I go anywhere, I'd like to talk to the senior partners. I was wondering if, since you've been sick, they might not let us make an exception and keep working together.'

'They might. We're a good team,' she smiled gratefully at him. 'And you'll be up for partner next year.'

'We'll talk to them,' he said calmly, 'but first Sam.'

'I haven't agreed yet,' she said, looking mischievous but loving.

'You will,' he said confidently, and he was right. By the end of the week, she had agreed. She was going to ask Sam for a divorce, and marry Brock as soon as it was final.

'I must be crazy,' she said distractedly, 'I'm twice your age.'

'You're ten years older, that doesn't even count, and you look younger than I do.' She did actually, she had dropped years since they had moved to Long Island. The effects of the chemo were falling away, her hair was thicker than it ever had been, and she had lost the bloat from the chemo. She looked the same as she had before the cancer, maybe better. And they were like kids as they played on the beach on the weekends. She was very relaxed when she and Brock drove in on Monday mornings. Carmen came out late on Sunday nights, so they could go back to the city on Monday in time to get to work. And they left work as early as they could on Thursdays and drove out to Long Island. Most of the lawyers took Fridays off in the summer, and the firm closed at noon, like many New York corporations.

And when they got back to their house at the beach, Annabelle was always waiting for them, happy and excited. During the week, Alex and Brock stayed at his place, or hers, whichever seemed the most convenient. It was the perfect summer.

Annabelle had heard from her father several times. He was in Cap d'Antibes by then. He had called her, and sent her a dozen postcards. But Alex hadn't talked to him, he never called when she was there. She didn't want to ask him for the divorce over the phone anyway. She had no doubts anymore. Brock had convinced her. He had done more than any man ever could to prove himself to her. And as long as he knew what he was doing, and what he wanted, she had no reason to question him any further. She knew that she loved him. She felt very lucky to be with him.

And she was surprised when they were lying on the beach in mid July, and she saw him looking at her bathing suit, and then he leaned over and kissed her.

'You're beautiful,' he said warmly, and she smiled

363

at him. Annabelle was nearby, but the prospect of a little 'nap' after lunch was very appealing.

'You're blind,' she responded, squinting at him in the sun, and then he gently touched her breast with one hand, and she could feel her whole body tingle.

'I think we should see a plastic surgeon sometime soon.'

'Why?' She tried to sound casual, but she didn't like talking about it. In spite of his gentleness with her, she was still selfconscious about the way she looked. And most of the time she wore a prosthesis.

'I just think you should,' he said kindly.

'Want me to get a new nose, or a face-lift?'

'Don't be such a twit. You're too young to spend the rest of your life hiding. You should be parading around naked all the time.' He was actually fairly circumspect, but she knew he was trying to make her feel better about her missing breast.

'You mean you want me to run around naked like Sam's little English girl? I don't think so.' The thought of Daphne still annoyed her.

'Never mind that. You know what I mean. At least talk to a doctor, find out what's involved. You could do it this summer and get it over with, and then you'd have two boobs forever.'

'It sounds awful, and it hurts a lot.'

'How do you know?'

'I've talked to other women in my support group, and Dr Webber told me. It sounded disgusting.'

'Don't be such a wimp.' They both knew she was anything but a wimp. But he also wanted her to feel self-confident, and whole again. He nagged her about it, and even gave her the name of a well-known reconstructive plastic surgeon he'd found through a surgeon friend. Brock was always very resourceful.

'I made an appointment for you,' he said bluntly, one afternoon at work, and she stared up at him in amazement.

'That's a pushy thing to do.' She didn't want to go, and she argued with him about it for half an hour. 'I'm not going.'

'Yes you are, I'm taking you. Just talk to the guy. It can't hurt you.'

She was still fuming about it when the day of the appointment came, but in the end, she went with him, and she was surprised how different this doctor was from her other surgeon. Where the other one was cold and methodical and dealing with hard facts and undeniable dangers, this one was dealing with improving things, and making people feel better about themselves. He was round and short, and gentle, and he had a good sense of humor. He had her laughing after a few minutes, and gently worked the conversation around to the procedure that had brought them to see him. He examined Alex's breast, or where it had been, and looked at the other one too, and told her he thought they could do a good job for her. They could either put an implant in or do a tissue expansion, which would require two months of weekly injections of saline solution to obtain the desired form. If anything, Alex preferred the immediacy of the implant. But in any case, she wasn't convinced yet. He explained that the surgery would be costly, of course, and not without pain, but they could take care of most of that for her, and at her age, he told her he thought it was well worth it.

'You don't want to look like that for the rest of your life, Mrs Parker. We can give you a beautiful breast.' He had suggested nipple sharing and a tattoo to complete the picture. And in spite of everything he said to encourage her, Alex still thought it sounded awful.

But after they made love that night, she asked Brock if it mattered to him if she didn't do it.

'Of course not,' he said honestly. 'I just thought you should. For you. But it's up to you. I'd love you with no boobs. God forbid.' Once was enough for a lifetime.

But without saying anything to him, she thought about it for two weeks, and at the end of July, she surprised him one morning in East Hampton.

'I'm doing it,' she said, sitting down at the table with him after finishing the dishes. He was deep in the Sunday paper.

'Doing what?' he asked, looking up at her, confused, but always interested in what she had to tell him. 'Are we doing something today?'

'Not today. I'm going to call on Monday.'

'Call who?' He felt as though he had already missed an important part of the conversation.

'Greenspan.'

'Who's that?' His mind was blank. He was half asleep. Maybe a new client.

'The doctor you took me to. The plastic surgeon.' She looked very determined, and kind of nervous.

'You are?' He beamed, he was happy for her. He thought she'd be pleased afterwards. 'Good for you!' He kissed her, and on Monday, true to her word, she called him and told him she had decided on the implant. She was terrified, about the surgery, and more pain, but once she decided to go ahead with it, she was determined to do it. He had had a cancellation at the end of the week, and he told her to expect to spend four days in the hospital, but after that she could go back to work. It would be

366

painful for a while, more painful than her previous surgery, he confessed, but nothing like the discomfort she had experienced with chemo.

She took Thursday off that week, and Carmen agreed to stay in East Hampton with Annabelle. Alex told Annabelle that she had to go away on business. She didn't want to worry her with telling her about the hospital. The only one she told was Carmen, who was concerned at first, but then relieved when Alex told her why she was going. She thought it was a good idea too, and so did Liz. Everyone was excited about it, except Alex, who was terrified, and had second thoughts at the last minute.

On Wednesday night, she lay awake all night, next to Brock, wishing she hadn't said she would do it.

Brock took her to Lenox Hill at seven a.m. the next day, and a nurse and an anesthesiologist explained all the procedures to them. They gave Alex a hospital gown, and the nurse started an IV, and as soon as she did, Alex started to cry uncontrollably. All she could think of was having chemo, and her last surgery, and she felt utterly stupid.

Dr Greenspan arrived and ordered a shot of Valium for her. 'We believe in keeping everyone happy around here,' he smiled, and then looked at Brock with amusement, 'would you like one too?'

'I'd love it.'

She was already half asleep when they wheeled her toward surgery, and Brock waited nervously in her room, and paced the halls, until five hours later when Dr Greenspan came and told him she had done well. He was very pleased. It was a complicated procedure but everything had gone smoothly.

'I think she'll be very happy with the results.' He had put an implant in, and as her original breast had been small, it did not require extensive tissue expansion although of course there had been some to obtain the desired form. There had been other options as well, but Alex preferred the immediacy of the implant, although she understood that it had to be carefully monitored in case of leakage, and she would have to be part of a control group, to provide data on silicone implants. 'She'll have to come back in a month or two for some final adjustments.' They had told her that the final nipple reconstruction and tattoos could be done with a local. 'But I think she'll do fine,' Greenspan reassured him.

It was another two hours before she came down from the recovery room, and when she did, she was still very woozy.

'Hi,' she whispered to him, 'how did it go?'

'It looks great,' he reassured her, although of course he hadn't seen it.

The next four days in the hospital were uncomfortable for her, more than she'd expected, and she was still in a fair amount of pain when she went back to the office on Monday. But it had none of the implications of her earlier surgery, and none of the dangers.

The bandage was cumbersome, but she still managed to do a fair amount of work, and a lot of the partners were away on vacation, so no one seemed to be aware of her situation. She stayed in her office, and she was wearing one of Brock's shirts over the bandages. He brought her lunch, and at the end of the day they went back to his apartment. And on Thursday, a week after the surgery, the dressing had come off, and the stitches were removed, before they went back to East Hampton. Annabelle was ecstatic to see them, and Alex moved a little gingerly while she held her.

'Did you hurt yourself, Mommy?' she asked worriedly, suddenly afraid again. Annabelle had bad memories too, and Alex didn't want to scare her.

'No, I'm fine,' she reassured her.

'Are you sick again?' Annabelle's eyes were huge as she looked at her mother, and Alex pulled her even closer, as she felt her little girl shaking.

'I'm fine,' she said gently, holding her in her arms, but then Alex realized she had to explain it. She told her very simply that when she had hurt her breast, ten months before, they had had to take some of it away, and now they'd put it back. It seemed the simplest explanation, but when her father called that night she told him that Mommy had found her breast and put it back on again, which she considered good news, and startled her father. He assumed that Annabelle had seen Alex's prosthesis. It never occurred to him that she'd had surgery again, and he didn't ask to speak to her since Daphne was standing right near him.

They were on the yacht by then, and some of Daphne's fancy English friends had joined them. It was a very worldly group with very sophisticated pastimes, and they were spending a lot of time visiting people on other yachts, and in villas along the Riviera. And in a few days they were going to Sardinia.

And every day, Brock reminded Alex that she had to talk to Sam as soon as he got home from Europe. He was very anxious to get married.

'I know, I know,' she smiled at him, kissing him gently to reassure him. 'Relax. As soon as he gets home, I'll call him.' If they filed by the fall, she and Brock could be married in the spring. It was all he wanted. Sometimes his youthful zeal made her feel ancient, but in other ways, she loved it. Most of the time she didn't feel the difference in their ages,

369

but there were undeniably times when a little bit of maturity was lacking, but she tried to ignore it. Their experiences, and their viewpoints, were occasionally a little different.

The summer flew by all too quickly for all of them. Daphne hated to come back from Europe, and only her passion for Sam brought her back to New York at all. She admitted to him that she was getting very homesick for London. Life in the States just wasn't the same for her, but he was hoping that she would be distracted by the new apartment. And he promised her that they would travel more, and start spending more time abroad. It wasn't easy for him with his business obligations in New York, but he had a lot of clients abroad too, and he would have done anything to keep her happy. He was spending so much time with her that for months he had seriously neglected his business. She was proving to be a very demanding girl, and she was obviously used to having what she wanted.

And by the time Sam came home, Alex and Brock were thinking with regret of the end of the summer. They had the house in East Hampton till Labor Day, and the first weekend he was back, Sam took Annabelle to Bridgehampton with him. He was staying there with friends, and after six and a half weeks away, Daphne agreed to let him bring Annabelle with them.

'Do you suppose they'll do better this time?' Alex asked Brock seriously. Annabelle had been so unhappy the last time she'd seen Daphne. But when Sam brought her back to East Hampton early on Sunday afternoon, it was obvious that something had happened. He was very terse when he dropped her off, and he was alone, and although she knew Brock was anxious for her to talk to him, there was no opportunity before he got in his car and sped off. He had scarcely said two words to Alex.

She looked down at Annabelle as soon as he had left and questioned her. 'What happened?'

'I don't know. Daddy got a lot of phone calls. He was on the phone all the time, and he shouted a lot at the people who called him. And today he said he had to go. He packed my suitcase and brought me home. Daphne shouted a lot too. She said if he wasn't nice to her, she was going back to England. That would be good. I think she's really mean, and stupid.'

It was obvious that something had gone wrong, but it was impossible to decipher it from Annabelle's description.

It was only the next morning, as she and Brock rode into town on the train, that Alex gave a start and stared at the front page of the papers. There were photographs of Sam and Larry and Tom. They were being indicted by the grand jury for fraudulent investments, and a variety of very impressive charges, including embezzlement.

'Holy shit,' she said, handing the paper to Brock. It was incredible. Sam had always been meticulously honest.

'Wow!' He whistled as he read it. The charges were very serious, and Simon was being implicated too, although he had not yet been indicted. It was the three original partners who were being accused of at least a dozen counts of fraud, and embezzlement. 'He's in big trouble, no wonder he was upset yesterday.' Brock looked over at her, and Alex was stunned. What had he done with his life in the past months? What stupidity had he gotten himself into? He could wind up in jail for twenty or thirty years on the charges they were bringing against him. What in hell had happened?

'I'll call him when we get to the office,' she said pensively. She still couldn't believe what she'd been reading.

But when she got to the office, there were already two calls from him. She walked into her office and closed the door, and dialed his office. He came on the line in an instant.

'Thanks for returning my call.' He sounded extremely nervous.

'What's happening?' she asked him, still stunned. She had thought she had known him.

'I'm not sure yet. I know some of it. But not all. I'm not sure I'll ever know everything. But I know enough. I'm up the creek, Alex. I need help. I need a lawyer.' He had a very good lawyer, but he wasn't a criminal attorney.

'I don't do criminal, Sam,' she said softly, sorry for him, sorry that he had let his life get away from him so completely, or had gone so far astray he couldn't see what he was doing. She wondered if the girl had anything to do with it, she felt sure Simon did, although he hadn't yet been indicted.

'You're a litigator. You can at least advise me about what I should do now. Can I talk to you? Can I come and see you, Alex? Please?' He was begging her, and after seventeen years, she felt she owed it to him at least to listen. Besides, despite everything that had happened to them, in a way, she still loved him.

'I'll see what I can do. But I'm going to refer you to a criminal attorney eventually, Sam. I'm not dumb enough to try to help you, and hurt you as a result of my ignorance. But I'll do the best I can if you want to tell me what happened. When do you want to come in?'

'Now?' He couldn't stand the tension a moment longer.

It was ten o'clock and she had an appointment at one-thirty, but she was free until then. 'Okay. Come on in.' Her paperwork could wait, and she went to tell Brock what she was doing.

'Shouldn't you turn him over to one of the criminal guys right now?'

'I want to talk to him first. Will you sit in with me?' It was an odd request, but this was a professional meeting, and she respected Brock's opinion.

'If you want me to. Can I punch him in the nose when he's finished?' he said with a grin. He couldn't think of a more fitting end to a bastard like Sam Parker than twenty years in jail. The only reason he was willing to listen was for Alex, but he was not particularly inclined to help him.

'You can't hit him till he pays his bill,' she smiled back at him. Her life was with Brock now, not with Sam, whatever his problems.

'Well, don't forget to ask him the million-dollar question.' He was reminding her about the divorce, but this was hardly the moment.

'Relax. This is business.'

Sam was there twenty minutes later, looking pale under his suntan. There were dark circles under his eyes, and when he sat across the conference table from Alex and Brock, his hands were visibly shaking. The man was in shock. His reputation was down the drain, and his entire life had fallen apart, seemingly all in six weeks, while he was in Europe with Daphne.

Alex had asked him if he minded having Brock in on the meeting with them, and though he wasn't enthusiastic about it, he agreed, if she thought it would be useful. He wanted all the help he could get, and he was very grateful to Alex. He told her she was the best attorney he knew, and he valued her opinion. He did not say more than that but the look that passed between them was old and familiar. They had known and loved each other for a long time, it was hard to forget that.

The story he told was not a pretty one, and as he had told her, he didn't yet have all the answers. What appeared to have happened, as far as he could discern, was that Simon had been slowly and steadily introducing unscrupulous clients into their business, and falsifying their histories and reports from various banks in Europe. And then, in ways Sam had not yet completely figured out, Simon had begun juggling money. He had embezzled from them, and stolen money from the legitimate clients, and he had begun laundering huge amounts from disreputable sources in Europe. It had apparently gone on for months, and Sam admitted, without accusing her, that during the time of her illness and the stress between them, he had stopped paying as close attention as he should to his business. He didn't want to tell her, unless he had to, that he had also been distracted by his affair with Daphne.

He did explain though that he was not yet sure if she had been introduced into the business by Simon, as a decoy. But her arrival had been very timely, along with the distraction she provided.

Sam admitted to her then, that by the spring he had begun to suspect something was wrong in Simon's dealings with one of their clients, and certain funds seemed to have been mishandled. But when he had confronted his partners about it, they had reassured him and insisted that it was not as it appeared, and he had decided that he was worried about nothing. He realized now that he had wanted to believe their story. And oddly enough, he confessed, it was at precisely that time that Alex had reminded him of her own suspicions about Simon again, and he had vehemently denied them.

'I was a damn fool all the way around,' he admitted now. 'Simon is as rotten as they come. You were right. And now I find out that Larry and Tom were in on it with him. Not at first, but in February they apparently caught on to something he'd done, and he bought them off. He paid them to keep quiet, and convinced them no one would ever know. He bought them off for a million bucks each, in a numbered account in Switzerland. So for the past six months, they've been in partnership with him, embezzling, stealing, making fraudulent deals. I can't believe how stupid and blind I was, or wanted to be. Simon even arranged to keep me out of the way in Europe for the last two months, when they made some of their worst deals. He found the yacht for me, and I walked right into it like a total fool,' with the help of Daphne. 'And while I was gone, someone at the bank got suspicious and reported us to the SEC and the FBI, and they brought in the Department of Justice, and the whole damn house of cards came down around us. And idiot that I was, they took me right down with them. When I got to London, something struck me wrong, when I talked to one of Simon's previous partners. I think he assumed I knew more than I did, which I didn't. But when I called Larry and Tom to ask what was going on, they covered for him, they were too scared not to. And while I was away they made twenty million dollars' worth of bad deals in my name. I'm up to my neck in the swamp with them.'

He looked devastated, and terrified. Everything he had built had been destroyed, and his reputation with it. His life was on the line now.

'But you weren't even here while they made those deals,' Alex said sensibly, 'will that help at all?'

'Those deals are only the tip of the iceberg. It's much worse than that, and I called in almost every day. They couriered things to me, I signed deal memos for them. They made them look quite respectable. And now I'm as responsible as they are. I wanted it all to be okay. I wanted my suspicions not to be true. I just didn't want to face what they were doing. But when I got home last week, and started asking questions, I got scared, and then I started to scratch the surface. You have no idea how much has gone on in the last year. I can't believe what a fool I was, or how much damage has been done, not just to my reputation, but to my business. It's all over, Alex.' He looked up at her with tears in his eyes. He hadn't cried for her, but he was crying for himself now. 'Everything I built is gone. Those two fools sold me out for a million dollars each, and now we're all going to wind up in jail thanks to Simon.' He closed his eyes, and tried to regain his composure again. She felt sorry for him, but not as sorry as she should be. In some ways, he had deserved this. He had trusted Simon when he shouldn't have, when his own instincts had warned him right from the beginning. And he had kept his eyes closed while Simon destroyed not only his business, but his life and his future. He opened his eyes wide and looked at her then, scared to death, and unafraid to show it. 'How bad is it?' He looked directly at her, and she hesitated, but only for a moment.

'Pretty bad, Sam. I made notes, and I want to call in one of our partners. But I don't think you're going to be able to just talk your way out of it. You've got too much implied responsibility here. It's going to be very hard to convince the grand jury, or anyone for that matter, that you didn't know what was going on, even if you didn't.'

'Do you believe me?'

'To a point,' she said honestly. 'I think you didn't want to know what was going on, and you let it happen without you.' Brock silently agreed with her completely.

'What do I do now?' He looked terrified, with good reason.

'Tell the truth. A lot of it. Particularly to your attorneys. Tell them everything you know, Sam. It'll be your only salvation. What about Simon?'

'They're indicting him this afternoon.'

'And the girl? His cousin? What part did she play in all this?' Other than destroying their marriage. He had really been set up by pros, and he'd been a complete fool, and he knew it.

'I don't know about her yet.' He looked away from Alex. 'She says she's not responsible, that she didn't know. I still think she knew when she came in, and then chose to stay out of it once she got here. Or maybe she didn't. Maybe she knew it all,' he said, running his hands through his hair as she watched him. He had paid a high price for his affair. He had paid with his business, his reputation, his money, possibly his life, if he wound up in prison. But she still wanted to help him. He was still her husband.

She went to the phone then, and called Phillip Smith, one of their senior partners. He specialized in tax fraud and SEC violations. It was similar enough. This was right up his alley, and he promised to be down in five minutes.

'What about you? Will you stay on it too?' Sam asked pathetically, and Brock wanted to hit him. She wasn't his any longer. He had done enough to her for one lifetime, but in spite of everything Alex still felt loyalties to him, if only because of their daughter.

'I wouldn't be any good to you,' Alex told Sam honestly, 'this isn't my area of expertise.' And in spite of feeling sorry for him, she didn't want to get too directly involved with him.

'Will you consult on it? Be an associate? Alex . . . please . . .' Brock turned away. He didn't want to see this. Sam was doing a number on her, and she felt obligated to help him.

'I'll see what I can do. But you don't need me, Sam. I'll see what Phillip Smith says after you talk to him.' She spoke to him very gently. And Brock was annoyed to see that, no matter what she said, and what Sam had done to her, there was still a bond between them.

'I do need you,' Sam said urgently in an undertone, as the senior partner arrived and Brock got called away for a few minutes.

She made the introductions and shared her notes with Phillip Smith. He nodded and frowned, and then sat down next to Alex, across the table from Sam.

'I should leave you alone,' she said, and stood up, looking down at Sam. He looked suddenly like a pathetic figure. He seemed broken by what had happened.

'Don't go.' He looked up at her like a frightened child and she was suddenly reminded of how she had felt when they told her she had cancer, how alone and afraid she had felt, and how he had refused to be there. He'd been out chasing Daphne, and letting criminals destroy his business, while he left Alex to puke her guts out.

378

'I'll be back,' she said quietly. She didn't want to encourage him to become dependent on her. This was going to be a complicated case, and she was sure it would go to trial. It would take months, if not years, and she wanted to be careful not to make too much of a commitment.

And when she got to her office, Brock was pacing the room with a look of fury.

'That whining sonofabitch,' he complained, glaring at her, as though it were all her fault. 'He hasn't done shit for you for a year, if he ever did before that, which I doubt, and now he shows up crying because he's about to go to jail. You know, you really ought to let him. It would do him good. It's really perfect. His fancy piece of ass and her cousin set him up for embezzlement and fraud and then he comes crying to you to save him.' He was so furious, he couldn't stop pacing. It was almost as though he had been betrayed, and not Alex.

'Relax, Brock,' she tried to calm him down, 'he's still my husband.'

'Not for long, I hope. What a slime bag. He sits there in his expensive suit and his ten-thousand-dollar watch, having just walked off a yacht in the South of France, and he's all surprised that his partners are crooks and he's been indicted by the grand jury. Well, I'm not surprised at all. I think he was probably in on it from the beginning.'

'I don't,' she said calmly, sitting at her desk while he paced, hating her husband. 'I think it probably happened pretty much the way he said. He was playing around and not paying attention, and they screwed him. That doesn't excuse him, he should have been watching what was going on. He had a responsibility, but he was playing, and hiding. And they were very busy while he was snoozing.'

'I still think he deserves it.'

'Maybe.' She wasn't sure what she thought yet. But after her one-thirty appointment left at two-fifteen, Sam was still talking to Phillip Smith, and a little while later they asked her to join them again. She went without Brock this time, which seemed simpler. She realized she'd been wrong to ask him in the first place. It was unfair to ask Brock to be objective.

'Well?' she said, as she sat down with them, and Sam noticed in spite of himself that her figure looked more natural again, and then he forced himself to think of his problems. 'Where are we?' she asked, focusing entirely on business. She was like a doctor with a patient, dispassionate and professional.

'Not in a very good place, I'm afraid.' Phillip Smith explained. He didn't pull any punches. He felt that Sam had a large degree of exposure, and that the grand jury indictment would most likely stick. In fact, there was a risk of additional charges. He felt sure that the matter would go to trial and what would happen in front of a jury was unpredictable. Sam had a good chance of losing. Particularly if the jury didn't believe him. The strongest thing he had going for him was the fact that he really hadn't known what had happened, until very late in the day. Phillip Smith felt that the partners would go down with Simon, but there was a faint chance of saving Sam if they could separate his case from theirs philosophically, and build up the sympathies of the jury. His wife had cancer, he was half out of his mind with worry over her, taking care of her, not paying attention to his business. He had trusted his partners, and in fact, he had not knowingly committed any crimes, he had been the pawn of Simon and his partners.

All of which sounded fair to her legally, but it seemed suddenly unfair to her that he should use her as his defense, when he had done so little for her. She understood it, it was a legal ploy, but it still irked her.

'In your opinion, will that fly?' Phillip asked her bluntly. He knew they were separated, and he wanted her reaction.

'It might,' she said cautiously, 'if no one looks too hard. I think most people knew that our marriage was falling apart, and that Sam was less than supportive.' Sam winced at her honesty, but he couldn't deny it. He said nothing to the two attorneys.

'Did people know he wasn't being "supportive" of you?'

'A few. I didn't advertise it. But I think Sam's life was fairly "involved" at the time.' She looked directly at him and he didn't expect what was coming. 'He has been rather conspicuously involved with someone else since last fall, or at least since well before Christmas.' Sam looked stunned as she said it, but was surprisingly calm. He had never realized how early she knew about Daphne.

Phillip Smith looked at him very coolly. 'Is that true?' Sam hated to admit it to him, and it shocked him to realize that Alex had known then. But he knew he had to be honest, as awkward as it was in front of Alex.

'Yes, it is true. It's the woman I told you about. Simon's cousin, Daphne Belrose.'

'Is she implicated too?'

'Not yet, but she's afraid she will be. She's talking about going back to England the minute anything happens.'

'That would be very foolish,' Smith said in stern

tones, 'it will make her an immediate fugitive, and they could very well extradite her from England. What is your situation with her now?'

'I'm living with her,' he said, feeling like a complete jerk, 'at least I was until this morning.'

'I see.' He nodded, taking it all in. 'Well, Mr Parker, I'd like some time to digest this, and let's see what the grand jury does. When do you testify before them?'

'In two days.'

'That gives us some time to decide on a course of action.' He didn't look pleased with the case and he didn't look as though he liked Sam, but he was willing to take the case for Alex. There was no question in his mind, it was going to be an interesting one, and a big one. Phillip Smith left them alone in the conference room then, and told Sam he'd call him in the morning. He told Alex he'd call her. And the two were left alone, to face each other. It was the first time they'd been alone since before the summer.

'I'm sorry. I didn't know how much you knew,' he said, looking genuinely pained, and unusually humble.

'I knew enough,' she said sadly, not wanting to talk about it with him. There was no point any longer. No matter what the remaining bond, or the child they shared, their marriage was over.

'I think you're in deep water, Sam. Very deep water. I'm sorry all of this happened. I hope Phillip can help you.'

'So do I.' And then, with an expression of real unhappiness he looked across the table at her. 'I'm sorry about dragging you into any of this, embarrassing you in any way. You don't deserve this.'

'Neither do you. You deserved a good kick in the ass,' she smiled sadly. 'But not this hard.'

'Maybe I did,' he said miserably, consumed with guilt for everything he'd done to her. 'When did you find out about Daphne?' He wanted to know now.

'I saw you come out of Ralph Lauren with her just before Christmas. The way you looked together said everything. It wasn't very difficult to figure the rest out. I guess, like you with Simon, I didn't want to see it. It was too painful, and I had too many other things to worry about.' It had been devastating, but she didn't say it. He knew just by looking at her, and he wished he could have turned the clock back, and changed things. But it was way too late now.

'I think I lost my mind for a while. All I could think of was when my mother died and what it had been like. I somehow got it into my head that you were her and you were going to die and take me with you, like my father. I panicked. Kind of like an insane déjà vu. I stopped thinking clearly and all my childhood rage at my mother came back on you. I was truly crazy. I suppose the affair with Daphne was crazy too. It was my way of hiding from reality. But I hurt everyone in the process. I don't even know what to think now. I don't know if she set me up, or if it was real. It's a terrible feeling. I'm not even sure I know her.' But he knew Alex, and how badly he had hurt her. And he hated himself for it. He knew now that he would pay for it for a lifetime.

'Maybe things happen the way they're meant to, Sam,' she said philosophically. It was too late for them, but at least he had come to his senses finally, and he also understood why he had hurt her. It had all been wrapped up in his terror of losing her, as he had his mother.

'I imagine you want out now,' he said, reading her perfectly, but as she looked at him, so vulnerable, so

383

hurt, so scared, his future so uncertain, she couldn't bring herself to press him.

'We can talk about it after you sort out your problems.' It didn't seem fair to dump that on him now, too. Despite Brock's eagerness for the divorce, there was really no great hurry. A month or two wouldn't make that much difference.

'You deserve so much better than I gave you,' he said miserably. For a moment he was going to say more but wisely made no move to approach her. He appreciated her graciousness, and didn't want to abuse it.

And she couldn't disagree with what he was saying to her. But she understood it a little better now. And fortunately, she had had Brock to get her through it.

'Maybe you didn't have a choice,' she said fairly. 'Maybe you couldn't help it.'

'I should have been kicked. I was such a damn fool.'

'You'll get out of this, Sam,' she said gently. 'You're a good man, fundamentally, and Phillip's a damn fine attorney.'

'So are you, and a good friend,' he said, fighting back tears as they stood across the conference room table from each other.

'Thanks, Sam,' she said with a smile. 'I'll keep track of what's happening. Call me if you need me.'

'Kiss Annabelle for me. I'll try to see her this weekend, if I'm not in jail,' he said ruefully, and she smiled at him from the doorway.

'You won't be. See ya.'

She went back to her office, and Brock was waiting for her. He was pacing again and very anxious. He knew she'd been in the conference room with Sam again. Liz had told him. And he'd seen Phillip leaving.

'Did you tell him?'

'More or less. He said he imagined I wanted a divorce, and I said we'd talk about it when he sorted this mess out.'

'*What?* Why didn't you tell him you want it *now?*' Brock was furious and she looked exasperated and exhausted. It was draining sitting there, discussing why their marriage had failed and also very upsetting, especially knowing how much trouble he was in. It was going to be very traumatic for Annabelle if he went to prison.

'I didn't tell him I wanted it now, because it doesn't make any difference if we file this month or next for heaven's sake. We're not going anywhere. Let's have a little respect for the guy, or at least compassion. He's under a grand jury indictment for embezzlement and fraud. He has just come home from Europe to find that out. And after seventeen years of marriage, and one child, I think I can give him a few weeks' grace to deal with his other problems.'

'How gracious was he with you last year? How "compassionate"? Do you remember?' he barked at her, which was unusual for him. She thought he was acting like a child, but she didn't say so.

'I remember it perfectly. But I still don't think I have to hit him over the head with it. It's over, Brock. It doesn't matter when we get the death certificate. My marriage to Sam is dead. We both know that.'

'With that sonofabitch, don't be so sure. And if his bimbo walks out on him, he'll be back knocking on your door in no time. I saw the way he looked at you today.'

'Oh for heaven's sake, stop it! That's utterly ridiculous.' She refused to discuss it with him any longer. He went back to his office in a fury, and she didn't see him again until they left the office together at seven o'clock that evening. But even then, Brock was in a bad mood, and he sulked at her all through dinner. She had never seen him behave that way, and it took endless cajoling to finally get him to stop it.

But at their penthouse on Fifth Avenue, Daphne was behaving no better with Sam. In fact, she was slamming doors, breaking glasses, and throwing things, and Sam was not finding her amusing.

'How dare you accuse me of that, you bastard!' she shouted at him. 'How dare you accuse me of "setting you up," as you put it. I wouldn't stoop to a thing like that. What a cheap trick, to try and put your crimes on me. Well, don't think you'll get away with it. Simon's already said he's going to hire a lawyer for me if I need one. But I'm not going to sit still for that either. I'm going back to London if these ridiculous charges stick. I'm not going to sit around and watch you go to jail, and try and take me with you.'

'Actually, darling, I think you'd be pretty poor company, from the looks of all this.' He looked at the debris of broken objects around them, and he didn't have the energy to fight her anymore. 'What would you think in my place? You dance me around your bed for the last year, very pleasantly, I might add, and all the while, Simon is destroying my business. It's hard to believe you knew nothing of what was happening, though I'd like to think you didn't. I found out that my wife knew about us all along, by the way. I must say, you have to give the poor woman credit. I gave her the worst deal any woman's ever had this side of hell, while she lies around half dead puking her brains out on chemo, and she's elegant enough not to admit she knows we're having an affair. Hats off to her. She's quite a lady.' Unlike Miss Daphne Belrose, he thought, but didn't say it.

'Why don't you go back to her then?' she asked, sitting on a black leather chair, and swinging one leg over the other, just enough for him to see what she had there. But he'd seen it before, and he was no longer bewitched. The spell had been broken.

'Alex is too smart to ever take me back,' he said quietly, in answer to Daphne's suggestion. 'I don't blame her a bit. I think I at least owe it to her not to go near her.'

'Maybe you two deserve each other. Mr and Mrs Perfect. Mr Honest. Mr Pure, who had no idea how Simon was multiplying his business by millions. Just how naive are you, Sam? Or to be perfectly blunt, how stupid? Don't tell me you didn't know anything. I didn't help him set it up, but for God's sake, even I could figure out what was happening. Don't tell me you couldn't.'

'The incredible stupidity of it all is that I wasn't paying attention. I was so busy trying to get under your skirts that I never saw what was going on around me. You blinded me, my dear. I was a total fool, and I suppose I deserve what's happening.'

'Nothing's happening, Sam. It's all over. You're finished,' she said derisively, as though it amused her.

'I know I am. Thanks to Simon.'

'You won't get a job as a bank clerk when this is all over.'

'And you, Daphne? How do you feel about that? Will you be around to make my dinner when I get home from a pathetic little job somewhere, selling thumbtacks?' He was looking at her with total contempt, and spoke to her in a voice dripping with sarcasm. He knew just who she was now.

'I don't think so,' she said, uncrossing her legs again, showing him everything he had wanted. He had lost a lifetime for what she had between her legs, and it hardly seemed worth it. 'The fun is over, Sam. It's time for me to move on. But it was fun, wasn't it?'

'Very much so,' he agreed, as she walked over to him slowly, and ran a hand inside his open shirt. She felt his nipples, and his chest, and his very firm stomach and he didn't move and then she tried to slide her hand slowly into his trousers, but he grabbed her hand before she got any further. It was the only thing they'd ever really had, raw sex, and a lot of it. But there was too high a price to pay for the pleasure.

'Will you miss me?' she asked, not pulling away from him, but on the contrary, moving closer. It was as though she wanted to prove something by casting a spell on him one more time, but he wouldn't let her.

'I'll miss you,' he said regretfully. 'I'll miss the illusion.' He had traded real life for a fantasy, and he knew it. It was a bitter admission. And he had lost Alex in the process.

Daphne pressed her lips down hard on his, and held him with her hands until she could feel him throbbing and he kissed her with the last of his passion for her, and then pulled away and looked at her unhappily, realizing that he would never know if she had collaborated in his destruction or if it had all been done by her cousin. It was terrible not knowing.

'One last time,' she asked in a hoarse voice. She had grown to like him better than she meant to. She was not one to get involved, or stay that way forever. And with him it had been different. But even she knew, it was all over.

He shook his head in answer to her question. He left the apartment for a long, quiet walk then. He had a lot to think about. And he came back two and a half hours later. There was no sound when he came in. And when he looked around, she was gone. The apartment was as empty as his heart. She had taken everything he'd given her, and left him nothing, except memories and questions. That night on the eleven o'clock news, they announced that Simon Barrymore had been indicted by the grand jury on sixteen counts of embezzlement and fraud. There was no mention of his cousin and possible accomplice, Daphne Belrose, who was, at that very moment, on the red-eye to London.

Chapter 20

Sam's appearance before the grand jury was awesome and frightening. It took all day. And at the end of it, their indictments remained as they had been made. Samuel Livingston Parker was ordered to stand trial on nine different charges. Each of his partners had been charged with thirteen, and Simon Barrymore with sixteen.

Alex had not gone to the hearings with Sam. But she called him after she saw Phillip Smith back in the office.

'I'm sorry, Sam,' she said quietly. She had thought the indictments would stick. But now he would have to fight them, or plea-bargain in some way, in the hope of reducing the charges. The trial had been set for November 19, and they had three months to prepare their defense.

Phillip Smith had already drafted three of the firm's best lawyers to help him. Another firm was representing Larry and Tom, and someone Alex had never heard of was representing Simon.

'What about the girl?' Alex asked matter-of-factly. 'They didn't get her at all. How'd she pull that off?'

'Luck, I guess.'

'She must be pleased,' Alex said coolly.

'I wouldn't know. She left for London. She figured the good times were over.' And she wasn't wrong. Sam knew what was in store for him. Success in the financial world was very fickle. Once the money and the hot deals were gone, and after a scandal like this, so was the respect and the recognition. He hadn't tried it yet, and had no immediate desire to, but he was sure that if he called La Grenouille or Le Cirque or the Four Seasons, all the reservations available to him would be at five-thirty and eleven-thirty, and the table would be in the kitchen. The champagne only flowed as long as the money.

And in a moment, even after two decades, the name Sam Parker would be forgotten.

The odd thing was that he had always told himself it didn't matter to him, but he realized now it did. Just knowing that his name was dirt, that his business had gone down the tubes, and the reputation he'd had along with it, made him feel finished. He suddenly realized what Alex had felt when she lost her breast, and with it her sense of femininity and sex appeal, and her ability to have children. She had felt diminished as a woman. And he of course hadn't helped by going out with another woman. Nice guy, he reminded himself. All he seemed to have were regrets now. But with the loss of his important position and his respectability based on it, he felt a loss of his manhood.

'Phillip is putting together a great team for you,' Alex said encouragingly on the phone. The worst of it for Sam was that she seemed to bear him no malice. It would almost have been easier if she'd hated him, but apparently she didn't. She seemed not to care about what he'd done to her at all. She had made her peace with everything that had happened to her. He had no idea how she'd done it. And clearly he hadn't figured out about her involvement with Brock yet. Alex gave away nothing, and even Annabelle's mentions of him didn't seem to imply anything but friendship.

'Are you going to be on that team?' Sam asked, embarrassed to even ask her. But he felt so insecure and so scared it was almost childish. He didn't even know what he was going to do with himself before the trial. They were closing the office, and liquidating their affairs. And all the company assets had already been frozen. He was trying to make up as much as he could to as many of their clients as possible, out of his own funds, but there were going to be staggering losses for many. Simon was responsible for most of them, but Tom and Larry had done their share of the damage too, and Sam had unwittingly helped them with some of the deals he had co-signed. He just hadn't been paying attention. He felt terribly guilty, but it was too late to change it. All he could do was pay the penalty, whatever it would be. Sometimes he thought he deserved to go to jail for sheer stupidity, and he said as much to Alex before she had a chance to answer his question.

'As far as I know, that's not a crime yet. And, no, I won't be on the team, but I'll watch from the sidelines.' He knew it was more than he deserved from her, and he didn't argue.

'Thank you. We're going to be closing the office in the next week or two. Almost everyone's gone now.' It had taken exactly three days to empty all the offices, and no one wanted to be associated with them for a moment longer than they had to. They were a pariah. 'I guess after that, it'll be all preparation for the trial.' And then, out of nowhere, 'I'm going to be selling the penthouse. I'm not going to need it now,' he had really bought it for Daphne, 'and frankly, I need the money. Besides, if I go to jail, you don't need the headache of liquidating that for me. I'm going to stay at the Carlyle.'

'Annabelle will like that.' She had tried to sound encouraging, but like her illness the year before, the prognosis was not great. He had some tough stuff to go through. He would be stripped to the bone, and bared for all to see, all his sins, and stupidities, and failings, and then he would be at the mercy of twelve good men, or women, a jury of his peers, who would determine his future. It was pretty scary.

And then she remembered that it was almost the Labor Day weekend. 'Are you still taking Annabelle?'

'I'd like to.' He was going to be alone with her, and it was going to be a relief not to have to fight with Daphne. He didn't think they'd go anywhere. He just wanted to be with Annabelle and enjoy her.

Carmen brought her in to the city and when he picked her up Alex was out. She didn't see him again in the office that week, although she knew he'd been in to see Phillip. She was trying to stay out of it officially, but still keep an eye on things, although from a distance. And she had promised Sam that she would sit through the trial with him, and go to as many meetings before that as she could. But she didn't want Phillip to feel that she was crowding him, or interfering.

And by the time she and Brock left for East Hampton for the weekend, on Friday afternoon, they were both exhausted. He was still annoyed that she hadn't taken the bull by the horns with Sam, and pressed him for an immediate divorce, and she thought Brock was being unreasonable and childish. They had a big fight about it again on Friday night, and for the first time in her five-month affair with him, they both went to bed angry.

But in the morning, as they woke up, he reached over and pulled her close to him and told her he was sorry.

'I'm sorry I'm such an idiot about all this, he just scares me,' he said, and Alex turned to look at him in amazement.

'Sam? Why, for heaven's sake? The poor guy's practically in jail. He's got plenty of problems of his own, what's to scare you?'

'History. Time. Annabelle. It doesn't matter what kind of sonofabitch the guy was to you last year, he's still your husband, and he had seventeen years with you before that. That carries a lot of weight. It's hard to fight that.' He looked at her knowingly, and she couldn't deny it, but she loved him too, and she wanted him to know it.

'You don't have to worry, Brock,' she said holding him close to her, and smoothing his hair with her hand, like a child. Sometimes she felt light-years older, but she was touched by what he was feeling, and he was right in some ways. The things he talked about had bound her to Sam for close to two decades. But Brock had a history with her too, a history of incredible kindness, and she couldn't ignore that either. Besides, she loved him. 'Don't worry about him. I'll get it all worked out after the trial. It just didn't seem right to do it before that. Like his moving out before I finished chemo. I'm sure he wanted to, but even as lousy as he was at the time, he stayed till I was finished. Sometimes it's just a question of basic decency and good manners.' She smiled and Brock smiled at her in answer. He relaxed for the first time in days and held her close to him.

'Just make sure good manners don't keep you married to him, or my manners are going to fall apart in a hurry. I may kill him.' Brock was the gentlest person she knew, and she knew he didn't mean it. He just wanted her out of her marriage to Sam, and she didn't blame him. She wanted that too. But in the right way, at the right time, without causing even more damage.

They spent an easy weekend on the beach, and packed up their things with regret on Monday. He had rented a station wagon to take everything home with them, and they were unpacking her things at her apartment when Sam came home with Annabelle. And she looked a lot happier than she did after her weekends with Daphne, but this time Sam looked a little startled. Suddenly, seeing Brock help her unload the car made Sam realize that there was more to it than just work at the office.

'Can I give you a hand?' Sam asked politely, carrying a box into the front hall. He suddenly felt like a stranger in what had been his home, and he realized he didn't belong there. Brock was painfully polite to him, and Alex was very pleasant, but when he saw Annabelle with them, he realized that this was a unit he could no longer interfere with. They were part of it, and he wasn't.

He left shortly afterwards, feeling depressed, and Brock looked pleased. There was no question. The message had been clear. 'She's mine now,' and Sam had got it.

Chapter 21

Annabelle went back to nursery school after Labor Day, and the rest of them went back to their usual routine. Alex had taken on her full workload again, and she appeared in court almost daily. Brock was still helping her, but he had his own cases too, and they didn't work as constantly together as they had while she was in chemo. And they both agreed that they missed it.

Several of her partners had commended her for her fortitude in hanging in while she was sick, and she had become something of a legend in the law firm. And in spite of the amount of time they still spent together almost every day, no one had yet figured out that she and Brock were seriously involved with each other. It had remained a well-kept secret.

Brock spent every night with them after work, but he still kept his own apartment, and most of the time, he slept there. Neither of them thought it would be good for Annabelle to have him living there full time, so he forced himself to get up in the middle of the night and go home, which they both hated. He only spent the night there, in the guest room, on weekends. And both Brock and Alex were anxious to tell Sam about the divorce, and get their life in order quickly, if only to get a good night's sleep, as Brock put it. But Annabelle was crazy about him, and probably wouldn't have minded if he'd moved in completely.

In September, Sam's trial was more than two months away. And by October, his meetings at the firm had stepped up radically with Phillip Smith and the team he'd created to mount Sam's defense. It was going to be a tough case to win, and they all knew it. Even Sam had few illusions. He'd closed his office by then, and all of the employees had been discharged. In the end, they had cheated people out of roughly twenty-nine million dollars. It could have been a lot worse, but Sam had done what he could to minimize clients' losses, and he was trying to activate whatever insurance policies he could to reimburse people for the difference. But no matter how you looked at it, it was ugly. His efforts to help people recoup what they could was not to improve his defense but simply part of who he always had been. If anything, he seemed more himself now. He seemed happier and more at peace, although when Alex saw him at meetings with Phillip, he was strained, and often nervous. The prospect of going to prison terrified him, but he also realized it was a strong possibility. Phillip had told him more than once that keeping him out of jail was going to be a long shot.

By late October, deals were being made, and the prosecutors were trying to get all of them to plead guilty, but so far no one would do it. They were offered shortened sentences as an exchange, but even that wasn't too appealing. Particularly to Sam, whose defense was still that he had been extremely stupid, but not intentionally dishonest.

'Think it'll fly?' Brock asked her honestly, one weekend when they were watching Annabelle in the playground. And she thought about it for a minute, before she answered.

'I'm not sure,' she said honestly. 'I hope it does, for his sake. But if I were on a jury and he told me he was too dumb to know that his partners were ripping him off while he was busy getting laid, I think I'd laugh my ass off, and send him straight to prison.'

'That's how I figure it too,' he said, but he wasn't entirely sorry for him, and he still thought he deserved it. But Alex always disagreed with him.

'You can't send a guy to jail for being shitty to his wife when she's having chemo, Brock. That's bullshit. That doesn't make him a criminal, it makes him an asshole. The issue here isn't me, it's was he cheating people knowingly?' No matter what else they were, they were lawyers, and the conversation often turned to their cases.

'He knew, don't tell me he didn't. He didn't want to know. But he knew damn well Simon wasn't clean. You even said so.'

'I thought the guy was a crook,' she said thoughtfully, 'but Sam always defended him. It was all so easy, the money just kept rolling in, from what he said, I guess he wanted to believe it was on the level. He was naive to believe it, but again, that's not a felony.'

'He should have checked a lot more closely.'

'Yes, he should. That's where I think his love life got in the way.'

'It's going to be a juicy trial,' Brock predicted, and it was. The papers were full of it from the moment they started taking depositions. And by November fifteenth, people were taking bets in the financial

398

community as to who would go to prison, and who wouldn't. Everyone figured that Simon would somehow weasel out of it, he was just too slippery not to. He'd been continuing to do business in Europe while waiting for the trial, and was involved in half a dozen shady deals there, but nothing seemed to stop him. And it was predicted that Larry and Tom were going to go to jail. But Sam was the dark horse that no one could figure. Most people thought he would, but there were a few who thought he wouldn't. He had had an excellent reputation for a long time, and some of the old-timers bought his story, though the younger men on Wall Street didn't. They thought he should have known, or did know, and didn't want to hear it, which was what Brock thought too.

And when the trial began, Alex was there. She watched the jury selection and conferred with Sam in the halls, just to keep him distracted. He had four attorneys, and there were five others involved in the other three's defense. It was a huge event, and the courtroom was filled with reporters. Alex had asked Brock if he wanted to come too, but he said he didn't. They both knew it was going to be a circus.

Brock was still uptight about Sam, still anxious for her to divorce him. He said he wouldn't believe it was for real until she told Sam, and they filed. But she kept promising it was going to happen right after the trial, and she meant it. She and Brock had been physically involved for eight months, and close friends for a lot longer, and she really loved him. But she and Sam had known each other for eighteen years, and loved each other for as long. She owed him something too, and although he didn't like it, she knew Brock understood that. But in spite of himself, and all their reasoning, Brock was extremely jealous.

Alex was startled to realize it, but she also found it very touching.

The actual trial began on the afternoon of the third day, and there was an air of real tension in the courtroom. The jury had been selected carefully, and they'd been told that the matters before them would be both complicated and financial. There were four defendants, who were accused in varying degrees, and each case was explained in excruciating detail. Sam's was explained last, and Alex thought the judge spelled it out very clearly. He was a good judge and she'd always had good experiences with him, but that didn't mean anything now. The facts were all against Sam, unless the jury believed his story. He was an honest man, or at least he always had been, but the truth in this case was hard to swallow.

There were three weeks of testimony, and Thanksgiving came and went without too much attention. She and Brock cooked turkey at his place, and Annabelle ate at the Carlyle with Sam, but he was in no mood for holidays. And Alex couldn't help remembering that her extreme reaction to her illness the year before had finally been the straw that broke the camel's back, and Sam had gone berserk because she was too sick to come to the table. Sam remembered that the day's trauma had finally driven him into Daphne's arms, and bed, for the first time, and all he wished, more than anything, was that he could turn the clock back.

He looked very distinguished and tall as he stood in the courtroom in a dark suit the day after Thanksgiving, and when Alex saw him, she asked how he was doing. She knew how difficult it was for him, how worried he was, and how much he had at stake, his entire future. Or at least a decade or two of it. The realization of that made him tremble as he looked at Alex.

'Thanks for coming,' he whispered, and she nodded. She could see the worry in his eyes, but he seemed prepared to take whatever came his way. He already knew that if he lost, he would be given thirty days until sentencing to settle his affairs, before he went to prison, which meant after Christmas. It was a daunting thought, as the judge rapped for order in the courtroom.

The final week of trial came in the second week in December, Sam took the stand, and his testimony was emotional and very moving. He had had to stop once or twice, when he became overwrought, as the reporters took rapid note of it, but she believed his story. She knew what a nightmarish time it had been for both of them, they had both been out of their minds in their own way, and his affair with Daphne must have clouded his judgment further. She was surprised at how dispassionate she felt, listening to him, it was a fascinating case, but she couldn't allow herself to think that Sam might go to prison. She couldn't even allow herself to think that she had once loved him. It would have been too painful.

Afterwards four of the attorneys addressed the jury, in some cases movingly, and Alex thought Phillip's speech was very clear, and stated the facts clearly. It emphasized what Sam himself had said on the witness stand, that between his wife's illness and his own foolishness, he had allowed himself to be lulled into thinking that what was going on was ethical when it wasn't. But the key was that he didn't know what the others were doing. He had never *knowingly* defrauded anyone, or been a party to what had happened. He had never knowingly been part of their collusion.

The jury took five days to deliberate, and called for evidence and testimony. They recalled everything they could, and then finally, it was over. Sam and the others sat looking very pale and were asked to stand when the jury entered the courtroom. Alex noticed that Simon tried to look contemptuous, but he was too pale for anyone to buy it. Just like the others, he was scared stiff, and the only one Alex felt sorry for was Sam. And poor little Annabelle. What if her Daddy went to prison? Someone at her school had told her about it, and Sam and Alex had tried to explain it to her simply, but it was much too confusing. And no, they didn't know if he was going away or not, but they hoped not. It had been a lousy resolution.

The foreman was a woman in this case, and she called out their verdicts loudly and clearly. They began with Tom, and named each of the thirteen charges against him, and to each of them she responded with a single word. Guilty. Guilty. Guilty. It droned on eternally, and again the same with Larry, and with Simon. There was a huge stir in the courtroom, and the press was going wild as the judge rapped his gavel furiously and called everyone to order.

And then it was Sam's turn, and this time, the verdict was 'not guilty' to all the charges of embezzlement, but to all the charges relating to fraud, and conspiracy to commit fraud, he was found guilty. Alex sat rooted to the spot, as she looked at him. He stood very quietly, listening to the judge, who was saying that they were to return thirty days from that date for sentencing, and he would take their cases, and their probation reports, under advisement until then. They were each being released on five-hundred-thousand-dollars bail, which meant a fifty-thousand-dollar bond, which Sam had put up for himself as soon as he was arrested. And then the judge reminded each of them that they were not to leave the state or country. He then rapped his gavel, and dismissed the court, and there was an instant uproar. Photographers flashed photographs of all of them and Alex had to fight to get where Sam was standing with Phillip.

Sam looked like he was in shock when she got to him, and there were tears in his eyes, understandably. Larry's and Tom's wives were sobbing openly, but she said nothing to them. And Simon left the courtroom almost immediately with his lawyer.

'I'm so sorry, Sam,' she said, just loud enough for him to hear her, as someone took their picture.

'Let's get out of here,' he said miserably, and she leaned over to Phillip then to ask him if he needed to talk to his client, but he shook his head. He was very disappointed by the verdict. Now all their efforts would be to reduce sentencing, but there was little chance of that now. Sam was going to prison.

She followed him outside, as news cameras and microphones were shoved into their faces, and finally they darted through the crowd and into a cab before anyone could stop them.

'Are you all right?' she asked him. He looked terrible, and she was suddenly worried he'd have a heart attack or a stroke. At fifty that wasn't completely impossible, although it was unlikely.

'I don't know. I think I'm numb. I kept telling myself I expected it, but I guess I didn't . . . let's go to the Carlyle.'

But at the hotel, they found reporters waiting for him. They went around to the Madison Avenue side, and hurried in, and he asked her if she'd come upstairs with him for a few minutes. And once there, he called room service and ordered drinks for both of them. Scotch for him, and coffee for her. She wasn't a drinker.

'I don't know what to say,' Alex said honestly, she was bereft of words. All she had left were feelings. Grief for him, and Annabelle who was about to lose her father, for twenty years or more. It was impossible to think of.

It was going to be hard on everyone until sentencing, but now they just had to live through it. 'Is there anything I can do?' she asked helplessly. She felt almost as helpless as he had when he found out she had cancer. There was nothing she could do to change it.

'Take good care of Annabelle,' he said, and then burst into tears. He sat with his face in his hands for a long time, sobbing, and she said nothing, and walked over to him and gently held his shoulders. When room service came, she signed for it, and brought the tray in herself, and handed him the Scotch. He took it gratefully, and apologized for his lack of composure.

'Don't be silly, Sam. It's all right,' she said gently, touching his shoulder. But there was nothing they could do. He had been found guilty, and he'd have to go to prison. They knew that.

He took a sip of his drink and looked at her. 'It can't have felt any better when they told you you had cancer.'

'It didn't,' she confirmed, and then smiled sadly. 'But I'd rather have chemotherapy than go to jail.'

He laughed cynically at what she'd said, and took another swig of Scotch. 'Thanks. I don't think they're offering the option.'

'Believe me, you wouldn't like it.'

'I remember that,' he said sorrowfully, feeling grim at how he had failed her. 'My God, you were sick. I kept blocking it out because I couldn't stand it. I even let Daphne help me do it. She kept feeling sorry for *me* instead of you, and I agreed with her completely. We were really nice people. Mr and Miss Terrific.' He looked into Alex's eyes, grateful beyond words that she had survived it.

'Have you heard from her?' she asked out of curiosity, and he shook his head.

'Not a word, the little dear. I'm sure she's moved on to greener pastures. She'll fall on her feet, wherever she is. Daphne's a smart girl, when it comes to Daphne.' And then he looked at his wife with an expression of immeasurable sadness. 'Why are you here? You shouldn't be by now.' It was true, but she was a faithful sort and they both knew that. Besides, Brock was right. Eighteen years had woven a powerful bond between them.

'I loved you for a long time. It's hard to forget that,' she said honestly, no longer afraid that he would hurt her. She knew he couldn't. She was too far removed now.

'You'd better forget it soon,' Sam said. 'Thirty days. I'll file before that, by the way. I'm sure your young lawyer friend will be relieved. The poor guy looks daggers at me everytime he sees me. Tell him he can relax now, I'm going.' She smiled at the irony of his words. They knew each other well. He had finally figured out who Brock was. Though he'd been a lot slower than she had been in figuring out Sam's relationship to Daphne. But there were no secrets between them now. 'Isn't he a little young for you?' There was a hint of jealousy in his voice when he asked, which reminded her of Brock and made her smile. They were both being silly.

'I say that to him every day, but he's very stubborn.' Alex smiled, thinking of Brock. 'He was incredible to me when I was sick. He spent the first five months with me throwing up on the bathroom floor of my office before he ever invited me anywhere.'

'He's a good man,' Sam said fairly. 'I wish I'd been decent enough to do that.' And then he thought of the result of the trial again, and shrugged unhappily. 'Maybe it's just as well I didn't stick by you. I don't want to take you down with me on this. You need your freedom.'

'So do you,' she said gently.

'Tell it to the judge,' he said, and stood up. He knew he had no right to keep her any longer, and it only made him feel worse to be near her. It was so obviously over for her, it was hard being around her. 'Tell Annabelle I'll come by tomorrow to pick her up. I want to do lots of things with her this month.' He only had one month of freedom left, probably, and he was going to spend it all with her. He would have liked to spend it with Alex too, but he would never have asked that. He knew he couldn't.

Alex was sad when she went home to Annabelle that night, and Brock called to say he had seen it on the news and was sorry. He was working late, and he'd come over in a while, but when he did, Alex was irritated by his attitude about Sam. He was supercilious and overtly pleased that Sam had been convicted. He said that Sam had messed up his life in every way possible, and basically deserved what had happened.

'I think twenty years in jail might be a pretty high price for his mess, wouldn't you say? Who the hell hasn't made mistakes? He was stupid and self-centered, and naively trusting of his partners, but he doesn't deserve to lose everything, nor does Annabelle because of his mistakes. She needs her father.'

'He should have thought of that before he went into business with Simon. Hell, Alex, the guy was obvious. You said so yourself,' and she couldn't disagree. She had never trusted Simon. But Sam had, much to his chagrin now.

The next day when Sam came by to pick up Annabelle, looking drained, Alex thought that Brock was unnecessarily unpleasant to him, and after Sam left with Annabelle, she said so. 'The guy's got enough on his plate without your being rude to him on top of it.' It was rare for them to fight, but for Alex, it was an issue of loyalty and kindness.

'I was not rude, I was cool, there's a distinct difference.'

'You weren't cool, Brock,' she said, feeling like his mother, scolding him. 'You were nasty, that's different. It could have happened to any of us. He was swept away by a glamorous crowd, who were out to use him. Are you so sure you're invulnerable to that?' she asked him pointedly, and he insisted it could never happen to him, but Alex knew better. But it was her attitude that worried Brock. He didn't like the things she said, or the way she said them.

'Why are you defending him?' he asked, looking suddenly worried. 'Are you still in love with him?' His eyes bore into hers. He was the prosecutor and she was the defendant.

'I don't think so,' she said honestly, wanting to be fair to both of them. 'I care about him. I'm sorry about what happened.'

'Don't you think he deserved it?' Brock pressed. They were alone in her apartment after Annabelle had left with Sam, and Brock wasn't going to let go of the issues. He wanted to know what she was feeling.

'No, I don't think he deserved it,' Alex said sadly. 'It's right for him to lose his business, and his job . . . his standing in the community . . . even his reputation. He was foolish, he hurt a lot of people by being blind to what the others were doing. But he shouldn't go to prison for that, Brock, no more than he should for failing me . . . it's not right. I just don't think he deserves that.'

'You're too soft,' Brock said, watching her carefully, and then slowly he went to her, and put his arms around her. 'I guess that's why I love you,' and then he closed his eyes and pulled her so tightly against him she could hardly breathe. 'I don't want to lose you, that's all. That's what this is all about for me . . . I keep hearing what you're saying about him, and seeing something in your eyes that still hurts for him. It's not over yet, no matter what you say. He still lives in your heart somewhere . . . maybe that's normal after eighteen years, and a little girl . . . I don't know . . . I just don't want to lose you,' he said again, and kissed her. And when they came up for air, she smiled at him, and touched his lips with a gentle finger.

'You won't, Brock. I love you.' And she meant it.

'But you love him too,' he said wisely, and this time she didn't deny it.

'Maybe I do, and I don't know it. I don't love him in a romantic sense. But I love who he was, and what we had. We were together for a long time. I thought we had it all . . . and then everything fell apart. It was hard to understand that.' They shared a blood bond by now, like members of the same family, that was near impossible to sever. 'I feel his pain. I think I understand what he did. I know what he's feeling. It's hard to explain that to someone else, or to stop feeling it just because things have changed between us.'

'Are you sure they have?' he asked softly.

'Positive,' she said firmly. 'I'm not his wife now. I'm someone different than I was before. I don't know . . . I'm not sure you can ever go back, after all that happened to us. You can only go forward.' And she had, into Brock's arms, but she was not his wife either. She was no one's. She was her own, for the first time in years, and as lonely as it had been for a while, now at times she even liked it. She had the best of both worlds. A sense of herself she'd never had before, and Brock, whom she loved deeply.

'Just let me know if anything changes,' he said simply, watching her eyes, and only somewhat reassured by what he saw there. He knew she was torn by everything she was feeling. She felt sorry for Sam, and loyalty to Brock. And in her own way, she loved both of them, and Annabelle, and she wanted what was right for everyone. Sometimes that wasn't easy.

'Don't say things like that,' she chided him. 'Nothing's going to change. It's just going to be a hard time for him, and I'd like to at least be supportive.'

'Why? He didn't support you last year. Why should this be any different?'

'Maybe for old times' sake.' But Brock wanted that with her. He wanted the same ancient bond that tied her to Sam even now, even from a distance.

'Don't feel too sorry for him,' he warned, kissing her again gently. 'I need you,' he whispered.

'So do I,' she whispered back, and they made love that morning in the bed she had once shared with Sam, and knew she never would again. What she had said to Brock was true, and she believed it. The past was gone, and it was time to move forward. Besides, she loved him.

But Sam was in a pensive mood when she picked Annabelle up at the Carlyle late that afternoon, after their day together. It was as though in the past twenty-four hours, the verdict had really sunk in, and he was beginning to panic. He was about to lose everything, his freedom, his life, his little girl, even the last whispers of all he had once shared with Alex. And he was suddenly a lot less philosophical and less glib than he had been the night before over his Scotch after the verdict. Being with Annabelle had reminded him of all he would lose, and seeing Alex made it even more poignant.

He had told Annabelle that afternoon that things hadn't gone well for him. She still didn't understand what that meant, and he hadn't explained it fully with all the implications. He had said nothing about leaving her, or going to prison. He would have to deal with that later. He had another thirty days in which to do it.

'Did you two have fun?' Alex asked, smiling at them. She had come to pick Annabelle up, while Brock shopped for their dinner at Gristede's.

'We had a great time,' Sam said, looking better but still tense. 'We went skating.' And then he sent Annabelle into the other room to get her doll and her sweater, and he turned to Alex with a look of anguish. 'I'm sorry about your friend this morning.

410

He seemed annoyed. I think I upset him,' he said. She nodded, hesitating about how much to say to him, but as always she was honest.

'He's afraid of our history, Sam. I can't really blame him. Eighteen years is a long time, it's hard to explain that to someone else. He's afraid that loyalty is more powerful than love, which is foolish.'

'Is it?' he asked softly, daring to raise his eyes to hers, and he ached instantly at what he saw there. He saw a woman he had hurt deeply, and every moment he spent with her, he remembered. 'Is it only loyalty?' he asked thoughtfully. 'I'm sorry to hear it. I suppose I'm lucky there's still that, after what I did to you.' He had spent the previous night, and even that afternoon, thinking about her, and the pain he had caused her.

'Sam, don't . . .' she said gently. It was too late for recriminations. There were too many regrets, and bad memories, along with the good ones.

'Why not? I guess I shouldn't say anything, but I have this crazy sense of time running out suddenly, which we both know isn't so crazy, after Friday's verdict. Maybe it's important to say things now, just in case there's no chance to say them later.' She understood what he felt, but she couldn't help him. She could be there for him, to a point, she could help him with Annabelle, and sympathize with what he was going through, but she couldn't give him more than that. That part of her life was Brock's now. 'I still love you,' he said softly, and tore at her heart, as Annabelle skipped back into the room with her doll and her sweater. 'I mean it,' he said pointedly, and she turned away, ignoring him, wishing he hadn't said anything. He had no right to.

Alex helped Annabelle put her sweater on, and then her hat and coat with trembling hands and she didn't say a word to Sam until Annabelle went to ring for the elevator, and they followed.

'Don't make things harder than they have to be. I know this is a hard time for you, and I feel terrible, but Sam . . . don't hurt all of us again now.' If he toyed with her, it would only hurt her, and Brock, and Annabelle, and even himself. 'Don't do that.'

'I didn't mean to hurt you,' he said thoughtfully. There was suddenly so much he had to tell her. 'I guess I ought to have the guts to leave you alone, no matter what I feel, especially if I'm going to prison. I promised myself that. But maybe it's a bigger mistake to just let you slip away without at least telling you I love you. I know I have no right to you. Hell, I don't even feel like a man anymore. Everything I ever hooked my identity to is gone, money, success, position . . . I guess that's how you felt when you lost your breast, but we're both stupid. Your womanhood wasn't in your breast . . . my manhood wasn't in my office . . . it's in our hearts, our souls, who we are, what we believe in. I don't know why I never understood that before. I understand so much more now, and the bitch of it is that I've figured it all out too late, too late for us anyway . . . all I want is to turn the clock back a year and start over.' She was shocked by what he was saying.

'I can't, Sam,' she whispered, as she closed her eyes for a moment so she wouldn't have to see the pain in his eyes, or the love she suddenly saw there. Why hadn't he said it all a year before? It was too late now. 'Don't say these things to me . . . I can't go back again, and I can't do this to Brock.' She had promised him she wouldn't only that morning.

'What are you doing with him?' Sam said, sounding annoyed. 'He's a kid. A nice kid, I can see that.

412

And he's been good to you, but ten years from now where will you be? Can he really give you what you want?'

'It's not what he can give me,' she said firmly to Sam, 'he's already given me so much. It's my turn to give now.'

'You can't give him your life to make up for what he did for you, any more than I can make up to you for what I didn't. But I still love you, Alex . . . you're still my wife. Maybe I have no right to you anymore, I'm sure I don't. But I want you to know I'll always love you. Even at my craziest, at my worst . . . I always loved you. I didn't want to leave, but I couldn't stay either. I was running away from everything, you, my mother's ghost, reality. And I had to get that girl out of my blood. I know how wrong it was, but she was driving me crazy. And so were you. I was driving myself mad more than anything. But I never meant to hurt you.' He wanted her to hear all of it from him, before he went to prison. But it wasn't fair. He pulled a string that hadn't been severed yet, and touched a part of her that was still his, which hurt too much. She didn't want to love him.

Her voice was deep and sad when she answered him, and glanced ahead at Annabelle, waiting for them in the distance, in the hallway. 'It would be so much easier, Sam, if we left each other cleanly. Don't look back, don't cry over the past . . . what's the point now?'

'Maybe there is no point anymore. But there is no "clean" after eighteen years. I don't know where you stop and I begin,' he said, with tears in his eyes. 'Can you really walk away from it like that? Can you say you don't feel anything, only loyalty? I don't believe you.'

Neither did she, but she was suddenly furious at what he was doing. Suddenly, he wanted to confess all his sins, and bare his soul. At the eleventh hour, in spite of everything that he had done, he didn't want to lose her. 'What do you want from me, Sam?' she asked him angrily. 'To make me admit I love you, so you can feel good about it when you leave? . . . Let me go . . . let us both be free, just as you said yesterday after the verdict. We both need that. Don't carry this with you to prison.'

'I can't let go of it,' he said, in visible agony. He had been awake all night, thinking about her, and the verdict. And suddenly, everything was different. He wasn't willing to just let her slip away from him in silence. 'I don't know how to let go,' he said, touching her arm, and aching to kiss her. 'I still love you.'

'So do I, Sam,' she said miserably, and Brock knew it too, he had said so. 'But it's too late now.' They both knew it, but he wasn't ready to give up yet, and she looked at him, Annabelle waved and the elevator door opened. 'Don't do this, Sam . . . please . . . for both our sakes.' It had been much easier than this when he'd left her for Daphne. He had seemed so sure then, and now he seemed so broken, and she was no longer clear what she owed him.

'I'm sorry, Alex,' he apologized, looking desperately unhappy. 'Can I see you sometime?' He looked panicked. The elevator was waiting.

'No.' She shook her head and hurried toward Annabelle, sorry she had come at all. 'I can't, Sam . . .' She couldn't do that to Brock, or herself. She just couldn't. 'I'm sorry.'

She stepped into the elevator then, next to Annabelle, and his eyes blazed into hers as the doors closed. And all the way home to her apartment, she tried to force him from her mind, and everything he had said, and think of Brock, as she clung to her daughter.

'Was Daddy mad at you?' Annabelle glanced up at her, looking puzzled, in the chill wind, as Christmas shoppers hurried past them.

'No, sweetheart. He was fine,' she lied, wondering why children always saw all the things they shouldn't.

'He looked sad when we left.'

'He was probably just unhappy to see you go, but he wasn't mad. I promise.' Only sad. And very foolish.

It was a relief to get home to Brock, and the rich smells wafting from her kitchen. He was making spaghetti sauce and garlic bread, and Alex had promised to make soup and pasta and salad, and hot fudge sundaes.

'Everything go okay?' he asked, glancing at her as she took her coat off and warmed her hands. She seemed very cold and somewhat shaken.

'Fine,' she smiled, slipping her arms around him as he stood at the stove, and forcing herself to forget everything Sam had told her. But no matter what she did that night, or how tightly she clung to Brock as he lay beside her, Sam's words continued to drift around her like spirits.

Chapter 22

Annabelle spent a week with Sam, starting on Christmas Day, and Alex made a point of not seeing him when she dropped her off. She let her go up alone in the elevator at the Carlyle. Alex hadn't heard from him again since the last time she saw him, and she could only assume that he had come to his senses. And whether or not he was thinking clearly again, she knew she was.

Christmas Eve had been wonderful with Brock and Annabelle. And they had rented the same house in Vermont for the week between Christmas and New Year's. And this time she skied and had a great time. She had never felt better all year. Her hair had grown longer by then, and she was wearing it in a stylish bob that Brock said he loved, and thought was very sexy. And after a few days in Vermont with her, he relaxed about Sam. Brock knew how much Alex loved him, and he felt suddenly foolish to have been worried.

They also learned, while they were there, that Sam had filed for divorce just after Christmas. And Alex was particularly relieved to hear it. He had obviously come to his senses. Leaving the past behind was difficult for both of them, but there was no question in her mind that they had to do it.

She and Brock talked about getting married quietly in June, and she reminded him again that they still had to work things out at the law firm. They even talked about their honeymoon as they lay by the fire on New Year's Eve, and Alex said dreamily that she would love to go to Europe.

'I think that could be arranged,' he said, sounding warm and comfortable and sexy. They had just made love, and he was half asleep lying next to her, as she smiled up at him and smoothed his hair back. He looked like a boy to her sometimes, a huge over-grown child, so innocent and trusting, it made her love him even more as she held him.

And on New Year's Day they drove back to New York from Vermont. It was a long drive, and they went to the apartment first, and dropped off their skis and suitcases. And then she walked over to pick up Annabelle at the Carlyle still in ski clothes. She called Sam from the desk downstairs, and he asked her to come up just for a minute. She hesitated, and then decided there was no harm in it. He'd filed for the divorce while she was gone. He understood what she wanted.

But when she got upstairs and he opened the door to her, she was shocked when she saw him. He looked haunted.

Seeing him brought it all home to her again, and the agony of what he was facing. She suddenly ached for him, and hated the thought of his going to prison. And somehow, being faced with him again brought back all the emotions she'd been avoiding.

Annabelle still seemed unaware of the strain her

father was going through, and she said she'd had a wonderful time with her Daddy.

'I'm glad, sweetheart.' Alex kissed her and held her tight as Sam looked longingly at her over their daughter. She wanted to tell him to stop the moment she saw him. She was still tormented at times by what he had said the last time they met. And this time was no different.

'I missed you,' he said softly, as Annabelle packed her things in the next room. He didn't want her to hear him.

'You shouldn't,' Alex said quietly, and then she thanked him for filing for the divorce. She knew he had done it for her sake and she was grateful.

'I owe you that at least,' he said unhappily, searching her eyes for something that appeared not to be there, and if it was, she refused to show him. 'I owe you a lot of things, most of which I'll never be able to repay you.'

'You've done enough,' she said, and she didn't mean it unkindly. They had shared a lot of happy times, and especially now, she was deeply grateful for their daughter. 'You don't owe me anything.'

'If I stayed with you for a lifetime, I couldn't repay you for what I did.' It was all he could think of now, playing again and again in his head the horror of how he had failed her. He had too much time to think now.

'Don't be silly, Sam,' she said, trying to lighten the moment. 'Stop dwelling on all that. It's gone, it's over. You have to move on. We both do.'

'Do we?' he asked, moving slowly toward her, as Annabelle continued to pack her things in the bedroom, and Alex wished that she would hurry. She would have gone in to help, but she didn't want to walk into Sam's bedroom. And as she looked at him, she saw that he was standing breathlessly close to her, and she saw everything in his eyes that she had once loved there, all the tenderness and love and kindness that had drawn her to him in the first place. He was the same man, and he needed her so much, but she had changed. Now everything about her seemed different. Or was it? 'Alex . . .' He said her name so longingly and she looked up at him, just as he pulled her into his arms, and kissed her gently on the lips before she could stop him. She started to pull away from him, but as she did, he only pulled her closer, and suddenly she couldn't remember why he should stop, and why she hadn't wanted him to do that. It was as though nothing had changed, as though they had moved back in time, and she was his again. And then, suddenly she remembered Brock, and knew she wasn't Sam's anymore, and couldn't let this happen. She wondered suddenly why she had come upstairs again, if she had wanted this to happen. And thinking that made her feel guilty.

'Don't!' was the single word she said when they stopped, and she was breathless. She felt dazed, and suddenly very frightened. She didn't want him pulling her back to him, she didn't want to do this. 'Sam, I can't . . .' Her eyes filled with tears, and he felt like a total bastard. He was taking advantage of her, and he knew he had no right to. He would only be there for days, and then he would be gone for years. It was why he had agreed to divorce her. That and a thousand other reasons he forgot the moment he kissed her.

'I'm sorry, Alex . . . I can't seem to stay away from you.' He looked almost as guilty as she did. But he was also incredibly appealing as he stood there. He looked vulnerable and afraid, and in love with her, and painfully familiar.

'Just try to behave,' she said, sounding a little hoarse and very sexy. 'I know it's hard for you to do that,' she smiled at him ruefully. She wanted to be furious, but he was so outrageous and so desperately in need, somehow she couldn't, 'but just try, will you please?' He nodded, looking sheepish, and he grinned at her, as Annabelle came out with her tiny suitcase and the bag of presents Sam had given her for Christmas. They exchanged a look over her head, and Alex wanted to be angry at him, but she couldn't.

He took them both downstairs, and stood and waved as they walked away. Annabelle turned half a dozen times to wave at him and tell him she loved him, and Alex made a point of not looking back at him. She was too afraid of what she'd see if she did. And she didn't want to see it. Vulnerable or not, he had touched a part of her she had thought was no longer there, but she knew it was now. She had thought that part of her had died, and it terrified her now to realize it hadn't. She couldn't let herself give in to it. She couldn't love both of them. She couldn't afford the luxury of Sam now. She and Brock had a future. And the one thing she knew as she walked home was that she had to let go of Sam forever.

And when she got home, Brock was there to meet her. She threw her arms around his neck, and held him close while he kissed her.

'What's that all about?' he asked, looking pleased by the fervor of her kisses. Vermont had been good for them. It was just what they needed.

She and Brock cooked dinner together that night, and afterwards she helped Annabelle unpack her things, while he put some music on the stereo and cleaned up the kitchen. It seemed hours later when Annabelle was in bed, and Brock was in the shower, when Sam called.

She was sitting in their study, thinking about him, and hearing his voice made her jump. It was as though he had heard her thinking.

'I just want you to know I'm not sorry I kissed you,' he said, and she wanted to hang up on him. She didn't know whether to laugh or cry. But she had loved him too. That was the trouble. 'But I want to know one thing.'

'What?' she said, feeling guilty for talking to him at all. It was hard to believe he'd been her husband. He seemed more like an illicit lover.

'I want to know if you're sorry, Alex. If you are, if you don't love me anymore, I'll leave you alone, no matter what I feel for you.' He suddenly sounded confident and stronger, as though an important part of him had been restored when he kissed her.

'I don't love you,' she said unconvincingly, and he laughed, sounding like the young man of years before, and she felt a familiar flutter.

'You're a liar.' Sam seemed to grin as he said it.

'I meant it,' she said, feeling guiltier than ever toward Brock, but Sam was undaunted.

'You're not sorry for a minute. You kissed me back.' Sam sounded like a kid again and he was laughing, and she couldn't help smiling when she answered.

'You're a shit,' and then her voice sobered again. 'I don't need these complications in my life, Sam. I want to keep things simple.'

'Things are going to be very simple for you in a few weeks, when I'm in prison,' he said, pressing her. And then, 'I want to see you.'

'You just did,' she said firmly. More firmly than she

felt. There was something about hearing from him again that softened a place in her heart that still loved him, but she was too afraid to ever let it happen.

'You know what I mean,' he persisted. 'Let's have dinner.'

'I don't want to.'

'Please . . .' He sounded so appealing, she wanted to scream.

'Stop it!'

'Alex, please.' He was pleading with her and driving her crazy, and she steadfastly refused to see him, and a few minutes later she hung up on him, and Brock got out of the shower. He had no idea that anyone had called her.

She still felt awkward about it the next day when Sam called her again at the office. She didn't want to speak to him, but after eighteen years, she felt she owed him something. 'What do you want from me?' she said finally in exasperation.

'One evening, that's all, and after that, I won't bother you again,' he bargained, and she sighed.

'Why? What difference does it make now?'

'It would mean a lot to me,' he said quietly, and in the end, she agreed to meet him. Just once. She didn't tell Brock about it, and she felt terrible lying to him. But she did it on a night when she knew Brock was busy with clients, and she left Annabelle with Carmen.

'Did you have to sneak out?' Sam teased when they met.

'Don't flatter yourself,' she snapped at him with a look of disapproval. She felt wrong doing this, and he could see that.

'Sorry.'

They went to a little restaurant in the East Eighties,

and ordered pasta and wine, and for a little while it was like turning the clock back. It reminded her of the old days when they had been dating, and had first fallen in love, but now everything was different for both of them. This was the end, not the beginning. And they knew it. He was calmer than he'd been the past few times she'd seen him, and painfully aware that he was going to prison.

They walked back downtown slowly afterwards, remembering things, talking about people, and places where they'd been. They dredged up memories neither of them had thought of for years. It was a lot like looking at old albums. And then, as they walked along, they stopped at a corner for a red light and he pulled her closer to him and kissed her. It was cold, and as he held her, she hated herself for responding.

She didn't say anything, and they walked some more, and then he pulled her gently into a doorway to keep warm, and kissed her again.

'I couldn't have paid you to do this a year ago,' she said sadly and bluntly, and she hit her mark. He felt terrible after she said it.

'I was so stupid, Alex,' he said, kissing her again and then just holding her, and she let him. She remembered how lonely she had been for him, and how badly she had needed him, and how much she loved him. And how badly he had hurt her. She hadn't thought then that she'd ever recover. And yet now things seemed so different. It all seemed so far away, and being with him seemed so much more real and so much more important. She wondered if forgiveness was really more just a question of forgetting.

'I learned a lot of lessons last year,' she said thoughtfully, nestled in his arms.

'Like what?'

'Like not depending on anyone, like not living or surviving for anyone but yourself. In the end, I just survived on pure grit, because I refused to die . . . it was an important lesson . . . maybe you're going to need to remember that in prison.'

'I can't even imagine it,' he said quietly, and then he looked down at her and smiled warmly. 'Thank you for this, for letting me hold you . . . and kiss you . . . you could have hit me over the head with your shoe, or called the cops. I'm glad you didn't.'

'Me too,' she said sadly, and then she stopped resisting the idea of him. 'I'm going to miss you.'

'You shouldn't. You'll have Annabelle, and the boy wonder,' he added sarcastically, and she laughed, as they started walking home again.

'He's great to Annabelle,' she said kindly about Brock.

'I'm glad. Is he good to you?'

'Very.'

'Then I'm happy for you.' But he wasn't, and they both knew it. More than anything, even though he had known it couldn't lead anywhere, he had wanted her to know how much he still loved her.

'Take care of yourself,' she said as they turned up Seventy-sixth Street toward the Carlyle. She lived only half a block away, and she was determined to walk home alone, but he wouldn't let her.

'I'll try. I have no idea where they'll send me. Probably Leavenworth,' since there were both state and federal charges. 'I hope it's civilized at least.'

'Maybe Phillip will do something miraculous, like get you a deal at the last minute.' But he had held out no hope of that to Sam. He'd have to go to prison, though he hoped not for too long. And after the first few months, or years, maybe he'd get transferred to one of the 'country club' prisons.

When they passed the Carlyle, he tried to talk her into coming upstairs with him, but she wouldn't. She knew better than to trust him, or herself. And when they got to her building, she kissed him on the cheek, and thanked him for a nice evening. And as she went upstairs, she felt quiet and pensive. There was a lot to think about, a lot of feelings to sift through.

Brock didn't question where she'd been the night before, but there was an odd atmosphere between them all the next morning in the office. It was as though he knew, but refused to ask her. And then finally, at lunch, he couldn't stand it any longer.

'You were out with him last night, weren't you?'

'With whom?' she asked stupidly, feeling her heart pound and hating herself for lying as she ate her sandwich.

'Your husband,' he said coolly. He knew. He had good instincts.

'Sam?' She paused, prepared to lie finally, and then decided not to. She owed Brock more than that and she knew it. But his jealousy scared her. But so did her feelings. The worst thing was that she loved both of them, and she knew it. She owed Sam for years past, and Brock for the past year. But what did she owe herself? That was the question she just couldn't answer. 'He wanted to have dinner to talk about Annabelle . . . I didn't think you'd mind,' she said, lying to him again, but he knew it. She felt so uncomfortable and so confused. She wanted to hate Sam for it, but she didn't.

'Why didn't you tell me?' Brock asked her, looking worried and unhappy.

'Because I was scared,' she said honestly, 'that you'd be angry, and I wanted to see him.' It was hard telling him the truth, but she knew she had to.

'Why did you want to see him?'

'Because he's going away for a long time, and I feel sorry for him, and as you put it, he's still my husband.' She looked sad and confused and unhappy. And her eyes told their own story.

'Did he kiss you?' He was no fool. And his jealousy jumped out on his skin like gooseflesh.

'Brock, stop it.' She tried to avoid him but he wouldn't let her.

'You didn't answer my question.' He was pushing at her, pressing her, daring her to answer, and then finally she snapped, mostly out of guilt, but also out of anger.

'What difference does it make?'

'It makes a difference to me.' She almost wondered if he'd followed them, but she didn't think he'd do that.

'All right, I kissed him. So what? That's all that happened.'

'That guy is a real sonofabitch,' he blazed, as he stormed around her office. 'He's going to jail, and he wants to get you wound up again. What does he want? For you to wait for him for twenty years? How nice for you. What a great guy he is, or don't you see that? He's completely selfish.'

'Okay, you win, he's selfish. But he's also human, and scared, and in his own way, he loves me.'

'And do you love him?'

'I was married to him for eighteen years, that's worth something. Friendship, if nothing else. I think all he wants is to make peace before he goes, to heal old wounds, and settle his affairs. He knows he's going. He's not trying to take me with him. He filed for divorce, didn't he?'

'And if he doesn't go?' He turned suddenly on her, and she was startled.

'He's not going to get off, Brock. He doesn't have a chance of that. You know that.'

'And if he did, would you stay married to him? Would you go back?' It was a difficult question, and she didn't want to answer it. For herself as much as him. There was no chance of his not going to prison. She knew that and so did Sam. Phillip Smith had left him no illusions. But the issue was not whether or not Sam was going to prison. The issue was not that simple.

'It doesn't have anything to do with that. If I really loved him, I'd be with him, whether or not he went to prison. I'm with you, Brock. That must mean something.'

'It does, but when he's gone, he'll be writing to you, wanting you to visit. You're still in love with him, Alex. Why don't you just face it?' He was hard on her, and she was angry at him for it. He wanted everything all at once, and life didn't work that way. She knew that better than he did.

'It takes old wounds time to heal, Brock. It doesn't happen in an instant. Be patient.'

'Why don't you admit what you're feeling? I think you're going to go back to him.'

'Why don't you grow up, Brock, and stop pushing?' she snapped at him in answer.

'Because I love you.' There were tears in his eyes suddenly when he said it. He loved her, and he wanted her, but there was no use denying that she still loved Sam. She did, and he knew it. He just didn't know what she'd want to do about it, in spite of all her denials.

She clung to him then, and they both cried. Nothing

was ever simple. But she wanted to explain to Brock that she needed time to mourn Sam, and to change the subject, she started talking about his sister. And as soon as she did, he looked stricken. She asked him why, but, at first, he wouldn't tell her, and then finally he knew he had to. He had meant to for a long time, but it had been better not to, for her sake. It had been particularly difficult when he and Alex talked about getting married, and she said she wanted to invite his sister.

'My sister's dead, Alex,' he said miserably. 'She's been dead for ten years. She had just what you had. She had a mastectomy, and chemo, and she couldn't take it. It was too hard for her, and she decided to stop the chemo, and die instead. Actually, her cancer had already spread before they took her breast off. But she gave up.' He started to cry as he remembered, and Alex stared at him in silent amazement. He had never told her. He had encouraged her to believe that his sister had made it, so she would stick with her treatment. 'She just quit. She wouldn't take the chemo. It took her a year to die . . . I was twenty-one, and I took care of her for a year. I wanted to make her live, but she was just too sick. And her husband was a real bastard, like Sam.' He looked at her pointedly. 'He never lifted a finger for her till she died, and he remarried six months later. She was thirty-two, and so beautiful . . .' He sat silent for a long time, as Alex held him and cried for both of them.

'Oh God, I'm so sorry, why didn't you tell me?' She felt terrible. He had given her so much hope, and now she realized all he must have gone through with his sister.

'I didn't want you to give up,' Brock explained, as he wiped away tears, remembering his sister, and loving Alex more than ever. In a way, loving Alex had been like a second chance to save her. And in some ways, Alex was a great deal like her.

'That's why I kept wanting you to do your chemo . . . I didn't want it to happen to you, and I didn't want you to know she'd died, or I thought you'd give up, like she did.'

'You should have told me.' He said nothing, he only sat quietly remembering, as Alex watched him. 'I should have known,' Alex reproached herself, as he blew his nose in a paper napkin she handed him. She wondered what else he hadn't told her, but not telling her about his sister had been a kindness.

'I'm just so scared,' he admitted to her as they sat in her office. 'I'm so scared you'll go back to him . . . he still loves you. I saw it all over his face . . . I can't stand seeing you with him.' She knew what he said was true, about Sam loving her. And she couldn't change it. She knew she loved Sam too. But it was too late. It was over. And he'd be gone soon, and then she wouldn't have to see him anymore, or ask herself what she felt. It would only be memories, and regrets, and disappointments. And the happier memories from before she got sick. But those were the memories Brock was afraid of.

They went back to work after that, and the next day she had to get ready for Annabelle's birthday. But she knew Sam would come too, and she hoped Brock wouldn't go crazy. In the end, he decided it would be easier for everyone if he wasn't there. And Alex didn't disagree with him, although Annabelle was disappointed.

'I wonder how old I'll be when I get out,' Sam said matter-of-factly, as he ate birthday cake, and Alex groaned at the lack of subtlety. Sometimes he couldn't resist a little dark humor, but ever since their dinner together, he seemed in better spirits.

'A hundred, I hope, and too old to remember you ever knew me,' she answered.

'Don't count on it.' And then, as he set the cake down, 'I'd like to have dinner with you again next week, before sentencing, if that's convenient. There are a lot of details about Annabelle I want to go over with you. I still have some money set aside for her support and education.' He had sold the apartment the month before, some of it was going to pay for his attorneys, and the rest he wanted to give to Alex for their daughter.

'Can I trust you?' she asked, and he laughed. The problem was she couldn't trust herself. The trouble was that neither of them could be trusted, and she knew it. He was still so attractive to her, but she had promised herself she would never give in to him. She was Brock's now.

'You can bring a bodyguard if you like, just don't bring the boy wonder.'

'Stop calling him that. His name is Brock.' Sam could at least be respectful of him. He was wonderful to their daughter.

'Sorry. I didn't realize you were so sensitive about him.' And with a sad look, he touched her arm, serious finally, as she was. 'Will he be Annabelle's stepfather?'

'I think so,' she said softly. They loved each other deeply, although things had been tense lately because of Sam, but she assumed that once Sam was gone, things would go back to normal. Gone. She hated the sound of that word now. Gone. Sam would be *gone* forever.

'Will you have dinner with me anyway?' he pressed, and she nodded.

'I'll try.'

'I don't have much time, Alex. Don't play games with me. Monday night at the Carlyle?'

'All right. I'll be there.'

'Thank you.'

But when she told Brock this time, he hit the ceiling.

'Oh for heaven's sake. I could have lied to you, and I didn't.'

'Why does he have to see you?'

'Because he wants to give me money for Annabelle. That's a perfectly reasonable explanation,' and she believed him.

'Tell him to send you a check.'

'No,' she said angrily, she was tired of his jealous tantrums. He had been a lot better behaved when she'd been throwing up on the floor of her office. 'Stop behaving like a four-year-old, and work this one out for yourself. I'm having dinner with my ex-husband.' She slammed the door to her bedroom then, and when she came out again, he was gone. He had gone back to his own apartment, and for once, she wasn't even sorry. He was putting too much pressure on her.

She arrived on schedule on Monday night at Sam's suite at the Carlyle Hotel, and he looked very serious in a dark gray suit and a white shirt, and navy Hermès tie. He had spent the afternoon with his lawyers, but he hadn't seen Alex at the law firm.

'How'd it go today?' she asked casually, sitting down on the couch, and noticing that he looked very tired. He was looking older lately, understandably. He was incredibly strained over what was about to happen.

'It didn't go too well,' he answered simply, 'Phillip Smith thinks the judge is going to put me away for quite a while, which brings me to why we're here.' He took out two checks and put them on the table. 'I got a million eight for the apartment last month. And after paying a few debts Miss Daphne Belrose left me with, and the agents' fees, I am left with a million five. I am giving you five hundred thousand here for Annabelle, and anything you might need for her. I want you to put it in trust for her. And I'm keeping five hundred thousand for me if I ever get out of jail again. And the last five hundred thousand is for you, as a settlement, if you want to call it that. You deserve more than that, but that's all that's left, kiddo. The business had nothing left but debts, and responsibilities for the money they embezzled.'

'Good Lord,' she was stunned. 'I don't want money from you, Sam.' She looked genuinely startled.

'You deserve it.'

'For what? Being married to you? Hell, I should get a lot more than that,' she heckled him, and he laughed. 'Never mind. I can't take this from you. Keep it, or give it to Annabelle.' But he wouldn't agree to either plan. He wanted her to keep it. But she already knew she would put it back in an account for him, he was going to need it a lot more than she did. She had her job, and her needs had never been very expensive.

He ordered dinner for them after that. Steak for himself and fish for Alex. She was careful about her diet. And they chatted easily about a variety of things, like old friends, and they stayed away from the subjects of court or prisons. She was glad she had come. The evening was entirely civilized. He had calmed down considerably in the past couple of weeks, he didn't pressure her, and he didn't lay a hand on her until she put her coat on, and then very gently he bent down to her and kissed her.

'Good night . . . thank you for coming . . .' he said,

and kissed her again, and she didn't move. She was always stunned by her own inability to resist him. There was something about the familiarity of him that was mesmerizing. It was as though, even after all this time, she had to be with him.

'We'd better stop this now,' she said softly, and then, stunned at herself, she put her arms around his neck and kissed him, just for old times' sake, she told herself. It didn't mean anything except to them. And Brock Stevens.

'Why stop now?' he whispered, and she laughed, as he kissed her again.

'I'm trying to remember,' she said, feeling guilty, but enjoying it anyway. And there was something very odd about feeling guilty with him. After all, he was still her husband. But Brock had made such a fuss about him. And it wasn't right for them to be kissing. She was involved with Brock, and she and Sam were divorcing.

'I love you,' he whispered, and she suddenly drew back from him, as though she realized it could go no further. She didn't want anyone to get hurt, or to let Sam hurt her again. But at the look in her eyes, he pulled her closer, and felt her heart pounding against his. And this time, when he kissed her, it wasn't gentle. It was urgent. In two days he would be leaving for decades, and he would never hold her again, and they both knew it. Gently he unbuttoned her coat and dropped it on a chair behind her, as she reminded herself to resist him. And then ever so carefully, he ran a hand up her right side, feeling the familiar breast that had nursed his daughter. He was careful not to touch the left, and then his hands touched her, he looked startled and she smiled at him, amused at his surprise over the implant.

'It grew back,' she said wickedly, and he looked embarrassed. It felt surprisingly realistic and he wondered when she'd done it.

'Why didn't you tell me?' he reproached gently and then kissed her again.

'It was none of your business,' she said softly, excited by him, and not wanting to be. And he wanted her desperately, not just for old times' sake, but for the present.

They were slowly, deliberately, unbuttoning each other's clothes, and she felt frightened as she did it. Their attraction to each other was irresistible and relentless, and there was no stopping what they were feeling.

'You're beautiful.' He pulled away and looked at her, and slowly unbuttoned her blouse and her skirt, and she let her clothes fall to the ground around her. In some ways, she knew she was crazy to do this. But he was going away for a long time, and she loved him. It was a way of saying good-bye, of letting go, of telling him how much she had once loved him, but she knew that they would never have a future. This was all they had now.

'I love you, Sam,' she said simply.

'I love you too . . . so very, very much . . .' He could barely speak, he was so excited. He wanted her one last time and then he had promised himself he would let go of her forever. He had no right to ruin her life. He had done enough. He wanted only this last gift from her, and it was obvious as they kissed that, in spite of all her warnings to herself, she wanted it as much as he did. She thought of nothing as she clung to him, except how much she had always loved him.

They made love quietly, and there was a certain peace and beauty to it. It was something they had both

434

wanted for a long time, and hadn't dared to acknowledge. There was passion and comfort and forgiveness. They felt as though they belonged in each other's arms, and they lay there afterwards, knowing it would never happen again, but they would long remember.

'I loved you so much,' she said, as she looked at him.

'So did I,' he said with tears in his eyes, but he was smiling. 'I still do. I always will. Not because I'm going to prison, but because I'm a fool and I learned my lessons too late. Be smarter than I was, Allie . . . don't fuck your life up.'

'You didn't,' she said gently.

'How can you say that now?' he asked softly. 'Look at where I'm going day after tomorrow. What a fool I was.' He lay on his back, thinking about all of it, and wishing he could undo it. And then she bent down and kissed him. He looked into her eyes and saw all the tenderness in life there. Brock Stevens was a lucky man. And Sam knew he didn't deserve her. He hoped things worked out for her. The boy was too young. But maybe he'd learn. Maybe he'd be smarter than Sam was.

She wanted to spend the night with him, but she didn't dare. If Annabelle woke up, she'd be upset, and if Brock called, he'd go crazy. He knew she was out with Sam, and he was frantic about it.

'I should go home,' she said sadly, hating to leave him.

'It's stupid, isn't it?' he said. 'We're married and we can't spend the night together.' It was all so ironic. And then he looked at her seriously. There was something else he had to tell her. 'I want you to know that I wish I had done things differently. When you got sick, I mean. I was too scared. I couldn't even listen. It's too late now to change any of it, but if I had it to do again, Alex, I'd be there. I don't think I'd be good at it, not as good as your friend was. But I'll never forgive myself for not being there for you. I learned a terrible lesson.' He had lost his wife over it, and chased after a falling star named Daphne, all because he'd been afraid and was running away from his mother.

'I know how frightened you were,' she said, forgiving him for the pain he had caused her. He really did sound as though he'd learned something from it.

'You can't even begin to know how frightened I was. I was crazed. I couldn't even see you. All I saw was my mother. I was such a damn fool,' he said, holding her, as she tried not to remember.

'I know,' she said softly. 'Things work out strangely sometimes,' she said philosophically, willing to accept what was, rather than what had been. She knew he was sorry. There was no point tormenting him over what had happened, though Brock would have been incensed that she forgave him. He would have been incensed over many things. But this wasn't his night, it was hers and Sam's, and it was very precious.

He walked her slowly home after that. They lingered, with his arm around her shoulders. And then he kissed her again. They stood that way for ages outside his old house, and she wanted to ask him up, but she knew she couldn't. They couldn't go on clinging to the past. They had to let go now. At least they were leaving each other something warm to remember.

'Thank you,' she whispered, as she kissed him for the last time. 'I'll see you tomorrow.' He was coming to say good-bye to Annabelle, which was going to be ghastly. Alex had taken his check for their daughter with her, but she had left his check for her on the table at the Carlyle, but he hadn't seen it.

'I love you,' he said for a last time, overwhelmed with how beautiful she was, and how much he loved her. He watched her go inside, and as he walked back to the hotel, there were tears running down his cheeks as he wondered how he could have been so stupid. He had blown his entire life and now he had nothing. No future, and no Alex. It was hardly worth living.

And alone in her bed, Alex remembered what it had been like making love to him. It was just like old times, she thought with a smile, only better. They had both learned a lot in the last year, about loving, and forgiveness. She only prayed that, wherever he went, he would be safe, and find something worthwhile to keep him going. She couldn't be there for him now. She owed too much to Brock. And no matter how much she still loved Sam, she knew she had to leave him. But Lord, how she would miss him.

Chapter 23

When Sam came to say good-bye to Annabelle, it almost killed all of them. Sam was sobbing when he left, and Annabelle, and Alex and Carmen were crying. All he had been able to explain to her was that he had worked with some men who had done bad things, and he hadn't paid attention to what they were doing. They had taken people's money, which was wrong, and now he and the bad men had to go to jail to make up for taking the money.

He could have told her that he was going on a long trip. But he didn't. He said that one day she could come to see him, but it wasn't a nice place, and he'd like her to be a little older. He told her to be a good girl, take care of Mommy, and always, always remember how much he loved her. He held her tightly in his arms while they all cried, but no one more than Sam or Alex. Annabelle was confused by what was happening, and she was upset that he was going, and that bad men had taken money. But she had no concept of twenty or thirty years. None of them did. It was beyond them. It simply felt like forever.

Alex walked out to the elevator with him, and clung to him. She had asked Brock not to come until later that evening. And just after he left, she called Sam at the Carlyle.

'Are you all right?' She was worried about him. This was too much for anyone, especially given the minor degree of his involvement. His main sin had been letting it happen.

'I'm okay. I didn't think I could ever leave her. I didn't think I could leave you either.' But he had, and now he knew what it was like to die. He felt like he'd already done it. He had nothing else to lose now.

'I'll be there tomorrow,' she said, wishing she could be there that night. But it didn't seem wise to do that again. After one night together, they both already felt as though they were still married and belonged together. And that would only complicate things for both of them. She had Brock, and he had to go away. There was no point dragging it out now.

But she still felt as though she belonged to Sam, as she talked to him, or stood next to him. All the old bonds had been re-formed in a single moment, and it wasn't fair to either of them. It would just make it harder for both of them when he left tomorrow. And he knew it too. He didn't ask her to come over. Making love to her again had reminded him of how much he loved her, and wanted to protect her. And leaving her now was going to be even more painful.

'I'll see you in court,' he said lightly, elegant to the end, Alex thought as she hung up, thinking about him again. And by the time Brock came by that night, they were all still very upset, even Carmen. Annabelle had cried herself to sleep, despite all of Alex's efforts to console her. And Alex didn't feel like eating dinner or talking.

'Christ, I'll be glad when this is over with,' Brock said tartly, and his tone annoyed her. It was like waiting for an execution and it seemed ghoulish to Alex.

'So will I. I don't think any of us are enjoying it, not even Sam,' Alex said curtly. Why couldn't he be more understanding? He had nothing to fear from Sam now.

'He's the one who created this mess,' Brock pointed out tersely, 'let's not forget that.'

'I don't think that's entirely true. Aren't you over-looking the facts here?'

'Oh give it up, Alex. The guy's a crook, whether or not he's your husband.' He made her want to scream as she listened to him. He was so worried he was going to lose Alex to Sam, all he wanted was for the guy to go to jail as soon as possible. For Brock, it was the best news of the year, and there were times when she hated him for it.

Eventually, they argued for so long, that he decided not to spend the night with her again, but before he left, they got into another argument over her going to court with Sam the next morning.

'I want to be there when they sentence him,' she explained as though he were retarded.

'Is that like going to the guillotine with someone?' he said nastily, and he set her off again. But the real heart of it came up a few minutes later. 'What if he doesn't go, Alex? Then what? Is he back in the picture?'

'Why do you hound me about this all the time? You're obsessed with him. What do I know what would happen?'

'You're still in love with him,' he accused.

'I'm in love with you,' she tried to reason with him, but he didn't want to hear it.

'But you're in love with him too, aren't you?'

'Brock, stop it!' she screamed, no longer caring if she woke Annabelle or Carmen. 'I love you. You've been there for me when no one else was. You got me through the last year. I would have died without you. Isn't that enough for you? Do you have to wipe out my whole past just to prove I love you? He's the father of my child. He's the man I married. He hurt me terribly. It's over. And he's going away now. That's the best I can do. I can't tell you what would happen if he stayed. But it doesn't matter anyway, he's not staying.'

'I can tell you what would happen if he did,' he said darkly, and she shook her head in despair. This was gruesome.

'You're destroying us while you're trying to destroy him. Stop, before you kill us, Brock. Please . . . don't do this.' She was crying then, for him, for herself, for Sam, for Annabelle, for all of them, all those who had suffered, even his sister.

'If he stays, I'm going back to Illinois.' It was the first she had heard of it, but she suddenly realized how tormented he must have been to make plans like that without her.

'Why?'

'Because I don't belong here. You belong with him. I know that. No matter how lousy he's been, or how badly he's hurt you, you still belong to him. I know that in my gut.' He was crying as he said it to her, but she couldn't deny the truth of what he was saying. 'If he goes, then you'd be alone anyway. You'd be free. But if he doesn't, I'm going home, Alex. I think I'm ready to go back now. I left because of my sister, but you helped me heal those wounds. I always felt responsible because she quit taking her chemo. I always felt I should have made her do it. I know now that I couldn't have changed anything. She did what

441

she wanted.' He sounded peaceful and more mature than she had ever heard him. It was hard growing up. It was always so damn painful.

'You saved my life, Brock.' She said it without reservation.

'You'd have done it anyway, because you're that kind of woman. You're not a quitter. That's why you still love him. You just won't give up, will you?' There was more truth to it than she'd ever realized, but Brock had made a difference in her chemo, and her survival. He had kept her at it.

'I think you made the difference,' she said, giving him the credit he deserved.

'That's nice to hear, but you never know.' He looked at her with a sad smile then, 'I'll always love you, you know.'

'You make it sound like you're leaving, and not Sam,' she said with tears in her eyes, and he shrugged.

'Maybe I should anyway,' he said sadly. The last three months had taken a terrible toll on them. Oddly enough, it had been better between them when he was helping her get through chemo.

'Don't go, Brock. He doesn't have a chance of getting off now.' She was trying to reassure him, but it only saddened her more.

'Even if he goes, you'll always love him.'

'That's true,' she admitted, 'I will. But he's the past, and you're the future. You have to decide if you can face that. If you can live with knowing that I loved him.' He nodded, but he didn't answer, and when he left the apartment, she had a strange feeling that he wasn't coming back, that he would never be able to accept the relationship she'd had with Sam, and the fact that she'd really loved him. He wanted her to hate him, but she didn't. He wanted her not to have a history with anyone, no bond to a man she still cared about so deeply. But life was never that simple. It never dealt the easy hands. The quick wins. There were always the difficult combinations, the tough choices, to deal with. But there were no choices for her now. Sam was going. And Brock would either grow up or he wouldn't. He would either live with her past or he'd leave her. She had a feeling, though, that in the long run, the ten years between them was a chasm beyond bridging, and that Brock knew it too. He seemed ready to go now. In a way, they had healed each other, and perhaps their time together was over. It was sad even thinking of that, but she had learned a lot in the past year about acceptance. And she knew that if she had to be, she could be alone now. But it was odd feeling that she was about to lose both of the men in her life. Maybe it was time for her to be on her own.

And as she lay in bed that night, she thought of Brock and all he'd done for her, but it was Sam she thought of constantly until morning, Sam who needed her thoughts and her strength now. Sam who seemed to be woven into her very soul, who seemed to be a part of her forever. And as she realized that, she felt strangely peaceful. There was no fighting it, he had become an unalterable part of her long since, and she had never even noticed.

She was up at six o'clock, and dressed in a black suit at seven. She didn't tell Annabelle where she was going, but Carmen knew. And Alex looked serious at breakfast and she left for the courthouse early so she would be there when Sam arrived. She wanted to be there for him.

The courthouse was already full when she got there, and she didn't want to crowd the counsel's table, although she could have. There was a huge row going on, because Simon Barrymore had fled the country the night before, and jumped bail, and the judge was in a furor. But once that was taken care of, and a warrant issued for Simon's arrest for jumping bail, the judge was prepared to deal with the others.

Once again, Larry and Tom went first. And each was sentenced to ten years in prison, with a million-dollar fine each. There was a gasp in the courtroom, and as usual, the reporters went wild and had to be reprimanded.

The judge was frantically pounding his gavel, and then he asked Sam to stand up. He looked very serious and very calm, and there was a stir in the courtroom. There had always been recognition that Sam's case was different from the others. He had maintained till the end that he hadn't known what they were doing, and due to the extenuating circumstances of his wife's illness, and his own stupidity, not to mention his affair with Daphne, he had been temporarily lulled into paying far too little attention to the practices of his partners. The jury had recognized the merit of that too, which was why they had cleared him of the embezzlement charges, but the charges of fraud had stood and he had been found guilty.

The judge looked at him long and hard. And then with a slow, deliberate voice he spoke Sam's sentence. 'Samuel Livingston Parker, I hereby sentence you to a fine, paid out of your personal funds, of five hundred thousand dollars, and ten years in prison.' The crowd roared, and every photographer in the place pressed toward him, as the judge shouted and continued to rap his gavel. Sam closed his eyes, but only for a split second, and Alex felt so nauseous suddenly it almost felt like chemo. 'Ten years in prison,' he repeated, glaring at the crowd and then at Sam, for silence, 'with your sentence to be reduced as of this date to ten years probation, and the court recommends that you find some other line of work, Mr Parker. Dog-catching, if you like, but stay out of the venture capital business, and stay off Wall Street.' Sam stood staring at the judge, as did everyone in the courtroom. For an instant there was silence. Ten years probation. He was free, or as good as. Alex couldn't believe it.

And then pandemonium broke loose in the courtroom.

The lawyers were all shaking hands as Larry and Tom were led away, and Sam stood looking dazed while court was adjourned and photographers from every paper in the country took his picture. Alex couldn't even get to him for the next twenty minutes, and she just stood staring at him in amazement. Phillip Smith had done an incredible job, but so had the judge, and the probation office itself had recommended for probation. They had concluded that Sam was a fool, but not a criminal, and no real purpose would be served by sending him to prison. And as she thought of it, she remembered the five-hundred-thousand-dollar check she had refused to take from him two days before. He was going to find it very useful.

She waited until he was out in the hallway to talk to him. She congratulated Phillip Smith, and the rest of his team, and then suddenly she found herself looking up at Sam, and he was smiling at her, almost shyly.

'This comes as a surprise, doesn't it?' he said, still looking dazed.

'I almost fell over when he said it,' Alex admitted. 'I figured you were gone for good.' She smiled and he laughed, feeling new again, just as she had when she'd finished chemo.

'Poor Annabelle . . . everything we put her through for nothing . . . let's pick her up at school,' Sam said, and then he looked down at Alex with an odd expression, and spoke to her softly in the lull of the crowd. 'Let's go somewhere and talk.'

'What about your hotel?' she whispered in his ear, and he nodded agreement.

'I'll meet you there in half an hour,' he said, and followed Phillip Smith out of the courthouse.

She thought of calling Brock, but she didn't know what to say to him. He had predicted this, and all the complications that went with it. She couldn't face reassuring him again, but worse than that, she wasn't sure what she felt now. She had come to terms with a lot of things the night before, and she suspected Brock had too when he left her. He had never called her.

Sam was suddenly back in her life, with no warning. It made her think of the time they had spent in bed together only two days before, and all the memories it had evoked for both of them. She didn't know anything anymore. She knew she still loved Sam, but did she trust him? Would he be there for her if it happened again, or would he fail her? Were his promises real, or was the nightmare? And where was Brock in all this? What did she owe him, or want from him? But the issue was not Brock now. It was Sam, with all his strengths and failings. The issue was them, and what they would do now. They both knew life gave no guarantees, only promises, and wishes and dreams, and terrible heartache when the dreams were broken.

Her head was reeling as she took a cab uptown to the Carlyle. And when she got there, she found him waiting for her, pacing up and down outside the hotel, as though he couldn't wait another moment. The cab slowed as they got there, and the doorman opened the door for her. And as she stepped out, Sam looked into her eyes, and she knew that Brock was right. They loved each other. It was that simple.

Sam had forgotten the rules for a while but she never had. For better or worse . . . it was all still there, in spite of all the pain and the heartbreak he had caused her. She wanted to tell Brock he was wrong. She wanted to be bigger than that, to be different, or modern, or very strong. But she wasn't. She was human. She was loyal. And she still loved her husband.

'Hello, Sam,' she said softly as he took her hand, and tucked it into his arm to walk her into the hotel. He was still shaken and stunned by what had just happened in court. He felt very humble, and incredibly lucky.

'Is it all right if we go upstairs?' he asked her politely, and she smiled and nodded, as they went through the revolving door and down the stairs into the lobby.

'It's all right,' she said softly. They were starting over. They were still friends, even though he had hurt her so badly. But she wasn't sure if they were more than that now. There was no way to tell about the future.

She stood next to him in the elevator, wondering what would happen now, how they would put all the pieces back together and try to forget what had happened, what they would say to Annabelle, and what she would tell Brock. It would be hard to tell him, but he already knew. He was packing that morning. They had said goodbye the night before, although neither of them knew it when it happened.

And all her worries seemed to fade as they got out on the eighth floor and Sam turned to look at her. He took out his key and held it for a long moment, looking at her, as she smiled at him. There was sadness in her smile, and truth, and knowledge, and wisdom. They had taught each other so much. So many hard lessons. And Brock had been right, in spite of all of it, Sam was still her husband.

He took the key and turned it in the lock, and gently pushed open the door, and left it standing, as he swept her into his arms, and carried her across the threshold. He looked at her questioningly as he did it, wanting to be sure that it was what she wanted too. But she looked at him and nodded. They'd been given a second chance. A rare, rare gift in any life. They had each gotten a second chance. It was time to grab it, and start over. And as he set her down, she smiled at him, and pushed the door gently closed behind them.

THE END